OXFORD WORLD'S CLASSICS

THE PRIVATE MEMOIRS AND CONFESSIONS OF A JUSTIFIED SINNER

Hogg + Burns, both self marketed 'rustic,

JAMES HOGG was born at Ettrick Farm, Ettrick, in 1770. He was *uneducat.* the second son of Robert Hogg, ex-shepherd and tenant farmer. In *self-* 1788 he was hired as a shepherd, and in 1793 he started writing *taught'* poetry. His poetical gift was discovered by Scott, for whom he *writers* collected ballads for the *Border Minstrelsy*. In 1807 his own early ballads were published under the title of *The Mountain Bard*. In 1810 he went to Edinburgh, where he met Wordsworth, Southey, and De Quincey. He achieved fame in 1813 with *The Queen's Wake*, and in 1815 *The Pilgrims of the Sun* was published. In the same year, the Duke of Buccleuch granted him the farm of Altrive in Yarrow, where he resided mainly for the rest of his life. His prose works include *The Three Perils of Man* (1822), *The Confessions of a Justified Sinner* (1824), and *The Domestic Manners and Private Life of Sir Walter Scott* (1834). He died in 1835.

JOHN CAREY is Merton Professor of English Literature at Oxford University. His books include *The Violent Effigy: A Study of Dickens' Imagination*, *Thackeray: Prodigal Genius*, *John Donne: Life, Mind and Art*, *Original Copy, Collected Reviews and Journalism, 1969–86*, and *The Intellectuals and the Masses: Pride and Prejudice among the Literary Intelligentsia, 1880–1939*.

OXFORD WORLD'S CLASSICS

*For over 100 years Oxford World's Classics have brought
readers closer to the world's great literature. Now with over 700
titles—from the 4,000-year-old myths of Mesopotamia to the
twentieth century's greatest novels—the series makes available
lesser-known as well as celebrated writing.*

*The pocket-sized hardbacks of the early years contained
introductions by Virginia Woolf, T. S. Eliot, Graham Greene,
and other literary figures which enriched the experience of reading.
Today the series is recognized for its fine scholarship and
reliability in texts that span world literature, drama and poetry,
religion, philosophy and politics. Each edition includes perceptive
commentary and essential background information to meet the
changing needs of readers.*

OXFORD WORLD'S CLASSICS

═══

JAMES HOGG

The Private Memoirs and Confessions of a Justified Sinner

═══

Edited with an Introduction and Notes by
JOHN CAREY

OXFORD
UNIVERSITY PRESS

OXFORD

UNIVERSITY PRESS

Great Clarendon Street, Oxford OX2 6DP

Oxford University Press is a department of the University of Oxford.
It furthers the University's objective of excellence in research, scholarship,
and education by publishing worldwide in

Oxford New York

Athens Auckland Bangkok Bogotá Buenos Aires Calcutta
Cape Town Chennai Dar es Salaam Delhi Florence Hong Kong Istanbul
Karachi Kuala Lumpur Madrid Melbourne Mexico City Mumbai
Nairobi Paris São Paulo Shanghai Singapore Taipei Tokyo Toronto Warsaw

with associated companies in Berlin Ibadan

Oxford is a registered trade mark of Oxford University Press
in the UK and in certain other countries

Published in the United States
by Oxford University Press Inc., New York

Introduction, Notes, and Chronology
© Oxford University Press 1969
Glossary © Graham Tulloch 1990
Bibliography © John Carey 1995

The moral rights of the author have been asserted

Database right Oxford University Press (maker)

First published in the Oxford English Novels Series by
Oxford University Press 1969
First issued as a World's Classics paperback 1981
Reissued with a new bibliography 1995
Reissued as an Oxford World's Classics paperback 1999

British Library Cataloguing in Publication Data

Data available

Library of Congress Cataloging in Publication Data

Data available

ISBN 0–19–283590–4

5 7 9 10 8 6 4

Printed in Great Britain by
Clays Ltd, St Ives plc

CONTENTS

ACKNOWLEDGEMENTS

I AM grateful to the General Editor of *Oxford English Novels*, Professor James Kinsley, for his helpful suggestions. Others who have placed me in their debt are Miss Edith Batho, and Professor A. L. Strout of Eastern Montana College, who were prompt in answering queries, Mr J. C. Maxwell of Balliol College, who first suggested to me the connection between Hogg's novel and Hoffmann, Mr D. H. Merry of the Bodleian Library, who aided me in my search for the putative 1895 reissue of the *Confessions*, and the Revd Fr. M. Jarrett-Kerr, CR, of Leeds University, and Mr James O'Neale of University College, Oxford, who brought to my notice contemporary reviews. I should like to record my thanks to each of them.

INTRODUCTION Antinomianism

THE events of the *Confessions of a Justified Sinner* are narrated twice, first by the 'editor', then by the 'sinner' himself. The editor's narrative begins in 1687 with the marriage of the old laird of Dalcastle to a pious girl who owes her strict Calvinism to the tuition of a minister, Robert Wringhim. The marriage soon breaks up, the laird and his wife occupying different parts of the house, and a Miss Arabella Logan comes to live with the laird as 'housekeeper'. Lady Dalcastle, however, produces two sons. The elder, George Colwan, turns out an upstanding youth and is brought up by the laird; Robert, the younger, is educated by his mother and Wringhim, whose name he takes and who, in the laird's opinion, is his real father. The brothers first meet in Edinburgh when George is playing tennis. Young Wringhim interferes, George knocks him down and publicly denies his legitimacy. From that hour George is haunted by his 'fiendish' brother wherever he goes until one morning, climbing Arthur's Seat, he is startled to see a giant apparition of his brother in the mist, and a 'halo of glory' round his own head. Turning, he collides with his brother crouching behind him, and eventually forces him to promise to follow him no longer. Shortly after, George is found dead. The inquiry decides that he was killed in a duel with one of his companions, the Hon. Thomas Drummond. The old laird dies heartbroken, and young Wringhim inherits Dalcastle. Miss Logan, convinced he is the murderer, cannot prove it until she meets a prostitute, Bell Calvert, who was an eyewitness of the crime, and confirms that Wringhim and a mysterious companion were the culprits. The two women

go to Dalcastle, find Wringhim, and tie him up. They hurry
to Edinburgh to inform the authorities, and officers are dispatched, but Wringhim has disappeared.

Wringhim's own memoir follows. It recounts his joyful
admittance by his stepfather into the number of God's elect,
and his meeting with an uncanny stranger, under whose
influence he murders George. The stranger, who calls himself Gil-Martin, but whom the reader soon recognizes as
Satan, assures Wringhim that no sin can affect the salvation
of an elect person: this concurs with his stepfather's teaching. Wringhim comes to believe that he has a criminal
doppelgänger, since he finds himself accused of crimes, including the seduction and murder of a girl, and the murder
of his own mother, of which he has no recollection. He runs
away from Dalcastle, finds various jobs, and has his
memoir printed; but he cannot shake off his terrible con-
federate.

The last part of the novel tells of the exhumation of
Wringhim's mummified corpse by two local youths in 1823.
This was first made public, the editor says, in a letter from
James Hogg to *Blackwood's*. (Hogg's letter really was published in the magazine a year before his novel came out.)
The editor, his friend J. G. Lockhart, and other gentlemen,
plan to exhume the body a second time. Hogg, whom they
come across at the Thirlestane ewe fair, dourly refuses to
act as guide, but another shepherd obliges, and Wringhim's
memoir is discovered in the grave.

The *Confessions* makes Hogg's other fiction look so ama-
teurish that George Saintsbury decided Lockhart must
have helped. This notion, seconded by Andrew Lang, was
indignantly countered by Hogg's daughter with the incon-
clusive argument that the manuscript, in her possession,
was 'clearly and neatly written' by Hogg throughout. The
picture of the Ettrick Shepherd calling on a classically edu-

cated friend to have his masterpiece knocked into shape lingered. When Earle Welby revived the *Confessions* in 1924, he assured his readers that the Lockhart-debt could 'hardly be disputed'. The best antidote to Saintsbury's theory is Lockhart's own novels. Their pedestrian plotting, with nothing more important in view than flimsy melodrama, and their confusion of evil with ungentlemanliness, put an end to any serious association of their author with a work which Walter Allen has proposed as the most convincing representation of a power of evil in our literature, and which succeeds largely because of its subtle structure and relentlessly prosaic tone.

Hogg boasted, untruthfully, that he avoided books, so as to preserve his originality, and he perhaps evolved the novel's double-account scheme for himself; but it had been common in epistolary novels since Richardson, and when he reworked elements from the *Confessions* in his *Strange Letter of a Lunatic*, Hogg, too, adopted the letter-form. The scheme as Hogg employs it is not simple, though to imagine, with Marius Bewley, that the editor's narrative presents 'an objective account of the facts of Colwan's life' would be to make it so. For one thing the editor is a bluff Tory, Lockhart's college-friend. His hero, seen through other eyes, is a young rowdy who slanders his mother in public and goes to church to spy on girls. The editor's complacency about the superior reactions of a 'man of science' in the halo-of-glory scene, and his perplexity over evidence 'not consistent with reason' in the summing-up, reveal him as a victim of Hogg's wit. Neither he nor Lockhart comes well out of the grave-robbing episode, which Hogg, in the novel, will not be a party to and had, it turns out, taken steps to forestall by giving a false location in his *Blackwood's* letter. Attracted by the editor's tone, David Craig has imagined Hogg himself to be 'an eighteenth-century man of

sense, derisive of "enthusiasm"', but Hogg, the believer in
fairies and fervent admirer of the Covenanters, will not
wear this label. The editor's limitations and separateness
from Hogg receive early advertisement when a girl's desperate evasion of her disgusting old bridegroom strikes him
as comic and wrong. Bell Calvert's home truths, later, about
Miss Logan's 'old unnatural master' straighten Colwan-
père's account, and it is worth remembering that he and Gil-
Martin are the only figures in the novel who refuse to pray.
The balance of the work requires that the editor's prejudices should be, in their way, as warping as Wringhim's, and
indeed Wringhim's cool self-exposure, as in 'My heart was
greatly cheered by this remark; and I sighed very deeply',
has a surer appeal than anything at the editor's disposal.

Further, the editor does not supply 'the facts'. He repeats
traditions which, he admits, may go no further back than
the printers of Wringhim's memoir. Consequently the
novel remains indecisive about whether the devil was a
delusion or an objective figure. The external evidence for
the whole affair is unsettlingly flawed: the old laird marries
after succeeding to Dalcastle in 1687, but his second son is
17 on 25 March 1704; Colwans and Wringhims go to Edinburgh in 1704 to attend a session of parliament that took
place in 1703; Mrs Calvert sees Drummond's claymore
glittering in the moon, and the surgeons testify that this
sword fits George's wounds, whereas Wringhim, by his
own and Mrs Calvert's account, carried a rapier; George's
body is found on a 'little washing green', but Mrs Calvert
remembers it as 'not a very small one'; she thinks she sees
him 'pierced through his body' twice, but examination
reveals only one fatal wound; Wringhim sees his mother's
body being carried to the house, but in the traditional
account she is lost without trace. The landlady, hysterically
repeating Miss Logan's 'It *is* he', does her bit to discredit

traditional evidence. Meanwhile intimations that Gil-Martin is a part of Wringhim are plentiful. He says himself, 'I feel as if I were the same person', and grows haggard along with his victim. Wringhim's anxiety about 'the red-letter side of the book of life' produces a devil whose 'bible' is 'intersected with red lines, and verses'. At first Gil-Martin asserts only what Wringhim needs to believe: that his state is 'to be envied', that he should possess Dalcastle, that he killed his brother fairly. And the crimes Wringhim later commits—murdering his mother and the girl he has seduced—seem, like his vision of a 'pure' woman at moments of stress, outgrowths of his own repression—('I brought myself to despise, if not abhor, the beauty of women'). On the other hand, Gil-Martin becomes an independent figure by virtue of his sense of humour, which constantly escapes Wringhim (as when he assures him that he does not expect acceptance with God on account of good works), and his grisly promises of advancement, so calmly received by this innocent Faust ('I bowed again, lifting my hat').

The novel's intricacy is increased by a mirroring technique, most obvious in the repeated confrontations of Scots- and English-speaking characters (the Scots habitually coarse but splendid)—Lady Dalcastle with her father, the elder Wringhim with John Barnet, the younger with Samuel Scrape, and so on—which back up James Hogg's rout of the gentry at Thirlestane. Among these exchanges, Bessy Gillies's 'flippant and fearless' vindication of a legal scruple against the Crown prosecutor reflects and redeems Robert's assertion of his 'right and the rights of his fellow-citizens' to the common field. Comparably, Mrs Calvert's growth from supplication to obstinacy in the prison scene reproduces Robert's treatment of George on the mountain (the link is spelt out: Robert, 'the unaccountable monster';

Mrs Calvert, 'the unaccountable culprit'), just as what we hear of her life, wrecked by a 'lordly fiend', suggests his.

Hogg's fiction is mostly expendable because of his belief in 'the fire and rapidity of true genius'. He never (so he said) knew when he wrote one line of a novel what the next would be, and he disagreed with revision on principle. But among the sweepings, elements which generate power in the *Confessions* can be picked out. He was always concerned with outcasts, from the winsome vagabond Duncan Campbell to Baron Guillaume de Iskar in his underground casino, and he rightly considered himself one. His ambitions necessarily isolated him from his peasant background. When he and other young shepherds started a literary society, for example, it was suspected of devil-raising, and blamed for the great storm of 1794. Returning to Ettrick in 1809, after failure as a tenant-farmer, he found himself friendless— 'even those whom I had loved, and trusted most, disowned me'. He remained sensitive to cold shoulders: 'I know I have always been looked on by the learned part of the community as an intruder.' In the *Confessions*, Robert is 'born an outcast in the world', disowned by his father, saddled with a 'sternness of demeanour from which other boys shrunk', and eventually beaten from every door; George is hissed and pointed at in the Edinburgh streets; Bell Calvert is whipped, banished, and driven to prostitution. Gil-Martin, the primal outcast, expounds a theology which thrives on the fear of exclusion.

Also near to the book's core is the complex of repulsion and attraction which colours Robert's relationship with Gil-Martin and with George. It features again in *The Brownie of the Black Haggs* and *The Marvellous Doctor. The Hunt of Eildon* has a shepherd who finds himself turned into a pig (Hogg's nickname among the *literati*), and rushes about 'trying to escape from himself'. Later he is trussed,

screaming and struggling, ready for slaughter, his girl-
friend lending her garters to strengthen his bonds. This
refinement combines with Hogg's everlasting phobia about
old women to produce the binding of Wringhim with
garters by Miss Logan and Mrs Calvert, and the similar
tableau in *A Strange Secret* with MacTavish bound hand and
foot and two murderous crones 'laughing immoderately at
my terrors'. The scene where Wringhim hangs upside
down, unclothed, and is beaten in front of the weaver's wife,
suggests a similar sexual deviation. A complementary
interest in a young bride's subjection to an elderly husband
informs both the *Confessions* and *The Bridal of Polmood*
(written when Hogg was about to marry a girl twenty years
younger). The preservation of dead bodies is another aber-
ration Hogg found endlessly fascinating. In *The Baron St
Gio*, the detail of long-dead flesh dimpling when handled
reappears, and the body half-destroyed and half-intact
is twice returned to in *The Surpassing Adventures of Allan
Gordon*.

Apart from these obsessive topics, particular narrative
counters recur. The hatred of a dark, studious youth for his
fair, athletic brother is the groundwork of *The Laird of
Cassway*. The 'halo of glory' and giant apparition which
startle George were seen by Hogg himself when he was
nineteen, and he recalls, in *Nature's Magic Lantern*, that the
shadow 'appeared to my affrighted imagination as the
enemy of mankind'. The details of the duel—the green
place, the moonlight, a supernatural voice calling out the
living, two wounds (one slight, one deadly) are repeated in
Adam Bell and *The Cameronian Preacher's Tale*.

Hogg's own involvement in Wringhim's religious
dilemma is borne out by his treatment of elements from the
Confessions in other stories. The superficial classification of
the book as a satire on Calvinism, sponsored by Ernest

Baker, suffers from a reading of, say, *The Prodigal Son*, where a saintly old minister, bearing every mark of Hogg's esteem, expresses the same scorn for 'moral harangues' as Wringhim, or of *The Wife of Lochmaber*, where the story of the pious wife with a devout friend, and the profligate husband who brings a 'buxom quean' to live under the same roof, is retold very much to the wife's advantage: she returns obligingly from the dead to report 'all that we believe of a Saviour and future state of existence is true'. The stern theology behind the *Confessions* is, after all, not very different from Wringhim's, except that he is the reprobate, not George. Hogg himself was punctilious about religious observances: on the one occasion he was away from his family in London, he wrote a book of prayers specially for their use. The implications of his novel are nearer to the Bunyanesque 'Then I saw that there was a way to Hell even from the Gates of Heaven', than to the jocularity of *Holy Willie's Prayer*, with which it is often compared.

The book's style can also be recognized in Hogg's lesser works. The attractive shamelessness of Wringhim's disclosures had been perfected in *The Adventures of Basil Lee*, and mimicry of the King James version (which spills over from Wringhim's part into the editor's with turns of phrase like 'But he mocked at them, and said' or 'The face was the face of his brother') had been in his repertoire since the *Chaldee Manuscript*.

Turning from the question of how Hogg managed to write the *Confessions* to why he wrote it in 1824, brings us up against his relations with the *Blackwood's* group, a crucial factor in his life from 1817 onwards. Early in the 1820s it dawned on him that the magazine which had at first welcomed and profited from his help was easing him out: 'no wonder I begin to feel a cold side to a work which holds such an avowed one to me', he wrote to Blackwood. His articles were rejected and, worse, articles he had never written, associating him with *Blackwood's* policy, appeared instead. He tried to guard against this by signing all contributions, but Wilson and Lockhart 'signed my name as fast as I did'. Hogg found himself seconding the magazine's snobbish abuse of Keats, and other exhibitions of muscular Toryism. The Whig papers, the *Scotsman* and the *London Magazine*, protested at this misuse of Hogg's name: a 'true national poet' was being made to involve himself in 'the guilt and filth of all the most odious articles that have appeared in *Blackwood's Magazine....* He is made to enlarge upon the sympathy he cherishes with the assassin's blow, the mercenary outrage. And this is done, in his name, by the very assassin himself.' The battle went beyond words: John Scott, the *London Magazine's* brilliant young editor, was killed in a duel by Lockhart's friend, Christie, within two months of this protest. Hogg, like Wringhim, was used to finding 'acts of cruelty, injustice, defamation, and deceit' attributed to him, of which he was wholly ignorant. The explanation which occurs to Wringhim, that he has a second self, became, too, a reality for Hogg in December 1822, when he began to figure in the *Noctes Ambrosianae*. At first these were composite productions, and Hogg took a hand, but by August 1823 Wilson was making up the shepherd's speeches and turning him, as Lockhart put it, into a 'boozing buffoon'. Mrs Hogg, understandably, came to dread each new number, and readers of the *Noctes* who, like William Howitt, met the actual James Hogg later, were astonished to find him 'smooth, well-looking and gentlemanly'.

Wringhim's divided attitude to his 'elevated and dreaded friend' can, without much imagination, be paralleled in Hogg's relationship with Professor Wilson. Bogus and unstable, Wilson treated Hogg as he had Wordsworth, pretending affection and then (over the signature 'An Old

Friend with a New Face') reviewing him so viciously in
Blackwood's of August 1821 that Ballantyne, the printer, at
first refused to set it up. Hogg was staggered when he
found that the author of this 'beastly depravity' was a friend
'in whose heart I never, before at least, believed that any
malice or evil intent dwelt', and vowed not to forgive him;
but the friendship recommenced, and in October 1823
Wilson betrayed it again with a piece on Hogg's *Three
Perils of Woman* which even Blackwood sent back to be
watered down. 'I have a strange indefinable sensation with
regard to him', Hogg confided to Blackwood in January
1825, 'made up of a mixture of terror, admiration and
jealousy—just such a sentiment as one devil might be supposed to have for another.' In another letter Wilson and
Lockhart are 'two devils' who 'have banished me their too
much loved society'. Wilson, apparently, was flattered, and
made his puppet-shepherd accuse him of 'Mephistopheles
tricks' in the *Noctes*: 'I aften think you're an evil speerit in
disguise, and that your greatest delight is in confounding
truth and falsehood.'

It is hard to resist seeing George, 'always ready to
oblige', and Wringhim with his 'ardent and ungovernable
passions', as the two sections of Hogg's personality. He was
eager to be liked, but suspicious and truculent. Goaded by
the need for money, he alternates between *bonhomie* and insult in his letters to Blackwood, Murray, and Scott, following up his outbursts with muddled, pathetic apologies—
'you may guess how grieved I was at all this anger and
jealousy'. Typically, when Wilson loosed his broadside in
1821, Hogg wrote furiously to Scott, threatening to knock
out the reviewer's brains, and, the same day, to Grieve,
protesting 'it appears to me to be a joke'. And though he
was sucked into the gentlemanly swaggerings of the Edinburgh set, another part of him defected. On one occasion he

went with Blackwood to cudgel a Glasgow Whig, Douglas, who had horsewhipped the publisher, but, when Douglas's seconds called on him, sent a servant-girl for the police.

In June 1824, the month the *Confessions* appeared, Blackwood published an anonymous English translation of Hoffmann's *Die Elixiere des Teufels*, which is arguably related to Hogg's novel. The translator was R. P. Gillies, whose acquaintance with Hogg was, by his own account, 'kept up uninterruptedly and cordially from 1913, till my departure from Edinburgh for London in 1827'. Hoffmann's Medardus recalls, 'I began to look upon myself as the one elect,—the pre-eminently chosen of heaven.' He is haunted by an ambiguous 'tall haggard figure' in 'strange foreign garb', who has 'an unearthly glare in his large black staring eyes' and 'an expression of bitter scorn, of disdain mixed almost with hatred'. He believes this figure to be the Devil, and it incites him with talk of predestination: 'The work to which thou wert chosen, must, for thine own weal and salvation, be fulfilled. . . . The attempt to resist the eternal decrees of Omnipotence is not only sinful, but hopeless presumption.' His *doppelgänger*, for whose crimes he is blamed, has himself the 'fixed delusion' that his personality is 'split into two hostile and contending powers', and Medardus's reaction on encountering him ('methought I was, as if by an electrical shock, roused up') corresponds to Wringhim's ('A sensation resembling a stroke of electricity came over me'). Hoffmann's hero hears warning female voices at crises and, like Wringhim, comes upon his brother perched unsuspectingly over a ravine. As his brother falls: 'his mangled form must have dashed from point to point of the rocks in his descent. I heard one piercing yell of agony' (compare Wringhim, who thinks of George 'being dashed to pieces on the protruding rocks, and of hearing his shrieks as he descended the cloud'). Though he has committed murder,

Medardus is persuaded that what 'had many times appeared to me as an unpardonable crime was but the fulfilment of an unalterable decree'. Later, when he believes himself un-armed:

> I felt a painful pressure on my breast, which seemed to proceed from some hard substance in my waistcoat pocket. I grappled with it accordingly, and drew out, to my surprise, a small stiletto. It must, of necessity, be the same which had been held up to me by my mysterious double. I recognized the glittering heft.

Wringhim believes himself weaponless in the weaver's house, but the man points to

> something on the inside of the breast of my frock-coat. I looked at it, and there certainly was the gilded haft of a poniard, the same weapon I had seen and handled before, and which I knew my illus-trious companion always carried about with him.

'Antinomianism' (the belief that the elect are not subject to the moral law) 'is not merely possible,' announced the *Eclectic Review* in December 1824, 'it lives, and walks the earth, and is exerting its deadly influence on society.' The writer was siphoning most of his alarm from Joseph Cottle's *Strictures on the Plymouth Antinomians*, which had come out in 1823. Cottle's subjects, like Hogg's, are a father and son: Dr Hawker, the Vicar of Charles, and the Revd John, 'who surpasses even his sire in all that is extravagant, acri-monious, and antichristian'. Cottle busies himself driving his opponents to blasphemous extremes. Dr Hawker, he reports, 'declares that from the first moment his statement of the gospel is received, the proselyte is . . . at once ren-dered independent of the Shafts of Satan, though perchance wearing his livery, and acting as his slave'. Like Hogg, Cottle calls antinomianism a 'mildew', and demonstrates, as Robert does, that preaching is inconsistent with it. He re-commends the same 'divine test' to the Hawkers—'By their fruits shall ye know them'—as Scrape does to Wringhim. Of course, this is mostly commonplace, and antinomian scares were a chronic disease of high Calvinism. But whether Hogg (who might well have heard about Cottle from Southey) came across the *Strictures* or not, the convictions he represents with such power were not historical oddities (Louis Simpson has pointed to the early eighteenth-century antinomian controversy which involved the Ettrick minister Thomas Boston), but sources of current concern in the year he wrote.

NOTE ON THE TEXT

LONGMANS published the first edition of the *Confessions* in June 1824. It was anonymous ('it being a story replete with horrors, after I had written it I durst not venture to put my name to it', Hogg divulged in 1832: more probably, he guessed it would scandalize high Calvinists), and dedicated by the 'editor' to the Lord Provost of Glasgow, to imply Glasgow provenance. But the *Noctes Ambrosianae* for June 1824 immediately disclosed the author, one character, Maginn, telling Hogg that he would be dug up 'quite fresh and lovely, like this new hero of yours, one hundred summers hence'. Hogg hurriedly contacted Blackwood, explaining that he wanted anonymity, and that it would give 'scope and freedom' for an ovation in the magazine. Obediently, the July number carried a note from Maginn regretting his mistake—'It is, as it professes to be, the performance of a Glasgow Literateur'—detecting 'the hand of a master', and advising Wilson to review it for *Blackwood's*. The only reviews it received, so far as I can discover, were, however, far from complimentary (see Appendix). Longmans had advanced £100 on the *Confessions* and *Queen Hynde* (1825), but according to Hogg (admittedly unreliable), when Blackwood agreed to take a share in the *Confessions*, which was selling slowly, he insisted on repayment of the advance. So, Hogg protests, he got not 'one penny for these two works', though when he went to London in 1832 he was suprised to find that Longmans had been sold out of both 'for a number of years'.

'In 1828', says the 'Publisher's Note' of the 1895 edition (see below), Hogg's novel was 'either reprinted, or more probably reissued with a cancel title page, as *The Suicide's Grave*, this time bearing the author's name.' I have been unable to trace a copy of this reissue, or any mention of it in the periodical lists of new publications for 1828. Possibly Longmans tried to accelerate sale with a new title and a well-known name, but if such a reissue existed it seems plain Hogg knew nothing of it. He never uses the new title and, though he gives a blow-by-blow account in 1832 of his dealings with Longmans, no reissue is alluded to. Indeed, he blames the book's failure on its anonymity. Had he known Longmans had sold out a reissue bearing his name, he would hardly have withheld such satisfying evidence.

In 1837 the novel figured as *The Private Memoirs and Confessions of a Fanatic* in the selected *Tales and Sketches* edited by D. O. Hill. The *Advertisement* claims that this selection 'occupied the attention of the author for several years before his lamented decease' and 'received the final corrections of his pen', and that 'a large portion' of it is 'printed from a copy which had been read by Sir Walter Scott, and which had received many of his corrections and emendations'. In all, 113 passages are chopped out of the *Confessions*, varying in length from one or two words to several pages. Three principles dictate the revision: bowdlerization, tinkering with the structure, and theological timidity. The first accounts for the disappearance of anything approaching profanity, and of the 'bagnio' visited by George and his friends which becomes 'another tavern'. The damage here is relatively slight, though the erasure of Gil-Martin's 'I'll have your soul, sir' and 'Ah, hell has it!' decidedly simplifies George's death scene. The second disposes of the John Barnet episode, the Auchtermuchty story, and the intervention of Hogg himself at the novel's end. The third discards references to the infallibility of the elect, empties the Wringhims's and Gil-Martin's speeches of serious theo-

logical content, and deprives Robert of his prayers, unshaken faith, and assurance of justification. The doctrinal
and psychological hinges of the work are thus patiently un-
screwed. Though the first edition did give offence—Longmans refused Hogg's next work on the grounds that his last
'had been found fault with in some very material points'—
it is hard to believe that, even in old age, Hogg would have
countenanced this vandalism, and the result is worthless
whether he did or not.

Thomson's edition of Hogg's *Works* in 1865 accepts the
1837 version.

In 1895 J. Shiells and Co. published *The Suicide's Grave,
Being the Private Memoirs and Confessions of a Justified
Sinner*, explaining that 'the text here followed is that of the
original edition'. It contains errors or omissions, mostly
minor, on all but three of its 266 pages. There are some
crude illustrations by R. Easton Stuart, one of which inter-
estingly represents Old Colwan and Mrs Logan as young
lovers, and Wringhim, lecturing them, as a doddering
patriarch.

In 1924 T. Earle Welby revived the *Confessions* as No. 1
of the Campion Reprints, and in 1947 the Cresset Press
published an edition with an introduction by André Gide.
Both return to *1824* for their text but tone down Hogg's
rather deliberate punctuation and smooth away irregularities in spelling. Some loss of flavour is involved.

The present text follows *1824*, but admits *1837* readings
in seven places where it seems clear that *1824* misprints:

    p. 63   l. 4. which] with which *1824*
    p. 113 l. 10. least] lest *1824*
    p. 137 l. 33. there] their *1824*
    p. 157 l. 26. undertaking] understanding *1824*
    p. 179 l. 34. trusty] trust *1824*

p. 206 l. 30. round and] round an' *1824*
p. 216 l. 23. effort] effect *1824*

The *1824* running titles have been retained.

SELECT BIBLIOGRAPHY

Abbreviations:

ScLJ   *Scottish Literary Journal*
SSL   *Studies in Scottish Literature*
SHW   *Studies in Hogg and His World*
ELH   *English Literary History*

Bibliography

W. D. Hogg, 'The First Editions of the Writings of James Hogg', *Publications of the Edinburgh Bibliographical Society*, 12 (1924), 53–68; E. C. Batho, *The Ettrick Shepherd*, 1927 (Miss Batho's *Bibliography*, pp. 183–221, is the best available. Corrections and additions are made by her in *Library*, 16 (1935), 309–26, and by B. M. H. Carr, 'The Ettrick Shepherd: Two Unnoted Articles', *N & Q* (2 Sept. 1950), 388–90); F. E. Pierce, 'James Hogg: the Ettrick Shepherd', *Yale University Library Gazette*, 5 (1931), 37–41; Douglas S. Mack, *Hogg's Prose: an Annotated Listing*, Stirling, 1985.

Collected Works

There is no complete edition of Hogg's poetry or prose, but the bulk of both is reprinted in *The Works of the Ettrick Shepherd*, ed. T. Thomson, 1865. Thomson's text is not always dependable, and he chooses the mutilated 1837 version of the *Confessions*.

Life and Letters

Hogg wrote four versions of his autobiography: 'Further particulars in the Life of James Hogg', *Scots Magazine* (July and Nov. 1805), 501–3, 820–3; 'Memoir of the Life of James Hogg' in *The Mountain Bard*, 1807; 'A Memoir of the Author's Life' in *The Mountain Bard*, third edition, 1821; and 'Memoir of the Author's Life' in *Altrive Tales*, 1832. *Memoir of the Author's Life*, ed. D. S. Mack, 1972, follows the *Altrive Tales* text, giving the variants between it and the earlier texts. Later studies include: [R. P. Gillies], 'Some Recollections of James Hogg', *Frasers' Magazine* (Oct. 1839), 414–30; Mrs Garden, *Memorials of James Hogg*, 1885; Sir G. Douglas, *James Hogg*, 1899; E. C. Batho, *The Ettrick Shepherd*, 1927; R. B. Adam, *Works, Letters and Manuscripts of James Hogg*, 1930; D. Carswell, *Sir Walter: a Four-Part Study in Biography*, 1930; A. L. Strout, *Life and Letters of James Hogg*, i. *1770–1825*, 1946; 'Hogg's "Chaldee Manuscript"', *PMLA* 65 (1950), 695–718; 'Maga and the Ettrick Shepherd', *SSL* 4 (1966), 48–51; Nelson C. Smith, *James Hogg*, 1980; David Groves, *James Hogg: The Growth of a Writer*, 1988.

Criticism

L. Simpson, *James Hogg: A Critical Study*, 1962; D. Gifford, *James Hogg*, 1976; Silvia Mergenthal, *James Hogg: Selbstbild und Bild*, 1990.

On the Confessions

G. Saintsbury, *Essays in English Literature, 1780–1860*, 1890, pp. 33–66

A. Lang, 'Confessions of a Justified Sinner', *Illustrated London News* (24 Nov. 1894), Supplement, 12 (answered by Mrs Garden, *Athenaeum* (16 Nov. 1895), 681, and she by Lang, *Athenaeum* (30 Nov. 1895), 754)

E. A. Baker, *History of the English Novel*, vi, 1929, pp. 252–7

W. Allen, *The English Novel*, 1954, pp. 124–5

K. Wittig, *The Scottish Tradition in Literature*, 1958, pp. 245–50

D. Craig, *Scottish Literature and the Scottish People, 1680–1830*, 1961, pp. 190–6

M. Bewley, 'The Society of the Just', *New Statesman* (26 Oct. 1962), 580–2

T. Riese, 'James Hogg und der Roman der englischen Romantik', *Archiv*, 198 (1962), 145–64

C. O. Parsons, *Witchcraft and Demonology in Scott's Fiction*, 1964, pp. 286–97

L. L. Lee, 'The Devil's Figure: James Hogg's "Justified Sinner"', *SSL* 3 (1966), 230–9

D. Mack, 'Hogg's Religion and "The Confessions of a Justified Sinner"', *SSL* 7 (1970), 272–5

D. Eggenschwiler, 'James Hogg's "Confessions" and the Fall into Division', *SSL* 9 (1972), 26–39

I. Campbell, 'Author and Audience in Hogg's "Confessions"', *Scottish Literary News*, 2 (1972), 66–76

I. Campbell, 'Hogg's "Confessions of a Justified Sinner"', *Liturgical Review*, 2 (1972), 28–33

B. R. Bloedé, 'James Hogg's "Private Memoirs and Confessions of a Justified Sinner": the genesis of a double', *Études Anglaises*, 26 (1973), 174–86

R. Kiely, 'The Private Memoirs and Confessions of a Justified Sinner', in *The Romantic Novel in England*, 1973, pp. 208–32

M. Y. Mason, 'The Three Burials in Hogg's "Justified Sinner"', *SSL* 13 (1978), 1–23

M. S. Kearns, 'Intuition and Narration in James Hogg's "Confessions"', *SSL* 13 (1978), 81–91

I. Campbell, 'Hogg's "Confessions" and the "Heart of Darkness"', *SSL* 15 (1980), 187–99

David Groves, 'Parallel Narratives in Hogg's "Justified Sinner"', *ScLJ* 9 (1982), 37–44

Ian Campbell, 'James Hogg and the Bible', *ScLJ* 10 (1983), 14–29

David Groves, 'James Hogg's "Singular Dream" and the "Confessions"', *ScLJ* 10 (1983), 54–66

David Oakleaf, '"Not the Truth": The Doubleness of Hogg's "Confessions" and the 18th-Century Tradition', *SSL* 18 (1983), 59–74

Barbara Bloedé, '"The Confessions of a Justified Sinner": The Paranoiac Nucleus', in *Papers Given at the First James Hogg Society Conference*, ed. Gillian Hughes, 1983, pp. 15–28

Magdalene Redekop, 'Beyond Closure: Buried Alive with Hogg's "Justified Sinner"', *ELH* 52 (1985), 159–84

Philip Rogers, '"A name which may serve your turn"; James Hogg's Gil-Martin', *SSL* 21 (1986), 89–98

Barbara Bloedé, 'A 19th-Century Case of Double Personality: A Possible Source for "The Confessions"', in *Papers Given at the Second James Hogg Society Conference*, ed. Gillian Hughes, 1988, pp. 117–27

Douglas Jones, 'Double Jeopardy and the Chameleon Art in James Hogg's "Justified Sinner"', *SSL* 23 (1988), 164–85

Julie Fenwick, 'Psychological and Narrative Determinism in James Hogg's "Justified Sinner"', *ScLJ* 15 (1988), 61–9

Jill Rubenstein, 'Confession, Damnation and the Dissolution of Identity in Novels by James Hogg and Harold Frederic', *SHW* 1 (1990), 103–13

Allan Beveridge, 'James Hogg and Abnormal Psychology: Some Background Notes', *SHW* 2 (1991), 91–4

David Groves, '"W——m B——e, A Great Original": William Blake, "The Grave", and James Hogg's "Confessions"', *ScLJ* 18 (1991), 27–45

David Petrie, 'The Sinner versus the Scholar: two exemplary models of mis-re-membering and mis-taking signs in relation to Hogg's "Justified Sinner"', *SHW* 3 (1992), 57–67

Clarke Hutton, 'Kierkegaard, Antinomianism, and James Hogg's "Confessions"', *ScLJ* 20 (1993), 37–48.

CHRONOLOGY OF JAMES HOGG

1770 (Nov. ?) Born at Ettrickhall Farm, Ettrick, second of four sons of Robert Hogg, ex-shepherd and tenant-farmer, and Margaret (*née* Laidlaw), distant cousin of William Laidlaw, later Scott's amanuensis.

1777 Father bankrupt. H.'s few months of school-attendance end.

1785 Has worked, by this date, for 'a dozen masters' as cow-herd and labourer. 'All this while I neither read nor wrote; nor had I access to any book save the Bible.'

1788 Hired as shepherd.

1793 First tries writing poetry.

1794 (Oct.) Has poem accepted by *Scots Magazine*.

1800 Starts managing Ettrickhouse Farm for father. Makes popular hit with recruiting-song *Donald MacDonald* (which, however, circulates anonymously).

1801 (Jan.) Publishes slim volume of *Scottish Pastorals*. Starts collecting ballads for William Laidlaw to send to Scott.

1802 (Jan.) First volumes of Scott's *Border Minstrelsy* published; H., disappointed with its imitation-ballads, starts writing his own. (June ?) Meets Scott.

1804 Visits Harris, aiming to take a farm, but loses savings (£150) over legal technicality. Hired as shepherd.

1807 (Apr.) Constable publishes *The Mountain Bard* (imitation-ballads) and (June) *The Shepherd's Guide* (a treatise on sheep-diseases). H., on proceeds, takes Locherben Farm, Dumfriesshire, at ruinous rent.

1809 Bankrupt.

1810 (Feb.) Decamps to Edinburgh. Persuades Constable to publish *The Forest Minstrel* (songs); a failure. (Sept.) Starts literary weekly, *The Spy*, writing half each number himself. It runs for one year, but loses half its subscribers with a risqué story in numbers iii and iv.

1813 (Mar.) *The Queen's Wake* (historico-narrative poem with ballad insets), declined by Constable, published by Goldie: fame at last. Goldie bankrupt after the third edition; Blackwood buys up the remainder.

1814 (Aug.–Sept.) Meets Wordsworth in Edinburgh: 'I listened to him that night as to a superior being.' (Sept.) Dines with De Quincey at Dove Cottage. Meets Southey. (Oct.) Becomes croupier of 'Right, Wrong or Right Club'. Drinks himself into a dangerous fever.

1815 (Jan.) Duke of Buccleuch leases H. Moss End Farm and house (Altrive Lake), rent-free. (Feb.) Blackwood publishes *The Pilgrims of the Sun* ('wild and visionary' poem about a virgin's trip to heaven).

1816 Blackwood publishes *Mador of the Moor* (narrative-descriptive poem in five cantos, written in 1814). (Nov.) Longmans publish *The Poetic Mirror* (volume of parodies); first edition sells in six weeks.

1817 (Sept.) Pringle and Cleghorn (editors of *Edinburgh Monthly Magazine* begun by Blackwood in Apr.) desert to Constable. (Oct.) First number of *Blackwood's Edinburgh Magazine* contains the *Chaldee Manuscript* (parody of prophet Daniel, satirizing Constable, Pringle, Cleghorn and associates, originally by H. but enlarged by Wilson and Lockhart); outcry ensues; H. terrified; *Blackwood's* readership leaps to 10,000.

1818 (June) Blackwood publishes *The Brownie of Bodsbeck* (pro-Covenanter novel).

1820 (Apr.) Marries Margaret Phillips (aged 31). (May) Oliver and Boyd publish *Winter Evening Tales* ('the greater part' written while H. was a shepherd). (Oct.) H. angers Blackwood by arranging with Oliver and Boyd for new edition of *The Mountain Bard*.

1821 Takes 9-year lease of Mount-Benger Farm: great financial mistake. (Aug.) Wilson savages H. in *Blackwood's* (reviewing new edition of *The Mountain Bard*).

1822 (June) Constable publishes H.'s *Poetical Works* (four volumes). Longmans publish *The Three Perils of Man* (potboiler historical romance).

1823 (Aug.) Longmans publish *The Three Perils of Woman* (domestic Scottish stories). (Oct.) Sneering review by Wilson in *Blackwood's*.

1824 (June) Longmans publish *Confessions of a Justified Sinner*.

1825 Longmans and Blackwood publish *Queen Hynde* ('epic poem' begun and abandoned in 1817); a failure.

1829 Blackwood publishes *The Shepherd's Calendar* (short stories).

1831 Blackwood publishes *Songs, by the Ettrick Shepherd* ('a selection of my best'). (Dec.) H. embarks on the 'Edinburgh Castle' for London.

1832 (Jan.–Mar.) Lionized in London. (Mar.) Cochrane, young London publisher, brings out volume i of *Altrive Tales* (intended as complete edition of H.'s prose), then goes bankrupt. Disappointment affects H.'s health. Blackwood alienated by the introductory memoir. (Sept.) Scott dies.

1834 *Familiar Anecdotes of Sir Walter Scott* published in New York and (Oct.) in England as *The Domestic Manners and Private Life of Sir Walter Scott.* Lockhart outraged.

1835 (Mar.) Cochrane, in business again, publishes *Tales of the Wars of Montrose*; bankrupt within a few months. (21 Nov.) H. dies. (30 Nov.) Wordsworth sends *Extempore Effusion* to the *Athenaeum*.

THE
EDITOR'S NARRATIVE

It appears from tradition, as well as some parish registers still extant, that the lands of Dalcastle (or Dalchastel, as it is often spelled) were possessed by a family of the name of Colwan, about one hundred and fifty years ago, and for at least a century previous to that period. That family was supposed to have been a branch of the ancient family of Colquhoun, and it is certain that from it spring the Cowans that spread towards the Border. I find, that in the year 1687, George Colwan succeeded his uncle of the same name, in the lands of Dalchastel and Balgrennan; and this being all I can gather of the family from history, to tradition I must appeal for the remainder of the motley adventures of that house. But of the matter furnished by the latter of these powerful monitors, I have no reason to complain: It has been handed down to the world in unlimited abundance; and I am certain, that in recording the hideous events which follow, I am only relating to the greater part of the inhabitants of at least four counties of Scotland, matters of which they were before perfectly well informed.

This George was a rich man, or supposed to be so, and was married, when considerably advanced in life, to the sole heiress and reputed daughter of a Baillie Orde, of Glasgow. This proved a conjunction any thing but agreeable to the parties contracting. It is well known, that the

Reformation principles had long before that time taken a powerful hold of the hearts and affections of the people of Scotland, although the feeling was by no means general, or in equal degrees; and it so happened that this married couple felt completely at variance on the subject. Granting it to have been so, one would have thought that the laird, owing to his retired situation, would have been the one that inclined to the stern doctrines of the reformers; and that the young and gay dame from the city would have adhered to the free principles cherished by the court party, and indulged in rather to extremity, in opposition to their severe and carping contemporaries.

The contrary, however, happened to be the case. The laird was what his country neighbours called 'a droll, careless chap,' with a very limited proportion of the fear of God in his heart, and very nearly as little of the fear of man. The laird had not intentionally wronged or offended either of the parties, and perceived not the necessity of deprecating their vengeance. He had hitherto believed that he was living in most cordial terms with the greater part of the inhabitants of the earth, and with the powers above in particular: but woe be unto him if he was not soon convinced of the fallacy of such damning security! for his lady was the most severe and gloomy of all bigots to the principles of the Reformation. Hers were not the tenets of the great reformers, but theirs mightily overstrained and deformed. Theirs was an unguent hard to be swallowed; but hers was that unguent embittered and overheated until nature could not longer bear it. She had imbibed her ideas from the doctrines of one flaming predestinarian divine alone; and these were so rigid, that they became a stumbling-block to many of his brethren, and a mighty handle for the enemies of his party to turn the machine of the state against them.

The wedding festivities at Dalcastle partook of all the gaiety, not of that stern age, but of one previous to it. There was feasting, dancing, piping, and singing: the liquors were handed around in great fulness, the ale in large wooden bickers, and the brandy in capacious horns of oxen. The laird gave full scope to his homely glee. He danced,—he snapped his fingers to the music,—clapped his hands and shouted at the turn of the tune. He saluted every girl in the hall whose appearance was any thing tolerable, and requested of their sweethearts to take the same freedom with his bride, by way of retaliation. But there she sat at the head of the hall in still and blooming beauty, absolutely refusing to tread a single measure with any gentleman there. The only enjoyment in which she appeared to partake, was in now and then stealing a word of sweet conversation with her favourite pastor about divine things; for he had accompanied her home after marrying her to her husband, to see her fairly settled in her new dwelling. He addressed her several times by her new name, Mrs. Colwan; but she turned away her head disgusted, and looked with pity and contempt towards the old inadvertent sinner, capering away in the height of his unregenerated mirth. The minister perceived the workings of her pious mind, and thenceforward addressed her by the courteous title of Lady Dalcastle, which sounded somewhat better, as not coupling her name with one of the wicked: and there is too great reason to believe, that for all the solemn vows she had come under, and these were of no ordinary binding, particularly on the laird's part, she at that time despised, if not abhorred him, in her heart.

The good parson again blessed her, and went away. She took leave of him with tears in her eyes, entreating him often to visit her in that heathen land of the Amorite, the Hittite, and the Girgashite: to which he assented, on many solemn and qualifying conditions,—and then the comely bride retired to her chamber to pray.

It was customary, in those days, for the bride's-man and maiden, and a few select friends, to visit the new married couple after they had retired to rest, and drink a cup to their healths, their happiness, and a numerous posterity. But the laird delighted not in this: he wished to have his jewel to himself; and, slipping away quietly from his jovial party, he retired to his chamber to his beloved, and bolted the door. He found her engaged with the writings of the Evangelists, and terribly demure. The laird went up to caress her; but she turned away her head, and spoke of the follies of aged men, and something of the broad way that leadeth to destruction. The laird did not thoroughly comprehend this allusion; but being considerably flustered by drinking, and disposed to take all in good part, he only remarked, as he took off his shoes and stockings, 'that whether the way was broad or narrow, it was time that they were in their bed.'

'Sure, Mr. Colwan, you won't go to bed to-night, at such an important period of your life, without first saying prayers for yourself and me.'

When she said this, the laird had his head down almost to the ground, loosing his shoe-buckle; but when he heard of *prayers*, on such a night, he raised his face suddenly up, which was all over as flushed and red as a rose, and answered,—

'Prayers, Mistress! Lord help your crazed head, is this a night for prayers?'

He had better have held his peace. There was such a torrent of profound divinity poured out upon him, that the laird became ashamed, both of himself and his new-made spouse, and wist not what to say: but the brandy helped him out.

'It strikes me, my dear, that religious devotion would be somewhat out of place to-night,' said he. 'Allowing that it is ever so beautiful, and ever so beneficial, were we to ride on the rigging of it at all times, would we not be constantly making a farce of it: It would be like reading the Bible and the jest-book, verse about, and would render the life of man a medley of absurdity and confusion.'

But against the cant of the bigot or the hypocrite, no reasoning can aught avail. If you would argue until the end of life, the infallible creature must alone be right. So it proved with the laird. One Scripture text followed another, not in the least connected, and one sentence of the profound Mr. Wringhim's sermons after another, proving the duty of family worship, till the laird lost patience, and, tossing himself into bed, said, carelessly, that he would leave that duty upon her shoulders for one night.

The meek mind of Lady Dalcastle was somewhat disarranged by this sudden evolution. She felt that she was left rather in an awkward situation. However, to show her unconscionable spouse that she was resolved to hold fast her integrity, she kneeled down and prayed in terms so potent, that she deemed she was sure of making an impression on him. She did so; for in a short time the laird began to utter a response so fervent, that she was utterly astounded, and fairly driven from the chain of her orisons. He began, in truth, to sound a nasal bugle of no ordinary calibre,—the notes being little inferior to those of a military trumpet. The lady tried to proceed, but every returning note from the bed burst on her ear with a louder twang, and a longer peal, till the concord of sweet sounds became so truly pathetic, that the meek spirit of the dame was quite overcome; and after shedding a flood of tears, she arose from her knees, and retired to the chimney-corner with her Bible in her lap, there to spend the hours in holy meditation till such time as the inebriated trumpeter should awaken to a sense of propriety.

The laird did not awake in any reasonable time; for, he being overcome with fatigue and wassail, his sleep became sounder, and his Morphean measures more intense. These varied a little in their structure; but the general run of the bars sounded something in this way,— 'Hic-hoc-wheew!' It was most profoundly ludicrous; and could not have missed exciting risibility in any one, save a pious, a disappointed, and humbled bride.

The good dame wept bitterly. She could not for her life go and awaken the monster, and request him to make room for her: but she retired somewhere; for the laird, on awaking next morning, found that he was still lying alone. His sleep had been of the deepest and most genuine sort; and all the time that it lasted, he had never once thought of either wives, children, or sweethearts, save in the way of dreaming about them; but as his spirit began again by slow degrees to verge towards the boundaries of reason, it became lighter and more buoyant from the effects of deep repose, and his dreams partook of that buoyancy, yea, to a degree hardly expressible. He dreamed of the reel, the jig, the strathspey, and the corant; and the elasticity of his frame was such, that he was bounding over the heads of the maidens, and making his feet skimmer against the ceiling, enjoying, the while, the most extatic emotions. These grew too fervent for the shackles of the drowsy god to restrain. The nasal bugle ceased its prolonged sounds in one moment, and a sort of hectic laugh took its place. 'Keep it going,—play up, you devils!' cried the laird, without changing his position on the pillow. But this exertion to hold the fiddlers at their work, fairly awakened the delighted dreamer; and though he could not refrain from continuing his laugh, he at length, by tracing out a regular chain of facts, came to be sensible of his real situation. 'Rabina, where are you? What's become of you, my dear?' cried the laird. But there was no voice, nor any one that answered or regarded. He flung open the curtains, thinking to find her still on her knees, as he had seen her; but she was not there, either sleeping or waking. 'Rabina! Mrs. Colwan!' shouted he, as loud as he could call, and then added, in the same breath, 'God save the king,—I have lost my wife!'

He sprung up and opened the casement: the day-light was beginning to streak the east, for it was spring, and the nights were short, and the mornings very long. The laird half dressed himself in an instant, and strode through every room in the house, opening the windows as he went, and scrutinizing every bed and every corner. He came into the hall where the wedding festival had held;[1] and, as he opened the various window-boards, loving couples flew off like hares surprised too late in the morning among the early braird. 'Hoo-boo! Fie, be frightened!' cried the laird. 'Fie, rin like fools, as if ye were caught in an ill turn!'—His bride was not among them; so he was obliged to betake himself to farther search. 'She will be praying in some corner, poor woman,' said he to himself. 'It is an unlucky thing this praying. But, for my part, I fear I have behaved very ill; and I must endeavour to make amends.'

The laird continued his search, and at length found his beloved in the same bed with her Glasgow cousin, who had acted as bride's-maid. 'You sly and malevolent imp,' said the laird; 'you have played me such a trick when I was fast asleep! I have not known a frolic so clever, and, at the same time, so severe. Come along, you baggage you!'

'Sir, I will let you know, that I detest your principles

and your person alike,' said she. 'It shall never be said, Sir, that my person was at the controul of a heathenish man of Belial,—a dangler among the daughters of women, —a promiscuous dancer,—and a player at unlawful games. Forego your rudeness, Sir, I say, and depart away from my presence and that of my kinswoman.'

'Come along, I say, my charming Rab. If you were the pink of all puritans, and the saint of all saints, you are my wife, and must do as I command you.'

'Sir, I will sooner lay down my life than be subjected to your godless will; therefore, I say, desist, and begone with you.'

But the laird regarded none of these testy sayings: he rolled her in a blanket, and bore her triumphantly away to his chamber, taking care to keep a fold or two of the blanket always rather near to her mouth, in case of any outrageous forthcoming of noise.

The next day at breakfast the bride was long in making her appearance. Her maid asked to see her; but George did not choose that any body should see her but himself: he paid her several visits, and always turned the key as he came out. At length breakfast was served; and during the time of refreshment the laird tried to break several jokes; but it was remarked, that they wanted their accustomed brilliancy, and that his nose was particularly red at the top.

Matters, without all doubt, had been very bad between the new-married couple; for in the course of the day the lady deserted her quarters, and returned to her father's house in Glasgow, after having been a night on the road; stage-coaches and steam-boats having then no existence in that quarter. Though Baillie Orde had acquiesced in his wife's asseveration regarding the likeness of their only daughter to her father, he never loved or admired her greatly; therefore this behaviour nothing astounded him.

He questioned her strictly as to the grievous offence committed against her; and could discover nothing that warranted a procedure so fraught with disagreeable consequences. So, after mature deliberation, the baillie addressed her as follows:—

'Ay, ay, Raby! An' sae I find that Dalcastle has actually refused to say prayers with you when you ordered him; an' has guidit you in a rude indelicate manner, outstepping the respect due to my daughter,—as my daughter. But wi' regard to what is due to his own wife, of that he's a better judge nor me. However, since he has behaved in that manner to *my daughter*, I shall be revenged on him for aince; for I shall return the obligation to ane nearer to him: that is, I shall take pennyworths of his wife,—an' let him lick at that.'

'What do you mean, Sir?' said the astonished damsel.

'I mean to be revenged on that villain Dalcastle,' said he, 'for what he has done to my daughter. Come hither, Mrs. Colwan, you shall pay for this.'

So saying, the baillie began to inflict corporal punishment on the runaway wife. His strokes were not indeed very deadly, but he made a mighty flourish in the infliction, pretending to be in a great rage only at the Laird of Dalcastle. 'Villain that he is!' exclaimed he, 'I shall teach him to behave in such a manner to a child of mine, be she as she may: since I cannot get at himself, I shall lounder her that is nearest to him in life. Take you that, and that, Mrs. Colwan, for your husband's impertinence!'

The poor afflicted woman wept and prayed, but the baillie would not abate aught of his severity. After fuming, and beating her with many stripes, far drawn, and lightly laid down, he took her up to her chamber, five stories high, locked her in, and there he fed her on bread and water, all to be revenged on the presumptuous Laird of Dalcastle;

but ever and anon, as the baillie came down the stair from carrying his daughter's meal, he said to himself, 'I shall make the sight of the laird the blithest she ever saw in her life.'

Lady Dalcastle got plenty of time to read, and pray, and meditate; but she was at a great loss for one to dispute with about religious tenets; for she found, that without this advantage, about which there was a perfect rage at that time, her reading, and learning of Scripture texts, and sentences of intricate doctrine, availed her nought; so she was often driven to sit at her casement and look out for the approach of the heathenish Laird of Dalcastle.

That hero, after a considerable lapse of time, at length made his appearance. Matters were not hard to adjust; for his lady found that there was no refuge for her in her father's house; and so, after some sighs and tears, she accompanied her husband home. For all that had passed, things went on no better. She *would* convert the laird in spite of his teeth: The laird would not be converted. She *would* have the laird to say family prayers, both morning and evening: The laird would neither pray morning nor evening. He would not even sing psalms, and kneel beside her, while she performed the exercise; neither would he converse at all times, and in all places, about the sacred mysteries of religion, although his lady took occasion to contradict flatly every assertion that he made, in order that she might spiritualize him by drawing him into argument.

The laird kept his temper a long while, but at length his patience wore out; he cut her short in all her futile attempts at spiritualization, and mocked at her wire-drawn degrees of faith, hope, and repentance. He also dared to doubt of the great standard doctrine of absolute predestination, which put the crown on the lady's christian resentment. She declared her helpmate to be a limb of Antichrist, and one with whom no regenerated person could associate. She therefore bespoke a separate establishment, and before the expiry of the first six months, the arrangements of the separation were amicably adjusted. The upper, or third story of the old mansion-house, was awarded to the lady for her residence. She had a separate door, a separate stair, a separate garden, and walks that in no instance intersected the laird's; so that one would have thought the separation complete. They had each their own parties, selected from their own sort of people; and though the laird never once chafed himself about the lady's companies, it was not long before she began to inter-meddle about some of his.

'Who is that fat bouncing dame that visits the laird so often, and always by herself?' said she to her maid Martha one day.

'O dear, mem, how can I ken? We're banished frae our acquaintances here, as weel as frae the sweet gospel ordinances.'

'Find me out who that jolly dame is, Martha. You, who hold communion with the household of this ungodly man, can be at no loss to attain this information. I observe that she always casts her eye up toward our windows, both in coming and going; and I suspect that she seldom departs from the house empty-handed.'

That same evening Martha came with the information, that this august visitor was a Miss Logan, an old and intimate acquaintance of the laird's, and a very worthy respectable lady, of good connections, whose parents had lost their patrimony in the civil wars.

'Ha! very well!' said the lady; 'very well, Martha! But, nevertheless, go thou and watch this respectable lady's motions and behaviour the next time she comes to visit the laird,—and the next after that. You will not, I see, lack opportunities.'

Martha's information turned out of that nature, that prayers were said in the uppermost story of Dalcastle-house against the Canaanitish woman, every night and every morning; and great discontent prevailed there, even to anathemas and tears. Letter after letter was dispatched to Glasgow; and at length, to the lady's great consolation, the Rev. Mr. Wringhim arrived safely and devoutly in her elevated sanctuary. Marvellous was the conversation between these gifted people. Wringhim had held in his doctrines that there were eight different kinds of FAITH, all perfectly distinct in their operations and effects. But the lady, in her secluded state, had discovered other five,— making twelve[1] in all: the adjusting of the existence or fallacy of these five faiths served for a most enlightened discussion of nearly seventeen hours; in the course of which the two got warm in their arguments, always in proportion as they receded from nature, utility, and common sense. Wringhim at length got into unwonted fervour about some disputed point between one of these faiths and TRUST; when the lady, fearing that zeal was getting beyond its wonted barrier, broke in on his vehe-ment asseverations with the following abrupt discom-fiture:—'But, Sir, as long as I remember, what is to be done with this case of open and avowed iniquity?'

The minister was struck dumb. He leaned him back on his chair, stroked his beard, hemmed—considered, and hemmed again; and then said, in an altered and softened tone,—'Why, that is a secondary consideration; you mean the case between your husband and Miss Logan?'

'The same, Sir. I am scandalised at such intimacies going on under my nose. The sufferance of it is a great and crying evil.'

'Evil, madam, may be either operative, or passive. To them it is an evil, but to us none. We have no more to do with the sins of the wicked and unconverted here, than with those of an infidel Turk; for all earthly bonds and fellowships are absorbed and swallowed up in the holy community of the Reformed Church. However, if it is your wish, I shall take him to task, and reprimand and humble him in such a manner, that *he* shall be ashamed of his doings, and renounce such deeds for ever, out of mere self-respect, though all unsanctified the heart, as well as the deed, may be. To the wicked, all things are wicked; but to the just, all things are just and right.'

'Ah, that is a sweet and comfortable saying, Mr. Wringhim! How delightful to think that a justified person can do no wrong! Who would not envy the liberty where-with we are made free? Go to my husband, that poor unfortunate, blindfolded person, and open his eyes to his degenerate and sinful state; for well are you fitted to the task.'

'Yea, I will go in unto him, and confound him. I will lay the strong holds of sin and Satan as flat before my face, as the dung that is spread out to fatten the land.'

'Master, there's a gentleman at the fore-door wants a private word o'ye.'

'Tell him I'm engaged: I can't see any gentleman to-night. But I shall attend on him to-morrow as soon as he pleases.'

'He's coming straight in, Sir.——Stop a wee bit, Sir, my master is engaged. He cannot see you at present, Sir.'

'Stand aside, thou Moabite! my mission admits of no delay. I come to save him from the jaws of destruction!'

'An that be the case, Sir, it maks a wide difference; an', as the danger may threaten us a', I fancy I may as weel let ye gang by as fight wi'ye, sin' ye seem sae intent on't.——

The man says he's comin' to save ye, an' canna stop, Sir.— Here he is.'

The laird was going to break out into a volley of wrath against Waters, his servant; but before he got a word pronounced, the Rev. Mr. Wringhim had stepped inside the room, and Waters had retired, shutting the door behind him.

No introduction could be more *mal-a-propos:* it is impossible; for at that very moment the laird and Arabella Logan were both sitting on one seat, and both looking on one book, when the door opened. 'What is it, Sir?' said the laird fiercely.

'A message of the greatest importance, Sir,' said the divine, striding unceremoniously up to the chimney,— turning his back to the fire, and his face to the culprits.—'I think you should know me, Sir?' continued he, looking displeasedly at the laird, with his face half turned round.

'I think I should,' returned the laird. 'You are a Mr. How's-tey-ca'-him, of Glasgow, who did me the worst turn ever I got done to me in my life. You gentry are always ready to do a man such a turn. Pray, Sir, did you ever do a good job for any one to counterbalance that? for, if you have not, you ought to be ——.'

'Hold, Sir, I say! None of your profanity before me. If I do evil to any one on such occasions, it is because he will have it so; therefore, the evil is not of my doing. I ask you, Sir,—before God and this witness, I ask you, have you kept solemnly and inviolate the vows which I laid upon you that day? Answer me?'

'Has the partner whom you bound me to, kept hers inviolate? Answer me that, Sir? None can better do so than you, Mr. How's-tey-ca'-you.'

'So, then, you confess your backslidings, and avow the profligacy of your life. And this person here, is, I suppose, the partner of your iniquity,—she whose beauty hath caused you to err! Stand up, both of you, till I rebuke you, and show you what you are in the eyes of God and man.'

'In the first place, stand you still there, till I tell you what *you* are in the eyes of God and man: You are, Sir, a presumptuous, self-conceited pedagogue, a stirrer up of strife and commotion in church, in state, in families, and communities. You are one, Sir, whose righteousness consists in splitting the doctrines of Calvin into thousands of undistinguishable films, and in setting up a system of justifying-grace against all breaches of all laws, moral or divine. In short, Sir, you are a mildew,—a canker-worm in the bosom of the Reformed Church, generating a disease of which she will never be purged, but by the shedding of blood. Go thou in peace, and do these abominations no more; but humble thyself, lest a worse reproof come upon thee.'

Wringhim heard all this without flinching. He now and then twisted his mouth in disdain, treasuring up, mean time, his vengeance against the two aggressors; for he felt that he had them on the hip, and resolved to pour out his vengeance and indignation upon them. Sorry am I, that the shackles of modern decorum restrain me from penning that famous rebuke; fragments of which have been attributed to every divine of old notoriety throughout Scotland. But I have it by heart; and a glorious morsel it is to put into the hands of certain incendiaries. The metaphors were so strong, and so appalling, that Miss Logan could only stand them a very short time: she was obliged to withdraw in confusion. The laird stood his ground with much ado, though his face was often crimsoned over with the hues of shame and anger. Several times he was on the point of turning the officious sycophant to the door; but good manners, and an inherent respect that he entertained for the clergy, as the immediate servants of the Supreme Being, restrained him.

Wringhim, perceiving these symptoms of resentment, took them for marks of shame and contrition, and pushed his reproaches farther than ever divine ventured to do in a similar case. When he had finished, to prevent further discussion, he walked slowly and majestically out of the apartment, making his robes to swing behind him in a most magisterial manner; he being, without doubt, elated with his high conquest. He went to the upper story, and related to his metaphysical associate his wonderful success; how he had driven the dame from the house in tears and deep confusion, and left the backsliding laird in such a quandary of shame and repentance, that he could neither articulate a word, nor lift up his countenance. The dame thanked him most cordially, lauding his friendly zeal and powerful eloquence; and then the two again set keenly to the splitting of hairs, and making distinctions in religion where none existed.

They being both children of adoption, and secured from falling into snares, or any way under the power of the wicked one, it was their custom, on each visit, to sit up a night in the same apartment, for the sake of sweet spiritual converse; but that time, in the course of the night, they differed so materially on a small point, somewhere between justification and final election, that the minister, in the heat of his zeal, sprung from his seat, paced the floor, and maintained his point with such ardour, that Martha was alarmed, and, thinking they were going to fight, and that the minister would be a hard match for her mistress, she put on some clothes, and twice left her bed and stood listening at the back of the door, ready to burst in should need require it. Should any one think this picture over-strained, I can assure him that it is taken from nature and from truth; but I will not likewise aver, that the theologist was neither crazed nor inebriated. If the listener's words were to be relied on, there was no love, no accommodating principle manifested between the two, but a fiery burning zeal, relating to points of such minor importance, that a true Christian would blush to hear them mentioned, and the infidel and profane make a handle of them to turn our religion to scorn.

Great was the dame's exultation at the triumph of her beloved pastor over her sinful neighbours in the lower parts of the house; and she boasted of it to Martha in high-sounding terms. But it was of short duration; for, in five weeks after that, Arabella Logan came to reside with the laird as his house-keeper, sitting at his table, and carrying the keys as mistress-substitute of the mansion. The lady's grief and indignation were now raised to a higher pitch than ever; and she set every agent to work, with whom she had any power, to effect a separation between these two suspected ones. Remonstrance was of no avail: George laughed at them who tried such a course, and retained his house-keeper, while the lady gave herself up to utter despair; for though she would not consort with her husband herself, she could not endure that any other should do so.

But, to countervail this grievous offence, our saintly and afflicted dame, in due time, was safely delivered of a fine boy, whom the laird acknowledged as his son and heir, and had him christened by his own name, and nursed in his own premises. He gave the nurse permission to take the boy to his mother's presence if ever she should desire to see him; but, strange as it may appear, she never once desired to see him from the day that he was born. The boy grew up, and was a healthful and happy child; and, in the course of another year, the lady presented him with a brother. A brother he certainly was, in the eye of the law, and it is more than probable that he was his brother in reality. But the laird thought otherwise; and, though he knew and acknowledged that he was obliged to support and provide for him, he refused to acknowledge him in other respects. He neither would countenance the banquet, nor take the baptismal vows on him in the child's name; of course, the poor boy had to live and remain an alien from the visible church for a year and a day; at which time, Mr. Wringhim, out of pity and kindness, took the lady herself as sponsor for the boy, and baptized him by the name of Robert Wringhim,—that being the noted divine's own name.

George was brought up with his father, and educated partly at the parish-school, and partly at home, by a tutor hired for the purpose. He was a generous and kind-hearted youth; always ready to oblige, and hardly ever dissatisfied with any body. Robert was brought up with Mr. Wringhim, the laird paying a certain allowance for him yearly; and there the boy was early inured to all the sternness and severity of his pastor's arbitrary and unyielding creed. He was taught to pray twice every day, and seven times on Sabbath days; but he was only to pray for the elect, and, like David of old, doom all that were aliens from God to destruction. He had never, in that family into which he had been as it were adopted, heard ought but evil spoken of his reputed father and brother; consequently he held them in utter abhorrence, and prayed against them every day, often 'that the old hoary sinner might be cut off in the full flush of his iniquity, and be carried quick into hell; and that the young stem of the corrupt trunk might also be taken from a world that he disgraced, but that his sins might be pardoned, because he knew no better.'

Such were the tenets in which it would appear young Robert was bred. He was an acute boy, an excellent learner, had ardent and ungovernable passions, and withal, a sternness of demeanour from which other boys shrunk. He was the best grammarian, the best reader, writer, and accountant in the various classes that he attended, and was fond of writing essays on controverted points of theology, for which he got prizes, and great praise from his guardian and mother. George was much behind him in scholastic acquirements, but greatly his superior in personal prowess, form, feature, and all that constitutes gentility in deportment and appearance. The laird had often manifested to Miss Logan an earnest wish that the two young men should never meet, or at all events that they should be as little conversant as possible; and Miss Logan, who was as much attached to George as if he had been her own son, took every precaution, while he was a boy, that he should never meet with his brother; but as they advanced towards manhood, this became impraticable. The lady was removed from her apartments in her husband's house to Glasgow, to her great content; and all to prevent the young laird being tainted with the company of her and her second son; for the laird had felt the effects of the principles they professed, and dreaded them more than persecution, fire, and sword. During all the dreadful times that had overpast, though the laird had been a moderate man, he had still leaned to the side of the kingly prerogative, and had escaped confiscation and fines, without ever taking any active hand in suppressing the Covenanters.[1] But after experiencing a specimen of their tenets and manner in his wife, from a secret favourer of them and their doctrines, he grew alarmed at the prevalence of such stern and factious principles, now that there was no check nor restraint upon them; and from that time he began to set himself against them, joining with the cavalier party of that day in all their proceedings.

It so happened, that, under the influence of the Earls of Seafield and Tullibardine,[1] he was returned for a Member of Parliament in the famous session[2] that sat at Edinburgh, when the Duke of Queensberry was commissioner, and in which party spirit ran to such an extremity. The young laird went with his father to the court, and remained in town all the time that the session lasted; and as all interested people of both factions flocked to the town at that period, so the important Mr. Wringhim was there among the rest, during the greater part of the time, blowing the coal of revolutionary principles with all his might, in every society to which he could obtain admission. He was a great favourite with some of the west country gentlemen of that faction, by reason of his unbending impudence. No opposition could for a moment cause him either to blush, or retract one item that he had advanced. Therefore the Duke of Argyle[3] and his friends made such use of him as sportsmen often do of terriers, to start the game, and make a great yelping noise to let them know whither the chace is proceeding. They often did this out of sport, in order to teaze their opponent; for of all pesterers that ever fastened on man he was the most insufferable: knowing that his coat protected him from manual chastisement, he spared no acrimony, and delighted in the chagrin and anger of those with whom he contended. But he was sometimes likewise *of real use* to the heads of the presbyterian faction, and therefore was admitted to their tables, and of course conceived himself a very great man.

His ward accompanied him; and very shortly after their arrival in Edinburgh, Robert, for the first time, met with the young laird his brother, in a match at tennis. The prowess and agility of the young squire drew forth the loudest plaudits of approval from his associates, and his own exertion alone carried the game every time on the one side, and that so far as all along to count three for their one. The hero's name soon ran round the circle, and when his brother Robert, who was an onlooker, learned who it was that was gaining so much applause, he came and stood close beside him all the time that the game lasted, always now and then putting in a cutting remark by way of mockery.

George could not help perceiving him, not only on account of his impertinent remarks, but he, moreover, stood so near him that he several times impeded him in his rapid evolutions, and of course got himself shoved aside in no very ceremonious way. Instead of making him keep his distance, these rude shocks and pushes, accompanied sometimes with hasty curses, only made him cling the closer to this king of the game. He seemed determined to maintain his right to his place as an onlooker, as well as any of those engaged in the game, and if they had tried him at an argument, he would have carried his point: or perhaps he wished to quarrel with this spark of his jealousy and aversion, and draw the attention of the gay crowd to himself by these means; for like his guardian, he knew no other pleasure but what consisted in opposition. George took him for some impertinent student of divinity, rather set upon a joke than any thing else. He perceived a lad with black clothes, and a methodistical face, whose countenance and eye he disliked exceedingly, several times in his way, and that was all the notice he took of him the first time they two met. But the next day, and every succeeding one, the same devilish-looking youth attended him as constantly as his shadow; was always in his way as with intention to impede him, and ever and anon his deep and malignant eye met those of his elder brother with a glance so fierce that it sometimes startled him.

The very next time that George was engaged at tennis,

he had not struck the ball above twice till the same in-
trusive being was again in his way. The party played for
considerable stakes that day, namely, a dinner and wine
at the Black Bull tavern; and George, as the hero and
head of his party, was much interested in its honour; consequently, the sight of this moody and hellish-looking
student affected him in no very pleasant manner. 'Pray,
Sir, be so good as keep without the range of the ball,' said he.

'Is there any law or enactment that can compel me to
do so?' said the other, biting his lip with scorn.

'If there is not, they are here that shall compel you,'
returned George: 'so, friend, I rede you to be on your
guard.'

As he said this, a flush of anger glowed in his handsome
face, and flashed from his sparkling blue eye; but it was a
stranger to both, and momently took its departure. The
black-coated youth set up his cap before, brought his
heavy brows over his deep dark eyes, put his hands in the
pockets of his black plush breeches, and stepped a little
farther into the semi-circle, immediately on his brother's
right hand, than he had ever ventured to do before. There
he set himself firm on his legs, and, with a face as demure
as death, seemed determined to keep his ground. He pretended to be following the ball with his eyes; but every
moment they were glancing aside at George. One of the
competitors chanced to say rashly, in the moment of
exultation, 'That's a d——d fine blow, George!' On
which the intruder took up the word, as characteristic of
the competitors, and repeated it every stroke that was
given, making such a ludicrous use of it, that several of
the on-lookers were compelled to laugh immoderately;
but the players were terribly nettled at it, as he really
contrived, by dint of sliding in some canonical terms, to
render the competitors and their game ridiculous.

But matters at length came to a crisis that put them beyond sport. George, in flying backward to gain the point at which the ball was going to light, came inadvertently so rudely in contact with this obstreperous interloper, that he not only overthrew him, but also got a grievous fall over his legs; and, as he arose, the other made a spurn at him with his foot, which, if it had hit to its aim, would undoubtedly have finished the course of the young laird of Dalcastle and Balgrennan. George, being irritated beyond measure, as may well be conceived, especially at the deadly stroke aimed at him, struck the assailant with his racket, rather slightly, but so that his mouth and nose gushed out blood; and, at the same time, he said, turning to his cronies,—'Does any of you know who the infernal puppy is?'

'Do you not know, Sir?' said one of the onlookers, a stranger: 'The gentleman is your own brother, Sir—Mr. Robert Wringhim Colwan!'

'No, not Colwan, Sir,' said Robert, putting his hands in his pockets, and setting himself still farther forward than before,—'not a Colwan, Sir; henceforth I disclaim the name.'

'No, certainly not,' repeated George: 'My mother's son you may be,—but *not a Colwan*! There you are right.' Then turning round to his informer, he said, 'Mercy be about us, Sir! is this the crazy minister's son from Glasgow?'

This question was put in the irritation of the moment; but it was too rude, and too far out of place, and no one deigned any answer to it. He felt the reproof, and felt it deeply; seeming anxious for some opportunity to make an acknowledgment, or some reparation.

In the meantime, young Wringhim was an object to all of the uttermost disgust. The blood flowing from his

mouth and nose he took no pains to stem, neither did he
so much as wipe it away; so that it spread over all his
cheeks, and breast, even off at his toes. In that state did
he take up his station in the middle of the competitors;
and he did not now keep his place, but ran about, impeding
every one who attempted to make at the ball. They
loaded him with execrations, but it availed nothing; he
seemed courting persecution and buffetings, keeping stedfastly to his old joke of damnation, and marring the game
so completely, that, in spite of every effort on the part of
the players, he forced them to stop their game, and give
it up. He was such a rueful-looking object, covered with
blood, that none of them had the heart to kick him,
although it appeared the only thing he wanted; and as
for George, he said not another word to him, either in
anger or reproof.

When the game was fairly given up, and the party were
washing their hands in the stone fount, some of them
besought Robert Wringhim to wash himself; but he
mocked at them, and said, he was much better as he was.
George, at length, came forward abashedly toward him,
and said,—'I have been greatly to blame, Robert, and
am very sorry for what I have done. But, in the first instance, I erred through ignorance, not knowing you were
my brother, which you certainly are; and, in the second,
through a momentary irritation, for which I am ashamed.
I pray you, therefore, to pardon me, and give me your
hand.'

As he said this, he held out his hand toward his polluted
brother; but the froward predestinarian took not his from
his breeches pocket, but lifting his foot, he gave his
brother's hand a kick. 'I'll give you what will suit such a
hand better than mine,' said he, with a sneer. And then,
turning lightly about, he added,—'Are there to be no

more of these d——d fine blows, gentlemen? For shame, to give up such a profitable and edifying game!'

'This is too bad,' said George. 'But, since it is thus, I have the less to regret.' And, having made this general remark, he took no more note of the uncouth aggressor. But the persecution of the latter terminated not on the play-ground: he ranked up among them, bloody and disgusting as he was, and, keeping close by his brother's side, he marched along with the party all the way to the Black Bull. Before they got there, a great number of boys and idle people had surrounded them, hooting and incommoding them exceedingly, so that they were glad to get into the inn; and the unaccountable monster actually tried to get in alongst with them, to make one of the party at dinner. But the innkeeper and his men, getting the hint, by force prevented him from entering, although he attempted it again and again, both by telling lies and offering a bribe. Finding he could not prevail, he set to exciting the mob at the door to acts of violence; in which he had like to have succeeded. The landlord had no other shift, at last, but to send privately for two officers, and have him carried to the guard-house; and the hilarity and joy of the party of young gentlemen, for the evening, was quite spoiled, by the inauspicious termination of their game.

The Rev. Robert Wringham was now to send for, to release his beloved ward. The messenger found him at table, with a number of the leaders of the Whig faction, the Marquis of Annandale[1] being in the chair; and the prisoner's note being produced, Wringhim read it aloud, accompanying it with some explanatory remarks. The circumstances of the case being thus magnified and distorted, it excited the utmost abhorrence, both of the deed and the perpetrators, among the assembled faction. They declaimed against the act as an unnatural attempt on the character, and even the life, of an unfortunate brother, who had been expelled from his father's house. And, as party spirit was the order of the day, an attempt was made to lay the burden of it to that account. In short, the young culprit got some of the best blood of the land to enter as his securities, and was set at liberty. But when Wringhim perceived the plight that he was in, he took him, as he was, and presented him to his honourable patrons. This raised the indignation against the young laird and his associates a thousand fold, which actually roused the party to temporary madness. They were, perhaps, a little excited by the wine and spirits they had swallowed; else a casual quarrel between two young men, at tennis, could not have driven them to such extremes. But certain it is, that from one at first arising to address the party on the atrocity of the offence, both in a moral and political point of view, on a sudden there were six on their feet, at the same time, expatiating on it; and, in a very short time thereafter, every one in the room was up, talking with the utmost vociferation, all on the same subject, and all taking the same side in the debate.

In the midst of this confusion, some one or other issued from the house, which was at the back of the Canongate, calling out,—'A plot, a plot! Treason, treason! Down with the bloody incendiaries at the Black Bull!'

The concourse of people that were assembled in Edinburgh at that time was prodigious; and as they were all actuated by political motives, they wanted only a ready-blown coal to set the mountain on fire. The evening being fine, and the streets thronged, the cry ran from mouth to mouth through the whole city. More than that, the mob that had of late been gathered to the door of the Black Bull, had, by degrees, dispersed; but, they being young men, and idle vagrants, they had only spread themselves over the rest of the street to lounge in search of farther amusement: consequently, a word was sufficient to send them back to their late rendezvous, where they had previously witnessed something they did not much approve of.

The master of the tavern was astonished at seeing the mob again assembling; and that with such hurry and noise. But his inmates being all of the highest respectability, he judged himself sure of protection, or, at least, of indemnity. He had two large parties in his house at the time; the largest of which was of the Revolutionist faction. The other consisted of our young tennis-players, and their associates, who were all of the Jacobite order; or, at all events, leaned to the Episcopal side. The largest party were in a front-room; and the attack of the mob fell first on their windows, though rather with fear and caution. Jingle went one pane; then a loud hurra; and that again was followed by a number of voices, endeavouring to restrain the indignation from venting itself in destroying the windows, and to turn it on the inmates. The Whigs, calling the landlord, inquired what the assault meant: he cunningly answered, that he suspected it was some of the youths of the Cavalier, or High-Church party, exciting the mob against them. The party consisted mostly of young gentlemen, by that time in a key to engage in any row; and, at all events, to suffer nothing from the other party, against whom their passions were mightily inflamed.

The landlord, therefore, had no sooner given them the spirit-rousing intelligence, than every one, as by instinct, swore his own natural oath, and grasped his own natural weapon. A few of those of the highest rank were armed with swords, which they boldly drew; those of the subordinate orders immediately flew to such weapons as the room, kitchen, and scullery afforded;—such as tongs,

pokers, spits, racks, and shovels; and breathing vengeance
on the prelatic party, the children of Antichrist and the
heirs of d—n—t—n! the barterers of the liberties of their
country, and betrayers of the most sacred trust,—thus
elevated, and thus armed, in the cause of right, justice,
and liberty, our heroes rushed to the street, and attacked
the mob with such violence, that they broke the mass in a
moment, and dispersed their thousands like chaff before
the wind. The other party of young Jacobites, who sat in
a room farther from the front, and were those against
whom the fury of the mob was meant to have been directed,
knew nothing of this second uproar, till the noise of the
sally made by the Whigs assailed their ears; being then
informed that the mob had attacked the house on account
of the treatment they themselves had given to a young
gentleman of the adverse faction, and that another jovial
party had issued from the house in their defence, and was
now engaged in an unequal combat, the sparks likewise
flew to the field to back their defenders with all their
prowess, without troubling their heads about who they
were.

A mob is like a spring-tide in an eastern storm, that
retires only to return with more overwhelming fury. The
crowd was taken by surprise, when such a strong and well-
armed party issued from the house with so great fury,
laying all prostrate that came in their way. Those who
were next to the door, and were, of course, the first whom
the imminent danger assailed, rushed backward among
the crowd with their whole force. The Black Bull standing
in a small square half way between the High Street and
the Cowgate, and the entrance to it being by two closes,
into these the pressure outward was simultaneous, and
thousands were moved to an involuntary flight they knew
not why.

But the High Street of Edinburgh, which they soon reached, is a dangerous place in which to make an open attack upon a mob. And it appears that the entrances to the tavern had been somewhere near to the Cross, on the south side of the street; for the crowd fled with great expedition, both to the east and west, and the conquerors, separating themselves as chance directed, pursued impetuously, wounding and maiming as they flew. But, it so chanced, that before either of the wings had followed the flying squadrons of their enemies for the space of a hundred yards each way, the devil an enemy they had to pursue! the multitude had vanished like so many thousands of phantoms! What could our heroes do?—Why, they faced about to return toward their citadel, the Black Bull. But that feat was not so easily, nor so readily accomplished, as they divined. The unnumbered alleys on each side of the street had swallowed up the multitude in a few seconds; but from these they were busy reconnoitring; and, perceiving the deficiency in the number of their assailants, the rush from both sides of the street was as rapid, and as wonderful, as the disappearance of the crowd had been a few minutes before. Each close vomited out its levies, and these better armed with missiles than when they sought it for a temporary retreat. Woe then to our two columns of victorious Whigs! The mob actually closed around them as they would have swallowed them up; and, in the meanwhile, shower after shower of the most abominable weapons of offence were rained in upon them. If the gentlemen were irritated before, this inflamed them still farther; but their danger was now so apparent, they could not shut their eyes on it, therefore, both parties, as if actuated by the same spirit, made a desperate effort to join, and the greater part effected it; but some were knocked down, and others were separated from their friends, and blithe to become silent members of the mob.

The battle now raged immediately in front of the closes leading to the Black Bull; the small body of Whig gentlemen was hardly bested, and it is likely would have been overcome and trampled down every man, had they not been then and there joined by the young Cavaliers; who, fresh to arms, broke from the wynd, opened the head of the passage, laid about them manfully, and thus kept up the spirits of the exasperated Whigs, who were the men in fact that wrought the most deray among the populace.

The town-guard was now on the alert; and two companies of the Cameronian regiment, with the Hon. Captain Douglas, rushed down from the Castle to the scene of action; but, for all the noise and hubbub that these caused in the street, the combat had become so close and inveterate, that numbers of both sides were taken prisoners fighting hand to hand, and could scarcely be separated when the guardsmen and soldiers had them by the necks.

Great was the alarm and confusion that night in Edinburgh; for every one concluded that it was a party scuffle, and, the two parties being so equal in power, the most serious consequences were anticipated. The agitation was so prevailing, that every party in the town, great and small, was broken up; and the lord-commissioner thought proper to go to the council-chamber himself, even at that late hour, accompanied by the sheriffs of Edinburgh and Linlithgow, with sundry noblemen besides, in order to learn something of the origin of the affray.

For a long time the court was completely puzzled. Every gentleman brought in exclaimed against the treatment he had received, in most bitter terms, blaming a mob set on him and his friends by the adverse party, and matters looked extremely ill, until at length they began to perceive that they were examining gentlemen of both parties, and that they had been doing so from the beginning, almost alternately, so equally had the prisoners been taken from both parties. Finally, it turned out, that a few gentlemen, two-thirds of whom were strenuous Whigs themselves, had joined in mauling the whole Whig population of Edinburgh. The investigation disclosed nothing the effect of which was not ludicrous; and the Duke of Queensberry, whose aims was at that time to conciliate the two factions, tried all that he could to turn the whole *fracas* into a joke—an unlucky frolic, where no ill was meant on either side, and which yet had been productive of a great deal.

The greater part of the people went home satisfied; but not so the Rev. Robert Wringhim. He did all that he could to inflame both judges and populace against the young Cavaliers, especially against the young Laird of Dalcastle, whom he represented as an incendiary, set on by an unnatural parent to slander his mother, and make away with a hapless and only brother; and, in truth, that declaimer against all human merit had that sort of powerful, homely, and bitter eloquence, which seldom missed affecting his hearers: the consequence at that time was, that he made the unfortunate affair between the two brothers appear in extremely bad colours, and the populace retired to their homes impressed with no very favourable opinion of either the Laird of Dalcastle or his son George, neither of whom were there present to speak for themselves.

As for Wringhim himself, he went home to his lodgings, filled with gall and with spite against the young laird, whom he was made to believe the aggressor, and that intentionally. But most of all was he filled with indignation against the father, whom he held in abhorrence at all times, and blamed solely for this unmannerly attack made on his

favourite ward, namesake, and adopted son; and for the
public imputation of a crime to his own reverence, in
calling the lad *his* son, and thus charging him with a sin
against which he was well known to have levelled all
the arrows of church censure with unsparing might.

But, filled as his heart was with some portion of these
bad feelings, to which all flesh is subject, he kept, nevertheless, the fear of the Lord always before his eyes so
far as never to omit any of the external duties of religion,
and farther than that, man hath no power to pry. He
lodged with the family of a Mr. Miller, whose lady was
originally from Glasgow, and had been a hearer, and, of
course, a great admirer of Mr. Wringhim. In that family
he made public worship every evening; and that night, in
his petitions at a throne of grace, he prayed for so many
vials of wrath to be poured on the head of some particular
sinner, that the hearers trembled, and stopped their ears.
But that he might not proceed with so violent a measure,
amounting to excommunication, without due scripture
warrant, he began the exercise of the evening by singing
the following verses, which it is a pity should ever have
been admitted into a Christian psalmody, being so
adverse to all its mild and benevolent principles:—

> Set thou the wicked over him,
>   *And upon his right hand*
> *Give thou his greatest enemy,*
>   *Even Satan, leave to stand.*
> And when by thee he shall be judged,
>   Let him remembered be;
> And let his prayer be turned to sin,
>   When he shall call on thee.
> Few be his days; and in his room
>   His charge another take;
> His children let be fatherless;
>   His wife a widow make:

> Let God his father's wickedness
>   Still to remembrance call;
> And never let his mother's sin
>   Be blotted out at all.
> As he in cursing pleasure took,
>   So let it to him fall;
> As he delighted not to bless,
>   So bless him not at all.
> As cursing he like clothes put on,
>   Into his bowels so,
> Like water, and into his bones
>   Like oil, down let it go.

Young Wringhim only knew the full purport of this spiritual song; and went to his bed better satisfied than ever, that his father and brother were cast-aways, reprobates, aliens from the church and the true faith, and cursed in time and eternity.

The next day George and his companions met as usual,—all who were not seriously wounded of them. But as they strolled about the city, the rancorous eye and the finger of scorn was pointed against them. None of them was at first aware of the reason; but it threw a damp over their spirits and enjoyments, which they could not master. They went to take a forenoon game at their old play of tennis, not on a match, but by way of improving themselves; but they had not well taken their places till young Wringhim appeared in his old station, at his brother's right hand, with looks more demure and determined than ever. His lips were primmed so close that his mouth was hardly discernible, and his dark deep eye flashed gleams of holy indignation on the godless set, but particularly on his brother. His presence acted as a mildew on all social intercourse or enjoyment; the game was marred, and ended ere ever it was well begun. There were whisperings apart—the party separated; and, in order to shake off the the blighting influence of this dogged persecutor, they entered sundry houses of their acquaintances, with an understanding that they were to meet on the Links for a game at cricket.

They did so; and, stripping off part of their clothes, they began that violent and spirited game. They had not played five minutes, till Wringhim was stalking in the midst of them, and totally impeding the play. A cry arose from all corners of 'O, this will never do. Kick him out of the playground! Knock down the scoundrel; or bind him, and let him lie in peace.'

'By no means,' cried George: 'it is evident he wants nothing else. Pray do not humour him so much as to touch him with either foot or finger.' Then turning to a friend, he said in a whisper, 'Speak to him, Gordon; he surely will not refuse to let us have the ground to ourselves, if you request it of him.'

Gordon went up to him, and requested of him, civilly, but ardently, 'to retire to a certain distance, else none of them could or would be answerable, however sore he might be hurt.'

He turned disdainfully on his heel, uttered a kind of pulpit hem! and then added, 'I will take my chance of that; hurt me, any of you, at your peril.'

The young gentlemen smiled, through spite and disdain of the dogged animal. Gordon followed him up, and tried to remonstrate with him; but he let him know that 'it was his pleasure to be there at that time; and, unless he could demonstrate to him what superior right he and his party had to that ground, in preference to him, and to the exclusion of all others, he was determined to assert his right, and the rights of his fellow-citizens, by keeping possession of whatsoever part of that common field he chose.'

'You are no gentleman, Sir,' said Gordon.

'Are you one, Sir?' said the other.

'Yes, Sir, I will let you know that I am, by G——!'

'Then, thanks be to Him whose name you have profaned, I am none. If *one* of the party be a gentleman, *I do hope in God I am not!*'

It was now apparent to them all that he was courting obloquy and manual chastisement from their hands, if by any means he could provoke them to the deed; and, apprehensive that he had some sinister and deep-laid design in hunting after such a singular favour, they wisely restrained one another from inflicting the punishment that each of them yearned to bestow, personally, and which he so well deserved.

But the unpopularity of the Younger George Colwan could no longer be concealed from his associates. It was manifested wherever the populace were assembled; and his young and intimate friend, Adam Gordon, was obliged to warn him of the circumstance, that he might not be surprised at the gentlemen of their acquaintance withdrawing themselves from his society, as they could not be seen with him without being insulted. George thanked him; and it was agreed between them, that the former should keep himself retired during the daytime while he remained in Edinburgh, and that at night they should always meet together, along with such of their companions as were disengaged.

George found it every day more and more necessary to adhere to this system of seclusion; for it was not alone the hisses of the boys and populace that pursued him,—a fiend of more malignant aspect was ever at his elbow, in the form of his brother. To whatever place of amusement he betook himself, and however well he concealed his intentions of going there from all flesh living, there was his brother Wringhim also, and always within a few yards of him, generally about the same distance, and ever and anon darting looks at him that chilled his very soul. They were looks that cannot be described; but they were felt piercing to the bosom's deepest core. They affected even the on-lookers in a very particular manner, for all whose eyes caught a glimpse of these hideous glances followed them to the object toward which they were darted: the gentlemanly and mild demeanour of that object generally calmed their startled apprehensions; for no one ever yet noted the glances of the young man's eye in the black coat, at the face of his brother, who did not at first manifest strong symptoms of alarm.

George became utterly confounded; not only at the import of this persecution, but how in the world it came to pass that this unaccountable being knew all his motions, and every intention of his heart, as it were intuitively. On consulting his own previous feelings and resolutions, he found that the circumstances of his going to such and such a place were often the most casual incidents in nature—the caprice of a moment had carried him there, and yet he had never sat or stood many minutes till there was the self-same being, always in the same position with regard to himself, as regularly as the shadow is cast from the substance, or the ray of light from the opposing denser medium.

For instance, he remembered one day of setting out with the intention of going to attend divine worship in the High Church, and when within a short space of its door, he was overtaken by young Kilpatrick of Closeburn, who was bound to the Grey-Friars to see his sweetheart, as he said; 'and if you will go with me, Colwan,' said he, 'I will let you see her too, and then you will be just as far forward as I am.'

George assented at once, and went; and after taking his seat, he leaned his head forward on the pew to repeat over to himself a short ejaculatory prayer, as had always been his custom on entering the house of God. When he had done, he lifted his eyes naturally toward that point on his right hand where the fierce apparition of his brother had been wont to meet his view: there he was, in the same habit, form, demeanour, and precise point of distance, as usual! George again laid down his head, and his mind was so astounded, that he had nearly fallen into a swoon. He tried shortly after to muster up courage to look at the speaker, at the congregation, and at Captain Kilpatrick's sweetheart in particular; but the fiendish glances of the young man in the black clothes were too appalling to be withstood,—his eye caught them whether he was looking that way or not: at length his courage was fairly mastered, and he was obliged to look down during the remainder of the service.

By night or by day it was the same. In the gallery of the Parliament House, in the boxes of the play-house, in the church, in the assembly, in the streets, suburbs, and the fields; and every day, and every hour, from the first rencounter of the two, the attendance became more and more constant, more inexplicable, and altogether more alarming and insufferable, until at last George was fairly driven from society, and forced to spend his days in his own and his father's lodgings with closed doors. Even there, he was constantly harassed with the idea, that the next time he lifted his eyes, he would to a certainty see that face, the most repulsive to all his feelings of aught the earth contained. The attendance of that brother was now become like the attendance of a demon on some devoted being that had sold himself to destruction; his approaches as undiscerned, and his looks as fraught with hideous malignity. It was seldom that he saw him either following him in the streets, or entering any house or church after him; he only appeared in his place, George wist not how, or whence; and, having sped so ill in his first friendly approaches, he had never spoken to his equivocal attendant a second time.

It came at length into George's head, as he was pondering, by himself, on the circumstances of this extraordinary attendance, that perhaps his brother had relented, and, though of so sullen and unaccommodating a temper that he would not acknowledge it, or beg a reconciliation, it might be for that very purpose that he followed his steps night and day in that extraordinary manner. 'I cannot for my life see for what other purpose it can be,' thought he. 'He never offers to attempt my life; nor dares he, if he had the inclination; therefore, although his manner is peculiarly repulsive to me, I shall not have my mind burdened with the reflection, that my own mother's son yearned for a reconciliation with me, and was repulsed by my haughty and insolent behaviour. The next time he comes to my hand, I am resolved that I will accost him as one brother ought to address another, whatever it may cost me; and, if I am still flouted with disdain, then shall the blame rest with him.'

After this generous resolution, it was a good while before his gratuitous attendant appeared at his side again; and George began to think that his visits were discontinued. The hope was a relief that could not be calculated; but still George had a feeling that it was too supreme to last. His enemy had been too pertinacious to abandon his design, whatever it was. He, however, began to indulge in a little more liberty, and for several days he enjoyed it with impunity.

George was, from infancy, of a stirring active disposition,

and could not endure confinement; and, having been of late much restrained in his youthful exercises by this singular persecutor, he grew uneasy under such restraint, and, one morning, chancing to awaken very early, he arose to make an excursion to the top of Arthur's Seat, to breathe the breeze of the dawning, and see the sun arise out of the eastern ocean. The morning was calm and serene; and as he walked down the south back of the Canongate, toward the Palace, the haze was so close around him that he could not see the houses on the opposite side of the way. As he passed the lord-commissioner's house, the guards were in attendance, who cautioned him not to go by the Palace, as all the gates would be shut and guarded for an hour to come, on which he went by the back of St. Anthony's gardens, and found his way into that little romantic glade adjoining to the Saint's chapel and well. He was still involved in a blue haze, like a dense smoke, but yet in the midst of it the respiration was the most refreshing and delicious. The grass and the flowers were loaden with dew; and, on taking off his hat to wipe his forehead, he perceived that the black glossy fur of which his chaperon was wrought, was all covered with a tissue of the most delicate silver— a fairy web, composed of little spheres, so minute that no eye could discern any one of them; yet there they were shining in lovely millions. Afraid of defacing so beautiful and so delicate a garnish, he replaced his hat with the greatest caution, and went on his way light of heart.

As he approached the swire at the head of the dell,— that little delightful verge from which in one moment the eastern limits and shores of Lothian arise on the view,— as he approached it, I say, and a little space from the height, he beheld, to his astonishment, a bright halo in the cloud of haze, that rose in a semi-circle over his head like a pale rainbow. He was struck motionless at the view of the lovely vision; for it so chanced that he had never seen the same appearance before, though common at early morn. But he soon perceived the cause of the phenomenon, and that it proceeded from the rays of the sun from a pure unclouded morning sky striking upon this dense vapour which refracted them. But the better all the works of nature are understood, the more they will be ever admired. That was a scene that would have entranced the man of science with delight, but which the uninitiated and sordid man would have regarded less than the mole rearing up his hill in silence and in darkness.

George did admire this halo of glory, which still grew wider, and less defined, as he approached the surface of the cloud. But, to his utter amazement and supreme delight, he found, on reaching the top of Arthur's Seat, that this sublunary rainbow, this terrestrial glory, was spread in its most vivid hues beneath his feet. Still he could not perceive the body of the sun, although the light behind him was dazzling; but the cloud of haze lying dense in that deep dell that separates the hill from the rocks of Salisbury, and the dull shadow of the hill mingling with that cloud, made the dell a pit of darkness. On that shadowy cloud was the lovely rainbow formed, spreading itself on a horizontal plain, and having a slight and brilliant shade of all the colours of the heavenly bow, but all of them paler and less defined. But this terrestrial phenomenon of the early morn cannot be better delineated than by the name given of it by the shepherd boys, 'The little wee ghost of the rainbow.'

Such was the description of the morning, and the wild shades of the hill, that George gave to his father and Mr. Adam Gordon that same day on which he had witnessed them; and it is necessary that the reader should comprehend something of their nature, to understand what follows.

He seated himself on the pinnacle of the rocky precipice, a little within the top of the hill to the westward, and, with a light and buoyant heart, viewed the beauties of the morning, and inhaled its salubrious breeze. 'Here,' thought he, 'I can converse with nature without disturbance, and without being intruded on by any appalling or obnoxious visitor.' The idea of his brother's dark and malevolent looks coming at that moment across his mind, he turned his eyes instinctively to the right, to the point where that unwelcome guest was wont to make his appearance. Gracious Heaven! What an apparition was there presented to his view! He saw, delineated in the cloud, the shoulders, arms, and features of a human being of the most dreadful aspect. The face was the face of his brother, but dilated to twenty times the natural size. Its dark eyes gleamed on him through the mist, while every furrow of its hideous brow frowned deep as the ravines on the brow of the hill. George started, and his hair stood up in bristles as he gazed on this horrible monster. He saw every feature, and every line of the face, distinctly, as it gazed on him with an intensity that was hardly brookable. Its eyes were fixed on him, in the same manner as those of some carnivorous animal fixed on its prey; and yet there was fear and trembling, in these unearthly features, as plainly depicted as murderous malice. The giant apparition seemed sometimes to be cowering down as in terror, so that nothing but its brow and eyes were seen; still these never turned one moment from their object—again it rose imperceptibly up, and began to approach with great caution; and as it neared, the dimensions of its form lessened, still continuing, however, far above the natural size.

George conceived it to be a spirit. He could conceive it to be nothing else; and he took it for some horrid demon by which he was haunted, that had assumed the features of his brother in every lineament, but in taking on itself the human form, had miscalculated dreadfully on the size, and presented itself thus to him in a blown-up, dilated frame of embodied air, exhaled from the caverns of death or the regions of devouring fire. He was farther confirmed in the belief that it was a malignant spirit, on perceiving that it approached him across the front of a precipice, where there was not footing for thing of mortal frame. Still, what with terror and astonishment, he continued rivetted to the spot, till it approached, as he deemed, to within two yards of him; and then, perceiving that it was setting itself to make a violent spring on him, he started to his feet and fled distractedly in the opposite direction, keeping his eye cast behind him lest he had been seized in that dangerous place. But the very first bolt that he made in his flight he came in contact with a *real* body of flesh and blood, and that with such violence that both went down among some scragged rocks, and George rolled over the other. The being called out 'Murder;' and, rising, fled precipitately. George then perceived that it was his brother; and, being confounded between the shadow and the substance, he knew not what he was doing or what he had done; and there being only one natural way of retreat from the brink of the rock, he likewise arose and pursued the affrighted culprit with all his speed towards the top of the hill. Wringhim was braying out 'Murder! murder!' at which George being disgusted, and his spirits all in a ferment from some hurried idea of intended harm, the moment he came up with the craven he seized him rudely by the shoulder, and clapped his hand on his mouth. 'Murder, you beast!' said he; 'what do you mean by roaring out murder in that way? Who the devil is murdering you, or offering to murder you?'

Wringhim forced his mouth from under his brother's hand, and roared with redoubled energy, 'Eh! Egh! murder! murder!' &c. George had felt resolute to put down this shocking alarm, lest some one might hear it and fly to the spot, or draw inferences widely different from the truth; and, perceiving the terror of this elect youth to be so great that expostulation was vain, he seized him by the mouth and nose with his left hand, so strenuously, that he sunk his fingers into his cheeks. But the poltroon still attempting to bray out, George gave him such a stunning blow with his fist on the left temple, that he crumbled, as it were, to the ground, but more from the effects of terror than those of the blow. His nose, however, again gushed out blood, a system of defence which seemed as natural to him as that resorted to by the race of stinkards. He then raised himself on his knees and hams, and raising up his ghastly face, while the blood streamed over both ears, he besought his life of his brother, in the most abject whining manner, gaping and blubbering most piteously.

'Tell me then, Sir,' said George, resolved to make the most of the wretch's terror—'tell me for what purpose it is that you thus haunt my steps? Tell me plainly, and instantly, else I will throw you from the verge of that precipice.'

'Oh, I will never do it again! I will never do it again! Spare my life, dear, good brother! Spare my life! Sure I never did you any hurt?'

'Swear to me, then, by the God that made you, that you will never henceforth follow after me to torment me with your hellish threatening looks; swear that you will never again come into my presence without being invited. Will you take an oath to this effect?'

'O yes! I will, I will!'

'But this is not all: you must tell me for what purpose you sought me out here this morning?'

'Oh, brother! for nothing but your good. I had nothing at heart but your unspeakable profit, and great and endless good.'

'So then, you indeed knew that I was here?'

'I was told so by a friend, but I did not believe him; a—a—at least I did not know it was true till I saw you.'

'Tell me this one thing, then, Robert, and all shall be forgotten and forgiven,—Who was that friend?'

'You do not know him.'

'How then does he know me?'

'I cannot tell.'

'Was he here present with you to-day?'

'Yes; he was not far distant. He came to this hill with me.'

'Where then is he now?'

'I cannot tell.'

'Then, wretch, confess that the devil was that friend who told you I was here, and who came here with you? None else could possibly know of my being here.'

fore-shadowing

'Ah! how little you know of him! Would you argue that there is neither man nor spirit endowed with so much foresight as to deduce natural conclusions from previous actions and incidents but the devil? Alas, brother! But why should I wonder at such abandoned notions and principles? It was fore-ordained that you should cherish them, and that they should be the ruin of your soul and body, before the world was framed. Be assured of this, however, that I had no aim in seeking you *but your good!*'

'Well, Robert, I will believe it. I am disposed to be hasty and passionate: it is a fault in my nature; but I never meant, or wished you evil; and God is my witness that I would as soon stretch out my hand to my own life, or my father's, as to yours.'——At these words, Wringhim uttered a hollow exulting laugh, put his hands in his pockets, and withdrew a space to his accustomed distance. George continued: 'And now, once for all, I request that we may exchange forgiveness, and that we may part and remain friends.'

'Would such a thing be expedient, think you? Or consistent with the glory of God? I doubt it.'

'I can think of nothing that would be more so. Is it not consistent with every precept of the Gospel? Come, brother, say that our reconciliation is complete.'

'O yes, certainly! I tell you, brother, according to the flesh: it is just as complete as the lark's is with the adder; no more so, nor ever can. Reconciled, forsooth! To what would I be reconciled?'

As he said this, he strode indignantly away. From the moment that he heard his life was safe, he assumed his former insolence and revengeful looks—and never were they more dreadful than on parting with his brother that morning on the top of the hill. 'Well, go thy ways,' said George; 'some would despise, but I pity thee. If thou art not a limb of Satan, I never saw one.'

The sun had now dispelled the vapours; and the morning being lovely beyond description, George sat himself down on the top of the hill, and pondered deeply on the unaccountable incident that had befallen to him that morning. He could in nowise comprehend it; but, taking it with other previous circumstances, he could not get quit of a conviction that he was haunted by some evil genius in the shape of his brother, as well as by that dark and mysterious wretch himself. In no other way could he account for the apparition he saw that morning on the face of the rock, nor for several sudden appearances of the same being, in places where there was no possibility of any foreknowledge that he himself was to be there, and as little that the same being, if he were flesh and blood like other men, could always start up in the same position with regard to him. He determined, therefore, on reaching home, to relate all that had happened, from beginning to end, to his father, asking his counsel and his assistance, although he knew full well that his father was not the fittest man in the world to solve such a problem. He was now involved in party politics, over head and ears; and, moreover, he could never hear the names of either of the Wringhims mentioned without getting into a quandary of disgust and anger; and all that he would deign to say of them was, to call them by all the opprobrious names he could invent.

It turned out as the young man from the first suggested: old Dalcastle would listen to nothing concerning them with any patience. George complained that his brother harassed him with his presence at all times, and in all places. Old Dal asked why he did not kick the dog out of his presence, whenever he felt him disagreeable? George said, he seemed to have some demon for a familiar. Dal answered, that he did not wonder a bit at that, for the young spark was the third in a direct line who had all been children of adultery; and it was well known that all such were born half deils themselves, and nothing was more likely than that they should hold intercourse with their fellows. In the same style did he sympathise with all his son's late sufferings and perplexities.

In Mr. Adam Gordon, however, George found a friend who entered into all his feelings, and had seen and knew every thing about the matter. He tried to convince him, that at all events there could be nothing supernatural in the circumstances; and that the vision he had seen on the rock, among the thick mist, was the shadow of his brother approaching behind him. George could not swallow this, for he had seen his own shadow on the cloud, and, instead of approaching to aught like his own figure, he perceived nothing but a halo of glory round a point of the cloud, that was whiter and purer than the rest. Gordon said, if he would go with him to a mountain of his father's, which he named, in Aberdeenshire, he would show him a giant spirit of the same dimensions, any morning at the rising of the sun, provided he shone on that spot. This statement excited George's curiosity exceedingly; and, being disgusted with some things about Edinburgh, and glad to get out of the way, he consented to go with Gordon to the Highlands for a space. The day was accordingly set for their departure, the old laird's assent obtained; and the two young sparks parted in a state of great impatience for their excursion.

One of them found out another engagement, however, the instant after this last was determined on. Young Wringhim went off the hill that morning, and home to his upright gaurdian again, without washing the blood from his face and neck; and there he told a most woful story indeed: How he had gone out to take a morning's walk on the hill, where he had encountered with his reprobate brother among the mist, who had knocked him down and very near murdered him; threatening dreadfully, and with horrid oaths, to throw him from the top of the cliff.

The wrath of the great divine was kindled beyond measure. He cursed the aggressor in the name of the Most High; and bound himself, by an oath, to cause that wicked one's transgressions return upon his own head sevenfold. But before he engaged farther in the business of vengeance, he kneeled with his adopted son, and committed the whole cause unto the Lord, whom he addressed as one coming breathing burning coals of juniper, and casting his lightnings before him, to destroy and root out all who had moved hand or tongue against the children of the promise.

Thus did he arise confirmed, and go forth to certain conquest.

We cannot enter into the detail of the events that now occurred, without forestalling a part of the narrative of one who knew all the circumstances—was deeply interested in them, and whose relation is of higher value than any thing that can be retailed out of the stores of tradition and old registers; but, his narrative being different from these, it was judged expedient to give the account as thus publicly handed down to us. Suffice it, that, before evening, George was apprehended, and lodged in jail, on a criminal charge of an assault and battery, to the shedding of blood, with the intent of committing fratricide. Then was the old laird in great consternation, and blamed himself for treating the thing so lightly, which seemed to have been gone about, from the beginning, so systematically, and with an intent which the villains were now going to realize, namely, to get the young laird disposed of, and then his brother, in spite of the old gentleman's teeth, would be laird himself.

Old Dal now set his whole interest to work among the noblemen and lawyers of his party. His son's case looked exceedingly ill, owing to the former assault before witnesses, and the unbecoming expressions made use of by him on that occasion, as well as from the present assault, which George did not deny, and for which no moving cause or motive could be made to appear.

On his first declaration before the sheriff, matters looked no better: but then the sheriff was a Whig. It is well known how differently the people of the present day, in Scotland, view the cases of their own party-men, and those of opposite political principles. But this day is nothing to that in such matters, although, God knows, they are still sometimes barefaced enough. It appeared, from all the witnesses in the first case, that the complainant was the first aggressor—that he refused to stand out of the way, though apprised of his danger; and when his brother came against him inadvertently, he had aimed a blow at him with his foot, which, if it had taken effect, would have killed him. But as to the story of the apparition in fair day-light—the flying from the face of it—the running foul of his brother—pursuing him, and knocking him down, why the judge smiled at the relation; and saying, 'It was a very extraordinary story,' he remanded George to prison, leaving the matter to the High Court of Justiciary.

When the case came before that court, matters took a different turn. The constant and sullen attendance of the one brother upon the other excited suspicions; and these were in some manner, confirmed, when the guards at Queensberry-house deponed, that the prisoner went by them on his way to the hill that morning, about twenty minutes before the complainant, and when the latter passed, he asked if such a young man had passed before him, describing the prisoner's appearance to them; and that, on being answered in the affirmative, he mended his pace and fell a-running.

The Lord Justice, on hearing this, asked the prisoner if he had any suspicions that his brother had a design on his life.

He answered, that all along, from the time of their first unfortunate meeting, his brother had dogged his steps so constantly, and so unaccountably, that he was convinced it was with some intent out of the ordinary course of events; and that if, as his lordship supposed, it was indeed his shadow that he had seen approaching him through the mist, then, from the cowering and cautious manner that it advanced, there was too little doubt that his brother's design had been to push him headlong from the cliff that morning.

A conversation then took place between the Judge and the Lord Advocate; and, in the mean time, a bustle was seen in the hall; on which the doors were ordered to be guarded,—and, behold, the precious Mr. R. Wringhim was taken into custody, trying to make his escape out of court. Finally it turned out, that George was honourably acquitted, and young Wringhim bound over to keep the peace, with heavy penalties and securities.

That was a day of high exultation to George and his youthful associates, all of whom abhorred Wringhim; and the evening being spent in great glee, it was agreed between Mr. Adam Gordon and George, that their visit to the Highlands, though thus long delayed, was not to be abandoned; and though they had, through the machinations of an incendiary, lost the season of delight, they would still find plenty of sport in deer-shooting. Accordingly, the day was set a second time for their departure; and, on the day preceding that, all the party were invited by George to dine with him once more at the sign of the Black Bull of Norway. Every one promised to attend, anticipating nothing but festivity and joy. Alas, what short-sighted improvident creatures we are, all of us; and how often does the evening cup of joy lead to sorrow in the morning!

The day arrived—the party of young noblemen and gentlemen met, and were as happy and jovial as men could be. George was never seen so brilliant, or so full of spirits; and exulting to see so many gallant young chiefs and gentlemen about him, who all gloried in the same principles of loyalty, (perhaps this word should have been written *disloyalty*,) he made speeches, gave toasts, and sung songs, all leaning slily to the same side, until a very late hour. By that time he had pushed the bottle so long and so freely, that its fumes had taken possession of every brain to such a degree, that they held Dame Reason rather at the staff's end, overbearing all her counsels and expostulations; and it was imprudently proposed by a wild inebriated spark, and carried by a majority of voices, that the whole party should adjourn to a bagnio for the remainder of the night.

They did so; and it appears from what follows, that the house to which they retired, must have been somewhere on the opposite side of the street to the Black Bull Inn, a little farther to the eastward. They had not been an hour in that house, till some altercation chanced to arise between George Colwan and a Mr. Drummond, the younger son of a nobleman of distinction. It was perfectly casual, and no one thenceforward, to this day, could ever tell what it was about, if it was not about the misunderstanding of some word, or term, that the one had uttered. However it was, some high words passed between them; these were followed by threats; and in less than two minutes from the commencement of the quarrel, Drummond left the house in apparent displeasure, hinting to the other that they two should settle that in a more convenient place.

The company looked at one another, for all was over before any of them knew such a thing was begun. 'What the devil is the matter?' cried one. 'What ails Drummond?' cried another. 'Who has he quarrelled with?' asked a third.

'Don't know.'—'Can't tell, on my life.'—'He has quarrelled with his wine, I suppose, and is going to send it a challenge.'

Such were the questions, and such the answers that passed in the jovial party, and the matter was no more thought of.

But in the course of a very short space, about the

length of which the ideas of the company were the next day at great variance, a sharp rap came to the door: It was opened by a female; but there being a chain inside, she only saw one side of the person at the door. He appeared to be a young gentleman, in appearance like him who had lately left the house, and asked, in a low whispering voice, 'if young Dalcastle was still in the house?' The woman did not know,—'If he is,' added he, 'pray tell him to speak with me for a few minutes.' The woman delivered the message before all the party, among whom there were then sundry courteous ladies of notable distinction, and George, on receiving it, instantly rose from the side of one of them, and said, in the hearing of them all, 'I will bet a hundred merks that is Drummond.'—'Don't go to quarrel with him, George,' said one.—'Bring him in with you,' said another. George stepped out; the door was again bolted, the chain drawn across, and the inadvertent party, left within, thought no more of the circumstance till the next morning, that the report had spread over the city, that a young gentleman had been slain, on a little washing-green at the side of the North Loch, and at the very bottom of the close where this thoughtless party had been assembled.

Several of them, on first hearing the report, hasted to the dead-room in the old Guard-house, where the corpse had been deposited, and soon discovered the body to be that of their friend and late entertainer, George Colwan. Great were the consternation and grief of all concerned, and, in particular, of his old father and Miss Logan; for George had always been the sole hope and darling of both, and the news of the event paralysed them so as to render them incapable of all thought or exertion. The spirit of the old laird was broken by the blow, and he descended at once from a jolly, good-natured, and active man, to a mere driveller, weeping over the body of his son, kissing his wound, his lips, and his cold brow alternately; denouncing vengeance on his murderers, and lamenting that he himself had not met the cruel doom, so that the hope of his race might have been preserved. In short, finding that all further motive of action and object of concern or of love, here below, were for ever removed from him, he abandoned himself to despair, and threatened to go down to the grave with his son.

But although he made no attempt to discover the murderers, the arm of justice was not idle; and it being evident to all, that the crime must infallibly be brought home to young Drummond, some of his friends sought him out, and compelled him, sorely against his will, to retire into concealment till the issue of the proof that should be led was made known. At the same time, he denied all knowledge of the incident with a resolution that astonished his intimate friends and relations, who to a man suspected him guilty. His father was not in Scotland, for I think it was said to me that this young man was second son to a John, Duke of Melfort,[1] who lived abroad with the royal family of the Stuarts; but this young gentleman lived with the relations of his mother, one of whom, an uncle, was a Lord of Session: these having thoroughly effected his concealment, went away, and listened to the evidence; and the examination of every new witness convinced them that their noble young relative was the slayer of his friend.

All the young gentlemen of the party were examined, save Drummond, who, when sent for, could not be found, which circumstance sorely confirmed the suspicions against him in the minds of judges and jurors, friends and enemies; and there is little doubt, that the care of his relations in concealing him, injured his character, and his cause. The young gentlemen, of whom the party was composed, varied considerably, with respect to the quarrel between him and the deceased. Some of them had neither heard nor noted it; others had, but not one of them could tell how it began. Some of them had heard the threat uttered by Drummond on leaving the house, and one only had noted him lay his hand on his sword. Not one of them could swear that it was Drummond who came to the door, and desired to speak with the deceased, but the general impression on the minds of them all, was to that effect; and one of the women swore that she heard the voice distinctly at the door, and every word that voice pronounced; and at the same time heard the deceased say, that it was Drummond's.

On the other hand, there were some evidences on Drummond's part, which Lord Craigie, his uncle, had taken care to collect. He produced the sword which his nephew had worn that night, on which there was neither blood nor blemish; and above all, he insisted on the evidence of a number of surgeons, who declared that both the wounds which the deceased had received, had been given behind. One of these was below the left arm, and a slight one; the other was quite through the body, and both evidently inflicted with the same weapon, a two-edged sword, of the same dimensions as that worn by Drummond.

Upon the whole, there was a division in the court, but a majority decided it. Drummond was pronounced guilty of the murder; outlawed for not appearing, and a high reward offered for his apprehension. It was with the greatest difficulty that he escaped on board of a small trading vessel, which landed him in Holland, and from thence, flying into Germany, he entered into the service of the Emperor Charles VI. Many regretted that he was not taken, and made to suffer the penalty due for such a crime, and the melancholy incident became a pulpit theme over a great part of Scotland, being held up as a proper warning to youth to beware of such haunts of vice and depravity, the nurses of all that is precipitate, immoral, and base, among mankind.

After the funeral of this promising and excellent young man, his father never more held up his head. Miss Logan, with all her art, could not get him to attend to any worldly thing, or to make any settlement whatsoever of his affairs, save making her over a present of what disposable funds he had about him. As to his estates, when they were mentioned to him, he wished them all in the bottom of the sea, and himself along with them. But whenever she mentioned the circumstance of Thomas Drummond having been the murderer of his son, he shook his head, and once made the remark, that 'It was all a mistake, a gross and fatal error; but that God, who had permitted such a flagrant deed, would bring it to light in his own time and way.' In a few weeks he followed his son to the grave, and the notorious Robert Wringhim took possession of his estates as the lawful son of the late laird, born in wedlock, and under his father's roof. The investiture was celebrated by prayer, singing of psalms, and religious disputation. The late guardian and adopted father, and the mother of the new laird, presided on the grand occasion, making a conspicuous figure in all the work of the day; and though the youth himself indulged rather more freely in the bottle, than he had ever been seen to do before, it was agreed by all present, that there had never been a festivity so sanctified within the great hall of Dalcastle. Then, after due thanks returned, they parted rejoicing in spirit; which thanks, by the by, consisted wholly in telling the Almighty what he was; and informing him, with very particular precision, what *they* were who addressed him; for Wringhim's whole system of popular declamation consisted it seems in this,—to denounce all men and women to destruction, and then hold out hopes to his adherents that they were the chosen few, included in the promises, and who could never fall away. It would appear that this pharisaical doctrine is a very delicious one, and the most grateful of all others to the worst characters.

But the ways of heaven are altogether inscrutable, and soar as far above and beyond the works and the comprehensions of man, as the sun, flaming in majesty, is above the tiny boy's evening rocket. It is the controller of Nature alone, that can bring light out of darkness, and order out of confusion. Who is he that causeth the mole, from his secret path of darkness, to throw up the gem, the gold, and the precious ore? The same, that from the mouths of babes and sucklings can extract the perfection of praise, and who can make the most abject of his creatures instrumental in bringing the most hidden truths to light.

Miss Logan had never lost the thought of her late master's prediction, that Heaven would bring to light the truth concerning the untimely death of his son. She perceived that some strange conviction, too horrible for expression, preyed on his mind from the moment that the fatal news reached him, to the last of his existence; and in his last ravings, he uttered some incoherent words about justification by faith alone, and absolute and eternal predestination having been the ruin of his house. These, to be sure, were the words of superannuation, and of the last and severest kind of it; but for all that, they sunk deep into Miss Logan's soul, and at last she began to think with herself, 'Is it possible the Wringhims, and the sophisticating wretch who is in conjunction with them, the mother of my late beautiful and amiable young master, can have effected his destruction? if so, I will spend my days, and my little patrimony, in endeavours to rake up and expose the unnatural deed.'

In all her outgoings and incomings, Mrs. Logan (as she was now styled) never lost sight of this one object. Every new disappointment only whetted her desire to fish up some particulars concerning it; for she thought so long, and so ardently upon it, that by degrees it became settled in her mind as a sealed truth. And as woman is always most jealous of her own sex in such matters, her suspicions were fixed on her greatest enemy, Mrs. Colwan, now the Lady Dowager of Dalcastle. All was wrapt in a chaos of confusion and darkness; but at last by dint of a thousand sly and secret inquiries, Mrs. Logan found out where Lady Dalcastle had been, on the night that the murder happened, and likewise what company she had kept, as well as some of the comers and goers; and she had hopes of having discovered a cue, which, if she could keep hold of the thread, would lead her through darkness to the light of truth.

Returning very late one evening from a convocation of family servants, which she had drawn together in order to fish something out of them, her maid having been in attendance on her all the evening, they found on going home, that the house had been broken, and a number of valuable articles stolen therefrom. Mrs. Logan had grown quite heartless before this stroke, having been altogether unsuccessful in her inquiries, and now she began to entertain some resolutions of giving up the fruitless search.

In a few days thereafter, she received intelligence that her clothes and plate were mostly recovered, and that she for one was bound over to prosecute the depredator, provided the articles turned out to be hers, as libelled in the indictment, and as a king's evidence had given out.

She was likewise summoned, or requested, I know not
which, being ignorant of these matters, to go as far as
the town of Peebles on Tweedside, in order to survey
these articles on such a day, and make affidavit to their
identity before the Sheriff. She went accordingly; but on
entering the town by the North Gate, she was accosted
by a poor girl in tattered apparel, who with great earnestness inquired if her name was not Mrs. Logan? On being
answered in the affirmative, she said that the unfortunate
prisoner in the tolbooth requested her, as she valued all
that was dear to her in life, to go and see her before she
appeared in court, at the hour of cause, as she (the prisoner)
had something of the greatest moment to impart to her.
Mrs. Logan's curiosity was excited, and she followed the
girl straight to the tolbooth, who by the way said to her,
that she would find in the prisoner a woman of a superior
mind, who had gone through all the vicissitudes of life.
'She has been very unfortunate, and I fear very wicked,'
added the poor thing, 'but she is my mother, and God
knows, with all her faults and failings, she has never been
unkind to me. You, madam, have it in your power to save
her; but she has wronged you, and therefore if you will
not do it for her sake, do it for mine, and the God of the
fatherless will reward you.'

Mrs. Logan answered her with a cast of the head, and
a hem! and only remarked, that 'the guilty must not
always be suffered to escape, or what a world must we be
doomed to live in!'

She was admitted to the prison, and found a tall emaciated figure, who appeared to have once possessed a sort of
masculine beauty in no ordinary degree, but was now
considerably advanced in years. She viewed Mrs. Logan
with a stern, steady gaze, as if reading her features as a
margin to her intellect; and when she addressed her it was

not with that humility, and agonized fervor, which are
natural for one in such circumstances to address to another,
who has the power of her life and death in her hands.

'I am deeply indebted to you, for this timely visit, Mrs.
Logan,' said she. 'It is not that I value life, or because I
fear death, that I have sent for you so expressly. But the
manner of the death that awaits me, has something
peculiarly revolting in it to a female mind. Good God!
when I think of being hung up, a spectacle to a gazing,
gaping multitude, with numbers of which I have had
intimacies and connections, that would render the moment
of parting so hideous, that, believe me, it rends to flinders
a soul born for another sphere than that in which it has
moved, had not the vile selfishness of a lordly fiend ruined
all my prospects, and all my hopes. Hear me then; for I
do not ask your pity: I only ask of you to look to yourself,
and behave with womanly prudence. If you deny this day,
that these goods are yours, there is no other evidence
whatever against my life, and it is safe for the present.
For as for the word of the wretch who has betrayed me,
it is of no avail; he has prevaricated so notoriously to save
himself. If you deny them, you shall have them all again
to the value of a mite, and more to the bargain. If you
swear to the identity of them, the process will, one way
and another, cost you the half of what they are worth.'

'And what security have I for that?' said Mrs. Logan.

'You have none but *my word*,' said the other proudly,
'and that never yet was violated. If you cannot take that,
I know the worst you can do—But I had forgot—I have
a poor helpless child without, waiting, and starving about
the prison door—Surely it was of her that I wished to
speak. This shameful death of mine will leave her in a
deplorable state.'

'The girl seems to have candour and strong affections,'

said Mrs. Logan; 'I grievously mistake if such a child would not be a thousand times better without such a guardian and director.'

'Then will you be so kind as come to the Grass Market, and see me put down?' said the prisoner. 'I thought a woman would estimate a woman's and a mother's feelings, when such a dreadful throw was at stake, at least in part. But you are callous, and have never known any feelings but those of subordination to your old unnatural master. Alas, I have no cause of offence! I have wronged you; and justice must take its course. Will you forgive me before we part?'

Mrs. Logan hesitated, for her mind ran on something else: On which the other subjoined, 'No, you will not forgive me, I see. But you will pray to God to forgive me? I know you will *do that.*'

Mrs. Logan heard not this jeer, but looking at the prisoner with an absent and stupid stare, she said, 'Did you know my late master?'

'Ay, that I did, and never for any good,' said she. 'I knew the old and the young spark both, and was by when the latter was slain.'

This careless sentence affected Mrs. Logan in a most peculiar manner. A shower of tears burst from her eyes ere it was done, and when it was, she appeared like one bereaved of her mind. She first turned one way and then another, as if looking for something she had dropped. She seemed to think she had lost her eyes, instead of her tears, and at length, as by instinct, she tottered close up to the prisoner's face, and looking wistfully and joyfully in it, said, with breathless earnestness, 'Pray, mistress, what is your name?'

'My name is Arabella Calvert,' said the other: 'Miss, mistress, or widow, as you chuse, for I have been all the three, and that not once nor twice only—Ay, and something beyond all these. But as for you, you have never been any thing!'

'Ay, ay! and so you are Bell Calvert? Well, I thought so—I thought so,' said Mrs. Logan; and helping herself to a seat, she came and sat down close by the prisoner's knee. 'So you are indeed Bell Calvert, so called once. Well, of all the world you are the woman whom I have longed and travailed the most to see. But you were invisible; a being to be heard of, not seen.'

'There have been days, madam,' returned she, 'when I *was* to be seen, and when there were few to be seen like me. But since that time there have indeed been days on which I was not to be seen. My crimes have been great, but my sufferings have been greater. So great, that neither you nor the world can ever either know or conceive them. I hope they will be taken into account by the Most High. Mine have been crimes of utter desperation. But whom am I speaking to? You had better leave me to myself, mistress.'

'Leave you to yourself? That I will be loth to do, till you tell me where you were that night my young master was murdered?'

'Where the devil would, I was! Will that suffice you? Ah, it was a vile action! A night to be remembered that was! Won't you be going? I want to trust my daughter with a commission.'

'No, Mrs. Calvert, you and I part not, till you have divulged that mystery to me.'

'You must accompany me to the other world, then, for you shall not have it in this.'

'If you refuse to answer me, I can have you before a tribunal, where you shall be sifted to the soul.'

'Such miserable inanity! What care I for your threatenings of a tribunal? I who must so soon stand before my last earthly one? What could the word of such a culprit avail? Or if it could, where is the judge that could enforce it?'

'Did you not say that there was some mode of accommodating matters on that score?'

'Yes, I prayed you to grant me my life, which is in your power. The saving of it would not have cost you a plack, yet you refused to do it. The taking of it will cost you a great deal, and yet to that purpose you adhere. I can have no parley with such a spirit. I would not have my life in a present from its motions, nor would I exchange courtesies with its possessor.'

'Indeed, Mrs. Calvert, since ever we met, I have been so busy thinking about who you might be, that I know not what you have been proposing. I believe, I meant to do what I could to save you. But once for all, tell me every thing that you know concerning that amiable young gentleman's death, and here is my hand there shall be nothing wanting that I can effect for you.'

'No, I despise all barter with such mean and selfish curiosity; and, as I believe *that* passion is stronger with you, than fear is with me, we part on equal terms. Do your worst; and my secret shall go to the gallows and the grave with me.'

Mrs. Logan was now greatly confounded, and after proffering in vain to concede every thing she could ask in exchange, for the particulars relating to the murder, she became the suppliant in her turn. But the unaccountable culprit, exulting in her advantage, laughed her to scorn; and finally, in a paroxysm of pride and impatience, called in the jailor and had her expelled, ordering him in her hearing not to grant her admittance a second time, on any pretence.

Mrs. Logan was now hard put to it, and again driven almost to despair. She might have succeeded in the attainment of that she thirsted for most in life so easily, had she known the character which she had to deal with—Had she known to have soothed her high and afflicted spirit: but that opportunity was past, and the hour of examination at hand. She once thought of going and claiming her articles, as she at first intended; but then, when she thought again of the Wringhims swaying it at Dalcastle, where she had been wont to hear them held in such contempt, if not abhorrence, and perhaps of holding it by the most diabolical means, she was withheld from marring the only chance that remained of having a glimpse into that mysterious affair.

Finally, she resolved not to answer to her name in the court, rather than to appear and assert a falsehood, which she might be called on to certify by oath. She did so; and heard the Sheriff give orders to the officers to make inquiry for Miss Logan from Edinburgh, at the various places of entertainment in town, and to expedite her arrival in court, as things of great value were in dependence. She also heard the man who had turned king's evidence against the prisoner, examined for the second time, and sifted most cunningly. His answers gave any thing but satisfaction to the Sheriff, though Mrs. Logan believed them to be mainly truth. But there were a few questions and answers that struck her above all others.

'How long is it since Mrs. Calvert and you became acquainted?'

'About a year and a half.'

'State the precise time, if you please; the day, or night, according to your remembrance.'

'It was on the morning of the 28th of February, 1705.'

'What time of the morning?'

'Perhaps about one.'

'So early as that? At what place did you meet then?'

'It was at the foot of one of the north wynds of Edin-burgh.'

'Was it by appointment that you met?'

'No, it was not.'

'For what purpose was it then?'

'For no purpose.'

'How is it that you chance to remember the day and hour so minutely, if you met that woman, whom you have accused, merely by chance, and for no manner of purpose, as you must have met others that night, perhaps to the amount of hundreds, in the same way?'

'I have good cause to remember it, my lord.'

'What was the cause?—No answer?—You don't choose to say what that cause was?'

'I am not at liberty to tell.'

The Sheriff then descended to other particulars, all of which tended to prove that the fellow was an accomplished villain, and that the principal share of the atrocities.had been committed by him. Indeed the Sheriff hinted, that he suspected the only share Mrs. Calvert had in them, was in being too much in his company, and too true to him. The case was remitted to the Court of Justiciary; but Mrs. Logan had heard enough to convince her that the culprits first met at the very spot, and the very hour, on which George Colwan was slain; and she had no doubt that they were incendiaries set on by his mother, to forward her own and her darling son's way to opulence. Mrs. Logan was wrong, as will appear in the sequel; but her antipathy to Mrs. Colwan made her watch the event with all care. She never quitted Peebles as long as Bell Calvert remained there, and when she was removed to Edinburgh, the other followed. When the trial came on, Mrs. Logan and her maid were again summoned as witnesses before the jury, and compelled by the prosecutor for the Crown to appear.

The maid was first called; and when she came into the witnesses' box, the anxious and hopeless looks of the prisoner were manifest to all: But the girl, whose name, she said, was Bessy Gillies, answered in so flippant and fearless a way, that the auditors were much amused. After a number of routine questions, the depute-advocate asked her if she was at home on the morning of the fifth of September last, when her mistress's house was robbed?

'Was I at hame, say ye? Na, faith-ye, lad! An I had been at hame, there had been mair to dee. I wad hae raised sic a yelloch!'

'Where were you that morning?'

'Where was I, say you? I was in the house where my mistress was, sitting dozing an' half sleeping in the kitchen. I thought aye she would be setting out every minute, for twa hours.'

'And when you went home, what did you find?'

'What found we? Be my sooth, we found a broken lock, an' toom kists.'

'Relate some of the particulars, if you please.'

'O, sir, the thieves didna stand upon particulars: they were halesale dealers in a' our best wares.'

'I mean, what passed between your mistress and you on the occasion?'

'What passed, say ye? O, there wasna muckle: I was in a great passion, but she was dung doitrified a wee. When she gaed to put the key i' the door, up it flew to the fer wa'.—"Bess, ye jaud, what's the meaning o' this?" quo she. "Ye hae left the door open, ye tawpie!" quo she.

"The ne'er o' that I did," quo I, "or may my shakel bane never turn another key." When we got the candle lightit, a' the house was in a hoad-road. "Bessy, my woman," quo she, "we are baith ruined and un-done creatures." "The deil a bit," quo I; "that I deny positively. H'mh! to speak o' a lass o' my age being ruined and undone! I never had muckle except what was within a good jerkin, an' let the thief ruin me there wha can." '

'Do you remember ought else that your mistress said on the occasion? Did you hear her blame any person?'

'O, she made a great deal o' grumphing an' groaning about the *misfortune*, as she ca'd it, an' I think she said it was a part o' the ruin wrought by the Ringans, or some sic name,—"they'll hae't a'! they'll hae't a'!" cried she, wringing her hands; "they'll hae't a', an' hell wi't, an' they'll get them baith." "Aweel, that's aye some satis-faction," quo I.'

'Whom did she mean by the Ringans, do you know?'

'I fancy they are some creatures that she has dreamed about, for I think there canna be as ill folks living as she ca's them.'

'Did you never hear her say that the prisoner at the bar there, Mrs. Calvert, or Bell Calvert, was the robber of her house; or that she was one of the Ringans?'

'Never. Somebody tauld her lately, that ane Bell Calvert robbed her house, but she disna believe it. Neither do I.'

'What reasons have you for doubting it?'

'Because it was nae woman's fingers that broke up the bolts an' the locks that were torn open that night.'

'Very pertinent, Bessy. Come then within the bar, and look at these articles on the table. Did you ever see these silver spoons before?'

'I hae seen some very like them, and whaever has seen siller spoons, has done the same.'

'Can you swear you never saw them before?'

'Na, na, I wadna swear to ony siller spoons that ever war made, unless I had put a private mark on them wi' my ain hand, an' that's what I never did to ane.'

'See, they are all marked with a C.'

'Sae are a' the spoons in Argyle, an' the half o' them in Edinburgh I think. A C is a very common letter, an' so are a' the names that begin wi't. Lay them by, lay them by, an' gie the poor woman her spoons again. They are marked wi' her ain name, an' I hae little doubt they are hers, an' that she has seen better days.'

'Ah, God bless her heart!' sighed the prisoner; and that blessing was echoed in the breathings of many a feeling breast.

'Did you ever see this gown before, think you?'

'I hae seen ane very like it.'

'Could you not swear that gown was your mistress's once?'

'No, unless I saw her hae't on, an' kend that she had paid for't. I am very scrupulous about an oath. *Like* is an ill mark. Sae ill indeed, that I wad hardly swear to ony thing.'

'But you say that gown is *very like* one your mistress used to wear.

'I never said sic a thing. It is like one I hae seen her hae out airing on the hay raip i' the back green. It is very like ane I hae seen Mrs. Butler in the Grass Market wearing too; I rather think it is the same. Bless you, sir, I wadna swear to my ain fore finger, if it had been as lang out o' my sight, an' brought in an' laid on that table.'

'Perhaps you are not aware, girl, that this scrupulousness of yours is likely to thwart the purposes of justice, and bereave your mistress of property to the amount of a thousand merks?' (*From the Judge.*)

'I canna help that, my lord: that's her lookout. For my part, I am resolved to keep a clear conscience, till I be married, at any rate.'

'Look over these things and see if there is any one article among them which you can fix on as the property of your mistress.'

'No ane o' them, sir, no ane o' them. An oath is an awfu' thing, especially when it is for life or death. Gie the poor woman her things again, an' let my mistress pick up the next she finds: that's my advice.'

When Mrs. Logan came into the box, the prisoner groaned, and laid down her head. But how she was astonished when she heard her deliver herself something to the following purport!—That whatever penalties she was doomed to abide, she was determined she would not bear witness against a woman's life, from a certain conviction that it could not be a woman who broke her house. 'I have no doubt that I may find some of my own things there,' added she, 'but if they were found in her possession, she has been made a tool, or the dupe, of an infernal set, who shall be nameless here. I believe she *did not* rob me, and for that reason I will have no hand in her condemnation.'

The Judge. 'This is the most singular perversion I have ever witnessed. Mrs. Logan, I entertain strong suspicions that the prisoner, or her agents, have made some agreement with you on this matter, to prevent the course of justice.'

'So far from that, my lord, I went into the jail at Peebles to this woman, whom I had never seen before, and proffered to withdraw my part in the prosecution, as well as my evidence, provided she would tell me a few simple facts; but she spurned at my offer, and had me turned insolently out of the prison, with orders to the jailor never to admit me again on any pretence.'

The prisoner's counsel, taking hold of this evidence, addressed the jury with great fluency; and finally, the prosecution was withdrawn, and the prisoner dismissed from the bar, with a severe reprimand for her past conduct, and an exhortation to keep better company.

It was not many days till a caddy came with a large parcel to Mrs. Logan's house, which parcel he delivered into her hands, accompanied with a sealed note, containing an inventory of the articles, and a request to know if the unfortunate Arabella Calvert would be admitted to converse with Mrs. Logan.

Never was there a woman so much overjoyed as Mrs. Logan was at this message. She returned compliments: Would be most happy to see her; and no article of the parcel should be looked at, or touched, till her arrival.— It was not long till she made her appearance, dressed in somewhat better style than she had yet seen her; delivered her over the greater part of the stolen property, besides many things that either never had belonged to Mrs. Logan, or that she thought proper to deny, in order that the other might retain them.

The tale that she told of her misfortunes was of the most distressing nature, and was enough to stir up all the tender, as well as abhorrent feelings in the bosom of humanity. She had suffered every deprivation in fame, fortune, and person. She had been imprisoned; she had been scourged, and branded as an impostor; and all on account of her resolute and unmoving fidelity and truth to *several* of the very worst of men, every one of whom had abandoned her to utter destitution and shame. But this story we cannot enter on at present, as it would perhaps mar the thread of our story, as much as it did the anxious anticipations of Mrs. Logan, who sat pining and longing for the relation that follows.

'Now I know, Mrs. Logan, that you are expecting a detail of the circumstances relating to the death of Mr. George Colwan; and in gratitude for your unbounded generosity, and disinterestedness, I will tell you all that I know, although, for causes that will appear obvious to you, I had determined never in life to divulge one circumstance of it. I can tell you, however, that you will be disappointed, for it was not the gentleman who was accused, found guilty, and would have suffered the utmost penalty of the law, had he not made his escape. *It was not he*, I say, who slew your young master, nor had he any hand in it.'

'I never thought he had. But, pray, how do you come to know this?'

'You shall hear. I had been abandoned in York, by an artful and consummate fiend; found guilty of being art and part concerned in the most heinous atrocities, and, in his place, suffered what I yet shudder to think of. I was banished the county—begged my way with my poor out-cast child up to Edinburgh, and was there obliged, for the second time in my life, to betake myself to the most degrading of all means to support two wretched lives. I hired a dress, and betook me, shivering, to the High Street, too well aware that my form and appearance would soon draw me suitors enow at that throng and intemperate time of the parliament. On my very first stepping out to the street, a party of young gentlemen was passing. I heard by the noise they made, and the tenor of their speech, that they were more than mellow, and so I resolved to keep near them, in order, if possible, to make some of them my prey. But just as one of them began to eye me, I was rudely thrust into a narrow close by one of the guards-men. I had heard to what house the party was bound, for the men were talking exceedingly loud, and making no secret of it: so I hasted down the close, and round below to the one where their rendezvous was to be; but I was too late, they were all housed and the door bolted. I resolved to wait, thinking they could not all stay long; but I was perishing with famine, and was like to fall down. The moon shone as bright as day, and I perceived, by a sign at the bottom of the close, that there was a small tavern of a certain description up two stairs there. I went up and called, telling the mistress of the house my plan. She approved of it mainly, and offered me her best apartment, provided I could get one of these noble mates to accompany me. She abused Lucky Sudds, as she called her, at the inn where the party was, envying her huge profits, no doubt, and giving me afterward something to drink, for which I really felt exceedingly grateful in my need. I stepped down stairs in order to be on the alert. The moment that I reached the ground, the door of Lucky Sudds' house opened and shut, and down came the Honourable Thomas Drummond, with hasty and impassioned strides, his sword rattling at his heel. I accosted him in a soft and soothing tone. He was taken with my address; for he instantly stood still and gazed intently at me, then at the place, and then at me again. I beckoned him to follow me, which he did without farther ceremony, and we soon found ourselves together in the best room of a house where every thing was wretched. He still looked about him, and at me; but all this while he had never spoken a word. At length, I asked if he would take any refreshment? "If you please," said he. I asked what he would have? but he only answered, "Whatever you choose, madam." If he was taken with my address, I was much more taken with his; for he was a complete gentleman, and a gentleman will ever act as one. At length, he began as follows:

' "I am utterly at a loss to account for this adventure, madam. It seems to me like enchantment, and I can hardly believe my senses. An English lady, I judge, and one, who from her manner and address should belong to the first class of society, in such a place as this, is indeed matter of wonder to me. At the foot of a close in Edinburgh! and at this time of the night! Surely it must have been no common reverse of fortune that reduced you to this?" I wept, or pretended to do so; on which he added. "Pray, madam, take heart. Tell me what has befallen you; and if I can do any thing for you, in restoring you to your country or your friends, you shall command my interest."

'I had great need of a friend then, and I thought now was the time to secure one. So I began and told him the moving tale I have told you. But I soon perceived that I had kept by the naked truth too unvarnishedly, and thereby quite overshot my mark. When he learned that he was sitting in a wretched corner of an irregular house, with a felon, who had so lately been scourged, and banished as a swindler and impostor, his modest nature took the alarm, and he was shocked, instead of being moved with pity. His eye fixed on some of the casual stripes on my arm, and from that moment he became restless and impatient to be gone. I tried some gentle arts to retain him, but in vain; so, after paying both the landlady and me for pleasures he had neither tasted nor asked, he took his leave.

'I showed him down stairs; and just as he turned the corner of the next land, a man came rushing violently by him; exchanged looks with him, and came running up to me. He appeared in great agitation, and was quite out of breath; and, taking my hand in his, we ran up stairs together without speaking, and were instantly in the apartment I had left, where a stoup of wine still stood untasted. "Ah, this is fortunate!" said my new spark, and helped himself. In the mean while, as our apartment was a corner one, and looked both east and north, I ran to the easter casement to look after Drummond. Now, note me well: I saw him going eastward in his tartans and bonnet, and the gilded hilt of his claymore glittering in the moon; and, at the very same time, I saw two men, the one in black, and the other likewise in tartans, coming toward the steps from the opposite bank, by the foot of the loch; and I saw Drummond and they eying each other as they passed. I kept view of *him* till he vanished towards Leith Wynd, and by that time the two strangers had come close up under our window. This is what I wish you to pay particular attention to. I had only lost sight of Drummond, (who had given me his name and address,) for the short space of time that we took in running up one pair of short stairs; and during that space he had halted a moment, for, when I got my eye on him again, he had not crossed the mouth of the next entry, nor proceeded above ten or twelve paces, and, *at the same time*, I saw the two men coming down the bank on the opposite side of the loch, at about three hundred paces distance. Both he and they were distinctly in my view, and never within speech of each other, until he vanished into one of the wynds leading toward the bottom of the High Street, at which precise time the two strangers came below my window; so that it was quite clear he neither could be one of them, nor have any communication with them.

'Yet, mark me again; for of all things I have ever seen, this was the most singular. When I looked down at the two strangers, *one of them was extremely like Drummond.* So like was he, that there was not one item in dress, form, feature, nor voice, by which I could distinguish the one from the other. I was certain it was not he, because I had seen the one going and the other approaching at the same time, and my impression at the moment was, that I looked upon some spirit, or demon, in his likeness. I felt a chillness creep all round my heart, my knees tottered, and, withdrawing my head from the open casement that lay in the dark shade, I said to the man who was with me, "Good God, what is this!"

'"What is it, my dear?" said he, as much alarmed as I was.

' "As I live, there stands an apparition!" said I.

'He was not so much afraid when he heard me say so, and peeping cautiously out, he looked and listened a-while, and then drawing back, he said in a whisper, "They are both living men, and one of them is he I passed at the corner."

' "That he is not," said I, emphatically. "To that I will make oath."

'He smiled and shook his head, and then added, "I never then saw a man before, whom I could not know again, particularly if he was the very last I had seen. But what matters it whether it be or not? As it is no concern of ours, let us sit down and enjoy ourselves."

' "But it *does* matter a very great deal with me, sir," said I.—"Bless me, my head is giddy—my breath quite gone, and I feel as if I were surrounded with fiends. Who are you, sir?"

' "You shall know that ere we two part, my love," said he: "I cannot conceive why the return of this young gentleman to the spot he so lately left, should discompose you? I suppose he got a glance of you as he passed, and has returned to look after you, and that is the whole secret of the matter."

' "If you will be so civil as to walk out and join him then, it will oblige me hugely," said I, "for I never in my life experienced such boding apprehensions of evil company. I cannot conceive how you should come up here without asking my permission? Will it please you to begone, sir?"—I was within an ace of prevailing. He took out his purse—I need not say more—I was bribed to let him remain. Ah, had I kept by my frail resolution of dismissing him at that moment, what a world of shame and misery had been evited! But that, though uppermost still in my mind, has nothing ado here.

'When I peeped over again, the two men were disputing in a whisper, the one of them in violent agitation and terror, and the other upbraiding him, and urging him on to some desperate act. At length I heard the young man in the Highland garb say indignantly, "Hush, recreant! It is God's work which you are commissioned to execute, and it must be done. But if you positively decline it, I will do it myself, and do you beware of the consequences."

' "Oh, I will, I will!" cried the other in black clothes, in a wretched beseeching tone. "You shall instruct me in this, as in all things else."

'I thought all this while I was closely concealed from them, and wondered not a little when he in tartans gave me a sly nod, as much as to say, "What do you think of this?" or, "Take note of what you see," or something to that effect, from which I perceived, that whatever he was about, he did not wish it to be kept a secret. For all that, I was impressed with a terror and anxiety that I could not overcome, but it only made me mark every event with the more intense curiosity. The Highlander, whom I still could not help regarding as the evil genius of Thomas Drummond, performed every action, as with the quickness of thought. He concealed the youth in black in a narrow entry, a little to the westward of my windows, and as he was leading him across the moonlight green by the shoulder, I perceived, for the first time, that both of them were armed with rapiers. He pushed him without resistance into the dark shaded close, made another signal to me, and hasted up the close to Lucky Sudds' door. The city and the morning were so still, that I heard every word that was uttered, on putting my head out a little. He knocked at the door sharply, and after waiting a considerable space, the bolt was drawn, and the door, as I conceived, edged up as far as the massy chain would let it. "Is young Dalcastle still in the house?" said he sharply.

'I did not hear the answer, but I heard him say, shortly after, "If he is, pray tell him to speak with me for a few minutes." He then withdrew from the door, and came slowly down the close, in a lingering manner, looking oft behind him. Dalcastle came out; advanced a few steps after him, and then stood still, as if hesitating whether or not he should call out a friend to accompany him; and that instant the door behind him was closed, chained, and the iron bolt drawn; on hearing of which, he followed his adversary without farther hesitation. As he passed below my window, I heard him say, "I beseech you, Tom, let us do nothing in this matter rashly;" but I could not hear the answer of the other, who had turned the corner.

'I roused up my drowsy companion, who was leaning on the bed, and we both looked together from the north window. We were in the shade, but the moon shone full on the two young gentlemen. Young Dalcastle was visibly the worse of liquor, and his back being turned toward us, he said something to the other which I could not make out, although he spoke a considerable time, and, from his tones and gestures, appeared to be reasoning. When he had done, the tall young man in the tartans drew his sword, and his face being straight to us, we heard him say distinctly, "No more words about it, George, if you please;

but if you be a man, as I take you to be, draw your sword, and let us settle it here."

'Dalcastle drew his sword, without changing his attitude; but he spoke with more warmth, for we heard his words, "Think you that I fear you, Tom? Be assured, sir, I would not fear ten of the best of your name, at each other's backs: all that I want is to have friends with us to see fair play, for if you close with me, you are a dead man."

'The other stormed at these words. "You are a braggart, sir," cried he, "a wretch—a blot on the cheek of nature—a blight on the Christian world—a reprobate— I'll have your soul, sir—You must play at tennis, and put down elect brethren in another world to-morrow." As he said this, he brandished his rapier, exciting Dalcastle to offence. He gained his point: The latter, who had previously drawn, advanced in upon his vapouring and licentious antagonist, and a fierce combat ensued. My companion was delighted beyond measure, and I could not keep him from exclaiming, loud enough to have been heard, "that's grand! that's excellent!" For me, my heart quaked like an aspen. Young Dalcastle either had a decided advantage over his adversary, or else the other thought proper to let him have it; for he shifted, and wore, and flitted from Dalcastle's thrusts like a shadow, uttering ofttimes a sarcastic laugh, that seemed to provoke the other beyond all bearing. At one time, he would spring away to a great distance, then advance again on young Dalcastle with the swiftness of lightning. But that young hero always stood his ground, and repelled the attack: he never gave way, although they fought nearly twice round the bleaching green, which you know is not a very small one. At length they fought close up to the mouth of the dark entry, where the fellow in black stood all this while concealed, and then the combatant in tartans closed with his antagonist, or pretended to do so; but the moment they began to grapple, he wheeled about, turning Colwan's back towards the entry, and then cried out, "Ah, hell has it! My friend, my friend!"

'That moment the fellow in black rushed from his cover with his drawn rapier, and gave the brave young Dalcastle two deadly wounds in the back, as quick as arm could thrust, both of which I thought pierced through his body. He fell, and rolling himself on his back, he perceived who it was that had slain him thus foully, and said, with a dying emphasis, which I never heard equalled, "Oh, dog of hell, is it you who has done this!"

'He articulated some more, which I could not hear for other sounds; for the moment that the man in black inflicted the deadly wound, my companion called out, "That's unfair, you rip! That's damnable! to strike a brave fellow behind! One at a time, you cowards! &c." to all which the unnatural fiend in the tartans answered with a loud exulting laugh; and then, taking the poor paralysed murderer by the bow of the arm, he hurried him into the dark entry once more, where I lost sight of them for ever.'

Before this time, Mrs. Logan had risen up; and when the narrator had finished, she was standing with her arms stretched upward at their full length, and her visage turned down, on which were pourtrayed the lines of the most absolute horror. 'The dark suspicions of my late benefactor have been just, and his last prediction is fulfilled,' cried she. 'The murderer of the accomplished George Colwan has been his own brother, set on, there is little doubt, by her who bare them both, and her directing angel, the self-justified bigot. Aye, and yonder they sit, enjoying the luxuries so dearly purchased, with perfect impunity! If the Almighty do not hurl them down, blasted with shame and confusion, there is no hope of retribution in this life. And, by his might, I will be the agent to accomplish it! Why did the man not pursue the foul murderers? Why did he not raise the alarm, and call the watch?'

'He? The wretch! He durst not move from the shelter he had obtained,—no, not for the soul of him. He was pursued for his life, at the moment when he first flew into my arms. But I did not know it; no, I did not *then* know him. May the curse of heaven, and the blight of hell, settle on the detestable wretch! He pursue for the sake of justice! No; his efforts have all been for evil, but never for good. But *I* raised the alarm; miserable and degraded as I was, I pursued and raised the watch myself. Have you not heard the name of Bell Calvert coupled with that hideous and mysterious affair?'

'Yes, I have. In secret often I have heard it. But how came it that you could never be found? How came it that you never appeared in defence of the Honourable Thomas Drummond; you, the only person who could have justified him?'

'I could not, for I then fell under the power and guidance of a wretch, who durst not for the soul of him be brought forward in the affair. And what was worse, his evidence would have overborne mine, for he would have sworn, that the man who called out and fought Colwan, was the same he met leaving my apartment, and there was an end of it. And moreover, it is well known, that this same man,—this wretch of whom I speak, never mistook one man for another in his life, which makes the mystery of the likeness between this incendiary and Drummond the more extraordinary.'

'If it was Drummond, after all that you have asserted, then are my surmises still wrong.'

'There is nothing of which I can be more certain, than

that it was not Drummond. We have nothing on earth but our senses to depend upon: if these deceive us, what are we to do. I own I cannot account for it; nor ever shall be able to account for it as long as I live.'

'Could you know the man in black, if you saw him again?'

'I think I could, if I saw him walk or run: his gait was very particular: He walked as if he had been flat-soled, and his legs made of steel, without any joints in his feet or ancles.'

'The very same! The very same! The very same! Pray will you take a few days' journey into the country with me, to look at such a man?'

'You have preserved my life, and for you I will do any thing. I will accompany you with pleasure: and I think I can say that I will know him, for his form left an impression on my heart not soon to be effaced. But of this I am sure, that my unworthy companion *will* recognize him, and that he will be able to swear to his identity every day as long as he lives.'

'Where is he? Where is he? O! Mrs. Calvert, where is he?'

'Where is he? He is the wretch whom you heard giving me up to the death; who, after experiencing every mark of affection that a poor ruined being could confer, and after committing a thousand atrocities of which she was ignorant, became an informer to save his diabolical life, and attempted to offer up mine as a sacrifice for all. We will go by ourselves first, and I will tell you if it is necessary to send any farther.'

The two dames, the very next morning, dressed themselves like country goodwives; and, hiring two stout ponies furnished with pillions, they took their journey westward, and the second evening after leaving Edinburgh they arrived at the village about two miles below Dalcastle, where they alighted. But Mrs. Logan, being anxious to have Mrs. Calvert's judgment, without either hint or preparation, took care not to mention that they were so near to the end of their journey. In conformity with this plan, she said, after they had sat a while, 'Heigh-ho, but I am weary! What suppose we should rest a day here before we proceed farther on our journey?'

Mrs. Calvert was leaning on the casement, and looking out when her companion addressed these words to her, and by far too much engaged to return any answer, for her eyes were riveted on two young men who approached from the farther end of the village; and at length, turning round her head, she said, with the most intense interest, 'Proceed farther on our journey, did you say? That we need not do; for, as I live, here comes the very man!'

Mrs. Logan ran to the window, and behold, there was indeed Robert Wringhim Colwan (now the Laird of Dalcastle) coming forward almost below their window, walking arm in arm with another young man; and as the two passed, the latter looked up and made a sly signal to the two dames, biting his lip, winking with his left eye, and nodding his head. Mrs. Calvert was astonished at this recognizance, the young man's former companion having made exactly such another signal on the night of the duel, by the light of the moon; and it struck her, moreover, that she had somewhere seen this young man's face before. She looked after him, and he winked over his shoulder to her; but she was prevented from returning his salute by her companion, who uttered a loud cry, between a groan and shriek, and fell down on the floor with a rumble like a wall that had suddenly been undermined. She had fainted quite away, and required all her companion's attention during the remainder of the evening, for she had scarcely ever well recovered out of one fit before she fell into another, and in the short intervals she raved like one distracted, or in a dream. After falling into a sound sleep by night, she recovered her equanimity, and the two began to converse seriously on what they had seen. Mrs. Calvert averred that the young man who passed next to the window, *was* the very man who stabbed George Colwan in the back, and she said she was willing to take her oath on it at any time when required, and was certain if the wretch Ridsley saw him, that he would make oath to the same purport, for that his walk was so peculiar, no one of common discernment could mistake it.

Mrs. Logan was in great agitation, and said, 'It is what I have suspected all along, and what I am sure my late master and benefactor was persuaded of, and the horror of such an idea cut short his days. That wretch, Mrs. Calvert, is the born brother of him he murdered, sons of the same mother they were, whether or not of the same father, the Lord only knows. But, O Mrs. Calvert, that is not the main thing that has discomposed me, and shaken my nerves to pieces at this time. Who do you think the young man was who walked in his company to night?'

'I cannot for my life recollect, but am convinced I have seen the same fine form and face before.'

'And did not he seem to know us, Mrs. Calvert? You who are able to recollect things as they happened, did he not seem to recollect us, and make signs to that effect?'

'He did, indeed, and apparently with great good humour.'

'O, Mrs. Calvert, hold me, else I shall fall into hysterics again! Who is he? Who is he? Tell me who you suppose he is, for I cannot say my own thought.'

'On my life, I cannot remember.'

'Did you note the appearance of the young gentleman

you saw slain that night? Do you recollect aught of the appearance of my young master, George Colwan?'

Mrs. Calvert sat silent, and stared the other mildly in the face. Their looks enountered, and there was an unearthly amazement that gleamed from each, which, meeting together, caught real fire, and returned the flame to their heated imaginations, till the two associates became like two statues, with their hands spread, their eyes fixed, and their chops fallen down upon their bosoms. An old woman who kept the lodging-house, having been called in before when Mrs. Logan was faintish, chanced to enter at this crisis with some cordial; and, seeing the state of her lodgers, she caught the infection, and fell into the same rigid and statue-like appearance. No scene more striking was ever exhibited; and if Mrs. Calvert had not resumed strength of mind to speak, and break the spell, it is impossible to say how long it might have continued. 'It is he, I believe,' said she, uttering the words as it were inwardly. 'It can be none other but he. But, no, it is impossible! I saw him stabbed through and through the heart; I saw him roll backward on the green in his own blood, utter his last words, and groan away his soul. Yet, if it is not he, who can it be?'

'It *is* he!' cried Mrs. Logan, hysterically.

'Yes, yes, it *is* he!' cried the landlady, in unison.

'It is who?' said Mrs. Calvert; 'whom do you mean, mistress?'

'Oh, I don't know! I don't know! I was affrighted.'

'Hold your peace then till you recover your senses, and tell me, if you can, who that young gentleman is, who keeps company with the new Laird of Dalcastle?'

'Oh, it is he! it is he!' screamed Mrs. Logan, wringing her hands.

'Oh, it is he! it is he!' cried the landlady, wringing hers.

Mrs. Calvert turned the latter gently and civilly out of the apartment, observing that there seemed to be some infection in the air of the room, and she would be wise for herself to keep out of it.

The two dames had a restless and hideous night. Sleep came not to their relief; for their conversation was wholly about the dead, who seemed to be alive, and their minds were wandering and groping in a chaos of mystery. 'Did you attend to his corpse, and know that he positively died and was buried?' said Mrs. Calvert.

'O, yes, from the moment that his fair but mangled corpse was brought home, I attended it till that when it was screwed in the coffin. I washed the long stripes of blood from his lifeless form, on both sides of the body—I bathed the livid wound that passed through his generous and gentle heart. There was one through the flesh of his left side too, which had bled most outwardly of them all. I bathed them, and bandaged them up with wax and perfumed ointment, but still the blood oozed through all, so that when he was laid in the coffin he was like one newly murdered. My brave, my generous young master! he was always as a son to me, and no son was ever more kind or more respectful to a mother. But he was butchered—he was cut off from the earth ere he had well reached to manhood—most barbarously and unfairly slain. And how is it, how can it be, that we again see him here, walking arm in arm with his murderer?'

'The thing cannot be, Mrs. Logan. It is a phantasy of our disturbed imaginations, therefore let us compose ourselves till we investigate this matter farther.'

'It cannot be in nature, that is quite clear,' said Mrs. Logan; 'yet how it should be that I should *think* so—I who knew and nursed him from his infancy—there lies the paradox. As you said once before, we have nothing but our senses to depend on, and if you and I believe that we see a person, why, we do see him. Whose word, or whose reasoning can convince us against our own senses? We will disguise ourselves, as poor women selling a few country wares, and we will go up to the Hall, and see what is to see, and hear what we can hear, for this is a weighty business in which we are engaged, namely, to turn the vengeance of the law upon an unnatural monster; and we will farther learn, if we can, who this is that accompanies him.'

Mrs. Calvert acquiesced, and the two dames took their way to Dalcastle, with baskets well furnished with trifles. They did not take the common path from the village, but went about, and approached the mansion by a different way. But it seemed as if some overruling power ordered it, that they should miss no chance of attaining the information they wanted. For ere ever they came within half a mile of Dalcastle, they perceived the two youths coming, as to meet them, on the same path. The road leading from Dalcastle toward the north-east, as all the country knows, goes along a dark bank of brushwood called the Bogle-heuch. It was by this track that the two women were going; and when they perceived the two gentlemen meeting them, they turned back, and the moment they were out of their sight, they concealed themselves in a thicket close by the road. They did this because Mrs. Logan was terrified for being discovered, and because they wished to reconnoitre without being seen. Mrs. Calvert now charged her, whatever she saw, or whatever she heard, to put on a resolution, and support it, for if she fainted there and was discovered, what was to become of her!

The two young men came on, in earnest and vehement conversation; but the subject they were on was a terrible one, and hardly fit to be repeated in the face of a Christian community. Wringhim was disputing the boundlessness of the true Christian's freedom, and expressing doubts, that, chosen as he knew he was from all eternity, still it might be possible for him to commit acts that would exclude him from the limits of the covenant. The other argued, with mighty fluency, that the thing was utterly impossible, and altogether inconsistent with eternal predestination. The arguments of the latter prevailed, and the laird was driven to sullen silence. But, to the women's utter surprise, as the conquering disputant passed, he made a signal of recognizance through the brambles to them, as formerly, and that he might expose his associate fully, and in his true colours, he led him backward and forward by the women more than twenty times, making him to confess both the crimes that he had done, and those he had in contemplation. At length he said to him, 'Assuredly I saw some strolling vagrant women on this walk, my dear friend: I wish we could find them, for there is little doubt that they are concealed here in your woods.'

'I wish we *could* find them,' answered Wringhim; 'we would have fine sport maltreating and abusing them.'

'That we should, that we should! Now tell me, Robert, if you found a malevolent woman, the latent enemy of your prosperity, lurking in these woods to betray you, what would you inflict on her?'

'I would tear her to pieces with my dogs, and feed them with her flesh. O, my dear friend, there is an old strumpet who lived with my unnatural father, whom I hold in such utter detestation, that I stand constantly in dread of her, and would sacrifice the half of my estate to shed her blood!'

'What will you give me if I will put her in your power, and give you a fair and genuine excuse for making away

with her; one for which you shall answer at any bar, here
or hereafter?'

'I should like to see the vile hag put down. She is in
possession of the family plate, that is mine by right, as
well as a thousand valuable relics, and great riches besides,
all of which the old profligate gifted shamefully away. And
it is said, besides all these, that she has sworn my destruction.'

'She has, she has. But I see not how she can accomplish
that, seeing the deed was done so suddenly, and in the
silence of the night?'

'It was said there were some on-lookers.—But where
shall we find that disgraceful Miss Logan?'

'I will show you her by and by. But will you then consent to the other meritorious deed? Come, be a man, and
throw away scruples.'

'If you can convince me that the promise is binding, I
will.'

'Then step this way, till I give you a piece of information.'

They walked a little way out of hearing, but went not
out of sight; therefore, though the women were in a
terrible quandary, they durst not stir, for they had some
hopes that this extraordinary person was on a mission of
the same sort with themselves, knew of them, and was
going to make use of their testimony. Mrs. Logan was
several times on the point of falling into a swoon, so
much did the appearance of the young man impress her,
until her associate covered her face that she might listen
without embarrassment. But this latter dialogue aroused
different feelings within them; namely, those arising from
imminent personal danger. They saw his waggish associate
point out the place of their concealment to Wringhim,
who came.toward them, out of curiosity to see what his

friend meant by what he believed to be a joke, manifestly without crediting it in the least degree. When he came running away, the other called after him, 'If she is too hard for you, call to me.' As he said this, he hasted out of sight, in the contrary direction, apparently much delighted with the joke.

Wringhim came rushing through the thicket impetuously, to the very spot where Mrs. Logan lay squatted. She held the wrapping close about her head, but he tore it off and discovered her. 'The curse of God be on thee!' said he: 'What fiend has brought thee here, and for what purpose art thou come? But, whatever has brought thee, *I have thee!*' and with that he seized her by the throat. The two women, when they heard what jeopardy they were in from such a wretch, had squatted among the underwood at a small distance from each other, so that he had never observed Mrs. Calvert; but no sooner had he seized her benefactor, than, like a wild cat, she sprung out of the thicket, and had both her hands fixed at his throat, one of them twisted in his stock, in a twinkling. She brought him back-over among the brushwood, and the two, fixing on him like two harpies, mastered him with ease. Then indeed was he wofully beset. He deemed for a while that his friend was at his back, and turning his bloodshot eyes toward the path, he attempted to call; but there was no friend there, and the women cut short his cries by another twist of his stock. 'Now, gallant and rightful Laird of Dalcastle,' said Mrs. Logan, 'what hast thou to say for thyself? Lay thy account to dree the weird thou hast so well earned. Now shalt thou suffer due penance for murdering thy brave and only brother.'

'Thou liest, thou hag of the pit! I touched not my brother's life.'

'I saw thee do it with these eyes that now look thee in

the face; ay, when his back was to thee too, and while he was hotly engaged with thy friend,' said Mrs. Calvert.

'I heard thee confess it again and again this same hour,' said Mrs. Logan.

'Ay, and so did I,' said her companion.—'Murder will out, though the Almighty should lend hearing to the ears of the willow, and speech to the seven tongues of the woodriff.'

'You are liars, and witches!' said he, foaming with rage, 'and creatures fitted from the beginning for eternal destruction. I'll have your bones and your blood sacrificed on your cursed altars! O, Gil-Martin! Gil-Martin! where art thou now? Here, here is the proper food for blessed vengeance!—Hilloa!'

There was no friend, no Gil-Martin there to hear or assist him: he was in the two women's mercy, but they used it with moderation. They mocked, they tormented, and they threatened him; but, finally, after putting him in great terror, they bound his hands behind his back, and his feet fast with long straps of garters which they chanced to have in their baskets, to prevent him from pursuing them till they were out of his reach. As they left him, which they did in the middle of the path, Mrs. Calvert said, 'We could easily put an end to thy sinful life, but our hands shall be free of thy blood. Nevertheless thou art still in our power, and the vengeance of thy country shall overtake thee, thou mean and cowardly murderer, ay, and that more suddenly than thou art aware!'

The women posted to Edinburgh; and as they put themselves under the protection of an English merchant, who was journeying thither with twenty horses loaden, and armed servants, so they had scarcely any conversation on the road. When they arrived at Mrs. Logan's house, then they spoke of what they had seen and heard, and agreed that they had sufficient proof to condemn young

Wringhim, who they thought richly deserved the severest doom of the law.

'I never in my life saw any human being,' said Mrs. Calvert, 'whom I thought so like a fiend. If a demon could inherit flesh and blood, that youth is precisely such a being as I could conceive that demon to be. The depth and the malignity of his eye is hideous. His breath is like the airs from a charnel house, and his flesh seems fading from his bones, as if the worm that never dies were gnawing it away already.'

'He was always repulsive, and every way repulsive,' said the other; 'but he is now indeed altered greatly to the worse. While we were handfasting him, I felt his body to be feeble and emaciated; but yet I know him to be so puffed up with spiritual pride, that I believe he weens every one of his actions justified before God, and instead of having stings of conscience for these, he takes great merit to himself in having effected them. Still my thoughts are less about him than the extraordinary being who accompanies him. He does every thing with so much ease and indifference, so much velocity and effect, that all bespeak him an adept in wickedness. The likeness to my late hapless young master is so striking, that I can hardly believe it to be a chance model; and I think he imitates him in every thing, for some purpose, or some effect on his sinful associate. Do you know that he is so like in every lineament, look, and gesture, that, against the clearest light of reason, I cannot in my mind separate the one from the other, and have a certain indefinable impression on my mind, that they are one and the same being, or that the one was a prototype of the other.'

'If there is an earthly crime,' said Mrs. Calvert, 'for the due punishment of which the Almighty may be supposed to subvert the order of nature, it is fratricide. But tell me, dear friend, did you remark to what the subtile and hellish villain was endeavouring to prompt the assassin?'

'No, I could not comprehend it. My senses were altogether so bewildered, that I thought they had combined to deceive me, and I gave them no credit.'

'Then hear me: I am almost certain he was using every persuasion to induce him to make away with his mother; and I likewise conceive that I heard the incendiary give his consent!'

'This is dreadful. Let us speak and think no more about it, till we see the issue. In the meantime, let us do that which is our bounden duty,—go and divulge all that we know relating to this foul murder.'

Accordingly the two women went to Sir Thomas Wallace of Craigie, the Lord Justice Clerk, (who was, I think, either uncle or grandfather to young Drummond, who was outlawed, and obliged to fly his country on account of Colwan's death,) and to that gentleman they related every circumstance of what they had seen and heard. He examined Calvert very minutely, and seemed deeply interested in her evidence—said he knew she was relating the truth, and in testimony of it, brought a letter of young Drummond's from his desk, wherein that young gentleman, after protesting his innocence in the most forcible terms, confessed having been with such a woman in such a house, after leaving the company of his friends; and that on going home, Sir Thomas's servant had let him in, in the dark, and from these circumstances he found it impossible to prove an *alibi*. He begged of his relative, if ever an opportunity offered, to do his endeavour to clear up that mystery, and remove the horrid stigma from his name in his country, and among his kin, of having stabbed a friend behind his back.

Lord Craigie, therefore, directed the two women to

the proper authorities, and after hearing their evidence there, it was judged proper to apprehend the present Laird of Dalcastle, and bring him to his trial. But before that, they sent the prisoner in the tolbooth, he who had seen the whole transaction along with Mrs. Calvert, to take a view of Wringhim privately; and his discrimination being so well known as to be proverbial all over the land, they determined secretly to be ruled by this report. They accordingly sent him on a pretended mission of legality to Dalcastle, with orders to see and speak with the proprietor, without giving him a hint what was wanted. On his return, they examined him, and he told them that he found all things at the place in utter confusion and dismay; that the lady of the place was missing, and could not be found, dead or alive. On being asked if he had ever seen the proprietor before, he looked astounded, and unwilling to answer. But it came out that he had; and that he had once seen him kill a man on such a spot at such an hour.

Officers were then despatched, without delay, to apprehend the monster, and bring him to justice. On these going to the mansion, and inquiring for him, they were told he was at home; on which they stationed guards, and searched all the premises, but he was not to be found. It was in vain that they overturned beds, raised floors, and broke open closets: Robert Wringhim Colwan was lost once and for ever. His mother also was lost; and strong suspicions attached to some of the farmers and house servants, to whom she was obnoxious, relating to her disappearance. The Honourable Thomas Drummond became a distinguished officer in the Austrian service, and died in the memorable year for Scotland, 1715; and this is all with which history, justiciary records, and tradition, furnish me relating to these matters.

I have now the pleasure of presenting my readers with an original document of a most singular nature, and preserved for their perusal in a still more singular manner. I offer no remarks on it, and make as few additions to it, leaving every one to judge for himself. We have heard much of the rage of fanaticism in former days, but nothing to this.

PRIVATE MEMOIRS

AND

CONFESSIONS OF A SINNER

WRITTEN BY HIMSELF

PRIVATE MEMOIRS

[handwritten annotation: Royal Society of Edinb. diagnosed a case of double personalities a few yrs b4 this was published]

CONFESSIONS OF A SINNER

M Y life has been a life of trouble and turmoil; of change
and vicissitude; of anger and exultation; of sorrow and of
vengeance. My sorrows have all been for a slighted gospel,
and my vengeance has been wreaked on its adversaries.
Therefore, in the might of heaven I will sit down and
write: I will let the wicked of this world know what I
have done in the faith of the promises, and justification
by grace, that they may read and tremble, and bless their
gods of silver and of gold, that the minister of heaven
was removed from their sphere before their blood was
mingled with their sacrifices.

I was born an outcast in the world, in which I was destined
to act so conspicuous a part. My mother was a burning
and a shining light, in the community of Scottish worthies,
and in the days of her virginity had suffered much in the
persecution of the saints. But it so pleased Heaven, that,
as a trial of her faith, she was married to one of the
wicked; a man all over spotted with the leprosy of sin. As
well might they have conjoined fire and water together,
in hopes that they would consort and amalgamate, as
purity and corruption: She fled from his embraces the
first night after their marriage, and from that time forth,

his iniquities so galled her upright heart, that she quitted his society altogether, keeping her own apartments in the same house with him.

I was the second son of this unhappy marriage, and, long ere ever I was born, my father according to the flesh disclaimed all relation or connection with me, and all interest in me, save what the law compelled him to take, which was to grant me a scanty maintenance; and had it not been for a faithful minister of the gospel, my mother's early instructor, I should have remained an outcast from the church visible. He took pity on me, admitting me not only into that, but into the bosom of his own household and ministry also, and to him am I indebted, under Heaven, for the high conceptions and glorious discernment between good and evil, right and wrong, which I attained even at an early age. It was he who directed my studies aright, both in the learning of the ancient fathers, and the doctrines of the reformed church, and designed me for his assistant and successor in the holy office. I missed no opportunity of perfecting myself particularly in all the minute points of theology in which my reverend father and mother took great delight; but at length I acquired so much skill, that I astonished my teachers, and made them gaze at one another. I remember that it was the custom, in my patron's house, to ask the questions of the Single Catechism round every Sabbath night. He asked the first, my mother the second, and so on, every one saying the question asked, and then asking the next. It fell to my mother to ask Effectual Calling at me. I said the answer with propriety and emphasis. 'Now, madam,' added I, 'my question to you is, What is *In*effectual Calling?'

'Ineffectual Calling? There is no such thing, Robert,' said she.

'But there is, madam,' said I; 'and that answer proves how much you say these fundamental precepts by rote, and without any consideration. Ineffectual Calling is, *the outward call of the gospel* without any effect on the hearts of unregenerated and impenitent sinners. Have not all these the same calls, warnings, doctrines, and reproofs, that we have? and is not this Ineffectual Calling? Has not Ardinferry the same? Has not Patrick M'Lure the same? *Has not the Laird of Dalcastle and his reprobate heir* the same? And will any tell me, that *this is not In*effectual Calling?'

'What a wonderful boy he is!' said my mother.

'I'm feared he turn out to be a conceited gowk,' said old Barnet, the minister's man.

'No,' said my pastor, and *father*, (as I shall henceforth denominate him,) 'No, Barnet, he *is* a wonderful boy; and no marvel, for I have prayed for these talents to be bestowed on him from his infancy: and do you think that Heaven would refuse a prayer so disinterested? No, it is impossible. But my dread is, madam,' continued he, turning to my mother, 'that he is yet in the bond of iniquity.'

'God forbid!' said my mother.

'I have struggled with the Almighty long and hard,' continued he; 'but have as yet had no certain token of acceptance in his behalf. I have indeed fought a hard fight, but have been repulsed by him who hath seldom refused my request; although I cited his own words against him, and endeavoured to hold him at his promise, he hath so many turnings in the supremacy of his power, that I have been rejected. How dreadful is it to think of our darling being still without the pale of the covenant! But I have vowed a vow, and in that there is hope.'

My heart quaked with terror, when I thought of being

still living in a state of reprobation, subjected to the awful issues of death, judgment, and eternal misery, by the slightest accident or casualty, and I set about the duty of prayer myself with the utmost earnestness. I prayed three times every day, and seven times on the Sabbath; but the more frequently and fervently that I prayed, I sinned still the more. About this time, and for a long period afterwards, amounting to several years, I lived in a hopeless and deplorable state of mind; for I said to myself, 'If my name is not written in the book of life from all eternity, it is in vain for me to presume that either vows or prayers of mine, or those of all mankind combined, can ever procure its insertion now.' I had come under many vows, most solemnly taken, every one of which I had broken; and I saw with the intensity of juvenile grief, that there was no hope for me. I went on sinning every hour, and all the while most strenuously warring against sin, and repenting of every one transgression, as soon after the commission of it as I got leisure to think. But O what a wretched state this unregenerated state is, in which every effort after righteousness only aggravates our offences! I found it vanity to contend; for after communing with my heart, the conclusion was as follows: 'If I could repent me of all my sins, and shed tears of blood for them, still have I not a load of original transgression pressing on me, that is enough to crush me to the lowest hell. I may be angry with my first parents for having sinned, but how I shall repent me of their sin, is beyond what I am able to comprehend.'

Still, in those days of depravity and corruption, I had some of those principles implanted in my mind, which were afterward to spring up with such amazing fertility among the heroes of the faith and the promises. In particular, I felt great indignation against all the wicked of this world, and often wished for the means of ridding it of such a noxious burden. I liked John Barnet, my reverend father's serving-man, extremely ill; but, from a supposition that he might be one of the justified, I refrained from doing him any injury. He gave always his word against me, and when we were by ourselves, in the barn or the fields, he rated me with such severity for my faults, that my heart could brook it no longer. He discovered some notorious lies that I had framed, and taxed me with them in such a manner that I could in nowise get off. My cheek burnt with offence, rather than shame; and he, thinking he had got the mastery of me, exulted over me most unmercifully, telling me I was a selfish and conceited blackguard, who made great pretences towards religious devotion to cloak a disposition tainted with deceit, and that it would not much astonish him if I brought myself to the gallows.

I gathered some courage from his over severity, and answered him as follows: 'Who made thee a judge of the actions or dispositions of the Almighty's creatures—thou who art a worm, and no man in his sight? How it befits thee to deal out judgments and anathemas! Hath he not made one vessel to honour, and another to dishonour, as in the case with myself and thee? Hath he not builded his stories in the heavens, and laid the foundations thereof in the earth, and how can a being like thee judge between good and evil, that are both subjected to the workings of his hand; or of the opposing principles in the soul of man, correcting, modifying, and refining one another?'

I said this with that strong display of fervor for which I was remarkable at my years, and expected old Barnet to be utterly confounded; but he only shook his head, and, with the most provoking grin, said, 'There he goes! sickan sublime and ridiculous sophistry I never heard come out of another mouth but ane. There needs nae aiths to be

sworn afore the session wha is your father, young goodman. I ne'er, for my part, saw a son sae like a dad, sin'my
een first opened.' With that he went away, saying, with
an ill-natured wince, 'You made to honour and me to dishonour! Dirty bowkail thing that thou be'st!'

'I will have the old rascal on the hip for this, if I live,'
thought I. So I went and asked my mother if John was
a righteous man? She could not tell, but supposed he was,
and therefore I got no encouragement from her. I went
next to my reverend father, and inquired his opinion,
expecting as little from that quarter. He knew the elect
as it were by instinct, and could have told you of all those
in his own, and some neighbouring parishes, who were
born within the boundaries of the covenant of promise, and
who were not.

'I keep a good deal in company with your servant, old
Barnet, father,' said I.

'You do, boy; you do, I see', said he.

'I wish I may not keep too much in his company,' said
I, 'not knowing what kind of society I am in;—is John a
good man, father?'

'Why, boy, he is but so, so. A morally good man John
is, but very little of the leaven of true righteousness, which
is faith, within. I am afraid old Barnet, with all his stock
of morality, will be a cast-away.'

My heart was greatly cheered by this remark; and I
sighed very deeply, and hung my head to one side. The
worthy father observed me, and inquired the cause? when
I answered as follows: 'How dreadful the thought, that I
have been going daily in company and fellowship with
one, whose name is written on the red-letter side of the
book of life; whose body and soul have been, from all
eternity, consigned over to everlasting destruction, and
to whom the blood of the atonement can never, never

reach! Father, this is an awful thing, and beyond my comprehension.'

'While we are in the world, we must mix with the inhabitants thereof,' said he; 'and the stains which adhere to us by reason of this admixture, which is unavoidable, shall all be washed away. It is our duty, however, to shun the society of wicked men as much as possible, lest we partake of their sins, and become sharers with them in punishment. John, however, is a morally good man, and may yet get a cast of grace.'

'I always thought him a good man till to day,' said I, 'when he threw out some reflections on your character, so horrible that I quake to think of the wickedness and malevolence of his heart. He was rating me very impertinently for some supposed fault, which had no being save in his own jealous brain, when I attempted to reason him out of his belief in the spirit of calm Christian argument. But how do you think he answered me? He did so, sir, by twisting his mouth at me, and remarking that such sublime and ridiculous sophistry never came out of another mouth but one, (meaning yours,) and that no oath before a kirk session was necessary to prove who was my dad, for that he had never seen a son so like a father as I was like mine.'

'He durst not for his soul's salvation, and for his daily bread, which he values much more, say such a word, boy; therefore take care what you assert,' said my reverend father.

'He said these very words, and will not deny them, sir,' said I.

My reverend father turned about in great wrath and indignation, and went away in search of John; but I kept out of the way, and listened at a back window; for John was dressing the plot of ground behind the house; and I hope it was no sin in me that I did rejoice in the dialogue

The Antinomian heresy proposed by Johannes Agricola in 1538 - those saved by divine grace outside the moral law which took place, it being the victory of righteousness over error.

'Well, John, this is a fine day for your delving work.'

'Ey, it's a tolerable day, sir.'

'Are you thankful in your heart, John, for such temporal mercies as these?'

'Aw doubt we're a' ower little thankfu', sir, baith for temporal an' speeritual mercies; but it isna aye the maist thankfu' heart that maks the greatest fraze wi' the tongue.'

'I hope there is nothing personal under that remark, John?'

'Gin the bannet fits ony body's head, they're unco welcome to it, sir, for me.'

'John, I do not approve of these innuendoes. You have an arch malicious manner of vending your aphorisms, which the men of the world are too apt to read the wrong way, for your dark hints are sure to have *one* very bad meaning.'

'Hout na, sir, it's only bad folks that think sae. They find ma bits o'gibes come hame to their hearts wi' a kind o' yerk, an' that gars them wince.'

'That saying is ten times worse than the other, John; it is a manifest insult: it is just telling me to my face, that you think me a bad man.'

'A body canna help his thoughts, sir.'

'No, but a man's thoughts are generally formed from observation. Now I should like to know, even from the mouth of a misbeliever, what part of my conduct warrants such a conclusion?'

'Nae particular pairt, sir; I draw a' my conclusions frae the haill o' a man's character, an' I'm no that aften far wrang.'

'Well, John, and what sort of general character do you suppose mine to be?'

'Yours is a Scripture character, sir, an' I'll prove it.'

'I hope so, John. Well, which of the Scripture characters do you think approximates nearest to my own?'

'Guess, sir, guess; I wish to lead a proof.'

'Why, if it be an Old Testament character, I hope it is Melchizedek, for at all events you cannot deny there is one point of resemblance: I, like him, am a preacher of righteousness. If it be a New Testament character, I suppose you mean the Apostle of the Gentiles, of whom I am an unworthy representative.'

'Na, na, sir, better nor that still, an'fer closer is the resemblance. When ye bring me to the point, I maun speak. Ye are the just Pharisee, sir, that gaed up wi' the poor publican to pray in the Temple; an' ye're acting the very same pairt at this time, an' saying i' your heart, "God, I thank thee that I am not as other men are, an' in nae way like this poor misbelieving unregenerate sinner, John Barnet."'

'I hope I may say so indeed.'

'There now! I tauld you how it was! But, d'ye hear, maister: Here stands the poor sinner, John Barnet, your beadle an' servant-man, wha wadna change chances wi' you in the neist world, nor consciences in this, for ten times a' that you possess,—your justification by faith an' awthegither.'

'You are extremely audacious and impertinent, John; but the language of reprobation cannot affect me: I came only to ask you one question, which I desire you to answer candidly. Did you ever say to any one that I was the boy Robert's natural father?'

'Hout na, sir! Ha—ha—ha! Aih, fie na, sir! I durstna say that for my life. I doubt the black stool, an' the sack gown, or maybe the juggs wad hae been my portion had I said sic a thing as that. Hout, hout! Fie, fie! Unco-like doings thae for a Melchizedek or a Saint Paul!'

'John, you are a profane old man, and I desire that you will not presume to break your jests on me. Tell me, dare you say, or dare you think, that I am the natural father of that boy?'

'Ye canna hinder me to think whatever I like, sir, nor can I hinder mysel.'

'But did you ever *say* to any one, that he resembled me, and fathered himself well enough?'

'I hae said mony a time, that he resembled you, sir. Naebody can mistake that.'

'But, John, there are many natural reasons for such likenesses, besides that of consanguinity. They depend much on the thoughts and affections of the mother; and, it is probable, that the mother of this boy, being deserted by her worthless husband, having turned her thoughts on me, as likely to be her protector, may have caused this striking resemblance.'

'Ay, it may be, sir. I coudna say.'

'I have known a lady, John, who was delivered of a blackamoor child, merely from the circumstance of having got a start by the sudden entrance of her negro servant, and not being able to forget him for several hours.'

'It may be, sir; but I ken this;—an I had been the laird, I wadna hae ta'en that story in.'

'So, then, John, you positively think, from a casual likeness, that this boy is my son?'

'Man's thoughts are vanity, sir; they come unasked, an gang away without a dismissal, an' he canna help them. I'm neither gaun to say that I *think* he's your son, nor that I think he's *no* your son: sae ye needna pose me nae mair about it.'

'Hear then my determination, John: If you do not promise to me, in faith and honour, that you never will say, or insinuate such a thing again in your life, as that that boy is my natural son, I will take the keys of the church from you, and dismiss you my service.'

John pulled out the keys, and dashed them on the gravel at the reverend minister's feet. 'There are the keys o' your kirk, sir! I hae never had muckle mense o' them sin' ye entered the door o't. I hae carried them this three an thretty year, but they hae aye been like to burn a hole i' my pouch sin' ever they were turned for your admittance. Tak them again, an' gie them to wha you will, and muckle gude may he get o' them. Auld John may dee a beggar in a hay barn, or at the back of a dike, but he sall aye be master o' his ain thoughts, an' gie them vent or no, as he likes.'

He left the manse that day, and I rejoiced in the riddance; for I disdained to be kept so much under, by one who was in the bond of iniquity, and of whom there seemed no hope, as he rejoiced in his frowardness, and refused to submit to that faithful teacher, his master.

It was about this time that my reverend father preached a sermon, one sentence of which affected me most disagreeably: It was to the purport, that every unrepented sin was productive of a new sin with each breath that a man drew; and every one of these new sins added to the catalogue in the same manner. I was utterly confounded at the multitude of my transgressions; for I was sensible that there were great numbers of sins of which I had never been able thoroughly to repent, and these momentary ones, by a moderate calculation, had, I saw, long ago, amounted to a hundred and fifty thousand in the minute, and I saw no end to the series of repentances to which I had subjected myself. A life-time was nothing to enable me to accomplish the sum, and then being, for any thing I was certain of, in my state of nature, and the grace of repentance withheld from me,—what was I to do, or what was to become of me? In the meantime, I went on sinning without measure; but I was still more troubled about the multitude than the magnitude of my transgressions, and the small minute ones puzzled me more than those that were more heinous, as the latter had generally some good effects in the way of punishing wicked men, froward boys, and deceitful women; and I rejoiced, even then in my early youth, at being used as a scourge in the hand of the Lord; another Jehu, a Cyrus, or a Nebuchadnezzar.

On the whole, I remember that I got into great confusion relating to my sins and repentances, and knew neither where to begin nor how to proceed, and often had great fears that I was wholly without Christ, and that I would find God a consuming fire to me. I could not help running into new sins continually; but then I was mercifully dealt with, for I was often made to repent of them most heartily, by reason of bodily chastisements received on these delinquencies being discovered. I was particularly prone to lying, and I cannot but admire the mercy that has freely forgiven me all these juvenile sins. Now that I know them all to be blotted out, and that I am an accepted person, I may the more freely confess them: the truth is, that one lie always paved the way for another, from hour to hour, from day to day, and from year to year; so that I found myself constantly involved in a labyrinth of deceit, from which it was impossible to extricate myself. If I knew a person to be a godly one, I could almost have kissed his feet; but against the carnal portion of mankind, I set my face continually. I esteemed the true ministers of the gospel; but the prelatic party, and the preachers up of good works I abhorred, and to this hour I account them the worst and most heinous of all transgressors.

There was only one boy at Mr. Wilson's class who

just like William Wilson

kept always the upper hand of me in every part of education. I strove against him from year to year, but it was all in vain; for he was a very wicked boy, and I was convinced he had dealings with the devil. Indeed it was believed all over the country that his mother was a witch; and I was at length convinced that it was no human ingenuity that beat me with so much ease in the Latin, after I had often sat up a whole night with my reverend father, studying my lesson in all its bearings. I often read as well and sometimes better than he; but the moment Mr. Wilson began to examine us, my opponent popped up above me. I determined, (as I knew him for a wicked person, and one of the devil's hand-fasted children,) to be revenged on him, and to humble him by some means or other. Accordingly I lost no opportunity of setting the Master against him, and succeeded several times in getting him severely beaten for faults of which he was innocent. I can hardly describe the joy that it gave to my heart to see a wicked creature suffering, for though he deserved it not for one thing, he richly deserved it for others. This may be by some people accounted a great sin in me; but I deny it, for I did it as a duty, and what a man or boy does for the right, will never be put into the sum of his transgressions.

This boy, whose name was M'Gill, was, at all his leisure hours, engaged in drawing profane pictures of beasts, men, women, houses, and trees, and, in short, of all things that his eye encountered. These profane things the Master often smiled at, and admired; therefore I began privately to try my hand likewise. I had scarcely tried above once to draw the figure of a man, ere I conceived that I had hit the very features of Mr. Wilson. They were so particular, that they could not be easily mistaken, and I was so tickled and pleased with the droll likeness that

I had drawn, that I laughed immoderately at it. I tried no other figure but this; and I tried it in every situation in which a man and a schoolmaster could be placed. I often wrought for hours together at this likeness, nor was it long before I made myself so much master of the outline, that I could have drawn it in any situation whatever, almost off hand. I then took M'Gill's account book of algebra home with me, and at my leisure put down a number of gross caricatures of Mr. Wilson here and there, several of them in situations notoriously ludicrous. I waited the discovery of this treasure with great impatience; but the book, chancing to be one that M'Gill was not using, I saw it might be long enough before I enjoyed the consummation of my grand scheme: therefore, with all the ingenuity I was master of, I brought it before our dominie's eye. But never shall I forget the rage that gleamed in the tyrant's phiz! I was actually terrified to look at him, and trembled at his voice. M'Gill was called upon, and examined relating to the obnoxious figures. He denied flatly that any of them were of his doing. But the Master inquiring at him whose they were, he could not tell, but affirmed it to be some trick. Mr. Wilson at one time, began, as I thought, to hesitate; but the evidence was so strong against M'Gill, that at length his solemn asseverations of innocence only proved an aggravation of his crime. There was not one in the school who had ever been known to draw a figure but himself, and on him fell the whole weight of the tyrant's vengeance. It was dreadful; and I was once in hopes that he would not leave life in the culprit. He, however, left the school for several months, refusing to return to be subjected to punishment for the faults of others, and I stood king of the class.

Matters were at last made up between M'Gill's parents and the schoolmaster, but by that time I had got the start

of him, and never in my life did I exert myself so much as
to keep the mastery. It was in vain; the powers of enchantment prevailed, and I was again turned down with the
tear in my eye. I could think of no amends but one, and
being driven to desperation, I put it in practice. I told a
lie of him. I came boldly up to the master, and told him
that M'Gill had in my hearing cursed him in a most
shocking manner, and called him vile names. He called
M'Gill, and charged him with the crime, and the proud
young coxcomb was so stunned at the atrocity of the
charge, that his face grew as red as crimson, and the
words stuck in his throat as he feebly denied it. His guilt
was manifest, and he was again flogged most nobly, and
dismissed the school for ever in disgrace, as a most in-
corrigible vagabond.

This was a great victory gained, and I rejoiced and
exulted exceedingly in it. It had, however, very nigh cost
me my life; for not long thereafter, I encountered M'Gill
in the fields, on which he came up and challenged me for a
liar, daring me to fight him. I refused, and said that I
looked on him as quite below my notice; but he would
not quit me, and finally told me that he should either *lick
me*, or I should *lick him*, as he had no other means of being
revenged on such a scoundrel. I tried to intimidate him,
but it would not do; and I believe I would have given all
that I had in the world to be quit of him. He at length
went so far as first to kick me, and then strike me on the
face; and, being both older and stronger than he, I
thought it scarcely became me to take such insults
patiently. I was, nevertheless, well aware that the
devilish powers of his mother would finally prevail; and
either the dread of this, or the inward consciousness of
having wronged him, certainly unnerved my arm, for I
fought wretchedly, and was soon wholly overcome. I was

so sore defeated, that I kneeled, and was going to beg his pardon; but another thought struck me momentarily, and I threw myself on my face, and inwardly begged aid from heaven; at the same time I felt as if assured that my prayer was heard, and would be answered. While I was in this humble attitude, the villain kicked me with his foot and cursed me; and I being newly encouraged, arose and encountered him once more. We had not fought long at this second turn, before I saw a man hastening toward us; on which I uttered a shout of joy, and laid on valiantly; but my very next look assured me, that the man was old John Barnet, whom I had likewise wronged all that was in my power, and between these two wicked persons I expected any thing but justice. My arm was again enfeebled, and that of my adversary prevailed. I was knocked down and mauled most grievously, and while the ruffian was kicking and cuffing me at his will and pleasure, up came old John Barnet, breathless with running, and at one blow with his open hand, levelled my opponent with the earth. 'Tak ye that, maister!' says John, 'to learn ye better breeding. Hout awa, man! an ye will fight, fight fair. Gude sauf us, ir ye a gentleman's brood, that ye will kick an' cuff a lad when he's down?'

When I heard this kind and unexpected interference, I began once more to value myself on my courage, and springing up, I made at my adversary; but John, without saying a word, bit his lip, and seizing me by the neck, threw me down. M'Gill begged of him to stand and see fair play, and suffer us to finish the battle; for, added he, 'he is a liar, and a scoundrel, and deserves ten times more than I can give him.'

'I ken he's a' that ye say, an' mair, my man,' quoth John: 'But am I sure that ye're no as bad, an' waur? It says nae muckle for ony o' ye to be tearing like tikes at ane anither here.'

John cocked his cudgel and stood between us, threatening to knock the one dead, who first offered to lift his hand against the other; but, perceiving no disposition in any of us to separate, he drove me home before him like a bullock, keeping close guard behind me, lest M'Gill had followed. I felt greatly indebted to John, yet I complained of his interference to my mother, and the old officious sinner got no thanks for his pains.

nothing is his fault the little bastard

As I am writing only from recollection, so I remember of nothing farther in these early days, in the least worthy of being recorded. That I was a great, a transcendent sinner, I confess. But still I had hopes of forgiveness, because I never sinned from principle, but accident; and then I always *tried* to repent of these sins by the slump, for individually it was impossible; and though not always successful in my endeavours, I could not help that; the grace of repentance being withheld from me, I regarded myself as in no degree accountable for the failure. Moreover, there were many of the most deadly sins into which I never fell, for I dreaded those mentioned in the Revelations as excluding sins, so that I guarded against them continually. In particular, I brought myself to despise, if not to abhor, the beauty of women, looking on it as the greatest snare to which mankind are subjected, and though young men and maidens, and even old women, (my mother among the rest,) taxed me with being an unnatural wretch, I gloried in my acquisition; and to this day, am thankful for having escaped the most dangerous of all snares.

I kept myself also free of the sins of idolatry, and misbelief, both of a deadly nature; and, upon the whole, I think I had not then broken, that is, absolutely broken, above four out of the ten commandments; but for all that, I had more sense than to regard either my good works, or my evil deeds, as in the smallest degree influencing the

good works & salvation

eternal decrees of God concerning me, either with regard to my acceptance or reprobation. I depended entirely on the bounty of free grace, holding all the righteousness of man as filthy rags, and believing in the momentous and magnificent truth, that the more heavily loaden with transgressions, the more welcome was the believer at the throne of grace. And I have reason to believe that it was this dependence and this belief that at last ensured my acceptance there.

I come now to the most important period of my existence,—the period that has modelled my character, and influenced every action of my life,—without which, this detail of my actions would have been as a tale that hath been told—a monotonous *farrago*—an uninteresting harangue—in short, a thing of nothing. Whereas, lo! it must now be a relation of great and terrible actions, done in the might, and by the commission of heaven. *Amen.*

Like the sinful king of Israel, I had been walking softly before the Lord for a season. I had been humbled for my transgressions, and, as far as I recollect, sorry on account of their numbers and heinousness. My reverend father had been, moreover, examining me every day regarding the state of my soul, and my answers sometimes appeared to give him satisfaction, and sometimes not. As for my mother, she would harp on the subject of my faith for ever; yet, though I knew her to be a Christian, I confess that I always despised her motley instructions, nor had I any great regard for her person. If this was a crime in me, I never could help it. I confess it freely, and believe it was a judgment from heaven inflicted on her for some sin of former days, and that I had no power to have acted otherwise toward her than I did

In this frame of mind was I, when my reverend father one morning arose from his seat, and, meeting me as I

declared as elect

entered the room, he embraced me, and welcomed me into the community of the just upon earth. I was struck speechless, and could make no answer save by looks of surprise. My mother also came to me, kissed, and wept over me; and after showering unnumbered blessings on my head, she also welcomed me into the society of *the just made perfect*. Then each of them took me by a hand, and my reverend father explained to me how he had wrestled with God, as the patriarch of old had done, not for a night, but for days and years, and that in bitterness and anguish of spirit, on my account; but that *he* had at last prevailed, and had now gained the long and earnestly desired assurance of my acceptance with the Almighty, in and through the merits and sufferings of his Son: That I was now a justified person, adopted among the number of God's children—my name written in the Lamb's book of life, and that no bypast transgression, nor any future act of my own, or of other men, could be instrumental in altering the decree. 'All the powers of darkness,' added he, 'shall never be able to pluck you again out of your Redeemer's hand. And now, my son, be strong and sted-fast in the truth. Set your face against sin, and sinful men, and resist even to blood, as many of the faithful of this land have done, and your reward shall be double. I am assured of your acceptance by the word and spirit of him who cannot err, and your sanctification and repentance unto life will follow in due course. Rejoice and be thankful, for you are plucked as a brand out of the burning, and now your redemption is sealed and sure.'

I wept for joy to be thus assured of my freedom from all sin, and of the impossibility of my ever again falling away from my new state. I bounded away into the fields and the woods, to pour out my spirit in prayer before the Almighty for his kindness to me: my whole frame seemed to be renewed; every nerve was buoyant with new life; I felt as if I could have flown in the air, or leaped over the tops of the trees. An exaltation of spirit lifted me, as it were, far above the earth, and the sinful creatures crawling on its surface; and I deemed myself as an eagle among the children of men, soaring on high, and looking down with pity and contempt on the grovelling creatures below.

As I thus wended my way, I beheld a young man of a mysterious appearance coming towards me. I tried to shun him, being bent on my own contemplations; but he cast himself in my way, so that I could not well avoid him; and more than that, I felt a sort of <u>invisible power</u> that drew me towards him, something like the <u>force of enchantment</u>, which I could not resist. As we approached each other, our eyes met, and I can never describe the strange sensations that thrilled through my whole frame at that impressive moment; a moment to me fraught with the most tremendous consequences; the beginning of a series of adventures which has puzzled myself, and will puzzle the world when I am no more in it. That time will now soon arrive, sooner than any one can devise who knows not the tumult of my thoughts, and the labour of my spirit; and when it hath come and passed over,—when my flesh and my bones are decayed, and my soul has passed to its everlasting home, then shall the sons of men ponder on the events of my life; wonder and tremble, and tremble and wonder how such things should be.

That stranger youth and I approached each other in silence, and slowly, with our eyes fixed on each other's eyes. We approached till not more than a yard intervened between us, and then stood still and gazed, measuring each other from head to foot. What was my astonishment, on perceiving that he was the same being as myself! The

clothes were the same to the smallest item. The fo[...]
the same; the apparent age; the colour of the hair; th[...]
and, as far as recollection could serve me from v[...]
my own features in a glass, the features too were the very
same. I conceived at first, that I saw a vision, and that
my guardian angel had appeared to me at this important
era of my life; but this singular being read my thoughts in my
looks, anticipating the very words that I was going to utter.

'You think I am your brother,' said he; 'or that I am
your second self. I am indeed your brother, not according
to the flesh, but in my belief of the same truths, and my
assurance in the same mode of redemption, than which, I
hold nothing so great or so glorious on earth.'

'Then you are an associate well adapted to my present
state,' said I. 'For this time is a time of great rejoicing in
spirit to me. I am on my way to return thanks to the Most
High for my redemption from the bonds of sin and misery.
If you will join with me heart and hand in youthful thanksgiving, then shall we two go and worship together; but
if not, go your way, and I shall go mine.'

'Ah, you little know with how much pleasure I will
accompany you, and join with you in your elevated devo-
tions,' said he fervently. 'Your state is a state to be envied
indeed; but I have been advised of it, and am come to be
a humble disciple of yours; to be initiated into the true
way of salvation by conversing with you, and perhaps by
being assisted by your prayers.'

My spiritual pride being greatly elevated by this address, I began to assume the preceptor, and questioned
this extraordinary youth with regard to his religious
principles, telling him plainly, if he was one who expected
acceptance with God at all, on account of good works, that
I would hold no communion with him. He renounced these
at once, with the greatest vehemence, and declared his

acquiescence in my faith. I asked if he believed in the eternal and irrevocable decrees of God, regarding the salvation and condemnation of all mankind? He answered that he did so: aye, what would signify all things else that he believed, if he did not believe in that? We then went on to commune about all our points of belief; and in every thing that I suggested, he acquiesced, and, as I thought that day, often carried them to extremes, so that I had a secret dread he was advancing blasphemies. Yet he had such a way with him, and paid such a deference to all my opinions, that I was quite captivated, and, at the same time, I stood in a sort of awe of him, which I could not account for, and several times was seized with an involuntary inclination to escape from his presence, by making a sudden retreat. But he seemed constantly to anticipate my thoughts, and was sure to divert my purpose by some turn in the conversation that particularly interested me. He took care to dwell much on the theme of the impossibility of those ever falling away, who were once accepted and received into covenant with God, for he seemed to know, that in that confidence, and that trust, my whole hopes were centred.

We moved about from one place to another, until the day was wholly spent. My mind had all the while been kept in a state of agitation resembling the motion of a whirlpool, and when we came to separate, I then discovered that the purpose for which I had sought the fields had been neglected, and that I had been diverted from the worship of God, by attending to the quibbles and dogmas of this singular and unaccountable being, who seemed to have more knowledge and information than all the persons I had ever known put together.

We parted with expressions of mutual regret, and when I left him I felt a deliverance, but at the same time a certain consciousness that I was not thus to get free of him, but that he was like to be an acquaintance that was to stick to me for good or for evil. I was astonished at his acuteness and knowledge about every thing; but as for his likeness to me, that was quite unaccountable. He was the same person in every respect, but yet he was not always so; for I observed several times, when we were speaking of certain divines and their tenets, that his face assumed something of the appearance of theirs; and it struck me, that by setting his features to the mould of other people's, he entered at once into their conceptions and feelings. I had been greatly flattered, and greatly interested by his conversation; whether I had been the better for it or the worse, I could not tell. I had been diverted from returning thanks to my gracious Maker for his great kindness to me, and came home as I went away, but not with the same buoyancy and lightness of heart. Well may I remember that day in which I was first received into the number, and made an heir to all the privileges of the children of God, and on which I first met this mysterious associate, who from that day forth contrived to wind himself into all my affairs, both spiritual and temporal, to this day on which I am writing the account of it. It was on the 25th day of March 1704, when I had just entered the eighteenth year of my age. Whether it behoves me to bless God for the events of that day, or to deplore them, has been hid from my discernment, though I have inquired into it with fear and trembling; and I have now lost all hopes of ever discovering the true import of these events until that day when my accounts are to make up and reckon for in another world.

When I came home, I went straight into the parlour, where my mother was sitting by herself. She started to her feet, and uttered a smothered scream. 'What ails you,

an extension of Robert's mind — overactive imagination

Robert?' cried she. 'My dear son, what is the matter with you?'

'Do you see any thing the matter with me?' said I. 'It appears that the ailment is with yourself, and either in your crazed head or your dim eyes, for there is nothing the matter with me.'

'Ah, Robert, you are ill!' cried she; 'you are very ill, my dear boy; you are quite changed; your very voice and manner are changed. Ah, Jane, haste you up to the study, and tell Mr. Wringhim to come here on the instant and speak to Robert.'

'I beseech you, woman, to restrain yourself,' said I. 'If you suffer your frenzy to run away with your judgment in this manner, I will leave the house. What do you mean? I tell you, there is nothing ails me: I never was better.'

She screamed, and ran between me and the door, to bar my retreat: in the meantime my reverend father entered, and I have not forgot how he gazed, through his glasses, first at my mother, and then at me. I imagined that his eyes burnt like candles, and was afraid of him, which I suppose made my looks more unstable than they would otherwise have been.

'What is all this for?' said he. 'Mistress! Robert! What is the matter here?'

'Oh, sir, our boy!' cried my mother; 'our dear boy, Mr. Wringhim! Look at him, and speak to him: he is either dying or translated, sir!'

He looked at me with a countenance of great alarm; mumbling some sentences to himself, and then taking me by the arm, as if to feel my pulse, he said, with a faltering voice, 'Something has indeed befallen you, either in body or mind, boy, for you are transformed, since the morning, that I could not have known you for the same person. Have you met with any accident?'

'No.'

'Have you seen any thing out of the ordinary course of nature?'

'No.'

'Then, Satan, I fear, has been busy with you, tempting you in no ordinary degree at this momentous crisis of your life?'

My mind turned on my associate for the day, and the idea that he might be an agent of the devil, had such an effect on me, that I could make no answer.

'I see how it is,' said he; 'you are troubled in spirit, and I have no doubt that the enemy of our salvation has been busy with you. Tell me this, has he overcome you, or has he not?'

'He has not, my dear father,' said I. 'In the strength of the Lord, I hope I have withstood him. But indeed, if he has been busy with me, I knew it not. I have been conversant this day with one stranger only, whom I took rather for an angel of light.'

'It is one of the devil's most profound wiles to appear like one,' said my mother.

'Woman, hold thy peace!' said my reverend father: 'thou pretendest to teach what thou knowest not. Tell me this, boy: Did this stranger, with whom you met, adhere to the religious principles in which I have educated you?'

'Yes, to every one of them, in their fullest latitude,' said I.

'Then he was no agent of the wicked one with whom you held converse,' said he; 'for that is the doctrine that was made to overturn the principalities and powers, the might and dominion of the kingdom of darkness.—Let us pray.'

After spending about a quarter of an hour in solemn and sublime thanksgiving, this saintly man and minister of

Christ Jesus, gave out that the day following should be kept by the family as a day of solemn thanksgiving, and spent in prayer and praise, on account of the calling and election of one of its members; or rather for the election of that individual being revealed on earth, as well as confirmed in heaven.

The next day was with me a day of holy exultation. It was begun by my reverend father laying his hands upon my head and blessing me, and then dedicating me to the Lord in the most awful and impressive manner. It was in no common way that he exercised this profound rite, for it was done with all the zeal and enthusiasm of a devotee to the true cause, and a champion on the side he had espoused. He used these remarkable words, which I have still treasured up in my heart:—'I give him unto Thee only, to Thee wholly, and to Thee for ever. I dedicate him unto Thee, soul, body, and spirit. Not as the wicked of this world, or the hirelings of a church profanely called by Thy name, do I dedicate this Thy servant to Thee: Not in words and form, learned by rote, and dictated by the limbs of Antichrist, but, Lord, I give him into Thy hand, as a captain putteth a sword into the hand of his sovereign, wherewith to lay waste his enemies. May he be a two-edged weapon in Thy hand, and a spear coming out of Thy mouth, to destroy, and overcome, and pass over; and may the enemies of Thy church fall down before him, and be as dung to fat the land!'

From that moment, I conceived it decreed, not that I should be a minister of the gospel, but a champion of it, to cut off the enemies of the Lord from the face of the earth; and I rejoiced in the commission, finding it more congenial to my nature to be cutting sinners off with the sword, than to be haranguing them from the pulpit, striving to produce an effect, which God, by his act of

absolute predestination, had for ever rendered impracticable. The more I pondered on these things, the more I
saw of the folly and inconsistency of ministers, in spending
their lives, striving and remonstrating with sinners, in
order to induce them to do that which they had it not in
their power to do. Seeing that God had from all eternity
decided the fate of every individual that was to be born of
woman, how vain was it in man to endeavour to save
those whom their Maker had, by an unchangeable decree,
doomed to destruction. I could not disbelieve the doctrine
which the best of men had taught me, and toward which
he made the whole of the Scriptures to bear, and yet it
made the economy of the Christian world appear to me as
an absolute contradiction. How much more wise would
it be, thought I, to begin and cut sinners off with the
sword! for till that is effected, the saints can never inherit
the earth in peace. Should I be honoured as an instrument
to begin this great work of purification, I should rejoice
in it. But then, where had I the means, or under what
direction was I to begin? There was one thing clear, I was
now the Lord's, and it behoved me to bestir myself in his
service. O that I had an host at my command, then would
I be as a devouring fire among the workers of iniquity!

Full of these great ideas, I hurried through the city,
and sought again the private path through the field and
wood of Finnieston, in which my reverend preceptor had
the privilege of walking for study, and to which he had
a key that was always at my command. Near one of the
stiles, I perceived a young man sitting in a devout posture,
reading on a Bible. He rose, lifted his hat, and made an
obeisance to me, which I returned and walked on. I had
not well crossed the stile, till it struck me I knew the face
of the youth, and that he was some intimate acquaintance,
to whom I ought to have spoken. I walked on, and

returned, and walked on again, trying to recollect who he was; but for my life I could not. There was, however, a fascination in his look and manner, that drew me back toward him in spite of myself, and I resolved to go to him, if it were merely to speak and see who he was.

I came up to him and addressed him, but he was so intent on his book, that, though I spoke, he lifted not his eyes. I looked on the book also, and still it seemed a Bible, having columns, chapters, and verses; but it was in a language of which I was wholly ignorant, and all intersected with red lines, and verses. A sensation resembling a stroke of electricity came over me, on first casting my eyes on that mysterious book, and I stood motionless. He looked up, smiled, closed his book, and put it in his bosom. 'You seem strangely affected, dear sir, by looking on my book,' said he mildly.

'In the name of God, what book is that?' said I: 'Is it a Bible?'

'It is *my* Bible, sir,' said he; 'but I will cease reading it, for I am glad to see you. Pray, is not this a day of holy festivity with you?'

I stared in his face, but made no answer, for my senses were bewildered.

'Do you not know me?' said he. 'You appear to be somehow at a loss. Had not you and I some sweet communion and fellowship yesterday?'

'I beg your pardon, sir,' said I. 'But surely if you are the young gentleman with whom I spent the hours yesterday, you have the cameleon art of changing your appearance; I never could have recognized you.'

'My countenance changes with my studies and sensations,' said he. 'It is a natural peculiarity in me, over which I have not full control. If I contemplate a man's features seriously, mine own gradually assume the very same appearance and character. And what is more, by contemplating a face minutely, I not only attain the same likeness, but, with the likeness, I attain the very same ideas as well as the same mode of arranging them, so that, you see, by looking at a person attentively, I by degrees assume his likeness, and by assuming his likeness I attain to the possession of his most secret thoughts. This, I say, is a peculiarity in my nature, a gift of the God that made me; but whether or not given me for a blessing, he knows himself, and so do I. At all events, I have this privilege,— I can never be mistaken of a character in whom I am interested.'

'It is a rare qualification,' replied I, 'and I would give worlds to possess it. Then, it appears, that it is needless to dissemble with you, since you can at any time extract our most secret thoughts from our bosoms. You already know my natural character?'

'Yes,' said he, 'and it is that which attaches me to you. By assuming your likeness yesterday, I became acquainted with your character, and was no less astonished at the profundity and range of your thoughts, than at the heroic magnanimity with which these were combined. And now, in addition to these, you are dedicated to the great work of the Lord; for which reasons I have resolved to attach myself as closely to you as possible, and to render you all the service of which my poor abilities are capable.'

I confess that I was greatly flattered by these compliments paid to my abilities by a youth of such superior qualifications; by one who, with a modesty and affability rare at his age, combined a height of genius and knowledge almost above human comprehension. Nevertheless, I began to assume a certain superiority of demeanour toward him, as judging it incumbent on me to do so, in order to keep up his idea of my exalted character. We conversed again till the day was near a close; and the things that he strove most to inculcate on my mind, were the infallibility of the elect, and the pre-ordination of all things that come to pass. I pretended to controvert the first of these, for the purpose of showing him the extent of my argumentative powers, and said, that 'indubitably there were degrees of sinning which would induce the Almighty to throw off the very elect.' But behold my hitherto humble and modest companion took up the argument with such warmth, that he put me not only to silence, but to absolute shame.

'Why, sir,' said he, 'by vending such an insinuation, you put discredit on the great atonement, in which you trust. Is there not enough of merit in the blood of Jesus to save thousands of worlds, if it was for these worlds that he died? Now, when you know, as you do, (and as every one of the elect may know of himself,) that this Saviour died for you, namely and particularly, dare you say that there is not enough of merit in his great atonement to annihilate all your sins, let them be as heinous and atrocious as they may? And, moreover, do you not acknowledge that God hath pre-ordained and decreed whatsoever comes to pass? Then, how is it that you should deem it in your power to eschew one action of your life, whether good or evil? Depend on it, the advice of the great preacher is genuine: 'What thine hand findeth to do, do it with all thy might, for none of us knows what a day may bring forth?' That is, none of us knows what is pre-ordained, but whatever is pre-ordained we *must* do, and none of these things will be laid to our charge.'

I could hardly believe that these sayings were genuine or orthodox; but I soon felt, that, instead of being a humble disciple of mine, this new acquaintance was to be my guide and director, and all under the humble guise of one stooping at my feet to learn the right. He said that he saw I was ordained to perform some great action for the cause of Jesus and his church, and he earnestly coveted being a partaker with me; but he besought of me never to think it possible for me to fall from the truth, or the favour of him who had chosen me, else that misbelief would baulk every good work to which I set my face.

There was something so flattering in all this, that I could not resist it. Still, when he took leave of me, I felt it as a great relief; and yet, before the morrow, I wearied and was impatient to see him again. We carried on our fellowship from day to day, and all the while I knew not who he was, and still my mother and reverend father kept insisting that I was an altered youth, changed in my appearance, my manners, and my whole conduct; yet something always prevented me from telling them more about my new acquaintance than I had done on the first day we met. I rejoiced in him, was proud of him, and soon could not live without him; yet, though resolved every day to disclose the whole history of my connection with him, I had it not in my power: Something always prevented me, till at length I thought no more of it, but resolved to enjoy his fascinating company in private, and by all means to keep my own with him. The resolution was vain: I set a bold face to it, but my powers were inadequate to the task; my adherent, with all the suavity imaginable, was sure to carry his point. I sometimes fumed, and sometimes shed tears at being obliged to yield to proposals against which I had at first felt every reasoning power of my soul rise in opposition; but, for all that, he never failed in carrying conviction along with him in effect, for he either forced me to acquiesce in his measures, and assent to the truth of his positions, or he put me so completely down, that I had not a word left to advance against them.

After weeks, and I may say months of intimacy, I observed, somewhat to my amazement, that we had never once prayed together; and more than that, that he had constantly led my attentions away from that duty, causing me to neglect it wholly. I thought this a bad mark of a man seemingly so much set on inculcating certain important points of religion, and resolved next day to put him to the test, and request of him to perform that sacred duty in name of us both. He objected boldly; saying there were very few people indeed, with whom he could join in prayer, and he made a point of never doing it, as he was sure they were to ask many things of which he disapproved, and that if he were to officiate himself, he was as certain to allude to many things that came not within the range of their faith. He disapproved of prayer altogether, in the manner it was generally gone about, he said. Man made it merely a selfish concern, and was constantly employed asking, asking, for every thing. Whereas it became all God's creatures to be content with their lot, and only to kneel before him in order to thank him for such benefits as he saw meet to bestow. In short, he argued with such energy, that before we parted I acquiesced, as usual, in his position, and never mentioned prayer to him any more.

Having been so frequently seen in his company, several people happened to mention the circumstance to my mother and reverend father; but at the same time had all described him differently. At length, they began to examine me with respect to the company I kept, as I absented myself from home day after day. I told them I kept company only with one young gentleman, whose whole manner of thinking on religious subjects, I found so congenial with my own, that I could not live out of his society. My mother began to lay down some of her old hackneyed rules of faith, but I turned from hearing her with disgust; for, after the energy of my new friend's reasoning, hers appeared so tame I could not endure it. And I confess with shame, that my reverend preceptor's religious dissertations began, about this time, to lose their relish very much, and by degrees became exceedingly tiresome to my ear. They were so inferior, in strength and sublimity, to the most common observations of my young friend, that in drawing a comparison the former appeared as nothing. He, however, examined me about many things relating to my companion, in all of which I satisfied him, save in one: I could neither tell him who my friend was, what was his name, nor of whom he was descended; and I wondered at myself how I had never once adverted to such a thing, for all the time we had been intimate.

I inquired the next day what his name was; as I said I was often at a loss for it, when talking with him. He replied, that there was no occasion for any one friend ever naming another, when their society was held in private, as ours was; for his part he had never once named me since we first met, and never intended to do so, unless by my own request. 'But if you cannot converse without naming me, you may call me Gil for the present,' added he; 'and if I think proper to take another name at any future period, it shall be with your approbation.'

'Gil!' said I; 'Have you no name but Gil? Or which of your names is it? Your Christian or surname?'

'O, you must have a surname too, must you!' replied he, 'Very well, you may call me Gil-Martin. It is not my *Christian* name; but it *is* a name which may serve your turn.'

'This is very strange!' said I. 'Are you ashamed of your parents, that you refuse to give your real name?'

'I have no parents save one, whom I do not acknowledge,' said he proudly; 'therefore, pray drop that subject for it is a disagreeable one. I am a being of a very peculiar temper, for though I have servants and subjects more than I can number, yet, to gratify a certain whim, I have left them, and retired to this city, and for all the society it contains, you see I have attached myself only to you. This is a secret, and I tell it you only in friendship, therefore pray let it remain one, and say not another word about the matter.'

I assented, and said no more concerning it; for it instantly struck me that this was no other than the Czar Peter of Russia,[1] having heard that he had been travelling through Europe in disguise, and I cannot say that I had not thenceforward great and mighty hopes of high preferment, as a defender and avenger of the oppressed Christian Church, under the influence of this great potentate. He had hinted as much already, as that it was more honourable, and of more avail to put down the wicked with the sword, than try to reform them, and I thought myself quite justified in supposing that he intended me for some great employment, that he had thus selected me for his companion out of all the rest in Scotland, and even pretended to learn the great truths of religion from my mouth. From that time I felt disposed to yield to such a great prince's suggestions without hesitation.

Nothing ever astonished me so much, as the uncommon powers with which he seemed invested. In our walk one day, we met with a Mr. Blanchard, who was reckoned a worthy, pious divine, but quite of the moral cast, who joined us; and we three walked on, and rested together in the fields. My companion did not seem to like him, but, nevertheless, regarded him frequently with deep attention, and there were several times, while he seemed contemplating him, and trying to find out his thoughts, that his face became so like Mr. Blanchard's, that it was impossible to have distinguished the one from the other. The antipathy between the two was mutual, and discovered itself quite palpably in a short time. When my companion the prince was gone, Mr. Blanchard asked me anent him, and I told him that he was a stranger in the city, but a very uncommon and great personage. Mr. Blanchard's answer to me was as follows: 'I never saw any body I disliked so much in my life, Mr. Robert; and if it be true that he is a stranger here, which I doubt, believe me he is come for no good.'

'Do you not perceive what mighty powers of mind he is possessed of?' said I, 'and also how clear and unhesitating he is on some of the most interesting points of divinity?'

'It is for his great mental faculties that I dread him,' said he. 'It is incalculable what evil such a person as he may do, if so disposed. There is a sublimity in his ideas, with which there is to me a mixture of terror; and when he talks of religion, he does it as one that rather dreads its truths than reverences them. He, indeed, pretends great strictness of orthodoxy regarding some of the points of doctrine embraced by the reformed church; but you do not seem to perceive, that both you and he are carrying these points to a dangerous extremity. Religion is a sublime and glorious thing, the bond of society on earth, and the connector of humanity with the Divine nature; but there is nothing so dangerous to man as the wresting of any of its principles, or forcing them beyond their due bounds: this is of all others the readiest way to destruction. Neither is there any thing so easily done. There is not an error into which a man can fall, which he may not press Scripture into his service as proof of the probity of, and though your boasted theologian shunned the full discussion of the subject before me, while you pressed it, I can easily see that both you and he are carrying your ideas of absolute predestination, and its concomitant appendages, to an extent that overthrows all religion and revelation together; or, at least, jumbles them into a chaos, out of which human capacity can never select what is good. Believe me, Mr. Robert, the less you associate with that illustrious stranger the better, for it appears to me that your creed and his carries damnation on the very front of it.'

I was rather stunned at this; but I pretended to smile with disdain, and said, it did not become youth to control age; and, as I knew our principles differed fundamentally, it behoved us to drop the subject. He, however, would not drop it, but took both my principles and me fearfully to task, for Blanchard was an eloquent and powerful-minded old man; and, before we parted, I believe I promised to drop my new acquaintance, and was *all but* resolved to do it.

As well might I have laid my account with shunning the light of day. He was constant to me as my shadow, and by degrees he acquired such an ascendency over me, that I never was happy out of his company, nor greatly so in it. When I repeated to him all that Mr. Blanchard had said, his countenance kindled with indignation and rage; and then by degrees his eyes sunk inward, his brow lowered, so that I was awed, and withdrew my eyes from looking at him. A while afterward, as I was addressing him, I chanced to look him again in the face, and the sight of him made me start violently. He had made himself so like Mr. Blanchard, that I actually believed I had been addressing that gentleman, and that I had done so in some absence of mind that I could not account for. Instead of being amused at the quandary I was in, he seemed offended: indeed, he never was truly amused with any thing. And he then asked me sullenly, if I conceived such personages as he to have no other endowments than common mortals?

I said I never conceived that princes or potentates had any greater share of endowments than other men, and frequently not so much. He shook his head, and bade me think over the subject again; and there was an end of it. I certainly felt every day the more disposed to acknowledge such a superiority in him, and from all that I could gather, I had now no doubt that he was Peter of Russia. Every thing combined to warrant the supposition, and, of course, I resolved to act in conformity with the discovery I had made.

For several days the subject of Mr. Blanchard's doubts and doctrines formed the theme of our discourse. My friend deprecated them most devoutly; and then again he would deplore them, and lament the great evil that such a man might do among the human race. I joined with him in allowing the evil in its fullest latitude; and, at length, after he thought he had fully prepared my nature for such a trial of its powers and abilities, he proposed calmly that we two should make away with Mr. Blanchard. I was so shocked, that my bosom became as it were a void, and the beatings of my heart sounded loud and hollow in it; my breath cut, and my tongue and palate became dry and speechless. He mocked at my cowardice, and began a-reasoning on the matter with such powerful eloquence, that before we parted, I felt fully convinced that it was my bounden duty to slay Mr. Blanchard; but my will was far, very far from consenting to the deed.

I spent the following night without sleep, or nearly so; and the next morning, by the time the sun arose, I was again abroad, and in the company of my illustrious friend. The same subject was resumed, and again he reasoned to the following purport: That supposing me placed at the head of an army of Christian soldiers, all bent on putting down the enemies of the church, would I have any hesitation in destroying and rooting out these enemies?—None surely.—Well then, when I saw and was convinced, that here was an individual who was doing more detriment to the church of Christ on earth, than tens of thousands of such warriors were capable of doing, was it not my duty to cut him off, and save the elect? 'He, who would be a champion in the cause of Christ and his Church, my brave young friend,' added he, 'must begin early, and no man can calculate to what an illustrious eminence small beginnings may lead. If the man Blanchard is worthy, he is only changing his situation for a better one; and if unworthy, it is better that one fall, than that a thousand souls perish. Let us be up and doing in our vocations. For me, my resolution is taken; I have but one great aim in this world, and I never for a moment lose sight of it.'

I was obliged to admit the force of his reasoning; for though I cannot from memory repeat his words, his eloquence was of that overpowering nature, that the subtility of other men sunk before it; and there is also little doubt that the assurance I had that these words were spoken by a great potentate, who could raise me to the highest eminence, (provided that I entered into his extensive and decisive measures,) assisted mightily in dispelling my youthful scruples and qualms of conscience; and I thought moreover, that having such a powerful back friend to support me, I hardly needed to be afraid of the consequences. I consented! But begged a little time to think of it. He said the less one thought of a duty the better; and we parted.

But the most singular instance of this wonderful man's power over my mind was, that he had as complete influence over me by night as by day. All my dreams corresponded exactly with his suggestions; and when he was absent from me, still his arguments sunk deeper in my heart than even when he was present. I dreamed that night of a great triumph obtained, and though the whole scene was but dimly and confusedly defined in my vision, yet the over-throw and death of Mr. Blanchard was the first step by which I attained the eminent station I occupied. Thus, by dreaming of the event by night, and discoursing of it by day, it soon became so familiar to my mind, that I almost conceived it as done. It was resolved on: which was the first and greatest victory gained; for there was no difficulty in finding opportunities enow of cutting off a man, who, every good day, was to be found walking by himself in private grounds. I went and heard him preach for two days, and in fact I held his tenets scarcely short of blas-phemy; they were such as I had never heard before, and his congregation, which was numerous, were turning up their ears and drinking in his doctrines with the utmost delight; for O, they suited their carnal natures and self-sufficiency to a hair! He was actually holding it forth, as a fact, that 'it was every man's own blame if he was not saved!' What horrible misconstruction! And then he was alleging, and trying to prove from nature and reason, that no man ever was guilty of a sinful action, who might not have declined it had he so chosen! 'Wretched contro-vertist!' thought I to myself an hundred times, 'shall not the sword of the Lord be moved from its place of peace for such presumptuous and absurd testimonies as these!'

When I began to tell the prince about these false doc-trines, to my astonishment I found that he had been in the church himself, and had every argument that the old divine had used *verbatim*; and he remarked on them with great concern, that these were not the tenets that corresponded with his views in society, and that he had agents in every city, and every land, exerting their powers to put them down. I asked, with great simplicity, 'Are all your subjects Christians, prince?'

'All my European subjects are, or deem themselves so,' returned he; 'and they are the most faithful and true subjects I have.'

Who could doubt, after this, that he was the Czar of Russia? I have nevertheless had reasons to doubt of his identity since that period, and which of my conjectures is right, I believe the God of heaven only knows, for I do not. I shall go on to write such things as I remember, and if any one shall ever take the trouble to read over these confessions, such a one will judge for himself. It will be observed, that since ever I fell in with this extraordinary person, I have written about him only, and I must continue to do so to the end of this memoir, as I have performed no great or interesting action in which he had not a principal share.

He came to me one day and said, 'We must not linger thus in executing what we have resolved on. We have much before our hands to perform for the benefit of mankind, both civil as well as religious. Let us do what we have to do here, and then we must wend our way to other cities, and perhaps to other countries. Mr. Blanchard is to hold forth in the high church of Paisley on Sunday next, on some particularly great occasion: this must be defeated; he must not go there. As he will be busy arranging his discourses, we may expect him to be walking by himself in Finnieston Dell the greater part of Friday and Saturday. Let us go and cut him off. What is the life of a man more than the life of a lamb, or any guiltless animal? It is not half so much, especially when we consider the immensity of the mischief this old fellow is working among our fellow-creatures. Can there be any doubt that it is the duty of one consecrated to God, to cut off such a mildew?'

'I fear me, great sovereign,' said I, 'that your ideas of retribution are too sanguine, and too arbitrary for the laws of this country. I dispute not that your motives are great and high; but have you debated the consequences, and settled the result?'

'I have,' returned he, 'and hold myself amenable for the action, to the laws of God and of equity; as to the enactments of men I despise them. Fain would I see the weapon of the Lord of Hosts, begin the work of vengeance that awaits it to do!'

I could not help thinking, that I perceived a little derision of countenance on his face as he said this, nevertheless I sunk dumb before such a man, and aroused myself to the task, seeing he would not have it deferred. I approved of it in theory, but my spirit stood aloof from the practice. I saw and was convinced that the elect of God would be happier, and purer, were the wicked and unbelievers all cut off from troubling and misleading them, but if it had not been the instigations of this illustrious stranger, I should never have presumed to begin so great a work myself. Yet, though he often aroused my zeal to the highest pitch, still my heart at times shrunk from the shedding of life-blood, and it was only at the earnest and unceasing instigations of my enlightened and voluntary patron, that I at length put my hand to the conclusive work. After I said all that I could say, and all had been overborne, (I remember my actions and words as well as it had been yesterday,) I turned round hesitatingly, and looked up to Heaven for direction; but there was a dimness came over my eyes that I could not see. The appearance was as if there had been a veil drawn over me, so nigh that I put up my hand to feel it; and then Gil-Martin (as this great sovereign was pleased to have himself called,) frowned, and asked me what I was grasping at? I knew not what to say, but answered, with fear and shame, 'I have no weapons, not one; nor know I where any are to be found.'

'The God whom thou servest will provide these,' said he; 'if thou provest worthy of the trust committed to thee.'

I looked again up into the cloudy veil that covered us, and thought I beheld golden weapons of every description let down in it, but all with their points towards me. I kneeled, and was going to stretch out my hand to take one, when my patron seized me, as I thought, by the clothes, and dragged me away with as much ease as I had been a lamb, saying, with a joyful and elevated voice,— 'Come, my friend, let us depart: thou art dreaming—thou art dreaming. Rouse up all the energies of thy exalted mind, for thou art an highly-favoured one; and doubt thou not, that he whom *thou* servest, will be ever at thy right and left hand, to direct and assist thee.'

These words, but particularly the vision I had seen, of the golden weapons descending out of Heaven, inflamed my zeal to that height that I was as one beside himself; which my parents perceived that night, and made some motions toward confining me to my room. I joined in the family prayers, and then I afterwards sung a psalm and prayed by myself; and I had good reasons for believing that that small oblation of praise and prayer was not turned to sin. But there are strange things, and unaccountable agencies in nature: He only who dwells between the Cherubim can unriddle them, and to him the honour must redound for ever. *Amen.*

I felt greatly strengthened and encouraged that night, and the next morning I ran to meet my companion, out of whose eye I had now no life. He rejoiced at seeing me so forward in the great work of reformation by blood, and said many things to raise my hopes of future fame and glory; and then, producing two pistols of pure beaten gold, he held them out and proffered me the choice of one, saying, 'See what thy master hath provided thee!' I took one of them eagerly, for I perceived at once that they were two of the very weapons that were let down from Heaven in the cloudy veil, the dim tapestry of the firmament; and I said to myself, 'Surely this is the will of the Lord.'

The little splendid and enchanting piece was so perfect, so complete, and so ready for executing the will of the donor, that I now longed to use it in his service. I loaded it with my own hand, as Gil-Martin did the other, and we took our stations behind a bush of hawthorn and bramble on the verge of the wood, and almost close to the walk. My patron was so acute in all his calculations that he never mistook an event. We had not taken our stand above a minute and a half, till old Mr. Blanchard appeared, coming slowly on the path. When we saw this, we cowered down, and leaned each of us a knee upon the ground, pointing the pistols through the bush, with an aim so steady, that it was impossible to miss our victim.

He came deliberately on, pausing at times so long, that we dreaded he was going to turn. Gil-Martin dreaded it, and I said I did, but wished in my heart that he might. He, however, came onward, and I will never forget the manner in which he came! No—I don't believe I ever can forget it, either in the narrow bounds of time or the ages of eternity! He was a boardly ill-shaped man, of a rude exterior, and a little bent with age; his hands were clasped behind his back, and below his coat, and he walked with a slow swinging air that was very peculiar. When he paused and looked abroad on nature, the act was highly impressive: he seemed conscious of being all alone, and conversant only with God and the elements of his creation. Never was there such a picture of human inadvertency! a man approaching step by step to the one that was to hurl him out of one existence into another, with as much ease and indifference as the ox goeth to the stall. Hideous vision, wilt thou not be gone from my mental sight! If not, let me bear with thee as I can!

When he came straight opposite to the muzzles of our pieces, Gil-Martin called out 'Eh!' with a short quick sound. The old man, without starting, turned his face and breast toward us, and looked into the wood, but looked over our heads. 'Now!' whispered my companion, and fired. But my hand refused the office, for I was not at that moment sure about becoming an assassin in the cause of Christ and his Church. I thought I heard a sweet voice behind me, whispering me to beware, and I was going to look round, when my companion exclaimed, 'Coward, we are ruined!'

I had no time for an alternative: Gil-Martin's ball had not taken effect, which was altogether wonderful, as the old man's breast was within a few yards of him. 'Hilloa!' cried Blanchard; 'what is that for, you dog!' and with that he came forward to look over the bush. I hesitated, as I said, and attempted to look behind me; but there was no time: the next step discovered two assassins lying in covert, waiting for blood. 'Coward, we are ruined!' cried my indignant friend; and that moment my piece was discharged. The effect was as might have been expected: the old man first stumbled to one side, and then fell on his back. We kept our places, and I perceived my companion's eyes gleaming with an unnatural joy. The wounded man raised himself from the bank to a sitting posture, and I beheld his eyes swimming; he, however, appeared sensible, for we heard him saying in a low and rattling voice, 'Alas,

alas! whom have I offended, that they should have been driven to an act like this! Come forth and shew yourselves, that I may either forgive you before I die, or curse you in the name of the Lord.' He then fell a-groping with both hands on the ground, as if feeling for something he had lost, manifestly in the agonies of death; and, with a solemn and interrupted prayer for forgiveness, he breathed his last.

I had become rigid as a statue, whereas my associate appeared to be elevated above measure. 'Arise, thou faint-hearted one, and let us be going,' said he. 'Thou hast done well for once; but wherefore hesitate in such a cause? This is but a small beginning of so great a work as that of purging the Christian world. But the first victim is a worthy one, and more of such lights must be extinguished immediately.'

We touched not our victim, nor any thing pertaining to him, for fear of staining our hands with his blood; and the firing having brought three men within view, who were hasting towards the spot, my undaunted companion took both the pistols, and went forward as with intent to meet them, bidding me shift for myself. I ran off in a contrary direction, till I came to the foot of the Pearman Sike, and then, running up the hollow of that, I appeared on the top of the bank as if I had been another man brought in view by hearing the shots in such a place. I had a full view of a part of what passed, though not of all. I saw my companion going straight to meet the men, apparently with a pistol in every hand, waving in a careless manner. They seemed not quite clear of meeting with him, and so he went straight on, and passed between them. They looked after him, and came onward; but when they came to the old man lying stretched in his blood, then they turned and pursued my companion, though not so quickly as they might have done; and I understood that from the first they saw no more of him.

Great was the confusion that day in Glasgow. The most popular of all their preachers of morality was (what they called) murdered in cold blood, and a strict and extensive search was made for the assassin. Neither of the accomplices was found, however, that is certain, nor was either of them so much as suspected; but another man was apprehended under circumstances that warranted suspicion.—This was one of the things that I witnessed in my life, which I never understood, and it surely was one of my patron's most dexterous tricks, for I must still say, what I have thought from the beginning, that like him there never was a man created. The young man who was taken up was a preacher; and it was proved that he had purchased fire arms in town, and gone out with them that morning. But the far greatest mystery of the whole was, that two of the men, out of the three who met my companion, swore, that that unfortunate preacher was the man whom they met with a pistol in each hand, fresh from the death of the old divine. The poor fellow made a confused speech himself, which there is not the least doubt was quite true; but it was laughed to scorn, and an expression of horror ran through both the hearers and jury. I heard the whole trial, and so did Gil-Martin; but we left the journeyman preacher to his fate, and from that time forth I have had no faith in the justice of criminal trials. If once a man is prejudiced on one side, he will swear any thing in support of such prejudice. I tried to expostulate with my mysterious friend on the horrid injustice of suffering this young man to die for our act, but the prince exulted in it more than the other, and said the latter was the most dangerous man of the two.

The alarm in and about Glasgow was prodigious. The

country being divided into two political parties, the court and the country party, the former held meetings, issued proclamations, and offered rewards, ascribing all to the violence of party spirit, and deprecating the infernal measures of their opponents. I did not understand their political differences; but it was easy to see that the true Gospel preachers joined all on one side, and the upholders of pure morality and a blameless life on the other, so that this division proved a test to us, and it was forthwith resolved, that we two should pick out some of the leading men of this unsaintly and heterodox cabal, and cut them off one by one, as occasion should suit.

Now, the ice being broke, I felt considerable zeal in our great work, but pretended much more; and we might soon have kidnapped them all through the ingenuity of my patron, had not our next attempt miscarried, by some awkwardness or mistake of mine. The consequence was, that he was discovered fairly, and very nigh seized. I also was seen, and suspected so far, that my reverend father, my mother, and myself were examined privately. I denied all knowledge of the matter; and they held it in such a ridiculous light, and their conviction of the complete groundlessness of the suspicion was so perfect, that their testimony prevailed, and the affair was hushed. I was obliged, however, to walk circumspectly, and saw my companion the prince very seldom, who was prowling about every day, quite unconcerned about his safety. He was every day a new man, however, and needed not to be alarmed at any danger; for such a facility had he in disguising himself, that if it had not been for a pass-word which we had between us, for the purposes of recognition, I never could have known him myself.

It so happened that my reverend father was called to Edinburgh about this time, to assist with his council in settling the national affairs. At my earnest request I was permitted to accompany him, at which both my associate and I rejoiced, as we were now about to move in a new and extensive field. All this time I never knew where my illustrious friend resided. He never once invited me to call on him at his lodgings, nor did he ever come to our house, which made me sometimes to suspect, that if any of our great efforts in the cause of true religion were discovered, he intended leaving me in the lurch. Consequently, when we met in Edinburgh (for we travelled not in company) I proposed to go with him to look for lodgings, telling him at the same time what a blessed religious family my reverend instructor and I were settled in. He said he rejoiced at it, but he made a rule of never lodging in any particular house, but took these daily, or hourly, as he found it convenient, and that he never was at a loss in any circumstance.

'What a mighty trouble you put yourself to, great sovereign!' said I, 'and all, it would appear, for the purpose of seeing and knowing more and more of the human race.'

'I never go but where I have some great purpose to serve,' returned he, 'either in the advancement of my own power and dominion, or in thwarting my enemies.'

'With all due deference to your great comprehension, my illustrious friend,' said I, 'it strikes me that you can accomplish very little either the one way or the other here, in the humble and private capacity you are pleased to occupy.'

'It is your own innate modesty that prompts such a remark' said, he. 'Do you think the gaining of *you* to my service, is not an attainment worthy of being envied by the greatest potentate in Christendom? Before I had missed such a prize as the attainment of your services, I would have travelled over one half of the habitable globe.'—I bowed with great humility, but at the same time how could I but feel proud and highly flattered? He continued. 'Believe me, my dear friend, for such a prize I account no effort too high. For a man who is not only dedicated to the King of Heaven, in the most solemn manner, soul, body, and spirit, but also chosen of him from the beginning, justified, sanctified, and received into a communion that never shall be broken, and from which no act of his shall ever remove him,—the possession of such a man, I tell you, is worth kingdoms; because every deed that he performs, he does it with perfect safety to himself and honour to me.'— I bowed again, lifting my hat, and he went on.—'I am now going to put his courage in the cause he has espoused, to a severe test—to a trial at which common nature would revolt, but he who is dedicated to be the sword of the Lord, must raise himself above common humanity. You have a father and a brother according to the flesh, what do you know of them?'

'I am sorry to say I know nothing good,' said I. 'They are reprobates, cast-aways, beings devoted to the wicked one, and, like him, workers of every species of iniquity with greediness.'

'They must both fall!' said he, with a sigh and melancholy look: 'It is decreed in the councils above, that they must both fall by your hand.'

'The God of heaven forbid it!' said I. 'They are enemies to Christ and his church, that I know and believe; but they shall live and die in their iniquity for me, and reap their guerdon when their time cometh. There my hand shall not strike.'

'The feeling is natural, and amiable,' said he; 'but you *must* think again. Whether are the bonds of carnal nature, or the bonds and vows of the Lord, strongest?'

'I will not reason with you on this head, mighty poten-tate,' said I, 'for whenever I do so it is but to be put down. I shall only express my determination, not to take ven-geance out of the Lord's hand in this instance. It availeth not. These are men that have the mark of the beast in their foreheads and right hands; they are lost beings themselves, but have no influence over others. Let them perish in their sins; for they shall not be meddled with by me.'

'How preposterously you talk, my dear friend!' said he. 'These people are your greatest enemies; they would re-joice to see you annihilated. And now that you have taken up the Lord's cause of being avenged on *his* enemies, wherefore spare those that are your own as well as his? Besides, you ought to consider what great advantages would be derived to the cause of righteousness and truth, were the estate and riches of that opulent house in your possession, rather than in that of such as oppose the truth and all manner of holiness.'

This was a portion of the consequence of following my illustrious adviser's summary mode of procedure, that had never entered into my calculation—I disclaimed all idea of being influenced by it; however, I cannot but say that the desire of being enabled to do so much good, by the posses-sion of these bad men's riches, made some impression on my heart, and I said I would consider of the matter. I did consider it, and that right seriously as well as frequently; and there was scarcely an hour in the day on which my resolves were not animated by my great friend, till at length I began to have a longing desire to kill my brother, in particular. Should any man ever read this scroll, he will wonder at this confession, and deem it savage and unnat-ural. So it appeared to me at first, but a constant thinking of an event changes every one of its features. I have done all for the best, and as I was prompted, by one who knew right and wrong much better that I did. I *had* a desire to slay him, it is true, and such a desire too as a thirsty man has to drink; but at the same time, this longing desire was mingled with a certain terror, as if I had dreaded that the drink for which I longed was mixed with deadly poison. My mind was so much weakened, or rather softened about this time, that my faith began a little to give way, and I doubted most presumptuously of the least tangible of all Christian tenets, namely, of *the infallibility of the elect.* I hardly comprehended the great work I had begun, and doubted of *my own* infallibility, or that of any created being. But I was brought over again by the unwearied diligence of my friend to repent of my backsliding, and view once more the superiority of the Almighty's counsels in its fullest latitude. *Amen.*

I prayed very much in secret about this time, and that with great fervor of spirit, as well as humility; and my satisfaction at finding all my requests granted is not to be expressed.

My illustrious friend still continuing to sound in my ears the imperious duty to which I was called, of making away with my sinful relations, and quoting many parallel actions out of the Scriptures, and the writings of the holy Fathers, of the pleasure the Lord took in such as executed his vengeance on the wicked, I was obliged to acquiesce in his measures, though with certain limitations. It was not easy to answer his arguments, and yet I was afraid that he soon perceived a leaning to his will on my part. 'If the acts of Jehu, in rooting out the whole house of his master, were ordered and approved of by the Lord,' said he, 'would it not have been more praiseworthy if one of Ahab's own sons had stood up for the cause of the God of Israel, and rooted out the sinners and their idols out of the land?'

'It would certainly,' said I. 'To our duty to God all other duties must yield.'

'Go thou then and do likewise,' said he. 'Thou art called to a high vocation; to cleanse the sanctuary of thy God in this thy native land by the shedding of blood; go thou forth then like a ruling energy, a master spirit of desolation in the dwellings of the wicked, and high shall be your reward both here and hereafter.'

My heart now panted with eagerness to look my brother in the face: On which my companion, who was never out of the way, conducted me to a small square in the suburbs of the city, where there were a number of young noblemen and gentlemen playing at a vain, idle, and sinful game, at which there was much of the language of the accursed going on; and among these blasphemers he instantly pointed out my brother to me. I was fired with indignation at seeing him in such company, and so employed; and I placed myself close beside him to watch all his motions, listen to his words, and draw inferences from what I saw and heard. In what a sink of sin was he wallowing! I resolved to take him to task, and if he refused to be admonished, to inflict on him some condign punishment; and knowing that my illustrious friend and director was looking on, I resolved to show some spirit. Accordingly, I waited until I heard him profane his Maker's name three times, and then, my spiritual indignation being roused above all restraint, I went up and kicked him. Yes, I went boldly up and struck him with my foot, and meant to have given him a more severe blow than it was my fortune to inflict. It had, however, the effect of rousing up his corrupt nature to quarrelling and strife, instead of taking the chastisement of the Lord in humility and meekness. He ran furiously against me in the choler that is always inspired by the wicked one; but I overthrew him, by reason of impeding the natural and rapid progress of his unholy feet, running to destruction. I also fell slightly; but his fall proving a severe one, he arose in wrath, and struck me with the mall which he held in his hand, until my blood flowed copiously; and from that moment I vowed his destruction in my heart. But I chanced to have no weapon at that time, nor any means of inflicting due punishment on the caitiff, which would not have been returned double on my head, by him and his graceless associates. I mixed among them at the suggestion of my friend, and following them to their den of voluptuousness and sin, I strove to be admitted among them, in hopes of finding some means of accomplishing my great purpose, while I found myself moved by the spirit within me so to do. But I was not only debarred, but, by the machinations of my wicked brother and his associates, cast into prison.

I was not sorry at being thus honoured to suffer in the cause of righteousness, and at the hands of sinful men; and as soon as I was alone, I betook myself to prayer, deprecating the long-suffering of God toward such horrid sinners. My jailer came to me, and insulted me. He was a rude unprincipled fellow, partaking much of the loose and carnal manners of the age; but I remembered of having read, in the Cloud of Witnesses,[1] of such men formerly, having been converted by the imprisoned saints; so I set myself, with all my heart, to bring about this man's repentance and reformation.

'Fat the deil are ye yoolling an' praying that gate for, man?' said he, coming angrily in. 'I thought the days o' praying prisoners had been a' ower. We had rowth o' them aince; an' they were the poorest an' the blackest bargains that ever poor jailers saw. Gie up your crooning, or I'll pit you to an in-by place, where ye sall get plenty o't.'

'Friend,' said I, 'I am making my appeal at that bar where all human actions are seen and judged, and where you shall not be forgot, sinful as you are. Go in peace, and let me be.'

'Hae ye naebody nearer-hand hame to mak your appeal to, man?' said he; 'because an ye haena, I dread you an' me may be unco weel acquaintit by an' by?'

I then opened up the mysteries of religion to him in a clear and perspicuous manner, but particularly the great doctrine of the election of grace; and then I added, 'Now, friend, you must tell me if you pertain to this chosen number. It is in every man's power to ascertain this, and it is every man's duty to do it.'

against the doctrines

'An' fat the better wad you be for the kenning o' this, man?' said he.

'Because, if you are one of my brethren, I will take you into sweet communion and fellowship,' returned I; 'but if you belong to the unregenerate, I have a commission to slay you.'

'The deil you hae, callant!' said he, gaping and laughing. 'An' pray now, fa was it that gae you siccan a braw commission?'

'My commission is sealed by the signet above,' said I, 'and that I will let you and all sinners know. I am dedicated to it by the most solemn vows and engagements. I am the sword of the Lord, and Famine and Pestilence are my sisters. Wo then to the wicked of this land, for they must fall down dead together, that the church may be purified!'

'Oo, foo, foo! I see how it is,' said he; 'yours is a very braw commission, but you will have the small opportunity of carrying it through here. Take my advising, and write a bit of a letter to your friends, and I will send it, for this is no place for such a great man. If you cannot steady your hand to write, as I see you have been at your great work, a word of a mouth may do; for I do assure you this is not the place at all, of any in the world, for your operations.'

The man apparently thought I was deranged in my intellect. He could not swallow such great truths at the first morsel. So I took his advice, and sent a line to my reverend father, who was not long in coming, and great was the jailer's wonderment when he saw all the great Christian noblemen of the land sign my bond of freedom.

My reverend father took this matter greatly to heart, and bestirred himself in the good cause till the transgressors were ashamed to shew their faces. My illustrious companion was not idle: I wondered that he came not to me in prison, nor at my release; but he was better employed, in stirring up the just to the execution of God's decrees; and he succeeded so well, that my brother and all his associates had nearly fallen victims to their wrath: But many were wounded, bruised, and imprisoned, and much commotion prevailed in the city. For my part, I was greatly strengthened in my resolution by the anathemas of my reverend father, who, privately, (that is in a family capacity,) in his prayers, gave up my father and brother, according to the flesh, to Satan, making it plain to all my senses of perception, that they were beings given up of God, to be devoured by fiends or men, at their will and pleasure, and that *whosoever* should slay them, would do God good service.

The next morning my illustrious friend met me at an early hour, and he was greatly overjoyed at hearing my sentiments now chime so much in unison with his own. I said, 'I longed for the day and the hour that I might look my brother in the face at Gilgal,[1] and visit on him the iniquity of his father and himself, for that I was now strengthened and prepared for the deed.'

'I have been watching the steps and movements of the profligate one,' said he; 'and lo, I will take you straight to his presence. Let your heart be as the heart of the lion, and your arms strong as the shekels of brass, and swift to avenge as the bolt that descendeth from Heaven, for the blood of the just and the good hath long flowed in Scotland. But already is the day of their avengement begun; the hero is at length arisen, who shall send all such as bear enmity to the true church, or trust in works of their own, to Tophet!'

Thus encouraged, I followed my friend, who led me directly to the same court in which I had chastised the miscreant on the foregoing day; and behold, there was the same group again assembled. They eyed me with terror in their looks, as I walked among them and eyed them with looks of disapprobation and rebuke; and I saw that the very eye of a chosen one lifted on these children of Belial, was sufficient to dismay and put them to flight. I walked aside to my friend, who stood at a distance looking on, and he said to me, 'What thinkest thou now?' and I answered in the words of the venal prophet,[1] 'Lo now, if I had a sword into mine hand, I would even kill him.'

'Wherefore lackest thou it?' said he. 'Dost thou not see that they tremble at thy presence, knowing that the avenger of blood is among them.'

My heart was lifted up on hearing this, and again I strode into the midst of them, and eyeing them with threatening looks, they were so much confounded, that they abandoned their sinful pastime, and fled every one to his house!

This was a palpable victory gained over the wicked, and I thereby knew that the hand of the Lord was with me. My companion also exulted, and said, 'Did not I tell thee? Behold thou dost not know one half of thy might, or of the great things thou art destined to do. Come with me and I will show thee more than this, for these young men cannot subsist without the exercises of sin. I listened to their councils, and I know where they will meet again.'

Accordingly he led me a little farther to the south, and we walked aside till by degrees we saw some people begin to assemble; and in a short time we perceived the same group stripping off their clothes to make them more expert in the practice of madness and folly. Their game was begun before we approached, and so also were the oaths and cursing. I put my hands in my pockets, and walked with dignity and energy into the midst of them. It was enough: Terror and astonishment seized them. A few of them cried out against me, but their voices were soon hushed amid the murmurs of fear. One of them, in the name of the rest, then came and besought of me to grant them liberty to amuse themselves; but I refused peremptorily, dared the whole multitude so much as to touch me with one of their fingers, and dismissed them in the name of the Lord.

Again they all fled and dispersed at my eye, and I went home in triumph, escorted by my friend, and some well-meaning young Christians, who, however, had not learned to deport themselves with soberness and humility. But my ascendency over my enemies was great indeed; for wherever I appeared I was hailed with approbation, and herever my guilty brother made his appearance, he was hooted and held in derision, till he was forced to hide his disgraceful head, and appear no more in public.

Immediately after this I was seized with a strange distemper, which neither my friends nor physicians could comprehend, and it confined me to my chamber for many days; but I knew, myself, that I was bewitched, and suspected my father's reputed concubine of the deed. I told my fears to my reverend protector, who hesitated concerning them, but I knew by his words and looks that he was conscious I was right. I generally conceived myself to be two people. When I lay in bed, I deemed there were two of us in it; when I sat up, I always beheld another person, and always in the same position from the place where I sat or stood, which was about three paces off me towards my left side. It mattered not how many or how few were present: this my second self was sure to be present in his place; and this occasioned a confusion in all my words and ideas that utterly astounded my friends, who all declared, that instead of being deranged in my intellect, they had never heard my conversation manifest so much energy or sublimity of conception; but for all that, over the singular delusion that I was two persons, my reasoning faculties had no power. The most perverse part of it was, that I rarely conceived *myself* to be any of the two persons. I thought for the most part that my companion was one of them, and my brother the other; and I found, that to be obliged to speak and answer in the character of another man, was a most awkward business at the long run.

Who can doubt, from this statement, that I was bewitched, and that my relatives were at the ground of it? The constant and unnatural persuasion that I was my brother, proved it to my own satisfaction, and must, I think, do so to every unprejudiced person. This victory of the wicked one over me kept me confined in my chamber, at Mr. Millar's house, for nearly a month, until the prayers of the faithful prevailed, and I was restored. I knew it was a chastisement for my pride, because my heart was lifted up at my superiority over the enemies of the church; nevertheless, I determined to make short work with the aggressor, that the righteous might not be subjected to the effect of his diabolical arts again.

I say I was confined a month. I beg he that readeth to take note of this, that he may estimate how much the word, or even the oath, of a wicked man, is to depend on. For a month I saw no one but such as came into my room, and for all that, it will be seen, that there were plenty of the same set to attest upon oath that I saw my brother every day during that period; that I persecuted him with my presence day and night, while all the time I never saw his face, save in a delusive dream. I cannot comprehend what manœuvres my illustrious friend was playing off with them about this time; for he, having the art of personating whom he chose, had peradventure deceived them, else so many of them had never all attested the same thing. I never saw any man so steady in his friendships and attentions as he; but as he made a rule of never calling at private houses, for fear of some discovery being made of his person, so I never saw him while my malady lasted; but as soon as I grew better, I knew I had nothing ado but to attend at some of our places of meeting, to see him again. He was punctual, as usual, and I had not to wait.

[margin, handwritten: crimes commott by supposed doppelg- during this time?]

My reception was precisely as I apprehended. There was no flaring, no flummery, nor bombastical pretensions, but a dignified return to my obeisance, and an immediate recurrence, in converse, to the important duties incumbent on us, in our stations, as reformers and purifiers of the Church.

'I have marked out a number of most dangerous characters in this city,' said he, 'all of whom must be cut off from cumbering the true vineyard before we leave this land. And if you bestir not yourself in the work to which you are called, I must raise up others who shall have the honour of it.'

'I am, most illustrious prince, wholly at your service,' said I. 'Show but what ought to be done, and here is the heart to dare, and the hand to execute. You pointed out my relations, according to the flesh, as brands fitted to be thrown into the burning. I approve peremptorily of the award; nay, I thirst to accomplish it; for I myself have suffered severely from their diabolical arts. When once that trial of my devotion to the faith is accomplished, then be your future operations disclosed.'

'You are free of your words and promises,' said he.

'So will I be of my deeds in the service of my master, and that shalt thou see,' said I. 'I lack not the spirit, nor the will, but I lack experience wofully; and because of that shortcoming, must bow to your suggestions.'

'Meet me here to-morrow betimes,' said he, 'and perhaps you may hear of some opportunity of displaying your zeal in the cause of righteousness.'

I met him as he desired me; and he addressed me with a hurried and joyful expression, telling me that my brother was astir, and that a few minutes ago he had seen him pass on his way to the mountain. 'The hill is wrapped in a cloud,' added he, 'and never was there such an opportunity of executing divine justice on a guilty sinner. You may trace him in the dew, and shall infallibly find him on the top of some precipice; for it is only in secret that he dares show his debased head to the sun.'

'I have no arms, else assuredly I would pursue him and discomfit him,' said I.

'Here is a small dagger,' said he; 'I have nothing of weapon-kind about me save that, but it is a potent one; and should you require it, there is nothing more ready or sure.'

'Will not you accompany me?' said I: 'Sure you will?'

'I will be with you, or near you,' said he. 'Go you on before.'

I hurried away as he directed me, and imprudently asked

some of Queensberry's guards if such and such a young man passed by them going out from the city. I was answered in the affirmative, and till then had doubted of my friend's intelligence, it was so inconsistent with a profligate's life to be so early astir. When I got the certain intelligence that my brother was before me, I fell a-running, scarcely knowing what I did; and looking several times behind me, I perceived nothing of my zealous and arbitrary friend. The consequence of this was, that by the time I reached St. Anthony's well, my resolution began to give way. It was not my courage, for now that I had once shed blood in the cause of the true faith, I was exceedingly bold and ardent; but whenever I was left to myself, I was subject to sinful doubtings. These always hankered on one point: I doubted if the elect were infallible, and if the Scripture promises to them were binding in all situations and relations. I confess this, and that it was a sinful and shameful weakness in me, but my nature was subject to it, and I could not eschew it. I never doubted that I was one of the elect myself; for, besides the strong inward and spiritual conviction that I possessed, I had my kind father's assurance; and these had been revealed to him in that way and measure that they could not be doubted.

In this desponding state, I sat myself down on a stone, and bethought me of the rashness of my undertaking. I tried to ascertain, to my own satisfaction, whether or not I really had been commissioned of God to perpetrate these crimes in his behalf, for in the eyes, and by the laws of men, they were great and crying transgressions. While I sat pondering on these things, I was involved in a veil of white misty vapour, and looking up to heaven, I was just about to ask direction from above, when I heard as it were a still small voice close by me, which uttered some words of derision and chiding. I looked intensely in the direction whence it seemed to come, and perceived a lady, robed in white, who hasted toward me. She regarded me with a severity of look and gesture that appalled me so much, I could not address her; but she waited not for that, but coming close to my side, said, without stopping, 'Preposterous wretch! how dare you lift your eyes to heaven with such purposes in your heart? Escape homeward, and save your soul, or farewell for ever!'

These were all the words that she uttered, as far as I could ever recollect, but my spirits were kept in such a tumult that morning, that something might have escaped me. I followed her eagerly with my eyes, but in a moment she glided over the rocks above the holy well, and vanished. I persuaded myself that I had seen a vision, and that the radiant being that had addressed me was one of the good angels, or guardian spirits, commissioned by the Almighty to watch over the steps of the just. My first impulse was to follow her advice, and make my escape home; for I thought to myself, 'How is this interested and mysterious foreigner, a proper judge of the actions of a free Christian?'

The thought was hardly framed, nor had I moved in a retrograde direction six steps, when I saw my illustrious friend and great adviser descending the ridge towards me with hasty and impassioned strides. My heart fainted within me; and when he came up and addressed me, I looked as one caught in a trespass. 'What hath detained thee, thou desponding trifler?' said he. 'Verily now shall the golden opportunity be lost which may never be recalled. I have traced the reprobate to his sanctuary in the cloud, and lo he is perched on the pinnacle of a precipice an hundred fathoms high. One ketch with thy foot, or toss with thy finger, shall throw him from thy sight into the foldings of the cloud, and he shall be no more seen, till found at the bottom of the cliff dashed to pieces. Make haste therefore, thou loiterer, if thou wouldst ever prosper and rise to eminence in the work of thy Lord and master.'

'I go no farther on this work,' said I, 'for I have seen a vision that has reprimanded the deed.'

'A vision?' said he: 'Was it that wench who descended from the hill?'

'The being that spake to me, and warned me of my danger, was indeed in the form of a lady,' said I.

'She also approached me and said a few words,' returned he; 'and I thought there was something mysterious in her manner. Pray, what did she say? for the words of such a singular message, and from such a messenger, ought to be attended to. If I understood her aright, she was chiding us for our misbelief and preposterous delay.'

I recited her words, but he answered that I had been in a state of sinful doubting at the time, and it was to these doubtings she had adverted. In short, this wonderful and clear-sighted stranger soon banished all my doubts and despondency, making me utterly ashamed of them, and again I set out with him in the pursuit of my brother. He showed me the traces of his footsteps in the dew, and pointed out the spot where I should find him. 'You have nothing more to do than go softly down behind him,' said he; 'which you can do to within an ell of him, without being seen; then rush upon him, and throw him from his seat, where there is neither footing nor hold. I will go, mean-while, and amuse his sight by some exhibition in the contrary direction, and he shall neither know nor perceive who has done him this *kind office*: for, exclusive of more weighty concerns, be assured of this, that the sooner he falls, the fewer crimes will he have to answer for, and his estate in the other world will be proportionally more tolerable, than if he spent a long unregenerate life steeped in iniquity to the loathing of the soul.'

'Nothing can be more plain or more pertinent,' said I: 'therefore I fly to perform that which is both a duty toward God and toward man!'

'You shall yet rise to great honour and preferment,' said he.

'I value it not, provided I do honour and justice to the cause of my master here,' said I.

'You shall be lord of your father's riches and demesnes,' added he.

'I disclaim and deride every selfish motive thereto relating,' said I, 'farther than as it enables me to do good.'

'Ay, but that is a great and a heavenly consideration, that *longing for ability to do good*,' said he;—and as he said so, I could not help remarking a certain derisive exultation of expression which I could not comprehend; and indeed I have noted this very often in my illustrious friend, and sometimes mentioned it civilly to him, but he has never failed to disclaim it. On this occasion I said nothing, but concealing his poniard in my clothes, I hasted up the mountain, determined to execute my purpose before any misgivings should again visit me; and I never had more ado, than in keeping firm my resolution. I could not help my thoughts, and there are certain trains and classes of thoughts that have great power in enervating the mind. I thought of the awful thing of plunging a fellow creature from the top of a cliff into the dark and misty void below— of his being dashed to pieces on the protruding rocks, and of hearing his shrieks as he descended the cloud, and beheld the shagged points on which he was to alight. Then I thought of plunging a soul so abruptly into hell, or, at the best, sending it to hover on the confines of that burning abyss—of its appearance at the bar of the Almighty to receive its sentence. And then I thought, 'Will there not be a sentence pronounced against me there, by a jury of the just made perfect, and written down in the registers of heaven?'

These thoughts, I say, came upon me unasked, and instead of being able to dispel them, they mustered, upon the summit of my imagination, in thicker and stronger array: and there was another that impressed me in a very particular manner, though, I have reason to believe, not so strongly as those above written. It was this: 'What if I should fail in my first effort? Will the consequence not be that I am tumbled from the top of the rock myself?' and then all the feelings anticipated, with regard to both body and soul, must happen to me! This was a spine-breaking reflection; and yet, though the probability was rather on that side, my zeal in the cause of godliness was such that it carried me on, maugre all danger and dismay.

I soon came close upon my brother, sitting on the dizzy pinnacle, with his eyes fixed stedfastly in the direction opposite to me. I descended the little green ravine behind him with my feet foremost, and every now and then raised my head, and watched his motions. His posture continued the same, until at last I came so near him I could have heard him breathe, if his face had been towards me. I laid my cap aside, and made me ready to spring upon him, and push him over. I could not for my life accomplish it! I do not think it was that *I durst not*, for I have always felt my courage equal to any thing in a good cause. But I had not the heart, or something that I ought to have had. In short, it was not done in time, as it easily might have been. These THOUGHTS are hard enemies wherewith to combat! And I was so grieved that I could not effect my righteous purpose, that I laid me down on my face and shed tears. Then, again, I thought of what my great enlightened friend and patron would say to me, and again my resolution rose indignant, and indissoluble save by blood. I arose on my right knee and left foot, and had just begun to advance the latter forward: the next step my great purpose had been accomplished, and the culprit had suffered the punishment due to his crimes. But what moved him I knew not: in the critical moment he sprung to his feet, and dashing himself furiously against me, he overthrew me, at the imminent peril of my life. I disencumbered myself by main force, and fled, but he overhied me, knocked me down, and threatened, with dreadful oaths, to throw me from the cliff. After I was a little recovered from the stunning blow, I aroused myself to the combat; and though I do not recollect the circumstances of that deadly scuffle very minutely, I know that I vanquished him so far as to force him to ask my pardon, and crave a reconciliation. I spurned at both, and left him to the chastisements of his own wicked and corrupt heart.

My friend met me again on the hill, and derided me, in a haughty and stern manner, for my imbecility and want of decision. I told him how nearly I had effected my purpose, and excused myself as well as I was able. On this, seeing me bleeding, he advised me to swear the peace against my brother, and have him punished in the mean time, he being the first aggressor. I promised compliance, and we parted, for I was somewhat ashamed of my failure, and was glad to be quit for the present of one of whom I stood so much in awe.

When my reverend father beheld me bleeding a second time by the hand of a brother, he was moved to the highest point of displeasure; and, relying on his high interest and the justice of his cause, he brought the matter at once before the courts. My brother and I were first examined face to face. His declaration was a mere romance:

mine was not the truth; but as it was by the advice of
my reverend father, and that of my illustrious friend,
both of whom I knew to be sincere Christians and true
believers, that I gave it, I conceived myself completely
justified on that score. I said, I had gone up into the
mountain early on the morning to pray, and had withdrawn myself, for entire privacy, into a little sequestered
dell—had laid aside my cap, and was in the act of
kneeling, when I was rudely attacked by my brother,
knocked over, and nearly slain. They asked my brother if
this was true. He acknowledged that it was; that I was
bare-headed, and in the act of kneeling when he ran foul
of me without any intent of doing so. But the judge took
him to task on the improbability of this, and put the profligate sore out of countenance. The rest of his tale told
still worse, insomuch that he was laughed at by all present,
for the judge remarked to him, that granting it was true
that he had at first run against me on an open mountain,
and overthrown me by accident, how was it, that after I had
extricated myself and fled, that he had pursued, overtaken,
and knocked me down a second time? Would he pretend that
all that was likewise by chance? The culprit had nothing to
say for himself on this head, and I shall not forget my
exultation and that of my reverend father, when the
sentence of the judge was delivered. It was, that my
wicked brother should be thrown into prison, and tried
on a criminal charge of assault and battery, with the intent
of committing murder. This was a just and righteous
judge, and saw things in their proper bearings, that is, he
could discern between a righteous and a wicked man, and
then there could be no doubt as to which of the two were
acting right, and which wrong.

Had I not been sensible that a justified person could
do nothing wrong, I should not have been at my ease

concerning the statement I had been induced to give on this occasion. I could easily perceive, that by rooting out the weeds from the garden of the Church, I heightened the growth of righteousness; but as to the tardy way of giving false evidence on matters of such doubtful issue, I confess I saw no great propriety in it from the beginning. But I now only moved by the will and mandate of my illustrious friend: I had no peace or comfort when out of his sight, nor have I ever been able to boast of much in his presence; so true is it that a Christian's life is one of suffering.

My time was now much occupied, along with my reverend preceptor, in making ready for the approaching trial, as the prosecutors. Our counsel assured us of a complete victory, and that banishment would be the mildest award of the law on the offender. Mark how different was the result! From the shifts and ambiguities of a wicked Bench, who had a fellow-feeling of iniquity with the defenders,—my suit was cast, the graceless libertine was absolved, and I was incarcerated, and bound over to keep the peace, with heavy penalties, before I was set at liberty.

I was exceedingly disgusted at this issue, and blamed the counsel of my friend to his face. He expressed great grief, and expatiated on the wickedness of our judicatories, adding, 'I see I cannot depend on you for quick and summary measures, but for your sake I shall be revenged on that wicked judge, and that you shall see in a few days.' The Lord Justice Clerk died that same week! But he died in his own house and his own bed, and by what means my friend effected it, I do not know. He would not tell me a single word of the matter, but the judge's sudden death made a great noise, and I made so many curious inquiries regarding the particulars of it, that some suspicions were like to attach to our family, of some unfair means used. For my part I know nothing, and rather think he died by the visitation of Heaven, and that my friend had foreseen it, by symptoms, and soothed me by promises of complete revenge.

It was some days before he mentioned my brother's meditated death to me again, and certainly he then found me exasperated against him personally to the highest degree. But I told him that I could not now think any more of it, owing to the late judgment of the court, by which, if my brother were missing or found dead, I would not only forfeit my life, but my friends would be ruined by the penalties.

'I suppose you know and believe in the perfect safety of your soul,' said he, 'and that that is a matter settled from the beginning of time, and now sealed and ratified both in heaven and earth?'

'I believe in it thoroughly and perfectly,' said I; 'and whenever I entertain doubts of it, I am sensible of sin and weakness.'

'Very well, so then am I,' said he. 'I think I can now divine, with all manner of certainty, what will be the high and merited guerdon of your immortal part. Hear me then farther: I give you my solemn assurance, and bond of blood, that no human hand shall ever henceforth be able to injure your life, or shed one drop of your precious blood, but it is on the condition that you walk always by my directions.'

'I will do so with cheerfulness,' said I; 'for without your enlightened counsel, I feel that I can do nothing. But as to your power of protecting my life, you must excuse me for doubting of it. Nay, were we in your own proper dominions, you could not ensure that.'

'In whatever dominion or land I am, my power accompanies me,' said he; 'and it is only against human might and human weapon that I ensure your life; on that will I keep an eye, and on that you may depend. I have never broken word or promise with you. Do you credit me?'

'Yes, I do,' said I; 'for I see you are in earnest. I believe, though I do not comprehend you.'

'Then why do you not at once challenge your brother to the field of honour? Seeing you now act without danger, cannot you also act without fear?'

'It is not fear,' returned I; 'believe me, I hardly know what fear is. It is a doubt, that on all these emergencies constantly haunts my mind, that in performing such and such actions I may fall from my upright state. This makes fratricide a fearful task.'

'This is imbecility itself,' said he. 'We have settled, and agreed on that point an hundred times. I would therefore advise that you challenge your brother to single combat. I shall ensure your safety, and he cannot refuse giving you satisfaction.'

'But then the penalties?' said I.

'We will try to evade these,' said he; 'and supposing you should be caught, if once you are Laird of Dalcastle and Balgrennan, what are the penalties to you?'

'Might we not rather pop him off in private and quietness, as we did the deistical divine?' said I.

'The deed would be alike meritorious, either way,' said he. 'But may we not wait for years before we find an opportunity? My advice is to challenge him, as privately as you will, and there cut him off.'

'So be it then,' said I. 'When the moon is at the full, I will send for him forth to speak with one, and there will I smite him and slay him, and he shall trouble the righteous no more.'

'Then this is the very night,' said he. 'The moon is nigh to the full, and this night your brother and his sinful mates hold carousal; for there is an intended journey to-morrow. The exulting profligate leaves town, where we must remain till the time of my departure hence; and then is he safe, and must live to dishonour God, and not only destroy his own soul, but those of many others. Alack, and wo is me! The sins that he and his friends will commit this very night, will cry to heaven against us for our shameful delay! When shall our great work of cleansing the sanctuary be finished, if we proceed at this puny rate?'

'I see the deed *must* be done, then,' said I; 'and since it is so, it shall be done. I will arm myself forthwith, and from the midst of his wine and debauchery you shall call him forth to me, and there will I smite him with the edge of the sword, that our great work be not retarded.'

'If thy execution were equal to thy intent, how great a man you soon might be!' said he. 'We shall make the attempt once more; and if it fail again, why, I must use other means to bring about my high purposes relating to mankind.—Home and make ready. I will go and procure what information I can regarding their motions, and will meet you in disguise twenty minutes hence, at the first turn of Hewie's lane beyond the loch.'

'I have nothing to make ready,' said I; 'for I do not choose to go home. Bring me a sword, that we may consecrate it with prayer and vows, and if I use it not to the bringing down of the wicked and profane, then may the Lord do so to me, and more also!'

We parted, and there was I left again to the multiplicity of my own thoughts for the space of twenty minutes, a thing my friend never failed in subjecting me to, and these were worse to contend with than hosts of sinful men. I prayed inwardly, that these deeds of mine might never be brought to the knowledge of men who were incapable of appreciating the high motives that led to them; and then I sung part of the 10th Psalm, likewise in spirit; but for all these efforts, my sinful doubts returned, so that when my illustrious friend joined me, and proffered me the choice of two gilded rapiers, I declined accepting any of them, and began, in a very bold and energetic manner, to express my doubts regarding the justification of all the deeds of perfect men. He chided me severely, and branded me with cowardice, a thing that my nature never was subject to; and then he branded me with falsehood, and breach of the most solemn engagements both to God and man.

I was compelled to take the rapier, much against my inclination; but for all the arguments, threats, and promises that he could use, I would not consent to send a challenge to my brother by his mouth. There was one argument only that he made use of which had some weight with me, but yet it would not preponderate. He told me my brother was gone to a notorious and scandalous habitation of women, and that if I left him to himself for ever so short a space longer, it might embitter his state through ages to come. This was a trying concern to me; but I resisted it, and reverted to my doubts. On this he said that he had meant to do me honour, but since I put it out of his power, he would do the deed, and take the responsibility on himself. 'I have with sore travail procured a guardship of your life,' added he. 'For my own, I have not; but, be that as it will, I shall not be baffled in my attempts to benefit my friends without a trial. You will at all events accompany me, and see that I get justice?'

'Certes, I will do thus much,' said I; 'and wo be to him if his arm prevail against my friend and patron!'

His lip curled with a smile of contempt, which I could hardly brook; and I began to be afraid that the eminence to which I had been destined by him was already fading from my view. And I thought what I should then do to ingratiate myself again with him, for without his countenance I had no life. 'I will be a man in act,' thought I, 'but in sentiment I will not yield, and for this he must surely admire me the more.'

As we emerged from the shadowy lane into the fair moonshine, I started so that my whole frame underwent the most chilling vibrations of surprise. I again thought I had been taken at unawares, and was conversing with another person. My friend was equipped in the Highland garb, and so completely translated into another being, that, save by his speech, all the senses of mankind could not have recognized him. I blessed myself, and asked whom it was his pleasure to personify to-night? He answered me carelessly, that it was a spark whom he meant should bear the blame of whatever might fall out to-night; and that was all that passed on the subject.

We proceeded by some stone steps at the foot of the North Loch, in hot argument all the way. I was afraid that our conversation might be overheard, for the night was calm and almost as light as day, and we saw sundry people crossing us as we advanced. But the zeal of my friend was so high, that he disregarded all danger, and continued to argue fiercely and loudly on my delinquency, as he was pleased to call it. I stood on one argument alone, which was, 'that I did not think the Scripture promises to the elect, taken in their utmost latitude, warranted the assurance that they could do no wrong; and that, therefore, it behoved every man to look well to his steps.'

There was no religious scruple that irritated my enlightened friend and master so much as this. He could not endure it. And the sentiments of our great covenanted reformers being on his side, there is not a doubt that I was wrong. He lost all patience on hearing what I advanced on this matter, and taking hold of me, he led me into a darksome booth in a confined entry; and, after a friendly but cutting reproach, he bade me remain there in secret and watch the event; 'and if I fall,' said he, 'you will not fail to avenge my death?'

I was so entirely overcome with vexation that I could make no answer, on which he left me abruptly, a prey to despair; and I saw or heard no more, till he came down to the moonlight green followed by my brother. They had quarrelled before they came within my hearing, for the first words I heard were those of my brother, who was in a state of intoxication, and he was urging a reconciliation, as was his wont on such occasions. My friend spurned at the suggestion, and dared him to the combat; and after a good deal of boastful altercation, which the turmoil of my spirits prevented me from remembering, my brother was compelled to draw his sword and stand on the defensive. It was a desperate and terrible engagement. I at first thought that the royal stranger and great champion of the faith would overcome his opponent with ease, for I considered heaven as on his side, and nothing but the arm of sinful flesh against him. But I was deceived: The sinner stood firm as a rock, while the assailant flitted about like a shadow, or rather like a spirit. I smiled inwardly, conceiving that these lightsome manœuvres were all a sham to show off his art and mastership in the exercise, and that whenever they came to close fairly, that instant my brother would be overcome. Still I was deceived: My brother's arm seemed invincible, so that the closer they fought the more palpably did it prevail. They fought round the green to the very edge of the water, and so round, till they came close up to the covert where I stood. There being no more room to shift ground, my brother then forced him to come to close quarters, on which, the

former still having the decided advantage, my friend
quitted his sword, and called out. I could resist no longer;
so, springing from my concealment, I rushed between
them with my sword drawn, and parted them as if they
had been two schoolboys: then turning to my brother, I
addressed him as follows:—'Wretch! miscreant! knowest
thou what thou art attempting? Wouldst thou lay thine
hand on the Lord's anointed, or shed his precious blood?
Turn thee to me, that I may chastise thee for all thy
wickedness, and not for the many injuries thou hast done
to me!' To it we went, with full thirst of vengeance on *diff.*
every side. The duel was fierce; but the might of heaven *in*
prevailed, and not my might. The ungodly and reprobate *narratives*
young man fell, covered with wounds, and with curses and
blasphemy in his mouth, while I escaped uninjured. Thereto his power extended not.

I will not deny, that my own immediate impressions of *Robs*
this affair in some degree differed from this statement. But *notices*
this is precisely as my illustrious friend described it to me *differ*
afterwards, and I can rely implicitly on his information, *in*
as he was at that time a looker-on, and my senses all in *narratives*
a state of agitation, and he could have no motive for
saying what was not the positive truth.

Never till my brother was down did we perceive that
there had been witnesses to the whole business. Our ears
were then astounded by rude challenges of unfair play,
which were quite appalling to me; but my friend laughed
at them, and conducted me off in perfect safety. As to the
unfairness of the transaction, I can say thus much, that my
royal friend's sword was down ere ever mine was presented. But if it still be accounted unfair to take up a
conqueror, and punish him in his own way, I answer:
That if a man is sent on a positive mission by his master,
and hath laid himself under vows to do his work, he

ought not to be too nice in the means of accomplishing it; and farther, I appeal to holy writ, wherein many instances are recorded of the pleasure the Lord takes in the final extinction of the wicked and profane; and this position I take to be unanswerable.

I was greatly disturbed in my mind for many days, knowing that the transaction had been witnessed, and sensible also of the perilous situation I occupied, owing to the late judgment of the court against me. But, on the contrary, I never saw my enlightened friend in such high spirits. He assured me there was no danger; and again repeated, that he warranted my life against the power of man. I thought proper, however, to remain in hiding for a week; but, as he said, to my utter amazement, the blame fell on another, who was not only accused, but pronounced guilty by the general voice, and outlawed for non-appearance! how could I doubt, after this, that the hand of heaven was aiding and abetting me? The matter was beyond my comprehension; and as for my friend, he never explained any thing that was past, but his activity and art were without a parallel.

He enjoyed our success mightily; and for his sake I enjoyed it somewhat, but it was on account of his comfort only, for I could not for my life perceive in what degree the church was better or purer than before these deeds were done. He continued to flatter me with great things, as to honours, fame, and emolument; and, above all, with the blessing and protection of him to whom my body and soul were dedicated. But after these high promises, I got no longer peace; for he began to urge the death of my father with such an unremitting earnestness, that I found I had nothing for it but to comply. I did so; and cannot express his enthusiasm of approbation. So much did he hurry and press me in this, that I was forced to devise some of the most openly violent measures, having no alternative. Heaven spared me the deed, taking, in that instance, the vengeance in its own hand; for before my arm could effect the sanguine but meritorious act, the old man followed his son to the grave. My illustrious and zealous friend seemed to regret this somewhat; but he comforted himself with the reflection, that still I had the merit of it, having not only consented to it, but in fact effected it, for by doing the one action I had brought about both.

No sooner were the obsequies of the funeral over, than my friend and I went to Dalcastle, and took undisputed possession of the houses, lands, and effects that had been my father's; but his plate, and vast treasures of ready money, he had bestowed on a voluptuous and unworthy creature, who had lived long with him as a mistress. Fain would I have sent her after her lover, and gave my friend some hints on the occasion; but he only shook his head, and said that we must lay all selfish and interested motives out of the question.

For a long time, when I awaked in the morning, I could not believe my senses, that I was indeed the undisputed and sole proprietor of so much wealth and grandeur; and I felt so much gratified, that I immediately set about doing all the good I was able, hoping to meet with all approbation and encouragement from my friend. I was mistaken: He checked the very first impulses towards such a procedure, questioned my motives, and uniformly made them out to be wrong. There was one morning that a servant said to me, there was a lady in the back chamber who wanted to speak with me, but he could not tell me who it was, for all the old servants had left the mansion, every one on hearing of the death of the late laird, and those who had come knew none of the people in the neighbourhood. From several circumstances, I had suspicions of private confabulations with women, and refused to go to her, but bid the servant inquire what she wanted. She would not tell; she could only state the circumstances to me; so I, being sensible that a little dignity of manner became me in my elevated situation, returned for answer, that if it was business that could not be transacted by my steward, it must remain untransacted. The answer which the servant brought back was of a threatening nature. She stated that she *must* see me, and if I refused her satisfaction there, she would compel it where I should not evite her.

My friend and director appeared pleased with my dilemma, and rather advised that I should hear what the woman had to say; on which I consented, provided she would deliver her mission in his presence. She came in with manifest signs of anger and indignation, and began with bold and direct charge against me of a shameful assault on one of her daughters; of having used the basest of means in order to lead her aside from the paths of rectitude; and on the failure of these, of having resorted to the most unqualified measures.

I denied the charge in all its bearings, assuring the dame that I had never so much as seen either of her daughters to my knowledge, far less wronged them; on which she got into great wrath, and abused me to my face as an accomplished vagabond, hypocrite, and sensualist; and she went so far as to tell me roundly, that if I did not *marry* her daughter, she would bring me to the gallows, and that in a very short time.

'Marry your daughter, honest woman!' said I, 'on the faith of a Christian, I never saw your daughter; and you may rest assured in this, that I will neither marry you nor her. Do you consider how short a time I have been in this place? How much that time has been occupied?

And how there was even a *possibility* that I could have accomplished such villainies?'

'And how long does your Christian reverence suppose you have remained in this place since the late laird's death?' said she.

'That is too well known to need recapitulation,' said I: only a very few days, though I cannot at present specify the exact number; perhaps from thirty to forty, or so. But in all that time, certes, I have never seen either you or any of your two daughters that you talk of. You must be quite sensible of that.'

My friend shook his head three times during this short sentence, while the woman held up her hands in amazement and disgust, exclaiming, 'There goes the self-righteous one! There goes the consecrated youth, who cannot err! You, sir, know, and the world shall know of the faith that is in this most just, devout, and religious miscreant! Can you deny that you have already been in this place four months and seven days? Or that in that time you have been forbid my house twenty times? Or that you have persevered in your endeavours to effect the basest and most ungenerous of purposes? Or that you *have* attained them? hypocrite and deceiver as you are! Yes, sir; I say, dare you deny that you *have* attained your vile, selfish, and degrading purposes towards a young, innocent, and unsuspecting creature, and thereby ruined a poor widow's only hope in this world? No, you cannot look in my face, and deny aught of this.'

'The woman is raving mad!' said I. 'You, illustrious sir, know, that in the first instance, I have not yet been in this place *one* month.' My friend shook his head again, and answered me, 'You are wrong, my dear friend; you are wrong. It is indeed the space of time that the lady hath stated, to a day, since you came here, and I came with you; and I am sorry that I know for certain that you have

[handwritten marginalia: "losing large spaces of time" and "his friend turns on him"]

been frequently haunting her house, and have often had private correspondence with one of the young ladies too. Of the nature of it I presume not to know.'

'You are mocking me,' said I. 'But as well may you try to reason me out of my existence, as to convince me that I have been here even one month, or that any of those things you allege against me has the shadow of truth or evidence to support it. I will swear to you, by the great God that made me; and by——'

'Hold, thou most abandoned profligate!' cried she violently, 'and do not add perjury to your other detestable crimes. Do not, for mercy's sake, any more profane that name whose attributes you have wrested and disgraced. But tell me what reparation you propose offering to my injured child?'

'I again declare, before heaven, woman, that to the best of my knowledge and recollection, I never saw your daughter. I now think I have some faint recollection of having seen your face, but where, or in what place, puzzles me quite.'

'And, why?' said she. 'Because for months and days you have been in such a state of extreme inebriety, that your time has gone over like a dream that has been forgotten. I believe, that from the day you came first to my house, you have been in a state of utter delirium, and that principally from the fumes of wine and ardent spirits.'

'It is a manifest falsehood!' said I; 'I have never, since I entered on the possession of Dalcastle, tasted wine or spirits, saving once, a few evenings ago; and, I confess to my shame, that I was led too far; but I have craved forgiveness and obtained it. I take my noble and distinguished friend there for a witness to the truth of what I assert; a man who has done more, and sacrificed more for the sake of genuine Christianity, than any this world contains. Him you will believe.'

'I hope you have attained forgiveness,' said he, seriously. 'Indeed it would be next to blasphemy to doubt it. But, of late, you have been very much addicted to intemperance. I doubt if, from the first night you tasted the delights of drunkenness, that you have ever again been in your right mind until Monday last. Doubtless you have been for a good while most diligent in your addresses to this lady's daughter.'

'This is unaccountable,' said I. 'It is impossible that I can have been doing a thing, and not doing it at the same time. But indeed, honest woman, there have several incidents occurred to me in the course of my life which persuade me I have a second self; or that there is some other being who appears in my likeness.' *doppelganger*

Here my friend interrupted me with a sneer, and a hint that I was talking insanely; and then he added, turning to the lady, 'I know my friend Mr. Colwan will do what is just and right. Go and bring the young lady to him, that he may see her, and he will then recollect all his former amours with her.'

'I humbly beg your pardon, sir,' said I. 'But the mention of such a thing as *amours* with any woman existing, to me, is really so absurd, so far from my principles, so far from the purity of nature and frame to which I was born and consecrated, that I hold it as an insult, and regard it with contempt.'

I would have said more in reprobation of such an idea, had not my servant entered, and said, that a gentleman wanted to see me on business. Being glad of an opportunity of getting quit of my lady visitor, I ordered the servant to show him in; and forthwith a little lean gentleman, with a long acquiline nose, and a bald head, daubed all over with powder and pomatum, entered. I thought I recollected having seen him too, but could not

remember his name, though he spoke to me with the
greatest familiarity; at least, that sort of familiarity that
an official person generally assumes. He bustled about
and about, speaking to every one, but declined listening
for a single moment to any. The lady offered to withdraw,
but he stopped her.

'No, no, Mrs. Keeler, you need not go; you need not
go; you *must* not go, madam. The business I came about,
concerns you—yes, that it does—Bad business yon of
Walker's? Eh? Could not help it—did all I could, Mr.
Wringhim. Done your business. Have it all cut and dry
here, sir—No, this is not it—Have it among them,
though—I'm at a little loss for your name, sir, (addressing
my friend,)—seen you very often, though—exceedingly
often—quite well acquainted with you.'

'No, sir, you are not,' said my friend, sternly.—The
intruder never regarded him; never so much as lifted his
eyes from his bundle of law papers, among which he was
bustling with great hurry and importance, but went on—

'*Im*possible! Have seen a face very like it, then—what
did you say your name was, sir?—very like it indeed. Is
it not the young laird who was murdered whom you
resemble so much?'

Here Mrs. Keeler uttered a scream, which so much
startled me, that it seems I grew pale. And on looking at
my friend's face, there was something struck me so forcibly
in the likeness between him and my late brother, that I
had very nearly fainted. The woman exclaimed, that it was
my brother's spirit that stood beside me.

'Im*poss*ible!' exclaimed the attorney; 'at least I hope
not, else his signature is not worth a pin. There is some
balance due on yon business, madam. Do you wish your
account? because I have it here, ready discharged, and it
does not suit letting such things lie over. This business of

Mr. Colwan's will be a severe one on you, madam,—
*ra*ther a severe one.'

'What business of mine, if it be your will, sir,' said I.
'For my part I never engaged you in business of any sort,
less or more.' He never regarded me, but went on. 'You
may appeal, though: Yes, yes, there are such things as
appeals for the refractory. Here it is, gentlemen,—here
they are all together—Here is, in the first place, sir, your
power of attorney, regularly warranted, sealed, and signed
with your own hand.'

'I declare solemnly that I never signed that document,'
said I.

'Ay, ay, the system of denial is not a bad one in general,'
said my attorney; 'but at present there is no occasion for it.
You do not deny your own hand?'

'I deny every thing connected with the business,' cried
I; 'I disclaim it *in toto*, and declare that I know no more
about it than the child unborn.'

'That is exceedingly good!' exclaimed he; 'I like your
pertinacity vastly! I have three of your letters, and three
of your signatures; that part is all settled, and I hope so
is the whole affair; for here is the original grant to your
father, which he has never thought proper to put in
requisition. Simple gentleman! But here have I, Lawyer
Linkum, in one hundredth part of the time that any other
notary, writer, attorney, or writer to the signet in Britain,
would have done it, procured the signature of his Majesty's
commissioner, and thereby confirmed the charter to you
and your house, sir, for ever and ever,—Begging your
pardon, madam.' The lady, as well as myself, tried several
times to interrupt the loquacity of Linkum, but in vain: he
only raised his hand with a quick flourish, and went on:—

'Here it is:—"JAMES, by the grace of God, King of
Great Britain, France, and Ireland, to his right trusty

cousin, sendeth greeting: And whereas his right leal and trust-worthy cousin, George Colwan, of Dalcastle and Balgrennan, hath suffered great losses, and undergone much hardship, on behalf of his Majesty's rights and titles; he therefore, for himself, and as prince and steward of Scotland, and by the consent of his right trusty cousins and councillors, hereby grants to the said George Colwan, his heirs and assignees whatsomever, heritably and irrevocably, all and haill the lands and others underwritten: *To wit*, All and haill, the five merk land of Kipplerig; the five pound land of Easter Knockward, with all the towers, fortalices, manor-places, houses, biggings, yards, orchards, tofts, crofts, mills, woods, fishings, mosses, muirs, meadows, commonties, pasturages, coals, coal-heughs, tenants, tenantries, services of free tenants, annexes, connexes, dependencies, parts, pendicles, and pertinents of the same whatsomever; to be peaceably brooked, joysed, set, used, and disposed of by him and his aboves, as specified, heritably. and irrevocably, in all time coming: And, in testimony thereof, His Majesty, for himself, and as prince and steward of Scotland, with the advice and consent of his foresaids, knowledge, proper motive, and kingly power, makes, erects, creates, unites, annexes, and incorporates, the whole lands above mentioned in an haill and free barony, by all the rights, miethes, and marches thereof, old and divided, as the same lies, in length and breadth, in houses, biggings, mills, multures, hawking, hunting, fishing; with court, plaint, herezeld, fock, fork, sack, sock, thole, thame, vert, wraik, waith, wair, venison, outfang thief, infang thief, pit and gallows, and all and sundry other commodities. Given at our Court of Whitehall, &c. &c. God save the King.

Compositio 5 lib. 13. 8.
Registrate 26th September, 1687."[1]

'See, madam, here are ten signatures of privy councillors of that year, and here are other ten of the present year, with his Grace the Duke of Queensberry at the head. All right—See here it is, sir,—all right—done your work. So you see, madam, this gentleman is the true and sole heritor of all the land that your father possesses, with all the rents thereof for the last twenty years, and upwards— Fine job for my employers!—sorry on your account, madam—can't help it.'

I was again going to disclaim all interest or connection in the matter, but my friend stopped me; and the plaints and lamentations of the dame became so overpowering, that they put an end to all farther colloquy; but Lawyer Linkum followed me, and stated his great outlay, and the important services he had rendered me, until I was obliged to subscribe an order to him for £100 on my banker.

I was now glad to retire with my friend, and ask seriously for some explanation of all this. It was in the highest degree unsatisfactory. He confirmed all that had been stated to me; assuring me, that I had not only been assiduous in my endeavours to seduce a young lady of great beauty, which it seemed I had effected, but that I had taken counsel, and got this supposed, old, false, and forged grant, raked up and new signed, to ruin the young lady's family quite, so as to throw her entirely on myself for protection, and be wholly at my will.

This was to me wholly incomprehensible. I could have freely made oath to the contrary of every particular. Yet the evidences were against me, and of a nature not to be denied. Here I must confess, that, highly as I disapproved of the love of women, and all intimacies and connections with the sex, I felt a sort of indefinite pleasure, an ungracious delight in having a beautiful woman solely at my disposal. But I thought of her spiritual good in the meantime. My friend spoke of my backslidings with concern; requesting me to make sure of my forgiveness, and to forsake them; and then he added some words of sweet comfort. But from this time forth I began to be sick at times of my existence. I had heart-burnings, longings, and yearnings, that would not be satisfied; and I seemed hardly to be an accountable creature; being thus in the habit of executing transactions of the utmost moment, without being sensible that I did them. I was a being incomprehensible to myself. Either I had a second self, who transacted business in my likeness, or else my body was at times possessed by a spirit over which it had no controul, and of whose actions my own soul was wholly unconscious. This was an anomaly not to be accounted for by any philosophy of mine, and I was many times, in contemplating it, excited to terrors and mental torments hardly describable. To be in a state of consciousness and unconsciousness, at the same time, in the same body and same spirit, was impossible. I was under the greatest anxiety, dreading some change would take place momently in my nature; for of dates I could make nothing: one-half, or two-thirds of my time, seemed to me to be totally lost. I often, about this time, prayed with great fervour, and lamented my hopeless condition, especially in being liable to the commission of crimes, which I was not sensible of, and could not eschew. And I confess, notwithstanding the promises on which I had been taught to rely, I began to have secret terrors, that the great enemy of man's salvation was exercising powers over me, that might eventually lead to my ruin. These were but temporary and sinful fears, but they added greatly to my unhappiness.

The worst thing of all was, what hitherto I had never felt, and, as yet, durst not confess to myself, that the presence of my illustrious and devoted friend was becoming irksome to me. When I was by myself, I breathed freer, and my step was lighter; but when he approached, a pang went to my heart, and, in his company, I moved and acted as if under a load that I could hardly endure. What a state to be in! And yet to shake him off was impossible—we were incorporated together—identified with one another, as it were, and the power was not in me to separate myself from him. I still knew nothing who he was, farther than that he was a potentate of some foreign land, bent on establishing some pure and genuine doctrines of Christianity, hitherto only half understood, and less than half exercised. Of this I could have no doubts, after all that he had said, done, and suffered in the cause. But, alongst with this, I was also certain, that he was possessed of some supernatural power, of the source of which I was wholly ignorant. That a man could be a Christian, and at the same time a powerful necromancer, appeared inconsistent, and adverse to every principle taught in our church; and from this I was led to believe, that he inherited his powers from on high, for I could not doubt either of the soundness of his principles, or that he accomplished things impossible to account for.

Thus was I sojourning in the midst of a chaos of confusion. I looked back on my bypast life with pain, as one looks back on a perilous journey, in which he has attained his end, without gaining any advantage either to himself, or others; and I looked forward, as on a darksome waste, full of repulsive and terrific shapes, pitfalls, and precipices, to which there was no definite bourne, and from which I turned with disgust. With my riches, my unhappiness was increased tenfold; and here, with another great acquisition of property, for which I had pleaded, and which I had gained in a dream, my miseries and difficulties were increasing. My principal feeling, about this time, was an insatiable

longing for something that I cannot describe or denominate properly, unless I say it was for *utter oblivion* that I
longed. I desired to sleep; but it was for a deeper and
longer sleep, than that in which the senses were nightly
steeped. I longed to be at rest and quiet, and close my
eyes on the past and the future alike, as far as this frail
life was concerned. But what had been formerly and finally
settled in the counsels above, I presumed not to call in
question.

In this state of irritation and misery, was I dragging
on an existence, disgusted with all around me, and in
particular with my mother, who, with all her love and
anxiety, had such an insufferable mode of manifesting them,
that ·she had by this time rendered herself exceedingly
obnoxious to me. The very sound of her voice at a distance,
went to my heart like an arrow, and made all my nerves
to shrink; and as for the beautiful young lady of whom they
told me I had been so much enamoured, I shunned all
intercourse with her or hers, as I would have done with
the devil. I read some of their letters and burnt them, but
refused to see either the young lady or her mother, on
any account.

About this time it was, that my worthy and reverend
parent came with one of his elders to see my mother and
myself. His presence always brought joy with it into our
family, for my mother was uplifted, and I had so few who
cared for me, or for whom I cared, that I felt rather gratified at seeing him. My illustrious friend was also much
more attached to him, than any other person, (except
myself,) for their religious principles tallied in every point,
and their conversation was interesting, serious, and sublime. Being anxious to entertain well and highly the man
to whom I had been so much indebted, and knowing that
with all his integrity and righteousness, he disdained not

the good things of this life, I brought from the late laird's well-stored cellars, various fragrant and salubrious wines, and we drank and became merry, and I found that my miseries and overpowering calamities, passed away over my head like a shower that is driven by the wind. I became elevated and happy, and welcomed my guests an hundred times; and then I joined them in religious conversation, with a zeal and enthusiasm which I had not often experienced, and which made all their hearts rejoice, so that I said to myself, 'Surely every gift of God is a blessing, and ought to be used with liberality and thankfulness.'

The next day I waked from a profound and feverish sleep, and called for something to drink. There was a servant answered whom I had never seen before, and he was clad in my servant's clothes and livery. I asked for Andrew Handyside, the servant who had waited at table the night before; but the man answered with a stare and a smile.

'What do you mean, sirrah,' said I. 'Pray what do you here? or what are you pleased to laugh at? I desire you to go about your business, and send me up Handyside. I want him to bring me something to drink.'

'Ye sanna want a drink, maister,' said the fellow: 'Tak a hearty ane, and see if it will wauken ye up something, sae that ye dinna ca' for ghaists through your sleep. Surely ye haena forgotten that Andrew Handyside has been in his grave these six months?'

This was a stunning blow to me. I could not answer farther, but sunk back on my pillow as if I had been a lump of lead, refusing to take a drink or any thing else at the fellow's hand, who seemed thus mocking me with so grave a face. The man seemed sorry, and grieved at my being offended, but I ordered him away, and continued sullen and thoughtful. Could I have again been for a season in utter oblivion to myself, and transacting business which I neither approved of, nor had any connection with! I tried to recollect something in which I might have been engaged, but nothing was pourtrayed on my mind subsequent to the parting with my friends at a late hour the evening before. The evening before it certainly was: but if so, how came it, that Andrew Handyside, who served at table that evening, should have been in his grave six months! This was a circumstance somewhat equivocal; therefore, being afraid to arise lest accusations of I knew not what might come against me, I was obliged to call once more in order to come at what intelligence I could. The same fellow appeared to receive my orders as before, and I set about examining him with regard to particulars. He told me his name was Scrape; that I hired him myself; of whom I hired him; and at whose recommendation. I smiled, and nodded so as to let the knave see I understood he was telling me a chain of falsehoods, but did not choose to begin with any violent asseverations to the contrary.

'And where is my noble friend and companion?' said I. 'How has he been engaged in the interim?'

'I dinna ken him, sir,' said Scrape; 'but have heard it said, that the strange mysterious person that attended you, him that the maist part of folks countit uncanny, had gane awa wi' a Mr. Ringan o' Glasko last year, and had never returned.'

I thanked the Lord in my heart for this intelligence, hoping that the illustrious stranger had returned to his own land and people, and that I should thenceforth be rid of his controlling and appalling presence. 'And where is my mother?' said I.—The man's breath cut short, and he looked at me without returning any answer.—'I ask you where my mother is?' said I.

'God only knows, and not I, where she is,' returned he. 'He knows where her soul is, and as for her body, if you dinna ken something o' it, I suppose nae man alive does.'

'What do you mean, you knave?' said I. 'What dark hints are these you are throwing out? Tell me precisely and distinctly what you know of my mother?'

'It is unco queer o' ye to forget, or pretend to forget every thing that gate, the day, sir,' said he. 'I'm sure you heard enough about it yestreen; an' I can tell you, there are some gayan ill-faurd stories gaun about that business. But as the thing is to be tried afore the circuit lords, it wad be far wrang to say either this or that to influence the public mind; it is best just to let justice tak its swee. I hae naething to say, sir. Ye hae been a good enough maister to me, and paid my wages regularly, <u>but ye hae muckle need to be innocent, for there are some heavy accusations rising against you.</u>'

'I fear no accusations of man,' said I, 'as long as I can justify my cause in the sight of Heaven; and that I can do this I am well aware. Go you and bring me some wine and water, and some other clothes than these gaudy and glaring ones.'

I took a cup of wine and water; put on my black clothes, and walked out. For all the perplexity that surrounded me, I felt my spirits considerably buoyant. It appeared that I was rid of the two greatest bars to my happiness, by what agency I knew not. <u>My mother, it seemed, was gone,</u> who had become a grievous thorn in my side of late, and my great companion and counsellor, who tyrannized over every spontaneous movement of my heart, had likewise taken himself off. This last was an unspeakable relief; for I found that for a long season I had only been able to act by the motions of his mysterious mind and spirit. I therefore thanked God for my deliverance, and strode through my woods with a daring and heroic step; with independence in my eye, and freedom swinging in my right hand.

At the extremity of the Colwan wood, I perceived a figure approaching me with slow and dignified motion. The moment that I beheld it, my whole frame received a shock as if the ground on which I walked had sunk suddenly below me. Yet, at that moment, I knew not who it was; it was the air and motion of some one that I dreaded, and from whom I would gladly have escaped; but this I even had not power to attempt. It came slowly onward, and I advanced as slowly to meet it; yet when we came within speech, I still knew not who it was. It bore the figure, air, and features of my late brother, I thought, exactly; yet in all these there were traits so forbidding, so mixed with an appearance of misery, chagrin, and despair, that I still shrunk from the view, not knowing on whose face I looked. But when the being spoke, both my mental and bodily frame received another shock more terrible than the first, for it was the voice of the great personage I had so long denominated my friend, of whom I had deemed myself for ever freed, and whose presence and counsels I now dreaded more than hell. It was his voice, but so altered—I shall never forget it till my dying day. Nay, I can scarce conceive it possible that any earthly sounds could be so discordant, so repulsive to every feeling of a human soul, as the tones of the voice that grated on my ear at that moment. They were the sounds of the pit, wheezed through a grated cranny, or seemed so to my distempered imagination.

'So! Thou shudderest at my approach now, dost thou?' said he. 'Is this all the gratitude that you deign for an attachment of which the annals of the world furnish no parallel? An attachment which has caused me to forego power and dominion, might, homage, conquest and adulation, all that I might gain one highly valued and sanctified spirit, to my great and true principles of reformation among mankind. Wherein have I offended? What have I done for evil, or what have I not done for your good, that you would thus shun my presence?'

'Great and magnificent prince,' said I humbly, 'let me request of you to abandon a poor worthless wight to his own wayward fortune, and return to the dominion of your people. I am unworthy of the sacrifices you have made for my sake; and after all your efforts, I do not feel that you have rendered me either more virtuous or more happy. For the sake of that which is estimable in human nature, depart from me to your own home, before you render me a being either altogether above, or below the rest of my fellow creatures. Let me plod on towards heaven and happiness in my own way, like those that have gone before me, and I promise to stick fast by the great principles which you have so strenuously inculcated, on condition that you depart and leave me for ever.'

'Sooner shall you make the mother abandon the child of her bosom; nay, sooner cause the shadow to relinquish the substance, than separate me from your side. Our beings are amalgamated, as it were, and consociated in one, and never shall I depart from this country until I can carry you in triumph with me.'

I can in nowise describe the effect this appalling speech had on me. It was like the announcement of death to one who had of late deemed himself free, if not of something worse than death, and of longer continuance. There was I doomed to remain in misery, subjugated, soul and body, to one whose presence was become more intolerable to me than ought on earth could compensate: And at that moment, when he beheld the anguish of my soul, he could not conceal that he enjoyed it. I was troubled for an answer, for which he was waiting: it became incumbent on me to say something after such a protestation of attachment; and, in some degree to shake the validity of it, I asked, with great simplicity, where he had been all this while?

'Your crimes and your extravagancies forced me from your side for a season,' said he; 'but now that I hope the day of grace is returned, I am again drawn towards you by an affection that has neither bounds nor interest; an affection for which I receive not even the poor return of gratitude, and which seems to have its radical sources in fascination. I have been far, far abroad, and have seen much, and transacted much, since I last spoke with you. During that space, I grievously suspect that you have been guilty of great crimes and misdemeanours, crimes that would have sunk an unregenerated person to perdition; but as I knew it to be only a temporary falling off, a specimen of that liberty by which the chosen and elected ones are made free, I closed my eyes on the wilful debasement of our principles, knowing that the transgressions could never be accounted to your charge, and that in good time you would come to your senses, and throw the whole weight of your crimes on the shoulders that had voluntarily stooped to receive the load.'

'Certainly I will,' said I, 'as I and all the justified have a good right to do. But what crimes? What misdemeanours and transgressions do you talk about? For my part, I am conscious of none, and am utterly amazed at insinuations which I do not comprehend.'

'You have certainly been left to yourself for a season,' returned he, 'having gone on rather like a person in a delirium, than a Christian in his sober senses. You are accused of having made away with your mother privately;

as also of the death of a beautiful young lady, whose affections you had seduced.'

'It is an intolerable and monstrous falsehood!' cried I, interrupting him; 'I never laid a hand on a woman to take away her life, and have even shunned their society from my childhood: I know nothing of my mother's exit, nor of that young lady's whom you mention—Nothing whatever.'

'I hope it is so,' said he. 'But it seems there are some strong presumptuous proofs against you, and I came to warn you this day that a precognition is in progress, and that unless you are perfectly convinced, not only of your innocence, but of your ability to prove it, it will be the safest course for you to abscond, and let the trial go on without you.'

'Never shall it be said that I shrunk from such a trial as this,' said I. 'It would give grounds for suspicions of guilt that never had existence, even in thought. I will go and show myself in every public place, that no slanderous tongue may wag against me. I have shed the blood of sinners, but of these deaths I am guiltless; therefore, I will face every tribunal, and put all my accusers down.'

'Asseveration will avail you but little,' answered he, composedly: 'It is, however, justifiable in its place, although to me it signifies nothing, who know too well that you *did* commit both crimes, in your own person, and with your own hands. Far be it from me to betray you; indeed, I would rather endeavour to palliate the offences; for though adverse to nature, I can prove them not to be so to the cause of pure Christianity, by the mode of which we have approved of it, and which we wish to promulgate.'

'If this that you tell me be true,' said I, 'then is it as true that I have two souls, which take possession of my bodily frame by turns, the one being all unconscious of what the other performs; for as sure as I have at this moment a spirit within me, fashioned and destined to eternal felicity, as sure am I utterly ignorant of the crimes you now lay to my charge.'

'Your supposition may be true in effect,' said he. 'We are all subjected to two distinct natures in the same person. I myself have suffered grievously in that way. The spirit that now directs my energies is not that with which I was endowed at my creation. It is changed within me, and so is my whole nature. My former days were those of grandeur and felicity. But, would you believe it? *I was not then a Christian.* Now I am. I have been converted to its truths by passing through the fire, and since my final conversion, my misery has been extreme. You complain that I have not been able to render you more happy than you were. Alas! do you expect it in the difficult and exterminating career which you have begun. I, however, promise you this—a portion of the only happiness which I enjoy, sublime in its motions, and splendid in its attainments—I will place you on the right hand of my throne, and show you the grandeur of my domains, and the felicity of my millions of true professors.'

I was once more humbled before this mighty potentate, and promised to be ruled wholly by his directions, although at that moment my nature shrunk from the concessions, and my soul longed rather to be inclosed in the deeps of the sea, or involved once more in utter oblivion. I was like Daniel in the den of lions, without his faith in divine support, and wholly at their mercy. I felt as one round whose body a deadly snake is twisted, which continues to hold him in its fangs, without injuring him, farther than in moving its scaly infernal folds with exulting delight, to let its victim feel to whose power he has subjected himself; and thus did I for a space drag an existence

from day to day, in utter weariness and helplessness; at one
time worshipping with great fervour of spirit, and at other
times so wholly left to myself, as to work all manner of vices
and follies with greediness. In these my enlightened friend
never accompanied me, but I always observed that he was
the first to lead me to every one of them, and then leave me
in the lurch. The next day, after these my fallings off, he
never failed to reprove me gently, blaming me for my venial
transgressions; but then he had the art of reconciling all,
by reverting to my justified and infallible state, which I
found to prove a delightful healing salve for every sore.

But, of all my troubles, this was the chief: I was every
day and every hour assailed with accusations of deeds of
which I was wholly ignorant; of acts of cruelty, injustice,
defamation, and deceit; of pieces of business which I
could not be made to comprehend; with law-suits, details,
arrestments of judgment, and a thousand interminable
quibbles from the mouth of my loquacious and conceited
attorney. So miserable was my life rendered by these
continued attacks, that I was often obliged to lock myself
up for days together, never seeing any person save my
man Samuel Scrape, who was a very honest blunt fellow,
a staunch Cameronian,[1] but withal very little conversant
in religious matters. He said he came from a place called
Penpunt, which I thought a name so ludicrous, that I
called him by the name of his native village, an appellation of which he was very proud, and answered every
thing with more civility and perspicuity when I denominated him Penpunt, than Samuel, his own Christian name.
Of this peasant was I obliged to make a companion on
sundry occasions, and strange indeed were the details
which he gave me concerning myself, and the ideas of
the country people concerning me. I took down a few of
these in writing, to put off the time, and here leave them

on record to show how the best and greatest actions are misconstrued among sinful and ignorant men.

'You say, Samuel, that I hired you myself—that I have been a good enough master to you, and have paid you your weekly wages punctually. Now, how is it that you say this, knowing, as you do, that I never hired you, and never paid you a sixpence of wages in the whole course of my life, excepting this last month?'

'Ye may as weel say, master, that water's no water, or that stanes are no stanes. But that's just your gate, an' it is a great pity aye to do a thing an' profess the clean contrair. Weel then, since you havena paid me ony wages, an' I can prove day and date when I was hired, an' came hame to your service, will you be sae kind as to pay me now? That's the best way o' curing a man o' the mortal disease o' leasing-making that I ken o'.'

'I should think that Penpunt and Cameronian principles, would not admit of a man taking twice payment for the same article.'

'In sic a case as this, sir, it disna hinge upon principles, but a piece o' good manners; an' I can tell you that at sic a crisis, a Cameronian is a gayan weel-bred man. He's driven to this, that he maun either make a breach in his friend's good name, or in his purse; an' O, sir, whilk o' thae, think you, is the most precious? For instance, an a Galloway drover had comed to the town o' Penpunt, an' said to a Cameronian, (the folk's a' Cameronians there,) "Sir, I want to buy your cow." "Vera weel," says the Cameronian, "I just want to sell the cow, sae gie me twenty punds Scots, an' take her w'ye." It's a bargain. The drover takes away the cow, an' gies the Cameronian his twenty pund Scots. But after that, he meets him again on the white sands, amang a' the drovers an' dealers o' the land, an' the Gallowayman, he says to the Cameronian, afore a' thae witnesses, "Come, Master Whiggam, I hae never paid you for yon bit useless cow, that I bought, I'll pay her the day, but you maun mind the luck-penny; there's muckle need for't,"—or something to that purpose. The Cameronian then turns out to be a civil man, an' canna bide to make the man baith a feele an' liar at the same time, afore a' his associates; an' therefore he pits his principles aff at the side, to be a kind o' sleepin partner, as it war, an' brings up his good breeding to stand at the counter: he pockets the money, gies the Galloway drover time o' day, an' comes his way. An' wha's to blame? *Man mind yoursel* is the first commandment. A Cameronian's principles never came atween him an' his purse, nor sanna in the present case; for as I canna bide to make you out a leear, I'll thank you for my wages.'

'Well, you shall have them, Samuel, if you declare to me that I hired you myself in this same person, and bargained with you with this same tongue, and voice, with which I speak to you just now.'

'That I do declare, unless ye hae twa persons o' the same appearance, and twa tongues to the same voice. But, od saif us, sir, do you ken what the auld wives o' the clachan say about you?'

'How should I, when no one repeats it to me?'

'Oo, I trow it's a' stuff;—folk shouldna heed what's said by auld crazy kimmers. But there are some o' them weel kend for witches too; an' they say,—lord have a care o' us!—they say the deil's often seen gaun sidie for sidie w'ye, whiles in ae shape, an' whiles in another. An' they say that he whiles takes your ain shape, or else enters into you, and then your turn a deil yoursel.'

I was so astounded at this terrible idea that had gone abroad, regarding my fellowship with the prince or darkness, that I could make no answer to the fellow's information, but sat like one in a stupor; and if it had not been for my well-founded faith, and conviction that I was a chosen and elected one before the world was made, I should at that moment have given into the popular belief, and fallen into the sin of despondency; but I was preserved from such a fatal error by an inward and unseen supporter. Still the insinuation was so like what I felt myself, that I was greatly awed and confounded.

The poor fellow observed this, and tried to do away the impression by some farther sage remarks of his own.

'Hout, dear sir, it is balderdash, there's nae doubt o't. It is the crownhead o' absurdity to tak in the havers o' auld wives for gospel. I told them that my master was a peeous man, an' a sensible man; an' for praying, that he could ding auld Macmillan[1] himsel. "Sae could the deil," they said, "when he liket, either at preaching or praying, if these war to answer his ain ends." "Na, na," says I, "but he's a strick believer in a' the truths o' Christianity, my master." They said, sae was Satan, for that he was the firmest believer in a' the truths of Christianity that was out o' heaven; an' that, sin' the Revolution that the gospel had turned sae rife, he had been often driven to the shift o' preaching it himsel, for the purpose o' getting some wrang tenets introduced into it, and thereby turning it into blasphemy and ridicule.'

I confess, to my shame, that I was so overcome by this jumble of nonsense, that a chillness came over me, and in spite of all my efforts to shake off the impression it had made, I fell into a faint. Samuel soon brought me to myself, and after a deep draught of wine and water, I was greatly revived, and felt my spirit rise above the sphere of vulgar conceptions, and the restrained views of un-regenerate men. The shrewd but loquacious fellow, per-ceiving this, tried to make some amends for the pain he had occasioned to me, by the following story, which I noted down, and which was brought on by a conversation to the following purport:—

'Now, Penpunt, you may tell me all that passed between you and the wives of the clachan. I am better of that stomach qualm, with which I am sometimes seized, and shall be much amused by hearing the sentiments of noted witches regarding myself and my connections.'

'Weel, you see, sir, I says to them, "It will be lang afore the deil intermeddle wi' as serious a professor, and as fervent a prayer as my master, for gin he gets the upper hand o' sickan men, wha's to be safe?" An', what think ye they said, sir? There was ane Lucky Shaw set up her lang lantern chafts, an' answered me, an' a' the rest shanned and noddit in assent an' approbation: "Ye silly, sauchless, Cameronian cuif!" quo she, "is that a' that ye ken about the wiles and doings o' the prince o' the air, that rules an' works in the bairns of disobedience? Gin ever he observes a proud professor, wha has mae than ordinary pretensions to a divine calling, and that reards and prays till the very howlets learn his preambles, *that's* the man Auld Simmie fixes on to mak a dishclout o'. He canna get rest in hell, if he sees a man, or a set of men o' this stamp, an' when he sets fairly to wark, it is seldom that he disna bring them round till his ain measures by hook or by crook. Then, O it is a grand prize for him, an' a proud deil he is, when he gangs hame to his ain ha', wi' a batch o' the souls o' sic strenuous professors on his back. Ay, I trow, auld Ingleby, the Liverpool packman, never came up Glasco street wi' prouder pomp, when he had ten horse-laids afore him o' Flanders lace, an' Hollin lawn, an' silks an' satins frae the eastern Indians, than Satan wad strodge into hell with a pack-laid o' the souls o' proud professors on his braid shoulders. Ha, ha, ha! I

think I see how the auld thief wad be gaun through his
gizened dominions, crying his wares, in derision, 'Wha
will buy a fresh, cauler divine, a bouzy bishop, a fasting
zealot, or a piping priest? For a' their prayers an' their
praises, their aumuses, an' their penances, their whinings,
their howlings, their rantings, an' their ravings, here they
come at last! Behold the end! Here go the rare and precious
wares! A fat professor for a bodle, an' a lean ane for half
a merk!''' I declare, I trembled at the auld hag's ravings
but the lave o' the kimmers applauded the sayings as
sacred truths. An' then Lucky went on: "There are many
wolves in sheep's claithing, among us, my man; mony
deils aneath the masks o' zealous professors, roaming
about in kirks and meeting-houses o' the land. It was but
the year afore the last, that the people o' the town o'
Auchtermuchty grew so rigidly righteous, that the meanest
hind among them became a shining light in ither towns
an' parishes. There was nought to be heard, neither night
nor day, but preaching, praying, argumentation, an'
catechising in a' the famous town o' Auchtermuchty. The
young men wooed their sweethearts out o' the Song o'
Solomon, an' the girls returned answers in strings o'
verses out o' the Psalms. At the lint-swinglings, they
said questions round; and read chapters, and sang hymns
at bridals; auld and young prayed in their dreams, an'
prophesied in their sleep, till the deils in the farrest nooks
o' hell were alarmed, and moved to commotion. Gin it
hadna been an auld carl, Robin Ruthven, Auchtermuchty
wad at that time hae been ruined and lost for ever. But
Robin was a cunning man, an' had rather mae wits than
his ain, for he had been in the hands o' the fairies when he
was young, an' a' kinds o' spirits were visible to his een,
an' their language as familiar to him as his ain mother
tongue. Robin was sitting on the side o' the West

Lowmond, ae still gloomy night in September, when he saw a bridal o' corbie craws coming east the lift, just on the edge o' the gloaming. The moment that Robin saw them, he kenned, by their movements, that they were craws o' some ither warld than this; so he signed himself, and crap into the middle o' his bourock. The corbie craws came a' an' sat down round about him, an' they poukit their black sooty wings, an' spread them out to the breeze to cool; and Robin heard ae corbie speaking, an' another answering him; and the tane said to the tither: 'Where will the ravens find a prey the night?'—'On the lean crazy souls o' Auchtermuchty,' quo the tither.—'I fear they will be o'er weel wrappit up in the warm flannens o' faith, an' clouted wi' the dirty duds o' repentance, for us to mak a meal o',' quo the first.—'Whaten vile sounds are these that I hear coming bumming up the hill?' 'O these are the hymns and praises o' the auld wives and creeshy louns o' Auchtermuchty, wha are gaun crooning their way to heaven; an' gin it warna for the shame o' being beat, we might let our great enemy tak them. For sic a prize as he will hae! Heaven, forsooth! What shall we think o' heaven, if it is to be filled wi' vermin like thae, amang whom there is mair poverty and pollution, than I can name.' 'No matter for that,' said the first, 'we cannot have our power set at defiance; though we should put them in the thief's hole, we must catch them, and catch them with their own bait too. Come all to church to-morrow, and I'll let you hear how I'll gull the saints of Auchtermuchty. In the mean time, there is a feast on the Sidlaw hills tonight, below the hill of Macbeth,—Mount, Diabolus, and fly.' Then, with loud croaking and crowing, the bridal of corbies again scaled the dusky air, and left Robin Ruthven in the middle of his cairn.

' "The next day the congregation met in the kirk of Auchtermuchty, but the minister made not his appearance. The elders ran out and in, making inquiries; but they could learn nothing, save that the minister was missing. They ordered the clerk to sing a part of the 119th Psalm, until they saw if the minister would cast up. The clerk did as he was ordered, and by the time he reached the 77th verse, a strange divine entered the church, by the *western door*, and advanced solemnly up to the pulpit. The eyes of all the congregation were riveted on the sublime stranger, who was clothed in a robe of black sackcloth, that flowed all around him, and trailed far behind, and they weened him an angel, come to exhort them, in disguise. He read out his text from the Prophecies of Ezekiel, which consisted of these singular words: 'I will overturn, overturn, overturn it; and it shall be no more, until he come, whose right it is, and I will give it him.'

' "From these words he preached such a sermon as never was heard by human ears, at least never by ears of Auchtermuchty. It was a true, sterling, gospel sermon— it was striking, sublime, and awful in the extreme. He finally made out the ɪᴛ, mentioned in the text, to mean, properly and positively, the notable town of Auchtermuchty. He proved all the people in it, to their perfect satisfaction, to be in the gall of bitterness and bond of iniquity, and he assured them, that God would overturn them, their principles, and professions; and that they should be no more, until the devil, the town's greatest enemy, came, and then it should be given unto him for a prey, for it was his right, and to him it belonged, if there was not forthwith a radical change made in all their opinions and modes of worship.

' "The inhabitants of Auchtermuchty were electrified— they were charmed; they were actually raving mad about the grand and sublime truths delivered to them, by this eloquent and impressive preacher of Christianity. 'He is a prophet of the Lord,' said one, 'sent to warn us, as Jonah was sent to the Ninevites.' 'O, he is an angel sent from heaven, to instruct this great city,' said another, 'for no man ever uttered truths so sublime before.' The good people of Auchtermuchty were in perfect raptures with the preacher, who had thus sent them to hell by the slump, tag, rag, and bobtail! Nothing in the world delights a truly religious people so much, as consigning them to eternal damnation. They wondered after the preacher— they crowded together, and spoke of his sermon with admiration, and still as they conversed, the wonder and the admiration increased; so that honest Robin Ruthven's words would not be listened to. It was in vain that he told them he heard a raven speaking, and another raven answering him: the people laughed him to scorn, and kicked him out of their assemblies, as a one who spoke evil of dignities; and they called him a warlock, an' a daft body, to think to mak language out o' the crouping o' craws.

' "The sublime preacher could not be heard of, although all the country was sought for him, even to the minutest corner of St. Johnston and Dundee; but as he had announced another sermon on the same text, on a certain day, all the inhabitants of that populous country, far and near, flocked to Auchtermuchty. Cupar, Newburgh, and Strathmiglo, turned out men, women, and children. Perth and Dundee gave their thousands; and from the East Nook of Fife to the foot of the Grampian hills, there was nothing but running and riding that morning to Auchtermuchty. The kirk would not hold the thousandth part of them. A splendid tent was erected on the brae north of the town, and round that the countless congregation assembled.

When they were all waiting anxiously for the great preacher, behold, Robin Ruthven set up his head in the tent, and warned his countrymen to beware of the doctrines they were about to hear, for he could prove, to their satisfaction, that they were all false, and tended to their destruction!

'"The whole multitude raised a cry of indignation against Robin, and dragged him from the tent, the elders rebuking him, and the multitude threatening to resort to stronger measures; and though he told them a plain and unsophisticated tale of the black corbies, he was only derided. The great preacher appeared once more, and went through his two discourses with increased energy and approbation. All who heard him were amazed, and many of them went into fits, writhing and foaming in a state of the most horrid agitation. Robin Ruthven sat on the outskirts of the great assembly, listening with the rest, and perceived what they, in the height of their enthusiasm, perceived not,—the ruinous tendency of the tenets so sublimely inculcated. Robin kenned the voice of his friend the corby-craw again, and was sure he could not be wrang: sae when public worship was finished, a' the elders an' a' the gentry flocked about the great preacher, as he stood on the green brae in the sight of the hale congregation, an' a' war alike anxious to pay him some mark o' respect. Robin Ruthven came in amang the thrang, to try to effect what he had promised; and, with the greatest readiness and simplicity, just took haud o' the side an' wide gown, an' in sight of a' present, held it aside as high as the preacher's knee, and behold, there was a pair o' cloven feet! The auld thief was fairly catched in the very height o' his proud conquest, an' put down by an auld carl. He could feign nae mair, but gnashing on Robin wi' his teeth, he dartit into the air like a fiery dragon, an' keust a reid rainbow our the taps o' the Lowmonds.

' "A' the auld wives an' weavers o' Auchtermuchty fell down flat wi' affright, an' betook them to their prayers aince again, for they saw the dreadfu' danger they had escapit, an' frae that day to this it is a hard matter to gar an Auchtermuchty man listen to a sermon at a', an' a harder ane still to gar him applaud ane, for he thinks aye that he sees the cloven foot peeping out frae aneath ilka sentence.

' "Now, this is a true story, my man," quo the auld wife; "an' whenever you are doubtfu' of a man, take auld Robin Ruthven's plan, an' look for the cloven foot, for it's a thing that winna weel hide; an' it appears whiles where ane wadna think o't. It will keek out frae aneath the parson's gown, the lawyer's wig, and the Cameronian's blue bannet; but still there is a gouden rule[1] whereby to detect it, an' that never, never fails."—The auld witch didna gie me the rule, an' though I hae heard tell o't often an' often, shame fa' me an I ken what it is! But ye will ken it well, an' it wad be nae the waur of a trial on some o' your friends, maybe; for they say there's a certain gentleman seen walking wi' you whiles, that, wherever he sets his foot, the grass withers as gin it war scoudered wi' a het ern. His presence be about us! What's the matter wi' you, master? Are ye gaun to take the calm o' the stamock again?'

The truth is, that the clown's absurd story, with the still more ridiculous application, made me sick at heart a second time. It was not because I thought my illustrious friend was the devil, or that I took a fool's idle tale as a counterbalance to divine revelation, that had assured me of my justification in the sight of God before the existence of time. But, in short, it gave me a view of my own state, at which I shuddered, as indeed I now always did, when the image of my devoted friend and ruler presented itself to my mind. I often communed with my heart on this, and wondered how a connection, that had the well-being of mankind solely in view, could be productive of fruits so bitter. I then went to try my works by the Saviour's golden rule, as my servant had put it into my head to do; and, behold, not one of them would stand the test. I had shed blood on a ground on which I could not admit that any man had a right to shed mine; and I began to doubt the motives of my adviser once more, not that they were intentionally bad, but that his was some great mind led astray by enthusiasm, or some overpowering passion.

He seemed to comprehend every one of these motions of my heart, for his manner towards me altered every day. It first became any thing but agreeable, then supercilious, and finally, intolerable; so that I resolved to shake him off, cost what it would, even though I should be reduced to beg my bread in a foreign land. To do it at home was impossible, as he held my life in his hands, to sell it whenever he had a mind; and besides, his ascendancy over me was as complete as that of a huntsman over his dogs. I was even so weak, as, the next time I met with him, to look stedfastly at his foot, to see if it was not cloven into two hoofs. It was the foot of a gentleman, in every respect, so far as appearances went, but the form of his counsels was somewhat equivocal, and if not double, they were amazingly crooked.

But, if I had taken my measures to abscond and fly from my native place, in order to free myself of this tormenting, intolerant, and bloody reformer, he had likewise taken his to expel me, or throw me into the hands of justice. It seems, that about this time, I was haunted by some spies connected with my late father and brother, of whom the mistress of the former was one. My brother's death had been witnessed by two individuals; indeed, I always had an impression that it was witnessed by more than one, having some faint recollection of hearing voices and challenges close beside me; and this woman had searched about until she found these people; but, as I shrewdly suspected, not without the assistance of the only person in my secret,—my own warm and devoted friend. I say this, because I found that he had them concealed in the neighbourhood, and then took me again and again where I was fully exposed to their view, without being aware. One time in particular, on pretence of gratifying my revenge on that base woman, he knew so well where she lay concealed, that he led me to her, and left me to the mercy of two viragos, who had very nigh taken my life. My time of residence at Dalcastle was wearing to a crisis. I could no longer live with my tyrant, who haunted me like my shadow; and besides, it seems there were proofs of murder leading against me from all quarters. Of part of these I deemed myself quite free, but the world deemed otherwise; and how the matter would have gone, God only knows, for, the case never having undergone a judicial trial, I do not. It perhaps, however, behoves me here to relate all that I know of it, and it is simply this:

On the first of June 1712, (well may I remember the day,) I was sitting locked in my secret chamber, in a state of the utmost despondency, revolving in my mind what I ought to do to be free of my persecutors, and wishing myself a worm, or a moth, that I might be crushed and at rest, when behold Samuel entered, with eyes like to start out of his head, exclaiming, 'For God's sake, master, fly and hide yourself, for your mother's found, an' as sure as you're a living soul, the blame is gaun to fa' on you!'

'My mother found!' said I. 'And, pray, where has she been all this while?' In the mean time, I was terribly discomposed at the thoughts of her return.

'Been, sir! Been? Why, she has been where ye pat her, it seems,—lying buried in the sands o' the linn. I can tell you, ye will see her a frightsome figure, sic as I never wish to see again. An' the young lady is found too, sir: an' it is said the devil—I beg pardon sir, *your friend*, I mean,—it is said your *friend* has made the discovery, an' the folk are away to raise officers, an' they will be here in an hour or two at the farthest, sir; an' sae you hae not a minute to lose, for there's proof, sir, strong proof, an' sworn proof, that ye were last seen wi' them baith; sae, unless ye can gie a' the better an account o' baith yoursel an' them, either hide, or flee for your bare life.'

'I will neither hide nor fly,' said I; 'for I am as guiltless of the blood of these women as the child unborn.'

'The country disna think sae, master; an' I can assure you, that should evidence fail, you run a risk o' being torn limb frae limb. They are bringing the corpse here, to gar ye touch them baith afore witnesses, an' plenty o' witnesses there will be!'

'They shall not bring them here,' cried I, shocked beyond measure at the experiment about to be made: 'Go, instantly, and debar them from entering my gate with their bloated and mangled carcases.'

'The body of your own mother, sir!' said the fellow emphatically. I was in terrible agitation; and, being driven to my wit's end, I got up and strode furiously round and round the room. Samuel wist not what to do, but I saw by his staring he deemed me doubly guilty. A tap came to the chamber door: we both started like guilty creatures; and as for Samuel, his hairs stood all on end with alarm, so that when I motioned to him, he could scarcely advance to open the door. He did so at length, and who should enter but my illustrious friend, manifestly in the utmost state of alarm. The moment that Samuel admitted him, the former made his escape by the prince's side as he entered, seemingly in a state of distraction. I was little better, when I saw this dreaded personage enter my chamber, which he had never before attempted; and being unable to ask his errand, I suppose I stood and gazed on him like a statue.

'I come with sad and tormenting tidings to you, my beloved and ungrateful friend,' said he; 'but having only a minute left to save your life, I have come to attempt it. There is a mob coming towards you with two dead bodies, which will place you in circumstances disagreeable enough: but that is not the worst, for of that you may be able to clear yourself. At this moment there is a party of officers, with a Justiciary warrant from Edinburgh, surrounding the house, and about to begin the search of it, for you. If you fall into their hands, you are inevitably lost; for I have been making earnest inquiries, and find that every thing is in train for your ruin.'

'Ay, and who has been the cause of all this?' said I, with great bitterness. But he stopped me short, adding, 'There is no time for such reflections at present: I gave you my word of honour that your life should be safe from the hand of man. So it shall, if the power remain with me to save it. I am come to redeem my pledge, and to save your life by the sacrifice of my own. Here,—Not one word of expostulation, change habits with me, and you may then pass by the officers, and guards, and even through the approaching mob, with the most perfect temerity. There is a virtue in this garb, and instead of offering to detain you, they shall pay you obeisance. Make haste, and leave this place for the present, flying

where you best may, and if I escape from these dangers
that surround me, I will endeavour to find you out, and
bring you what intelligence I am able.

I put on his green frock coat, buff belt, and a sort of a
turban that he always wore on his head, somewhat
resembling a bishop's mitre: he drew his hand thrice
across my face, and I withdrew as he continued to urge me.
My hall door and postern gate were both strongly
guarded, and there were sundry armed people within,
searching the closets; but all of them made way for me,
and lifted their caps as I passed by them. Only one superior
officer accosted me, asking if I had seen the culprit? I
knew not what answer to make, but chanced to say, with
great truth and propriety, 'He is safe enough.' The man
beckoned with a smile, as much as to say, 'Thank you,
sir, that is quite sufficient;' and I walked deliberately
away.

I had not well left the gate, till, hearing a great noise
coming from the deep glen toward the east, I turned that
way, deeming myself quite secure in this my new disguise,
to see what it was, and if matters were as had been described
to me. There I met a great mob, sure enough, coming
with two dead bodies stretched on boards, and decently
covered with white sheets. I would fain have examined
their appearance, had I not perceived the apparent fury in
the looks of the men, and judged from that how much more
safe it was for me not to intermeddle in the affray. I cannot tell how it was, but I felt a strange and unwonted
delight in viewing this scene, and a certain pride of heart
in being supposed the perpetrator of the unnatural crimes
laid to my charge. This was a feeling quite new to me;
and if there were virtues in the robes of the illustrious
foreigner, who had without all dispute preserved my life
at this time; I say, if there was any inherent virtue in

these robes of his, as he had suggested, this was one of their effects, that they turned my heart towards that which was evil, horrible, and disgustful.

I mixed with the mob to hear what they were saying. Every tongue was engaged in loading me with the most opprobrious epithets! One called me a monster of nature; another an incarnate devil; and another a creature made to be cursed in time and eternity. I retired from them, and winded my way southward, comforting myself with the assurance, that so mankind had used and persecuted the greatest fathers and apostles of the Christian church, and that their vile opprobrium could not alter the counsels of heaven concerning me.

On going over that rising ground called Dorington Moor, I could not help turning round and taking a look of Dalcastle. I had little doubt that it would be my last look, and nearly as little ambition that it should not. I thought how high my hopes of happiness and advancement had been on entering that mansion, and taking possession of its rich and extensive domains, and how miserably I had been disappointed. On the contrary, I had experienced nothing but chagrin, disgust, and terror; and I now consoled myself with the hope that I should henceforth shake myself free of the chains of my great tormentor, and for that privilege was I willing to encounter any earthly distress. I could not help perceiving, that I was now on a path which was likely to lead me into a species of distress hitherto unknown, and hardly dreamed of by me, and that was total destitution. For all the riches I had been possessed of a few hours previous to this, I found that here I was turned out of my lordly possessions without a single merk, or the power of lifting and commanding the smallest sum, without being thereby discovered and seized. Had it been possible for me to have escaped in my own clothes, I had a considerable sum secreted in these, but, by the sudden change, I was left without a coin for present necessity. But I had hope in heaven, knowing that the just man would not be left destitute; and that though many troubles surrounded him, he would at last be set free from them all. I was possessed of strong and brilliant parts, and a liberal education; and though I had somehow unaccountably suffered my theological qualifications to fall into desuetude, since my acquaintance with the ablest and most rigid of all theologians, I had nevertheless hopes that, by preaching up redemption by grace, pre-ordination, and eternal purpose, I should yet be enabled to benefit mankind in some country, and rise to high distinction.

These were some of the thoughts by which I consoled myself as I posted on my way southward, avoiding the towns and villages, and falling into the cross ways that led from each of the great roads passing east and west, to another. I lodged the first night in the house of a country weaver, into which I stepped at a late hour, quite overcome with hunger and fatigue, having travelled not less than thirty miles from my late home. The man received me ungraciously, telling me of a gentleman's house at no great distance, and of an inn a little farther away; but I said I delighted more in the society of a man like him, than that of any gentleman of the land, for my concerns were with the poor of this world, it being easier for a camel to go through the eye of a needle, than for a rich man to enter into the kingdom of heaven. The weaver's wife, who sat with a child on her knee, and had not hitherto opened her mouth, hearing me speak in that serious and religious style, stirred up the fire, with her one hand; then drawing a chair near it, she said, 'Come awa, honest lad, in by here: sin' it be sae that you belang to Him wha gies us a' that we hae, it is but right that you should share a part. You are a stranger, it is true, but *them* that winna entertain a stranger will never entertain an angel unawares.'

I never was apt to be taken with the simplicity of nature; in general I despised it; but, owing to my circumstances at the time, I was deeply affected by the manner of this poor woman's welcome. The weaver continued in a churlish mood throughout the evening, apparently dissatisfied with what his wife had done in entertaining me, and spoke to her in a manner so crusty that I thought proper to rebuke him, for the woman was comely in her person, and virtuous in her conversation; but the weaver her husband was large of make, ill-favoured, and pestilent; therefore did I take him severely to task for the tenor of his conduct; but the man was froward, and answered me rudely, with sneering and derision, and, in the height of his caprice, he said to his wife, 'Whan focks are sae keen of a chance o' entertaining angels, gudewife, it wad maybe be worth their while to tak tent what kind o' angels they are. It wadna wonder me vera muckle an ye had entertained your friend the deil the night, for aw thought aw fand a saur o' reek an' brimstane about him. *He's* nane o' the best o' angels, an' focks winna hae muckle credit by entertaining him.'

Certainly, in the assured state I was in, I had as little reason to be alarmed at mention being made of the devil as any person on earth: of late, however, I felt that the reverse was the case, and that any allusion to my great enemy, moved me exceedingly. The weaver's speech had such an effect on me, that both he and his wife were alarmed at my looks. The latter thought I was angry, and chided her husband gently for his rudeness; but the weaver himself rather seemed to be confirmed in his opinion that I was the devil, for he looked round like a startled roe-buck, and immediately betook him to the family Bible.

I know not whether it was on purpose to prove my identity or not, but I think he was going to desire me either to read a certain portion of Scripture that he had sought out, or to make family worship, had not the conversation at that instant taken another turn; for the weaver, not knowing how to address me, abruptly asked my name, as he was about to put the Bible into my hands. Never having considered myself in the light of a malefactor, but rather as a champion in the cause of truth, and finding myself perfectly safe under my disguise, I had never once thought of the utility of changing my name, and when the man asked me, I hesitated; but being compelled to say something, I said my name was Cowan. The man stared at me, and then at his wife, with a look that spoke a knowledge of something alarming or mysterious.

'Ha! Cowan?' said he. 'That's most extrordinar! Not Colwan, I hope?'

'No: Cowan is my sirname,' said I. 'But why not Colwan, there being so little difference in the sound?'

'I was feared ye might be that waratch that the deil has taen the possession o', an' eggit him on to kill baith his father an' his mother, his only brother, an' his sweetheart,' said he; 'an' to say the truth, I'm no that sure about you yet, for I see you're gaun wi' arms on ye.'

'Not I, honest man,' said I; 'I carry no arms; a man conscious of his innocence and uprightness of heart, needs not to carry arms in his defence now.'

'Ay, ay, maister,' said he; 'an' pray what div ye ca' this bit windlestrae that's appearing here?' With that he pointed to something on the inside of the breast of my frock-coat. I looked at it, and there certainly was the gilded haft of a poniard, the same weapon I had seen and handled before, and which I knew my illustrious companion always carried about with him; but till that moment I knew not that I was in possession of it. I drew it out: a more dangerous or insidious looking weapon could not be conceived. The weaver and his wife were both frightened, the latter in particular; and she being my friend, and I dependant on their hospitality, for that night, I said, 'I declare I knew not that I carried this small rapier, which has been in my coat by chance, and not by any design of mine. But lest you should think that I meditate any mischief to any under this roof, I give it into your hands, requesting of you to lock it by till to-morrow, or when I shall next want it.'

The woman seemed rather glad to get hold of it; and, taking it from me, she went into a kind of pantry out of my sight, and locked the weapon up; and then the discourse went on.

'There cannot be such a thing in reality,' said I, 'as the story you were mentioning just now, of a man whose name resembles mine.'

'It's likely that you ken a wee better about the story than I do, maister,' said he, 'suppose you do leave the *L* out of your name. An' yet I think sic a waratch, an' a murderer, wad hae taen a name wi' some gritter difference in the sound. But the story is just that true, that there were twa o' the Queen's officers here nae mair than an hour ago, in pursuit o' the vagabond, for they gat some intelligence that he had fled this gate; yet they said he had been last seen wi' black claes on, an' they supposed he was clad in black. His ain servant is wi' them, for the purpose o' kennin the scoundrel, an' they're galloping through the country like mad-men. I hope in God they'll get him, an' rack his neck for him!'

I could not say *Amen* to the weaver's prayer, and therefore tried to compose myself as well as I could, and made some religious comment on the causes of the nation's depravity. But suspecting that my potent friend had betrayed my flight and disguise, to save his life, I was very uneasy, and gave myself up for lost. I said prayers in the family, with the tenor of which the wife was delighted, but the weaver still dissatisfied; and, after a supper of the most homely fare, he tried to start an argument with me, proving, that every thing for which I had interceded in my prayer, was irrelevant to man's present state. But I, being weary and distressed in mind, shunned the contest, and requested a couch whereon to repose.

I was conducted into the other end of the house, among looms, treadles, pirns, and confusion without end; and there, in a sort of box, was I shut up for my night's repose, for the weaver, as he left me, cautiously turned the key of my apartment, and left me to shift for myself among the looms, determined that I should escape from the house with nothing. After he and his wife and children were crowded into their den, I heard the two mates contending furiously about me in suppressed voices, the one maintaining the probability that I was the murderer, and the other proving the impossibility of it. The husband, however, said as much as let me understand, that he had locked me up on purpose to bring the military, or officers of justice, to seize me. I was in the utmost perplexity, yet, for all that, and the imminent danger I was in, I fell asleep, and a more troubled and tormenting sleep never enchained a mortal frame. I had such dreams that they will not bear repetition, and early in the morning I awaked, feverish, and parched with thirst.

I went to call mine host, that he might let me out to the open air, but before doing so, I thought it necessary

to put on some clothes. In attempting to do this, a circumstance arrested my attention, (for which I could in nowise
account, which to this day I cannot unriddle, nor shall I
ever be able to comprehend it while I live,) the frock and
turban, which had furnished my disguise on the preceding
day, were both removed, and my own black coat and
cocked hat laid down in their place. At first I thought I was
in a dream, and felt the weaver's beam, web, and treadle-
strings with my hands, to convince myself that I was
awake. I was certainly awake; and there was the door
locked firm and fast as it was the evening before. I
carried my own black coat to the small window, and
examined it. It was my own in verity; and the sums of
money, that I had concealed in case of any emergency,
remained untouched. I trembled with astonishment; and
on my return from the small window, went doiting in
amongst the weaver's looms, till I entangled myself, and
could not get out again without working great deray
amongst the coarse linen threads that stood in warp from
one end of the apartment unto the other. I had no knife
whereby to cut the cords of this wicked man, and therefore
was obliged to call out lustily for assistance. The weaver
came half naked, unlocked the door, and, setting in his
head and long neck, accosted me thus:

'What now, Mr. Satan? What for are ye roaring that
gate? Are you fawn inna little hell, instead o' the big
muckil ane? Deil be in your reistit trams! What for have
ye abscondit yoursel into ma leddy's wab for?'

'Friend, I beg your pardon,' said I; 'I wanted to be at
the light, and have somehow unfortunately involved myself in the intricacies of your web, from which I cannot get
clear without doing you a great injury. Pray do, lend your
experienced hand to extricate me.'

'May aw the pearls o' damnation light on your silly

snout, an I dinna estricat ye weel enough! Ye ditit, donnart, deil's burd that ye be! what made ye gang howkin
in there to be a poor man's ruin? Come out, ye vile rag-of-
a-muffin, or I gar ye come out wi' mair shame and disgrace,
an' fewer haill banes in your body.'

My feet had slipped down through the double warpings
of a web, and not being able to reach the ground with
them, (there being a small pit below,) I rode upon a number
of yielding threads, and there being nothing else that I
could reach, to extricate myself was impossible. I was
utterly powerless; and besides, the yarn and cords hurt
me very much. For all that, the destructive weaver seized
a loomspoke, and began a-beating me most unmercifully,
while, entangled as I was, I could do nothing but shout
aloud for mercy, or assistance, whichever chanced to be
within hearing. The latter, at length, made its appearance,
in the form of the weaver's wife, in the same state of
dishabille with himself, who instantly interfered, and
that most strenuously, on my behalf. Before her arrival,
however, I had made a desperate effort to throw myself
out of the entanglement I was in; for the weaver continued
repeating his blows and cursing me so, that I determined
to get out of his meshes at any risk. This effort made my
case worse; for my feet being wrapt among the nether
threads, as I threw myself from my saddle on the upper
ones, my feet brought the others up through these, and I
hung with my head down, and my feet as firm as they had
been in a vice. The predicament of the web being thereby
increased, the weaver's wrath was doubled in proportion,
and he laid on without mercy.

At this critical juncture the wife arrived, and without
hesitation rushed before her offended lord, withholding
his hand from injuring me farther, although then it was
uplifted along with the loomspoke in overbearing ire.

'Dear Johnny! I think ye be gaen dementit this morning. Be quiet, my dear, an' dinna begin a Boddel Brigg¹ business in your ain house. What for ir ye persecutin' a servant o' the Lord's that gate, an' pitting the life out o' him wi' his head down an' his heels up?'

, 'Had ye said a servant o' the deil's, Nans, ye wad hae been nearer the nail, for gin he binna the auld ane himsel, he's gayan sib till him. There, didna I lock him in on purpose to bring the military on him; an' in place o' that, hasna he keepit me in a sleep a' this while as deep as death? An' here do I find him abscondit like a speeder i' the mids o' my leddy's wab, an' me dreamin' a' the night that I had the deil i' my house, an' that he was clapper-clawin me ayont the loom. Have at you, ye brunstane thief!' and, in spite of the good woman's struggles, he lent me another severe blow.

'Now, Johnny Dods, my man! O Johnny Dods, think if that be like a Christian, and ane o' the heroes o' Boddel Brigg, to entertain a stranger, an' then bind him in a web wi' his head down, an' mell him to death! O Johnny Dods, think what you are about! Slack a pin, an' let the good honest religious lad out.'

The weaver was rather overcome, but still stood to his point that I was the deil, though in better temper; and as he slackened the web to release me, he remarked, half laughing, 'Wha wad hae thought that John Dods should hae escapit a' the snares an' dangers that circum-fauldit him, an' at last should hae weaved a net to catch the deil.'

The wife released me soon, and carefully whispered me, at the same time, that it would be as well for me to dress and be going. I was not long in obeying, and dressed myself in my black clothes, hardly knowing what I did, what to think, or whither to betake myself. I was sore hurt by the blows of the desperate ruffian; and, what was worse, my ankle was so much strained, that I could hardly set my foot to the ground. I was obliged to apply to the weaver once more, to see if I could learn any thing about my clothes, or how the change was effected. 'Sir,' said I, 'how comes it that you have robbed me of my clothes, and put these down in their place over night?'

'Ha! thae claes? Me pit down thae claes!' said he, gaping with astonishment, and touching the clothes with the point of his fore-finger; 'I never saw them afore, as I have death to meet wi': So help me God!'

He strode into the work-house where I slept, to satisfy himself that my clothes were not there, and returned perfectly aghast with consternation. 'The doors were baith fast lockit,' said he. 'I could hae defied a rat either to hae gotten out or in. My dream has been true! My dream has been true! The Lord judge between thee and me; but, in his name, I charge you to depart out o' this house; an', gin it be your will, dinna tak the braidside o't w'ye, but gang quietly out at the door wi' your face foremost. Wife, let nought o' this enchanter's remain i' the house, to be a curse, an' a snare to us; gang an' bring him his gildit weapon, an' may the Lord protect a' his ain against its hellish an' deadly point!'

The wife went to seek my poniard, trembling so excessively that she could hardly walk, and shortly after, we heard a feeble scream from the pantry. The weapon had disappeared with the clothes, though under double lock and key; and the terror of the good people having now reached a disgusting extremity, I thought proper to make a sudden retreat, followed by the weaver's anathemas.

My state both of body and mind was now truly deplorable. I was hungry, wounded, and lame; an outcast and a vagabond in society; my life sought after with avidity, and all for doing that to which I was predestined by him who fore-ordains whatever comes to pass. I knew not whither to betake me. I had purposed going into England, and there making some use of the classical education I had received, but my lameness rendered this impracticable for the present. I was therefore obliged to turn my face towards Edinburgh, where I was little known—where concealment was more practicable than by skulking in the country, and where I might turn my mind to something that was great and good. I had a little money, both Scots and English, now in my possession, but not one friend in the whole world on whom I could rely. One devoted friend, it is true, I had, but he was become my greatest terror. To escape from him, I now felt that I would willingly travel to the farthest corners of the world, and be subjected to every deprivation; but after the certainty of what had taken place last night, after I had travelled thirty miles by secret and bye-ways, I saw not how escape from him was possible.

Miserable, forlorn, and dreading every person that I saw, either behind or before me, I hasted on towards Edinburgh, taking all the bye and unfrequented paths; and the third night after I left the weaver's house, I reached the West Port, without meeting with any thing remarkable. Being exceedingly fatigued and lame, I took lodgings in the first house I entered, and for these I was to pay two groats a-week, and to board and sleep with a young man who wanted a companion to make his rent easier. I liked this; having found from experience, that the great personage who had attached himself to me, and was now become my greatest terror among many surrounding evils, generally haunted me when I was alone, keeping aloof from all other society.

My fellow lodger came home in the evening, and was

glad at my coming. His name was Linton, and I changed mine to Elliot. He was a flippant unstable being, one to whom nothing appeared a difficulty, in his own estimation, but who could effect very little, after all. He was what is called by some a compositor, in the Queen's printing house, then conducted by a Mr. James Watson.[1] In the course of our conversation that night, I told him that I was a first-rate classical scholar, and would gladly turn my attention to some business wherein my education might avail me something; and that there was nothing would delight me so much as an engagement in the Queen's printing office. Linton made no difficulty in bringing about that arrangement. His answer was. 'Oo, gud sir, you are the very man we want. Gud bless your breast and your buttons, sir! Ay, that's neither here nor there— That's all very well—Ha-ha-ha—A byeword in the house, sir. But, as I was saying, you are the very *man* we want— You will get any money you like to ask, sir—*Any* money you like, sir. God bless your buttons!—That's settled— All done—Settled, settled—I'll do it, I'll do it—No more about it; no more about it. Settled, settled.'

The next day I went with him to the office, and he presented me to Mr. Watson as the most wonderful genius and scholar ever known. His recommendation had little sway with Mr. Watson, who only smiled at Linton's extravagancies, as one does at the prattle of an infant. I sauntered about the printing office for the space of two or three hours, during which time Watson bustled about with green spectacles on his nose, and took no heed of me. But seeing that I still lingered, he addressed me at length, in a civil gentlemanly way, and inquired concerning my views. I satisfied him with all my answers, in particular those to his questions about the Latin and Greek languages; but when he came to ask testimonials of my character and acquirements, and found that I could produce none, he viewed me with a jealous eye, and said he dreaded I was some ne'er-do-weel, run from my parents or guardians, and he did not chuse to employ any such. I said my parents were both dead; and that being thereby deprived of the means of following out my education, it behoved me to apply to some business in which my education might be of some use to me. He said he would take me into the office, and pay me according to the business I performed, and the manner in which I deported myself; but he could take no man into her Majesty's printing office upon a regular engagement, who could not produce the most respectable references with regard to morals.

I could not but despise the man in my heart who laid such a stress upon morals, leaving grace out of the question; and viewed it as a deplorable instance of human depravity and self conceit; but for all that, I was obliged to accept of his terms, for I had an inward thirst and longing to distinguish myself in the great cause of religion, and I thought if once I could print my own works, how I would astonish mankind, and confound their self wisdom and their esteemed morality—blow up the idea of any dependence on good works, and *morality*, forsooth! And I weened that I might thus get me a name even higher than if I had been made a general of the Czar Peter's troops against the infidels.

I attended the office some hours every day, but got not much encouragement, though I was eager to learn every thing, and could soon have set types considerably well. It was here that I first conceived the idea of writing this journal, and having it printed, and applied to Mr. Watson to print it for me, telling him it was a religious parable such as the Pilgrim's Progress. He advised me to print it close, and make it a pamphlet, and then if it did not sell, it would not cost me much; but that religious pamphlets, especially if they had a shade of allegory in them, were the very rage of the day. I put my work to the press, and wrote early and late; and encouraging my companion to work at odd hours, and on Sundays, before the press-work of the second sheet was begun, we had the work all in types, corrected, and a clean copy thrown off for farther revisal. The first sheet was wrought off; and I never shall forget how my heart exulted when at the printing house this day, I saw what numbers of my works were to go abroad among mankind, and I determined with myself that I would not put the Border name of Elliot, which I had assumed, to the work.

THUS far have my History and Confessions been carried.

I must now furnish my Christian readers with a key to the process, management, and winding up of the whole matter; which I propose, by the assistance of God, to limit to a very few pages.

Chesters, July 27, 1712.—My hopes and prospects are a wreck. My precious journal is lost! consigned to the flames! My enemy hath found me out, and there is no hope of peace or rest for me on this side the grave.

In the beginning of the last week, my fellow lodger came home, running in a great panic, and told me a story of the devil having appeared twice in the printing house, assisting the workmen at the printing of my book, and that some of them had been frightened out of their wits. That the story was told to Mr. Watson, who till that time had never paid any attention to the treatise, but who, out of curiosity, began and read a part of it, and thereupon flew into a great rage, called my work a medley of lies and blasphemy, and ordered the whole to be consigned to the flames, blaming his foreman, and all connected with the press, for letting a work go so far, that was enough to bring down the vengeance of heaven on the concern.

If ever I shed tears through perfect bitterness of spirit it was at that time, but I hope it was more for the ignorance and folly of my countrymen than the overthrow of my own hopes. But my attention was suddenly aroused to other matters, by Linton mentioning that it was said by some in the office the devil had inquired for me.

'Surely you are not such a fool,' said I, 'as to believe that the devil really was in the printing office?'

'Oo, gud bless you sir! saw him myself, gave him a nod, and good-day. Rather a gentlemanly personage—Green Circassian hunting coat and turban—Like a foreigner—Has the power of vanishing in one moment though—Rather a suspicious circumstance that. Otherwise, his appearance not much against him.'

If the former intelligence thrilled me with grief, this did so with terror. I perceived who the personage was that had visited the printing house in order to further the progress of my work; and at the approach of every person to our lodgings, I from that instant trembled every bone, lest it should be my elevated and dreaded friend. I could not say I had ever received an office at his hand that was not friendly, yet these offices had been of a strange tendency; and the horror with which I now regarded him was unaccountable to myself. It was beyond description, conception, or the soul of man to bear. I took my printed sheets, the only copy of my unfinished work existing; and, on pretence of going straight to Mr. Watson's office, decamped from my lodgings at Portsburgh a little before the fall of evening, and took the road towards England.

As soon as I got clear of the city, I ran with a velocity I knew not before I had been capable of. I flew out the way towards Dalkeith so swiftly, that I often lost sight of the ground, and I said to myself, 'O that I had the wings of a dove, that I might fly to the farthest corners of the earth, to hide me from those against whom I have no power to stand!'

I travelled all that night and the next morning, exerting myself beyond my power; and about noon the following day I went into a yeoman's house, the name of which was Ellanshaws, and requested of the people a couch of any sort to lie down on, for I was ill, and could not proceed on my journey. They showed me to a stable-loft where there were two beds, on one of which I laid me down; and, falling into a sound sleep, I did not awake till the evening, that other three men came from the fields to sleep in the same place, one of whom lay down beside me, at which I was exceedingly glad. They fell all sound asleep, and I was terribly alarmed at a conversation I overheard somewhere outside the stable. I could not make out a sentence, but trembled to think I knew one of the voices at least, and rather than not be mistaken, I would that any man had run me through with a sword. I fell into a cold sweat, and once thought of instantly putting hand to my own life, as my only means of relief, (May the rash and sinful thought be in mercy forgiven!) when I heard as it were two persons at the door, contending, as I thought, about their right and interest in me. That the one was forcibly preventing the admission of the other, I could hear distinctly, and their language was mixed with something dreadful and mysterious. In an agony of terror, I awakened my snoring companion with great difficulty, and asked him, in a low whisper, who these were at the door? The man lay silent, and listening, till fairly awake,

and then asked if I had heard any thing? I said I had heard
strange voices contending at the door.

'Then I can tell you, lad, it has been something neither
good nor canny,' said he: 'It's no for naething that our
horses are snorking that gate.'

For the first time, I remarked that the animals were
snorting and rearing as if they wished to break through
the house. The man called to them by their names, and
ordered them to be quiet; but they raged still the more
furiously. He then roused his drowsy companions, who
were alike alarmed at the panic of the horses, all of them
declaring that they had never seen either Mause or Jolly
start in their lives before. My bed-fellow and another
then ventured down the ladder, and I heard one of them
then saying, 'Lord be wi' us! What can be i' the house?
The sweat's rinning off the poor beasts like water.'

They agreed to sally out together, and if possible to
reach the kitchen and bring a light. I was glad at this, but
not so much so when I heard the one man saying to the
other, in a whisper, 'I wish that stranger man may be
canny enough.'

'God kens!' said the other: 'It doesnae look unco weel.'

The lad in the other bed, hearing this, set up his head
in manifest affright as the other two departed for the
kitchen; and, I believe, he would have been glad to have
been in their company. This lad was next the ladder, at
which I was extremely glad, for had he not been there,
the world should not have induced me to wait the return
of these two men. They were not well gone, before I
heard another distinctly enter the stable, and come towards the ladder. The lad who was sitting up in his bed,
intent on the watch, called out, 'Wha's that there?
Walker, is that you? Purdie, I say, is it you?'

The darkling intruder paused for a few moments, and

then came towards the foot of the ladder. The horses broke loose, and snorting and neighing for terror, raged through the house. In all my life I never heard so frightful a commotion. The being that occasioned it all, now began to mount the ladder toward our loft, on which the lad in the bed next the ladder sprung from his couch, crying out, 'the L—d A——y preserve us! what can it be?' With that he sped across the loft, and by my bed, praying lustily all the way; and, throwing himself from the other end of the loft into a manger, he darted, naked as he was, through among the furious horses, and making the door, that stood open, in a moment he vanished and left me in the lurch. Powerless with terror, and calling out fearfully, I tried to follow his example; but not knowing the situation of the places with regard to one another, I missed the manger, and fell on the pavement in one of the stalls. I was both stunned and lamed on the knee; but terror prevailing, I got up and tried to escape. It was out of my power; for there were divisions and cross divisions in the house, and mad horses smashing every thing before them, so that I knew not so much as on what side of the house the door was. Two or three times was I knocked down by the animals, but all the while I never stinted crying out with all my power. At length, I was seized by the throat and hair of the head, and dragged away, I wist not whither. My voice was now laid, and all my powers, both mental and bodily, totally overcome; and I remember no more till I found myself lying naked on the kitchen table of the farm house, and something like a horse's rug thrown over me. The only hint that I got from the people of the house on coming to myself was, that my absence would be good company; and that they had got me in a woful state, one which they did not chuse to describe, or hear described.

As soon as day-light appeared, I was packed about my business, with the hisses and execrations of the yeoman's family, who viewed me as a being to be shunned, ascribing to me the visitations of that unholy night. Again was I on my way southward, as lonely, hopeless, and degraded a being as was to be found on life's weary round. As I limped out the way, I wept, thinking of what I might have been, and what I really had become: of my high and flourishing hopes, when I set out as the avenger of God on the sinful children of men; of all that I had dared for the exaltation and progress of the truth; and it was with great difficulty that my faith remained unshaken, yet was I preserved from that sin, and comforted myself with the certainty, that the believer's progress through life is one of warfare and suffering.

My case was indeed a pitiable one. I was lame, hungry, fatigued, and my resources on the very eve of being exhausted. Yet these were but secondary miseries, and hardly worthy of a thought, compared with those I suffered inwardly. I not only looked around me with terror at every one that approached, but I was become a terror to myself; or rather, my body and soul were become terrors to each other; and, had it been possible, I felt as if they would have gone to war. I dared not look at my face in a glass, for I shuddered at my own image and likeness. I dreaded the dawning, and trembled at the approach of night, nor was there one thing in nature that afforded me the least delight.

In this deplorable state of body and mind, was I jogging on towards the Tweed, by the side of the small river called Ellan, when, just at the narrowest part of the glen, whom should I meet full in the face, but the very being in all the universe of God I would the most gladly have shunned. I had no power to fly from him, neither durst I, for the spirit within me, accuse him of falsehood, and renounce his fellowship. I stood before him like a condemned criminal, staring him in the face, ready to be winded, twisted, and tormented as he pleased. He regarded me with a sad and solemn look. How changed was now that majestic countenance, to one of haggard despair—changed in all save the extraordinary likeness to my late brother, a resemblance which misfortune and despair tended only to heighten. There were no kind greetings passed between us at meeting, like those which pass between the men of the world; he looked on me with eyes that froze the currents of my blood, but spoke not, till I assumed as much courage as to articulate—'You here! I hope you have brought me tidings of comfort?'

'Tidings of despair!' said he. 'But such tidings as the timid and the ungrateful deserve, and have reason to expect. You are an outlaw, and a vagabond in your country, and a high reward is offered for your apprehension. The enraged populace have burnt your house, and all that is within it; and the farmers on the land bless themselves at being rid of you. So fare it with every one who puts his hand to the great work of man's restoration to freedom, and draweth back, contemning the light that is within him! Your enormities caused me to leave you to yourself for a season, and you see what the issue has been. You have given some evil ones power over you, who long to devour you, both soul and body, and it has required all my power and influence to save you. Had it not been for my hand, you had been torn in pieces last night; but for once I prevailed. We must leave this land forthwith, for here there is neither peace, safety, nor comfort for us. Do you now, and here, pledge yourself to one who has so often saved your life, and has put his own at stake to do so? Do you pledge yourself that you will henceforth be guided by my counsel, and follow me whithersoever I chuse to lead?'

'I have always been swayed by your counsel,' said I, 'and for your sake, principally, am I sorry, that all our measures have proved abortive. But I hope still to be useful in my native isle, therefore let me plead that your highness will abandon a poor despised and outcast wretch to his fate, and betake you to your realms, where your presence cannot but be greatly wanted.'

'Would that I could do so!' said he wofully. 'But to talk of that is to talk of an impossibility. I am wedded to you so closely, that I feel as if I were the same person. Our essences are one, our bodies and spirits being united, so, that I am drawn towards you as by magnetism, and wherever you are, there must my presence be with you.'

Perceiving how this assurance affected me, he began to chide me most bitterly for my ingratitude; and then he assumed such looks, that it was impossible for me longer to bear them; therefore I staggered out the way, begging and beseeching of him to give me up to my fate, and hardly knowing what I said; for it struck me, that, with all his assumed appearance of misery and wretchedness, there were traits of exultation in his hideous countenance, manifesting a secret and inward joy at my utter despair.

It was long before I durst look over my shoulder, but when I did so, I perceived this ruined and debased potentate coming slowly on the same path, and I prayed that the Lord would hide me in the bowels of the earth, or depths of the sea. When I crossed the Tweed, I perceived him still a little behind me; and my despair being then at its height, I cursed the time I first met with such a tormentor; though, on a little recollection it occurred, that it was at that blessed time when I was solemnly dedicated to the Lord, and assured of my final election, and confirmation, by an eternal decree never to be annulled. This being my sole and only comfort, I recalled my curse upon the time, and repented me of my rashness.

After crossing the Tweed, I saw no more of my persecutor that day, and had hopes that he had left me for a season; but, alas, what hope was there of my relief after the declaration I had so lately heard! I took up my lodgings that night in a small miserable inn in the village of Ancrum, of which the people seemed alike poor and ignorant. Before going to bed, I asked if it was customary with them to have family worship of evenings? The man answered, that they were so hard set with the world, they often could not get time, but if I would be so kind as officiate they would be much obliged to me. I accepted the invitation, being afraid to go to rest lest the commotions of the foregoing night might be renewed, and continued the worship as long as in decency I could. The poor people thanked me, hoped my prayers would be heard both on their account and my own, seemed much taken with my abilities, and wondered how a man of my powerful eloquence chanced to be wandering about in a condition so forlorn. I said I was a poor student of theology, on my way to Oxford. They stared at one another with expressions of wonder, disappointment, and fear. I afterwards came to learn, that the term *theology* was by them quite misunderstood, and that they had some crude conceptions that nothing was taught at Oxford but the *black arts*, which ridiculous idea prevailed over all the south of Scotland. For the present I could not understand what the people meant, and less so, when the man asked me, with deep concern, 'If I was serious in my intentions of going to Oxford? He hoped not, and that I would be better guided.'

I said my education wanted finishing;—but he remarked, that the Oxford arts were a bad finish for a religious man's education.—Finally, I requested him to sleep with me, or in my room all the night, as I wanted some serious and religious conversation with him, and likewise to convince him that the study of the fine arts, though not absolutely necessary, were not incompatible with the character of a Christian divine. He shook his head, and wondered how I could call them *fine arts*— hoped I did not mean to convince him by any ocular demonstration, and at length reluctantly condescended to sleep with me, and let the lass and wife sleep together for one night. I believe he would have declined it, had it not been some hints from his wife, stating, that it was a good arrangement, by which I understood there were only two beds in the house, and that when I was preferred to the lass's bed, she had one to shift for.

The landlord and I accordingly retired to our homely bed, and conversed for some time about indifferent matters, till he fell sound asleep. Not so with me: I had that within which would not suffer me to close my eyes; and about the dead of night, I again heard the same noises and contention begin outside the house, as I had heard the night before; and again I heard it was about a sovereign and peculiar right in me. At one time the noise was on the top of the house, straight above our bed, as if the one party were breaking through the roof, and the other forcibly preventing it; at another time it was at the door, and at a third time at the window; but still mine host lay sound by my side, and did not waken. I was seized with terrors indefinable, and prayed fervently, but did not attempt rousing my sleeping companion until I saw if no better could be done. The women, however, were alarmed, and, rushing into our apartment, exclaimed that all the devils in hell were besieging the house. Then, indeed, the landlord awoke, and it was time for him, for the tumult had increased to such a degree, that it shook the house to its foundations, being louder and more furious than I could have conceived the heat of battle to be when the volleys of artillery are mixed with groans, shouts, and blasphemous cursing. It thundered and lightened; and there were screams, groans, laughter, and execrations, all intermingled.

I lay trembling and bathed in a cold perspiration, but was soon obliged to bestir myself, the inmates attacking me one after the other.

'O, Tam Douglas! Tam Douglas! haste ye an' rise out fra-yont that incarnal devil!' cried the wife: 'Ye are in ayont the auld ane himsel, for our lass Tibbie saw his cloven cloots last night.'

'Lord forbid!' roared Tam Douglas, and darted over the bed like a flying fish. Then, hearing the unearthly tumult with which he was surrounded, he returned to the side of the bed, and addressed me thus, with long and fearful intervals:

'If ye be the deil, rise up, an' depart in peace out o' this house—afore the bedstrae take kindling about ye, an' than it'll maybe be the waur for ye—Get up—an' gang awa out amang your cronies, like a good—lad—There's nae body here wishes you ony ill—D'ye hear me?'

'Friend,' said I, 'no Christian would turn out a fellow creature on such a night as this, and in the midst of such a commotion of the villagers.'

'Na, if ye be a mortal man,' said he, 'which I rather think, from the use you made of the holy book—Nane o' your practical jokes on strangers an' honest foks. These are some o' your Oxford tricks, an' I'll thank you to be ower wi' them.—Gracious heaven, they are brikkin through the house at a' the four corners at the same time!'

The lass Tibby, seeing the innkeeper was not going

to prevail with me to rise, flew toward the bed in desperation, and seizing me by the waist, soon landed me on the
floor, saying: 'Be ye deil, be ye chiel, ye's no lie there till
baith the house an' us be swallowed up!'

Her master and mistress applauding the deed, I was
obliged to attempt dressing myself, a task to which my
powers were quite inadequate in the state I was in, but I
was readily assisted by every one of the three; and as soon
as they got my clothes thrust on in a loose way, they shut
their eyes lest they should see what might drive them
distracted, and thrust me out to the street, cursing me,
and calling on the fiends to take their prey and begone.

The scene that ensued is neither to be described, nor
believed, if it were. I was momently surrounded by a
number of hideous fiends, who gnashed on me with their
teeth, and clenched their crimson paws in my face; and
at the same instant I was seized by the collar of my coat
behind, by my dreaded and devoted friend, who pushed
me on, and, with his gilded rapier waving and brandishing
around me, defended me against all their united attacks.
Horrible as my assailants were in appearance, (and they
had all monstrous shapes,) I felt that I would rather have
fallen into their hands, than be thus led away captive by my
defender at his will and pleasure, without having the right
or power to say my life, or any part of my will, was my
own. I could not even thank him for his potent guardian-
ship, but hung down my head, and moved on I knew
not whither, like a criminal led to execution, and still the
infernal combat continued, till about the dawning, at
which time I looked up, and all the fiends were expelled
but one, who kept at a distance; and still my persecutor
and defender pushed me by the neck before him.

At length he desired me to sit down and take some rest,
with which I complied, for I had great need of it, and

wanted the power to withstand what he desired. There, for a whole morning did he detain me, tormenting me with reflections on the past, and pointing out the horrors of the future, until a thousand times I wished myself non-existent. 'I have attached myself to your wayward fortune,' said he; 'and it has been my ruin as well as thine. Ungrateful as you are, I cannot give you up to be devoured; but this is a life that it is impossible to brook longer. Since our hopes are blasted in this world, and all our schemes of grandeur overthrown; and since our everlasting destiny is settled by a decree which no act of ours can invalidate, let us fall by our own hands, or by the hands of each other; die like heroes; and, throwing off this frame of dross and corruption, mingle with the pure ethereal essence of existence, from which we derived our being.'

I shuddered at a view of the dreadful alternative, yet was obliged to confess that in my present circumstances existence was not to be borne. It was in vain that I reasoned on the sinfulness of the deed, and on its damning nature; he made me condemn myself out of my own mouth, by allowing the absolute nature of justifying grace, and the impossibility of the elect ever falling from the faith, or the glorious end to which they were called; and then he said, this granted, self-destruction was the act of a hero, and none but a coward would shrink from it, to suffer a hundred times more every day and night that passed over his head.

I said I was still contented to be that coward; and all that I begged of him was, to leave me to my fortune for a season, and to the just judgment of my creator; but he said his word and honour were engaged on my behoof, and these, in such a case, were not to be violated. 'If you will not pity yourself, have pity on me,' added he: 'turn your eyes on me, and behold to what I am reduced.'

Involuntarily did I turn round at the request, and caught a half glance of his features. May no eye destined to reflect the beauties of the New Jerusalem inward upon the beatific soul, behold such a sight as mine then beheld! My immortal spirit, blood, and bones, were all withered at the blasting sight; and I arose and withdrew, with groanings which the pangs of death shall never wring from me.

Not daring to look behind me, I crept on my way, and that night reached this hamlet on the Scottish border; and being grown reckless of danger, and hardened to scenes of horror, I took up my lodging with a poor hind, who is a widower, and who could only accommodate me with a bed of rushes at his fire-side. At midnight I heard some strange sounds, too much resembling those to which I had of late been inured; but they kept at a distance, and I was soon persuaded that there was a power protected that house superior to those that contended for, or had the mastery over me. Overjoyed at finding such an asylum, I remained in the humble cot. This is the third day I have lived under the roof, freed of my hellish assailants, spending my time in prayer, and writing out this my journal, which I have fashioned to stick in with my printed work, and to which I intend to add portions while I remain in this pilgrimage state, which, I find too well, cannot be long.

August 3, 1712.—This morning the hind has brought me word from Redesdale, whither he had been for coals, that a stranger gentleman had been traversing that country, making the most earnest inquiries after me, or one of the same appearance; and from the description that he brought of this stranger, I could easily perceive who it was. Rejoicing that my tormentor has lost traces of me for once, I am making haste to leave my asylum, on pretence of following this stranger, but in reality to conceal myself still more completely from his search. Perhaps this may be the last sentence ever I am destined to write. If so, farewell Christian reader! May God grant to thee a happier destiny than has been allotted to me here on earth, and the same assurance of acceptance above! *Amen*.

Ault-Righ, *August* 24, 1712.—Here am I, set down on the open moor to add one sentence more to my woful journal; and then, farewell all beneath the sun!

On leaving the hind's cottage on the Border, I hasted to the north-west, because in that quarter I perceived the highest and wildest hills before me. As I crossed the mountains above Hawick, I exchanged clothes with a poor homely shepherd, whom I found lying on a hill side, singing to himself some woful love ditty. He was glad of the change, and proud of his saintly apparel; and I was no less delighted with mine, by which I now supposed myself completely disguised; and I found moreover that in this garb of a common shepherd I was made welcome in every house. I slept the first night in a farm-house nigh to the church of Roberton, without hearing or seeing aught extraordinary; yet I observed next morning that all the servants kept aloof from me, and regarded me with looks of aversion. The next night I came to this house, where the farmer engaged me as a shepherd; and finding him a kind, worthy, and religious man, I accepted of his terms with great gladness. I had not, however, gone many times to the sheep, before all the rest of the shepherds told my master, that I knew nothing about herding, and begged of him to dismiss me. He perceived too well the truth of their intelligence; but being much taken with my learning, and religious conversation, he would not put me away, but set me to herd his cattle.

It was lucky for me, that before I came here, a report

had prevailed, perhaps for an age, that this farm-house was haunted at certain seasons by a ghost. I say it was lucky for me, for I had not been in it many days before the same appalling noises began to prevail around me about midnight, often continuing till near the dawning. Still they kept aloof, and without doors; for this gentleman's house, like the cottage I was in formerly, seemed to be a sanctuary from all demoniacal power. He appears to be a good man and a just, and mocks at the idea of supernatural agency, and he either does not hear these persecuting spirits, or will not acknowledge it, though of late he appears much perturbed.

The consternation of the menials has been extreme. They ascribe all to the ghost, and tell frightful stories of murders having been committed there long ago. Of late, however, they are beginning to suspect that it is I that am haunted; and as I have never given them any satisfactory account of myself, they are whispering that I am a murderer, and haunted by the spirits of those I have slain.

August 30.—This day I have been informed, that I am to be banished the dwelling-house by night, and to sleep in an out-house by myself, to try if the family can get any rest when freed of my presence. I have peremptorily refused acquiescence, on which my master's brother struck me, and kicked me with his foot. My body being quite exhausted by suffering, I am grown weak and feeble both in mind and bodily frame, and actually unable to resent any insult or injury. I am the child of earthly misery and despair, if ever there was one existent. My master is still my friend; but there are so many masters here, and every one of them alike harsh to me, that I wish myself in my grave every hour of the day. If I am driven from the family sanctuary by night, I know I shall be torn in pieces before morning; and then who will deign or dare to gather up my mangled limbs, and give them honoured burial.

My last hour is arrived: I see my tormentor once more approaching me in this wild. Oh, that the earth would swallow me up, or the hill fall and cover me! Farewell for ever!

September 7, 1712.—My devoted, princely, but sanguine friend, has been with me again and again. My time is expired, and I find a relief beyond measure, for he has fully convinced me that no act of mine can mar the eternal counsel, or in the smallest degree alter or extenuate one event which was decreed before the foundations of the world were laid. He said he had watched over me with the greatest anxiety, but perceiving my rooted aversion towards him, he had forborn troubling me with his presence. But now, seeing that I was certainly to be driven from my sanctuary that night, and that there would be a number of infernals watching to make a prey of my body, he came to caution me not to despair, for that he would protect me at all risks, if the power remained with him. He then repeated an ejaculatory prayer, which I was to pronounce, if in great extremity. I objected to the words as equivocal, and susceptible of being rendered in a meaning perfectly dreadful; but he reasoned against this, and all reasoning with him is to no purpose. He said he did not ask me to repeat the words, unless greatly straitened; and that I saw his strength and power giving way, and when perhaps nothing else could save me.

The dreaded hour of night arrived; and, as he said, I was expelled from the family residence, and ordered to a byre, or cow-house, that stood parallel with the dwelling-house behind, where, on a divot loft, my humble bedstead stood, and the cattle grunted and puffed below me. How unlike the splendid halls of Dalcastle! And to what I am now reduced, let the reflecting reader judge. Lord, thou knowest all that I have done for thy cause on earth! Why then art thou laying thy hands so sore upon me? Why hast thou set me as a butt of thy malice? But thy will must be done! Thou wilt repay me in a better world. *Amen*.

September 8.—My first night of trial in this place is overpast! Would that it were the last that I should ever see in this detested world! If the horrors of hell are equal to those I have suffered, eternity will be of short duration there, for no created energy can support them for one single month, or week. I have been buffeted as never living creature was. My vitals have all been torn, and every faculty and feeling of my soul racked, and tormented into callous insensibility. I was even hung by the locks over a yawning chasm, to which I could perceive no bottom, and then—not till then, did I repeat the tremendous prayer!—I was instantly at liberty; and what I now am, the Almighty knows! *Amen*.

September 18, 1712.—Still am I living, though liker to a vision than a human being; but this is my last day of mortal existence. Unable to resist any longer, I pledged myself to my devoted friend, that on this day we should die together, and trust to the charity of the children of men for a grave. I am solemnly pledged; and though I dared to repent, I am aware he will not be gainsaid, for he is raging with despair at his fallen and decayed majesty, and there is some miserable comfort in the idea that my tormentor shall fall with me. Farewell, world, with all thy miseries; for comforts or enjoyments hast thou none! Farewell, woman, whom I have despised and shunned; and man, whom I have hated; whom, nevertheless, I desire to leave in charity! And thou, sun, bright emblem of a far brighter effulgence, I bid farewell to thee also! I do not now take my last look of thee, for to thy glorious orb shall a poor suicide's last earthly look be raised. But, ah! who is yon that I see approaching furiously—his stern face blackened with horrid despair! My hour is at hand.—Almighty God, what is this that I am about to do! The hour of repentance is past, and now my fate is inevitable.—*Amen, for ever!* I will now seal up my little book, and conceal it; and cursed be he who trieth to alter or amend!

END OF THE MEMOIR

WHAT can this work be? Sure, you will say, it must be an allegory; or (as the writer calls it) a religious PARABLE, showing the dreadful danger of self-righteousness? I cannot tell. Attend to the sequel: which is a thing so extraordinary, so unprecedented, and so far out of the common course of human events, that if there were not hundreds of living witnesses to attest the truth of it, I would not bid any rational being believe it.

In the first place, take the following extract from an authentic letter, published in *Blackwood's Magazine for August*, 1823.[1]

'On the top of a wild height called Cowanscroft, where the lands of three proprietors meet all at one point, there has been for long and many years the grave of a suicide marked out by a stone standing at the head, and another at the feet. Often have I stood musing over it myself, when a shepherd on one of the farms, of which it formed the extreme boundary, and thinking what could induce a young man, who had scarcely reached the prime of life, to brave his Maker, and rush into his presence by an act of

his own erring hand, and one so unnatural and preposterous. But it never once occurred to me, as an object of
curiosity, to dig up the mouldering bones of the culprit,
which I considered as the most revolting of all objects.
The thing was, however, done last month, and a discovery
made of one of the greatest natural phenomena that I have
heard of in this country.

'The little traditionary history that remains of this
unfortunate youth, is altogether a singular one. He was
not a native of the place, nor would he ever tell from what
place he came; but he was remarkable for a deep, thoughtful, and sullen disposition. There was nothing against his
character that any body knew of here, and he had been a
considerable time in the place. The last service he was in
was with a Mr. Anderson of Eltrive, (Ault-Righ, *the
King's burn*,) who died about 100 years ago, and who had
hired him during the summer to herd a stock of young
cattle in Eltrive Hope. It happened one day in the month
of September, that James Anderson, his master's son,
went with this young man to the Hope to divert himself.
The herd had his dinner along with him, and about one
o'clock, when the boy proposed going home, the former
pressed him very hard to stay and take share of his dinner;
but the boy refused, for fear his parents might be alarmed
about him, and said he *would* go home: on which the herd
said to him, "Then, if ye winna stay with me, James, ye
may depend on't I'll cut my throat afore ye come back
again."

'I have heard it likewise reported, but only by one
person, that there had been some things stolen out of his
master's house a good while before, and that the boy had
discovered a silver knife and fork, that was a part of the
stolen property, in the herd's possession that day, and that
it was this discovery that drove him to despair.

'The boy did not return to the Hope that afternoon; and, before evening, a man coming in at the pass called *The Hart Loup*, with a drove of lambs, on the way for Edinburgh, perceived something like a man standing in a strange frightful position at the side of one of Eldinhope hay-ricks. The driver's attention was riveted on this strange uncouth figure, and as the drove-road passed at no great distance from the spot, he first called, but receiving no answer, he went up to the spot, and behold it was the above-mentioned young man, who had hung himself in the hay rope that was tying down the rick.

'This was accounted a great wonder; and every one said, if the devil had not assisted him it was impossible the thing could have been done; for, in general, these ropes are so brittle, being made of green hay, that they will scarcely bear to be bound over the rick. And the more to horrify the good people of this neighbourhood, the driver said, when he first came in view, *he could almost give his oath* that he saw two people busily engaged at the hay-rick, going round it and round it, and he thought they were dressing it.

'If this asseveration approximated at all to truth, it makes this evident at least, that the unfortunate young man had hanged himself after the man with the lambs came in view. He was, however, quite dead when he cut him down. He had fastened two of the old hay-ropes at the bottom of the rick on one side, (indeed they are all fastened so when first laid on,) so that he had nothing to do but to loosen two of the ends on the other side. These he had tied in a knot round his neck, and then slackening his knees, and letting himself down gradually, till the hay-rope bore all his weight, he had contrived to put an end to his existence in that way. Now the fact is, that if you try all the ropes that are thrown over all the outfield hay-ricks in Scotland, there is not one among a thousand of them will hang a colley dog; so that the manner of this wretch's death was rather a singular circumstance.

'Early next morning, Mr. Anderson's servants went reluctantly away, and, taking an old blanket with them for a winding sheet, they rolled up the body of the deceased, first in his own plaid, letting the hay-rope still remain about his neck, and then rolling the old blanket over all, they bore the loathed remains away to the distance of three miles or so, on spokes, to the top of Cowan's-Croft, at the very point where the Duke of Buccleuch's land, the Laird of Drummelzier's, and Lord Napier's, meet, and there they buried him, with all that he had on and about him, silver knife and fork and altogether. Thus far went tradition, and no one ever disputed one jot of the disgusting oral tale.

'A nephew of that Mr. Anderson's who was with the hapless youth that day he died, says, that, as far as he can gather from the relations of friends that he remembers, and of that same uncle in particular, it is one hundred and five years next month, (that is September, 1823), since that event happened; and I think it likely that this gentleman's information is correct. But sundry other people, much older than he, whom I have consulted, pretend that it is six or seven years more. They say they have heard that Mr. James Anderson was then a boy ten years of age; that he lived to an old age, upwards of fourscore, and it is two and forty years since he died. Whichever way it may be, it was about that period some way, of that there is no doubt.

'It so happened, that two young men, William Shiel and W. Sword, were out, on an adjoining height, this summer, casting peats, and it came into their heads to open this grave in the wilderness, and see if there were any of the bones of the suicide of former ages and centuries remaining. They did so, but opened only one half of the grave, beginning at the head and about the middle at the same time. It was not long till they came upon the old blanket—I think they said not much more than a foot from the surface. They tore that open, and there was the hay rope lying stretched down alongst his breast, so fresh that they saw at first sight that it was made of *risp*, a sort of long sword-grass that grows about marshes and the sides of lakes. One of the young men seized the rope and pulled by it, but the old enchantment of the devil remained,—it would not break; and so he pulled and pulled at it, till behold the body came up into a sitting posture, with a broad blue bonnet on its head, and its plaid around it, all as fresh as that day it was laid in! I never heard of a preservation so wonderful, if it be true as was related to me, for still I have not had the curiosity to go and view the body myself. The features were all so plain, that an acquaintance might easily have known him. One of the lads gripped the face of the corpse with his finger and thumb, and the cheeks felt quite soft and fleshy, but the dimples remained and did not spring out again. He had fine yellow hair, about nine inches long; but not a hair of it could they pull out till they cut part of it off with a knife. They also cut off some portions of his clothes, which were all quite fresh, and distributed them among their acquaintances, sending a portion to me, among the rest, to keep as natural curiosities. Several gentlemen have in a manner forced me to give them fragments of these enchanted garments: I have, however, retained a small portion for you, which I send along with this, being a piece of his plaid, and another of his waistcoat breast, which you will see are still as fresh as that day they were laid in the grave.

'His broad blue bonnet was sent to Edinburgh several weeks ago, to the great regret of some gentlemen connected with the land, who wished to have it for a keepsake. For my part, fond as I am of blue bonnets, and broad ones in particular, I declare I durst not have worn that one. There was nothing of the silver knife and fork discovered, that I heard of, nor was it very likely it should: but it would appear he had been very near run of cash, which I daresay had been the cause of his utter despair; for, on searching his pockets, nothing was found but three old Scots halfpennies. These young men meeting with another shepherd afterwards, his curiosity was so much excited that they went and digged up the curious remains a second time, which was a pity, as it is likely that by these exposures to the air, and from the impossibility of burying it up again as closely as it was before, the flesh will now fall to dust.'

*　　*　　*

The letter from which the above is an extract, is signed JAMES HOGG, and dated from Altrive Lake, *August 1st*, 1823. It bears the stamp of authenticity in every line; yet, so often had I been hoaxed by the ingenious fancies displayed in that Magazine, that when this relation met my eye, I did not believe it; but from the moment that I perused it, I half formed the resolution of investigating these wonderful remains personally, if any such existed; for, in the immediate vicinity of the scene, as I supposed, I knew of more attractive metal than the dilapidated remains of mouldering suicides.

Accordingly, having some business in Edinburgh in September last, and being obliged to wait a few days for the arrival of a friend from London, I took that opportunity to pay a visit to my townsman and fellow collegian,

Mr. L——t of C——d,[1] advocate. I mentioned to him Hogg's letter, asking him if the statement was founded at all on truth. His answer was, 'I suppose so. For my part I never doubted the thing, having been told that there has been a deal of talking about it up in the Forest for some time past. But, God knows! Hogg has imposed as ingenious lies on the public ere now.'

I said, if it was within reach, I should like exceedingly to visit both the Shepherd and the Scots mummy he had described. Mr. L——t assented at the first proposal, saying he had no objections to take a ride that length with me, and make the fellow produce his credentials: That we would have a delightful jaunt through a romantic and now classical country, and some good sport into the bargain, provided he could procure a horse for me, from his father-in-law, next day. He sent up to a Mr. L——w[2] to inquire, who returned for answer, that there was an excellent pony at my service, and that he himself would accompany us, being obliged to attend a great sheep fair at Thirlestane; and that he was certain the Shepherd would be there likewise.

Mr. L——t said that was the very man we wanted to make our party complete; and at an early hour next morning we started for the ewe fair of Thirlestane, taking Blackwood's Magazine for August along with us. We rode through the ancient royal burgh of Selkirk,—halted and corned our horses at a romantic village, nigh to some deep linns on the Ettrick, and reached the market ground at Thirlestane-green a little before midday. We soon found Hogg, standing near the *foot* of the market, as he called it, beside a great drove of *paulies*, a species of stock that I never heard of before. They were small sheep, striped on the backs with red chalk. Mr. L——t introduced me to him as a great wool-stapler, come to raise the price of that article; but he eyed me with distrust, and turning his back on us, answered, 'I hae sell'd mine.'

I followed, and shewing him the above-quoted letter, said I was exceedingly curious to have a look of these singular remains he had so ingeniously described; but he only answered me with the remark, that 'It was a queer fancy for a woo-stapler to tak.'

His two friends then requested him to accompany us to the spot, and to take some of his shepherds with us to assist in raising the body; but he spurned at the idea, saying, 'Od bless ye, lad! I hae ither matters to mind. I hae a' thae paulies to sell, an' a' yon Highland stotts down on the green every ane; an' then I hae ten scores o' yowes to buy after, an' if I canna first sell my ain stock, I canna buy nae ither body's. I hae mair ado than I can manage the day, foreby ganging to houk up hunder-year-auld banes.'

Finding that we could make nothing of him, we left him with his *paulies*, Highland stotts, grey jacket, and broad blue bonnet, to go in search of some other guide. L——w soon found one, for he seemed acquainted with every person in the fair. We got a fine old shepherd, named W——m B——e,[1] a great original, and a very obliging and civil man, who asked no conditions but that we should not speak of it, because he did not wish it to come to his master's ears, that he had been engaged in *sic a profane thing*. We promised strict secrecy; and accompanied by another farmer, Mr. S——t, and old B——e, we proceeded to the grave, which B——e described as about a mile and a half distant from the market ground.

We went into a shepherd's cot to get a drink of milk, when I read to our guide Mr. Hogg's description, asking him if he thought it correct? He said there was hardly a bit o't correct, for the grave was not on the hill of Cowan's-Croft, nor yet on the point where three lairds' lands met, but on the top of a hill called the Faw-Law, where there was no land that was not the Duke of Buccleuch's within a quarter of a mile. He added that it was a wonder how the poet could be mistaken there, who once herded the very ground where the grave is, and saw both hills from his own window. Mr. L——w testified great surprise at such a singular blunder, as also how the body came *not* to be buried at the meeting of three or four lairds' lands, which had always been customary in the south of Scotland. Our guide said he had always heard it reported, that the Eltrive men, with Mr. David Anderson at their head, had risen before day on the Monday morning, it having been on the Sabbath day that the man *put down* himself; and that they set out with the intention of burying him on Cowan's-Croft, where three marches met at a point. But it having been an invariable rule to bury such *lost sinners* before the rising of the sun, these five men were overtaken by day-light, as they passed the house of Berry-Knowe; and by the time they reached the top of the Faw-Law, the sun was beginning to skair the east. On this they laid down the body, and digged a deep grave with all expedition; but when they had done, it was too short, and the body being stiff, it would not go down, on which Mr. David Anderson looking to the east, and perceiving that the sun would be up on them in a few minutes, set his foot on the suicide's brow, and tramped down his head into the grave with his iron-heeled shoe, until his nose and skull crashed again, and at the same time uttered a terrible curse on the wretch who had disgraced the family, and given them all this trouble. This anecdote, our guide said, he had heard when a boy, from the mouth of

Robert Laidlaw, one of the five men who buried the body.

We soon reached the spot, and I confess I felt a singular sensation, when I saw the grey stone[1] standing at the head, and another at the feet, and the one half of the grave manifestly new digged, and closed up again as had been described. I could still scarcely deem the thing to be a reality, for the ground did not appear to be wet, but a kind of dry rotten moss. On looking around, we found some fragments of clothes, some teeth, and part of a pocket-book, which had not been returned into the grave, when the body had been last raised, for it had been twice raised before this, but only from the loins upward.

To work we fell with two spades, and soon cleared away the whole of the covering. The part of the grave that had been opened before, was filled with mossy mortar, which impeded us exceedingly, and entirely prevented a proper investigation of the fore parts of the body. I will describe every thing as I saw it before four respectable witnesses, whose names I shall publish at large if permitted. A number of the bones came up separately; for with the constant flow of liquid stuff into the deep grave, we could not see to preserve them in their places. At length great loads of coarse clothes, blanketing, plaiding, &c. appeared; we tried to lift these regularly up, and on doing so, part of a skeleton came up, but no flesh, save a little that was hanging in dark flitters about the spine, but which had no consistence; it was merely the appearance of flesh without the substance. The head was wanting; and I being very anxious to possess the skull, the search was renewed among the mortar and rags. We first found a part of the scalp, with the long hair firm on it; which, on being cleaned, is neither black nor fair, but of a darkish dusk, the most common of any other colour. Soon afterwards we found the skull, but it was not complete. A spade had damaged it, and one of the temple quarters was wanting. I am no phrenologist, not knowing one organ from another, but I thought the skull of that wretched man no study. If it was particular for any thing, it was for a smooth, almost perfect rotundity, with only a little protuberance above the vent of the ear.

When we came to the part of the grave that had never been opened before, the appearance of every thing was quite different. There the remains lay under a close vault of moss, and within a vacant space; and I suppose, by the digging in the former part of the grave, that part had been deepened, and drawn the moisture away from this part, for here all was perfect. The breeches still suited the thigh, the stocking the leg, and the garters were wrapt as neatly and as firm below the knee as if they had been newly tied. The shoes were all opened in the seams, the hemp having decayed, but the soles, upper leathers, and wooden heels, which were made of birch, were all as fresh as any of those we wore. There was one thing I could not help remarking, that in the inside of one of the shoes there was a layer of cow's dung, about one eighth of an inch thick, and in the hollow of the sole fully one fourth of an inch. It was firm, green, and fresh; and proved that he had been working in a byre. His clothes were all of a singular ancient cut, and no less singular in their texture. Their durability certainly would have been prodigious; for in thickness, coarseness, and strength, I never saw any cloth in the smallest degree to equal them. His coat was a frock coat, of a yellowish drab colour, with wide sleeves. It is tweeled, milled, and thicker than a carpet. I cut off two of the skirts and brought them with me. His vest was of striped serge, such as I have often seen worn by country people. It was lined and backed with white stuff. The breeches were a sort of striped plaiding, which I never saw worn, but which our guide assured us was very common in the country once, though, from the old clothes which he had seen remaining of it, he judged that it could not be less than 200 years since it was in fashion. His garters were of worsted, and striped with black or blue; his stockings gray, and wanting the feet. I brought samples of all along with me. I have likewise now got possession of the bonnet, which puzzles me most of all. It is not conformable with the rest of the dress. It is neither a broad bonnet, nor a Border bonnet; for there is an open behind, for tying, which no genuine Border bonnet, I am told, ever had. It seems to have been a Highland bonnet, worn in a flat way like a scone on the crown, such as is sometimes still seen in the west of Scotland. All the limbs, from the loins to the toes, seemed perfect and entire, but they could not bear handling. Before we got them returned again into the grave, they were all shaken to pieces, except the thighs, which continued to retain a kind of flabby form.

All his clothes that were sewed with linen yarn were lying in separate portions, the thread having rotten; but such as were sewed with worsted remained perfectly firm and sound. Among such a confusion, we had hard work to find out all his pockets, and our guide supposed, that, after all, we did not find above the half of them. In his vest pocket was a long clasp knife, very sharp; the haft was thin, and the scales shone as if there had been silver inside. Mr. Sc—t took it with him, and presented it to his neighbour, Mr. R——n of W—n L—e,[1] who still has it in his possession. We found a comb, a gimblet, a vial, a small neat square board, a pair of plated knee-buckles, and several samples of cloth of different kinds, rolled neatly up within one another. At length, while we were busy on the search, Mr. L——t picked up a leathern case, which seemed to have been wrapped round and round by some ribbon, or cord, that had been rotten from it, for the swaddling marks still remained. Both L——w and B——e called out that 'it was the tabacco spleuchan, and a well-filled ane too;' but on opening it out, we found, to our great astonishment, that it contained a *printed pamphlet*. We were all curious to see what sort of a pamphlet such a person would read; what it could contain that he seemed to have had such a care about? for the slough in which it was rolled, was fine chamois leather; what colour it had been, could not be known. But the pamphlet was wrapped so close together, and so damp, rotten, and yellow, that it seemed one solid piece. We all concluded, from some words that we could make out, that it was a religious tract, but that it would be impossible to make any thing of it. Mr. L——w remarked that it was a great pity if a few sentences could not be made out, for that it was a question what might be contained in that little book; and then he requested Mr. L——t to give it to me, as he had so many things of literature and law to attend to, that he would never think more of it. He replied, that either of us were heartily welcome to it, for that he had thought of returning it into the grave, if he could have made out but a line or two, to have seen what was its tendency.

'Grave, man!' exclaimed L——w, who speaks excellent strong broad Scots: 'My truly, but ye grave weel! I wad esteem the contents o' that spleuchan as the most precious treasure. I'll tell you what it is, sir: I hae often wondered how it was that this man's corpse has been miraculously preserved frae decay, a hunder times langer than ony other body's, or than even a tanner's. But now I could wager a guinea, it has been for the preservation o' that little book. And Lord kens what may be in't! It will maybe reveal some mystery that mankind disna ken naething about yet.'

'If there be any mysteries in it,' returned the other, 'it is not for your handling, my dear friend, who are too much taken up about mysteries already.' And with these words he presented the mysterious pamphlet to me. With very little trouble, save that of a thorough drying, I unrolled it all with ease, and found the very tract which I have here ventured to lay before the public, part of it in small bad print, and the remainder in manuscript. The title page is written, and is as follows:

THE PRIVATE MEMOIRS
AND CONFESSIONS
OF A JUSTIFIED SINNER:
WRITTEN BY HIMSELF.

FIDELI CERTA MERCES.

And, alongst the head, it is the same as given in the present edition of the work. I altered the title to *A Self-justified Sinner*, but my booksellers did not approve of it; and there being a curse pronounced by the writer on him that should dare to alter or amend, I have let it stand as it is. Should it be thought to attach discredit to any received principle of our church, I am blameless. The printed part ends at page 222, and the rest is in a fine old hand, extremely small and close. I have ordered the printer to procure a fac-simile of it, to be bound in with the volume.

With regard to the work itself, I dare not venture a judgment, for I do not understand it. I believe no person, man or woman, will ever peruse it with the same attention that I have done, and yet I confess that I do not comprehend the writer's drift. It is certainly impossible that these scenes could ever have occurred, that he describes as having himself transacted. I think it *may be* possible that he had some hand in the death of his brother, and yet I am disposed greatly to doubt it; and the numerous distorted traditions, &c. which remain of that event, may be attributable to the work having been printed and burnt, and of course the story known to all the printers, with their families and gossips. That the young Laird of Dalcastle came by a violent death, there remains no doubt; but that this wretch slew him, there is to me a good deal. However, allowing this to have been the case, I account all the rest either dreaming or madness; or, as he says to Mr. Watson, a religious parable, on purpose to illustrate something scarcely tangible, but to which he seems to have attached great weight. Were the relation at all consistent with reason, it corresponds so minutely with traditionary facts, that it could scarcely have missed to have been received as authentic; but in this day, and with the present generation, it will not go down, that a man should be daily tempted by the devil, in the semblance of a fellow-creature; and at length lured to self-destruction, in the hopes that this same fiend and tormentor was to suffer and fall along with him. It was a bold theme for an allegory, and would have suited that age well had it been taken up by one fully qualified for the task, which this writer was not. In short, we must either conceive him not only the greatest fool, but the greatest wretch, on whom was ever stamped the form of humanity; or, that he was a religious maniac, who wrote and wrote about a deluded creature, till he arrived at that height of madness, that he believed himself the very object whom he had been all along describing. And in order to escape from an ideal tormentor, committed that act for which, according to the tenets he embraced, there was no remission, and which consigned his memory and his name to everlasting detestation.

FINIS

APPENDIX

HOGG's novel was reviewed, anonymously, in the *British Critic* for July 1824, which found it 'uncouth and unpleasant', the *Quarterly Theological Review* for December 1824, which denied it 'one single attribute of a good and useful book', the *New Monthly Magazine* for November 1824, which pronounced it 'extraordinary trash', and the *Westminster Review* for October 1824, as follows:

Private Memoirs and Confessions of a Justified Sinner.
Written by Himself. Longman. 8vo. 1824.

THIS is a strange tale of Diablerie and Theology. The hero is born in lawful wedlock to a jolly Scotch laird by his outrageous saint of a wife, who is the disciple and admirer of an ultra-calvinist minister, and sits up with him o'nights to discuss the different kinds of faith. The youth becomes one of the elect, and falls in with a strange fellow, who seems to be no other than Satan himself in disguise, who instigates him to push his religious tenets to the most immoral consequences, and then carry them into practice by pistoling a worthy old Gospel preacher, conniving at the execution of a worthy young Gospel preacher for the murder, stabbing his own elder brother, breaking his lawful father's heart, getting rid, it does not appear exactly how, of his mother, revelling in all sorts of excess and atrocity while he possessed the paternal property, and when driven from its enjoyment by the dread of justice, saving its officers trouble by hanging himself upon a hay-stack. All this is represented as having taken place in the lowlands of Scotland, about the commencement of the last century.

There are three good reasons for reading books: first to be instructed by them; secondly to be amused; and thirdly, to review them. The first does not apply at all to the tale before us; as to the second, there are but few whose taste it will suit, and they may be much more highly gratified by many portions of the Newgate Calendar; the third carried us through with that proud consciousness of martyrdom for the public good, to which we are but too much accustomed when labouring in our vocation.

The author has managed the tale very clumsily, having made two distinct narratives of the same events; and, however true it may be in mathematics, it certainly does not always hold in story-telling, that two halves are equal to one whole. The events, up to the flight of the hero from his estate, are first told by the author from tradition, and then by himself. This expedient soon puts an end to all interest about the fate of the elder brother, who is almost the only personage in the book that does not richly merit the gallows here, and perdition hereafter. But soon to put an end to all interest about his best character, is not the best plan for a novelist who has any other object than that of providing materials for a monitory lecture to young writers of fiction. Unless this was the author's design, he must have adopted the plan for the sake of its originality. His ambition is commendable, for that praise has not hitherto been awarded to Scottish novels of the third rate, the class to which this production belongs.

If an author will introduce supernatural beings, he is at least bound to invent plausible motives for their interference in human concerns. The Royal One of the burning lake must have had much less business upon his hands than usual, or have been in a strangely capricious humour, when he became incarnate, and toiled so industriously, merely to get the soul of a raw Dominic Sampson, who was by nature wholly wicked and half-crazy. The devil is very difficult to manage; as much so poetically as theologically. He is sure to be disappointing, wearisome, or disgusting, unless made sublime enough for the reader to tremble at, or grotesque enough for him to laugh at. Our author is neither a Milton nor a Le Sage. His demon is no genius; nor is he.

In the supposed auto-biography of a victim of superstition, to preserve that unity which is essential to the production of a pleasurable impression on the reader, one of two obvious courses must be consistently adhered to. The phantoms of that superstition must either have a real, external being; or they must exist solely in the diseased imagination of the supposed writer. We can readily become, for the time, either believers or philosophers, to relish a good story; but the author must make his election, and adhere to it. The 'Justified Sinner' will not allow us to jog on comfortably with him in either character. He is mad enough, for all the arch-fiend's pranks to have been played in his own brain merely: so mad, that we are oft-times convinced they could have no other theatre; and yet, just as we are settling down into this conviction, the most preposterous of his tricks are seriously sworn to by some half-dozen witnesses in their sober senses, on the authority of their own eyes and ears. This inconsistency is as great an annoyance as if the audience were compelled to change their dresses three or four times during a performance, instead of the actors.

It is a still more serious objection, that the author has been unjust to a class of religionists, whose opinions are far from being obsolete, and of whom, though they might have much to answer for, he has given a delineation so grossly overcharged as to make it a hideous caricature. The ultra-calvinists of Scotland did vehemently decry ethical preaching; they did misapply texts of Scripture in a way very inconsistent with the peace of society and the rights of others; they were profoundly ignorant of the science of morals; but neither they nor any other sect, have ever advocated the practice of what they allowed to be vicious, or set themselves in open opposition to what they deemed virtue. The fanatic may think that the purest morals, without faith, will not keep a man out of hell; but he has still (controversy apart) all the reasons for speaking well of morality, and they are neither few nor small, which influence those who expect neither heaven nor hell; and he has all the inducements to its practice which arise from the connection of individual interest with the general good. The most outrageous votary of saving faith, would not brand the character of his own party by recording, that 'the true Gospel preachers joined all on one side, and the upholders of pure morality and a blameless life on the other.' There is great want of keeping in this and similar language. Men never select such colours for their own portraits; and to make them do so, offends as much against candour as against taste.

There are a few redeeming passages, especially the story of the Auchtermuchty preachment, which is told with some humour; but they only make us regret that the author did not employ himself better than in uselessly and disgustingly abusing his imagination, to invent wicked tricks for a mongrel devil, and blasphemous lucubrations for an insane fanatic.

EXPLANATORY NOTES

7 *had held*: had taken place (see *OED*: Hold *v.* II. 26); *1837* needlessly emends to 'had been held'.

12 *twelve*: *1837* corrects Hogg's arithmetic.

19 *Covenanters*: the party which, originating in the Reformation movement, bound itself by 'covenants' to maintain the Presbyterian doctrine and system of Church government. After the Restoration of Charles II, who renounced the covenants in 1662 and brought back episcopacy, they were repressed with great brutality by the forces of the Crown under John Graham of Claverhouse.

20 *the Earls of Seafield and Tullibardine*: James Ogilvy, created first Earl of Seafield in 1701 and appointed Lord High Chancellor of Scotland in 1702, was really committed to carrying out Godolphin's Scottish policy, and was among the most active promoters of the union with England. In order, though, to gain the support of the Tories in the 1703 parliament, he arranged for the office of Lord Privy Seal to be given to John Murray, created Earl of Tullibardine in 1696, and Duke of Atholl in 1703, who had begun as a Whig but became a fiery Jacobite.

the famous session: Feeling ran high in the 1703 parliament, the first to be elected since 1689, over the English Bill against Occasional Conformity, which would have deprived dissenters of civic status, and thus ensured the triumph of episcopacy. The house had a Whig and Presbyterian majority, and passed an Act of Security which declared that 20 days after the death of the reigning sovereign without issue, the Estates were to name a successor who should be a Protestant and descendant of the House of Stewart. Clearly this could not be acceptable to the Government, and the session closed with mutual recrimination between Queensberry, the Lord High Commissioner, and the House. The next session opened on 6 July 1704, with Tweeddale as Commissioner. Robert first meets Gil-Martin on 25 March 1704 (p. 119).

Duke of Argyle: Archibald Campbell, first Duke, who died on 29 September 1703.

25 *Marquis of Annandale*: William Johnstone, first Marquis, Lord President of the Privy Council. He had been appointed Lord High Commissioner to the General Assembly of the Kirk in 1701, and was concerned to ensure a Protestant succession.

53 *second son to a John, Duke of Melfort*: John Drummond, first Earl and
   titular Duke of Melfort, a Catholic, who was the most powerful nobleman in Scotland during the reign of James II, and went with him
   to St Germain. He died in Paris in 1714. The second son of his second marriage (to Euphemia Wallace, in 1680) was called Thomas
   and really did enter the Austrian service (see p. 92). Sir Thomas
   Wallace of Craigie was this boy's grandfather, not uncle (see pp. 54
   and 91), and was a Lord of Session, 1671–80.

130 *Czar Peter of Russia*: Peter the Great's European travels took place
    during 1697–8. He came to England in January 1698 for three
    months to study shipbuilding at Deptford.

149 *the Cloud of Witnesses*: an anachronism. *A Cloud of Witnesses, for the
    Royal Prerogatives of Jesus Christ; or, The Last Speeches and Testimonies
    of those who have suffered for the Truth, in Scotland, since the Year 1680*
    was first printed in 1714.

151 *Gilgal*: Joshua's camp (Josh. 5–10).

152 *venal prophet*: Balaam (Num. 22: 29).

180 *James . . . 1687*: Hogg's charter-style is authentic. Evidently he con-
    sulted some copies of charters, possibly those in William Maitland,
    History of Edinburgh, 1753, where the terms he uses can be found.

193 *Cameronian*: the Cameronians were extremist Covenanters, follow-
    ers of Richard Cameron (1648–80). After the religious settlement of
    1690, they became a separate church.

196 *Macmillan*: John Macmillan (1670–1753), minister of Balmaghie,
    who became minister to the Cameronians in 1706, amid much con-
    troversy. They were then known as the Macmillanites until 1743,
    when he founded the Reformed Presbyterian Church.

203 *gouden rule*: Matt. 7: 12.

217 *Boddel Brigg*: Bothwell Bridge where, on 22 June 1679, the Royal-
    ists under the Duke of Monmouth inflicted a crippling defeat on the
    Covenanters.

220 *James Watson*: publisher of the famous *Choice Collection of Comic and
    Serious Scottish Poems*, 1706–11. He became Queen's Printer in Scot-
    land in 1711.

240 *authentic letter . . . 1823*: Hogg reprints his own letter, with some
    omissions, from *Blackwood's*, 14 (1823), 188–90.

246 *Mr L——t of C——d*: John Gibson Lockhart of Chiefswood, Scott's
    son-in-law and biographer.

    Mr L——w: William Laidlaw, author of 'Lucy's Flittin', who
    became Scott's steward at Abbotsford in 1817.

247 *W——m B——e*: possibly the William Beattie of Hogg's *A Shep-·
     herd's Wedding* (*Tales and Sketches*, 1837, ii. 169). David Groves,
     ScLJ 18 (1991), 27–45 rather improbably proposes the poet William
     Blake.

249 *the grey stone*: A 2 ft. × 1 ft. slab, rather like a gravestone, still stands
     on top of a cairn on Fall Law. For this information I am indebted to
     Mr H. Kidd, Bursar of St. John's College, Oxford, who climbed Fall
     Law for me.

251 *Mr Sc——t . . . Mr R——n of W——n L——e*: It seems likely that
     the last two words are Wilton Lodge, a sizeable house on the edge
     of Hawick, about 13 miles east of Thirlestane. Neighbouring Mr
     Scotts in 1824 were H. E. Scott of Harden and J. C. Scott of Sinton,
     but the proprietor and occupant of Wilton Lodge was Mr James
     Anderson, a gentleman of 'intellectual treasures' and 'cultivated
     understanding' according to Robert Wilson, *Sketch of the History of
     Hawick*, 1825, p. 6 (see also pp. 345 and 352). Perhaps Hogg's 'A'
     was misread 'R'.

GLOSSARY

Compiled by Graham Tulloch

This glossary predominantly consists of Scots words and phrases used in the novel. It also includes some names of localities, obsolete or unusual English words, and Gaelic and Latin words and phrases. I have not included items in the long lists of Scots legal terms in the charter on p. 180 as Hogg has used them for their overall effect rather than their precise individual meaning, nor have I included words explained by Hogg. I have consulted the *Scottish National Dictionary*, *Concise Scots Dictionary*, and *Oxford English Dictionary*, and, occasionally, Jamieson's *Etymological Dictionary of the Scottish Language*.

a', all
ado, to do
ae, one
aff, off
afore, before, in front of
aften, often
ain, own
aince, once
aith, oath
Altrive, place in Selkirkshire
amang, among
amuses, plural of *awmous*, alms-giving
an, if
an', and
ane, one
aneath, beneath
anent, concerning
anither, another
Arthur's Seat, high rocky hill near Edinburgh
atween, between
auld, old
auld ane, the, the Devil

Ault-Righ, the king's stream (Hogg's Gaelic derivation for
  Altrive)
aw, all
aw, I
awthegither, altogether
aye, continually, always
ayont, beyond, beside

back green, grassy ground at the back of the house
baillie, town councillor
bairn, child
baith, both
bane, bone
bannet, flat cap worn by males
bedstrae, bedstraw
belang, belong
Belial, man of, wicked man
bicker, wooden drinking vessel
bigging, building
binna, is not
bit, small
blue bonnet, see *bannet*
boardly, burly
bodle, two pence Scots, one sixth of an English penny
body, person
bogle, fearsome ghost, bugbear
bonnet, see *bannet*
bourock, cottage
bouzy, fat
bowkail, cabbage
brae, hillside
braidside, whole side
braird, first sprouts of grain
braw, splendid
break, break into (a house)
brikk, break
brunstane, brimstone
bum, buzz, drone
burd, offspring
burgh, royal, borough with charter direct from the crown
burn, stream

ca', call
caddy, errand boy
callant, young man

calm, qualm, feeling of sickness

canna, cannot

canny, bringing good luck; with negative: not unnatural or supernatural (see *uncanny*)

Canongate, street near Holyrood House

carl, man, fellow

cast, n. chance, opportunity; toss (of the head)

cast, v. dig out, cut (peats)

Catechism, Single, the Shorter Catechism approved by the Church of Scotland in 1648

cauler, fresh, newly caught

cause, the hour of, the appointed time for a trial

chafts, cheeks

chiel, man

circuit lords, the judges of the High Court of Justiciary when going on circuit

circumfauld, surround

clachan, small village

claes, clothes

claithing, clothing

clapperclaw, possibly 'to strike a blow as a spider at a fly' (Jamieson)

claymore, large Highland sword

cloot, hoof

close, narrow alleyway, especially one leading to the entrance to a *land*

cock, raise

collegian, university student

commissioner, see *lord-commissioner*

contrair, contrary

corbie, raven

corby-craw, raven

Court of Justiciary, High, supreme criminal court of Scotland

crap, crept

craw, crow

creeshy, fat

croon, bellow, roar

Cross, the, the Mercat (Market) Cross on the High Street

crouping, croaking

cuif, fool

daft, crazy

dangler, someone who hangs around a woman

day, the, today

dee, do
dee, die
deil, devil
depone, testify
depute-advocate, a barrister appointed as a prosecutor in court
deray, disturbance, damage
Diabolus, Devil
didna, did not
dike, low wall
ding, beat
dinna, do not
disna, does not
ditit, foolish
div, do
divot, turf, peat
doesnae, does not
doit, stumble
doitrified, dazed
dominie, schoolmaster
donnart, stupid
doubt, fear
dree, suffer
dung, struck

easter, eastern
een, eyes
Eldinhope, place in Selkirkshire
ell, about four-fifths of the English measure
entry, an alley-way leading to an entrance
ern, iron
evite, avoid
extraordinar, extraordinary

fa, who
fand, found
fat, what
fawn, fallen
feele, fool
fer, far
fideli certa merces, an assured reward for the faithful one
Finnieston, formerly open ground, now part of city of Glasgow
flannen, flannel
flaring, flattery
flinders, shreds, fragments
flitters, shreds

flummery, flattery
fock, folk
foot, lower end (of a street, piece of ground)
foreby, let alone
fore-door, front door
frae, from
fra-yont, from the other side of
fraze, palaver

gae, go
gae, gave
gaed, went
gang, go
gar, make
gate, way
gaun, going
gayan, very
ghaist, ghost
gie, give
gin, if
gizened, withered
glaring, ostentatious
Glasco, Glasgow
glen, valley
gloaming, twilight
goodman, a term of address
goodwife, mistress of a house or farm
gowk, cuckoo, fool
Grass Market, the, wide street in Edinburgh formerly used for public executions
grit, great
grumphing, grumbling
gude, good; God
gudewife, mistress of a house; wife (used as a term of address)
guerdon, reward
guidit, treated
gull, fool, dupe

ha', house, home
hae, have
haena, have not
haill, whole
hale, whole
halesale, wholesale
halfpenny, Scots, equivalent to one-twelfth of the English coin

GLOSSARY

hame, home
hand-fast, make a contract by joining hands
havers, gossip
head of the passage, point where an alley enters the main street
heartless, disheartened
heritor, landed proprietor
het, hot
heuch, bank
High Church, one of the churches into which St. Giles in
  Edinburgh was formerly divided
High Street, street in centre of old Edinburgh
hind, farm-worker, ploughman
hoad-road, state of chaos
Hollin lawn, fine linen fabric
hope, small valley in midst of hills
horse-laid, horse-load
houk, dig
hout na, definitely no
howk, poke one's nose in
howlet, owl
hunder, hundred

in-by, *in by*, further in
ir, are
ither, other

jaud, worthless woman
juggs, pillory
Justice Clerk, *Lord*, vice president of the High Court of
  Justiciary

keek, peep
ken, know
ketch, toss
keust, cast
kimmer, gossip
kirk, church
kirk session, church court of a parish
kist, chest

lady, title formerly given to a laird's wife, as in *Lady
  Dalchastel*
laird, landed proprietor, owner of an estate held directly from
  the crown; the laird's male heir is known as the *young laird*
  and the laird himself, if he has a male heir, is known as the
  old laird

land, building, of several storeys or more, divided into flats
lang, long
lave, remainder
lay, silence (a voice)
lead, produce (proof, evidence)
learn, teach
leasing-making, telling lies
leear, liar
Leith Wynd, narrow street leading north from the Canongate
libel, state (in a law case)
like, likely
linn, ravine, gorge
lint-swingling, flax-beating
loaden, laden
lord-commissioner, the sovereign's representative in the Scottish parliament
loun, fellow
lounder, thrash
loup, leap
luckpenny, a sum returned to the buyer by the seller as a discount
lucky, landlady of a tavern; also used before the surname of an older woman

ma, my
mae, more
mair, more
maister, master
mak, make
mall, a mallet used for striking the ball in the game pall-mall
march, boundary
margin, explanatory note
maugre, in spite of
maun, must
meeting-house, place of worship
mell, thrash
mense, credit
merk, mark, two-thirds of a pound, the Scots money being valued at one-twelfth of the English
mind, remember
momently, instantly
mony, many
Morphean, associated with the god of dreams and sleep, sleepy
muckil, large

muckle, much
mysel, myself

na, no
nae, no
ne'er, the, the Devil
neist, next
no, not
North Loch, shallow lake north of Edinburgh Castle, later
  drained

o', of
od, God (in oaths and exclamations)
o'er, too
ony, any
outfield, poorer, outlying parts of a farm
overhie, overtake
ower, over; too

pack-laid, pack-load
packman, pedlar, travelling merchant
Palace, the, Holyrood House
pat, put
paulie, undersized, sickly lamb
Pearman Sike, watercourse near Finnieston
peats, pieces of peat cut for burning
peeous, pious
pennyworths of, tak, take revenge on
pink, finest example
pirn, spool
pit, put
plack, small coin; *not a plack*, nothing at all
plea, go to law
pose, interrogate
pouk, preen
precognition, preliminary investigation of a case
professor, someone making public profession of religious faith
put down, kill, put to death
put off, pass (time)

rack, stretch
raip, rope
reard, roar
rede, advise
reid, red
reist, bring to a stop, prevent from moving

Revolutionist, a supporter of the Glorious Revolution of 1688
rigging of it, *ride the*, be totally preoccupied with it
rin, run
rip, worthless fellow
rowth, abundance

sae, so
St. Anthony's chapel, small ruined hermitage in valley near
  Arthur's Seat
St. Johnston, Perth
Salisbury, rock of, Salisbury Craigs, a rocky ridge behind
  Holyrood House
sanna, shall not
sauchless, foolish
sauf, save
saur, smell
scouder, scorch
scragged, covered with stunted bushes or undergrowth
Session, Lord of, a judge of the Court of Session, supreme civil
  court of Scotland; some Lords of Session are also members of
  the High Court of Justiciary
shakel, wrist
shan, make a wry face
sheriff, chief officer of a county (with judicial functions,
  usually performed by a deputy)
sib, related
sic, such
siccan, sickan, such
sidie for sidie, side by side
siller, silver
Simmie, Auld, the Devil
sin', since
skair, illuminate
skimmer, glide easily, skim
slack, slacken
slump, by the, taken all together
snork, snort
speeder, spider
spleuchan, tobacco pouch
spoke, wooden bar used in carrying a coffin
stair, staircase
stamack, stomach
stane, stone
stint, stop

stool, black, seat in a church on which offenders sat while
  being publicly rebuked, a 'stool of repentance'
stott, bullock
strick, strict
strodge, stride, strut
swee, sway
swire, level place near the top of a hill

tak, take
tane, one
tap, top
tartans, full Highland dress
tauld, told
tawpie, scatterbrained young woman
tent, notice
thae, those
thief, the auld, the Devil
thief's hole, cell in a prison
thrang, throng
thretty, thirty
throng, busy
tither, other
tolbooth, town prison
toom, empty
trams, legs
trow, believe
twa, two
tweel, twill

uncanny, linked with dangerous supernatural powers
unco, very
unco-like, peculiar, extraordinary

vapouring, boastful
vera, very

wa', wall
wab, web
wad, would
wadna, would not
war, were
waratch, wretch
wark, work
warlock, male witch
wasna, was not
wauken, waken

waur, worse
wee, little
weel, well
weird, fate
West Port, one of the gates in the old Edinburgh city walls
wha, who
whaever, whoever
whan, when
whaten, what sort of
whiles, sometimes
wife, woman
windlestrae, dried stalk of grass; figuratively, a weapon
winna, will not
woodriff, woodruff
wore, moved cautiously
wrang, wrong
writer, solicitor, lawyer
Writer to the Signet, solicitor with special functions and
  privileges
wynd, narrow alley

yelloch, shriek
yerk, sudden throb of pain
ye's, you shall
yestreen, yesterday
yon, that
yooll, howl, bawl, wail
yowe, ewe

JANE AUSTEN	**Emma**
	Mansfield Park
	Persuasion
	Pride and Prejudice
	Sense and Sensibility
MRS BEETON	**Book of Household Management**
LADY ELIZABETH BRADDON	**Lady Audley's Secret**
ANNE BRONTË	**The Tenant of Wildfell Hall**
CHARLOTTE BRONTË	**Jane Eyre**
	Shirley
	Villette
EMILY BRONTË	**Wuthering Heights**
SAMUEL TAYLOR COLERIDGE	**The Major Works**
WILKIE COLLINS	**The Moonstone**
	No Name
	The Woman in White
CHARLES DARWIN	**The Origin of Species**
CHARLES DICKENS	**The Adventures of Oliver Twist**
	Bleak House
	David Copperfield
	Great Expectations
	Nicholas Nickleby
	The Old Curiosity Shop
	Our Mutual Friend
	The Pickwick Papers
	A Tale of Two Cities
GEORGE DU MAURIER	**Trilby**
MARIA EDGEWORTH	**Castle Rackrent**

TROLLOPE IN OXFORD WORLD'S CLASSICS

ANTHONY TROLLOPE

	Six French Poets of the Nineteenth Century
HONORÉ DE BALZAC	Cousin Bette
	Eugénie Grandet
	Père Goriot
CHARLES BAUDELAIRE	The Flowers of Evil
	The Prose Poems and Fanfarlo
BENJAMIN CONSTANT	Adolphe
DENIS DIDEROT	Jacques the Fatalist
ALEXANDRE DUMAS (PÈRE)	The Black Tulip
	The Count of Monte Cristo
	Louise de la Vallière
	The Man in the Iron Mask
	La Reine Margot
	The Three Musketeers
	Twenty Years After
	The Vicomte de Bragelonne
ALEXANDRE DUMAS (FILS)	La Dame aux Camélias
GUSTAVE FLAUBERT	Madame Bovary
	A Sentimental Education
	Three Tales
VICTOR HUGO	Notre-Dame de Paris
J.-K. HUYSMANS	Against Nature
PIERRE CHODERLOS DE LACLOS	Les Liaisons dangereuses
MME DE LAFAYETTE	The Princesse de Clèves
GUILLAUME DU LORRIS and JEAN DE MEUN	The Romance of the Rose

Émile Zola

L'Assommoir
The Attack on the Mill
La Bête humaine
La Débâde
Germinal
The Ladies' Paradise
The Masterpiece
Nana
Pot Luck
Thérèse Raquin

A SELECTION OF **OXFORD WORLD'S CLASSICS**

American Literature

British and Irish Literature

Children's Literature

Classics and Ancient Literature

Colonial Literature

Eastern Literature

European Literature

History

Medieval Literature

Oxford English Drama

Poetry

Philosophy

Politics

Religion

The Oxford Shakespeare

A complete list of Oxford Paperbacks, including Oxford World's Classics, Oxford Shakespeare, Oxford Drama, and Oxford Paperback Reference, is available in the UK from the Academic Division Publicity Department, Oxford University Press, Great Clarendon Street, Oxford OX2 6DP.

In the USA, complete lists are available from the Paperbacks Marketing Manager, Oxford University Press, 198 Madison Avenue, New York, NY 10016.

Oxford Paperbacks are available from all good bookshops. In case of difficulty, customers in the UK can order direct from Oxford University Press Bookshop, Freepost, 116 High Street, Oxford OX1 4BR, enclosing full payment. Please add 10 per cent of published price for postage and packing.

BOTANY BAY

*A man who has gone into a different climate
changes his nature, in part. But he cannot
change it altogether, for in his life's
beginning the destiny of his body was
determined.*

Ptolemy

To this entry in a ninth century manuscript at Berne,
an exile named Cormac added:
*So is it always with the Irish who
died in a foreign land.*

Title page illustration: The harbour at Cove with the mastless hulk *Surprise* in the centre of the
scene, *c.* 1840. Drawing by Maeve Costello from that of W. Willies in Mr & Mrs S. C. Hall's
Ireland (1841).

Mercier Press
PO Box 5 5 French Church Street Cork
16 Hume Street Dublin 2

First published by Mercier Press 1987
Reprinted 1996

© Con Costello 1987

A CIP record for this book is available from the British Library.

ISBN 0 85342 808 5
10 9 8 7 6 5 4 3 2 1

Printed in Ireland by ColourBooks Baldoyle Dublin 13

Botany Bay

The story of the convicts transported
from Ireland to Australia, 1791-1853

Con Costello

MERCIER PRESS

The Cove of Cork from an early nineteenth century print.

Contents

VAN DIEMEN'S LAND.

MARIA I.

HOBART

EAGLE HAWK NECK

PORT ARTHUR

EARLY

AUSTRALIA.

NEW SOUTH WALES

MORETON BAY

PORT MACQUARIE

PARRAMATTA

SYDNEY

NORFOLK I. (1050 MLS)

BOTANY BAY

PERTH.

FREMANTLE.

BALLARAT

MELBOURNE

VAN DIEMEN'S LAND

Map of early Australia (drawing: Maeve Costello).

Acknowledgements

I cannot, without doing violence to my feelings, omit this opportunity of making my acknowledgements to those gentlemen who have honoured me with their countenance and aid in my researches.
J. C. Walker, 1818

During the years that I have been researching the material for this book I have had helpful advice and information from many people; in thanking those listed below, I beg the indulgence of any whom I may have overlooked. For their constructive comments on the text I am indebted to Professor Colm Kiernan, Mr Keith Johnson, Director of the Library of Australian History, Lieutenant Colonel Michael Begley, Miss Anne Fitzsimons, Mark and Denis Costello and my wife Maeve.

The following individuals and Institutions in Australia were helpful: Alan Queale, Fr M. Palmer, Mrs M. O'Neill, Bro. A. I. Keenan, Mrs M. Fletcher, Mr C.E. McDonald, Mrs J. W. Simpson, Miss E. Snodgrass, Mr W. Stone, Mrs V. King, Mr K. S. Parker, Mr F. J. Butler, Mrs E. C. O'Dea, Mr G. A. Dillon, Rev. M. McEvoy, Dr F. Farrell, Mrs M. H. Sweeney, Mr F. Burke, Mr J. Vincent, Fr D. Mahony, Mr C. Bateson, Mr W.J. Hayes, Mrs J. Finucane, Mitchell Library, Sydney, State Library, Tasmania, John Oxley Library, Brisbane.

In Ireland the following gave assistance: Professor G. Mac Eoin, Mr Peter Pearson, Mr Tony O'Riordan, Mr R. Gallagher, Miss M. Scannell, Mr D. Ó Cionaola, Mr D. Ó Súilleabháin, Mr T. P. Ó Cuinn, Rev. J. L. Cairns, Mr A. T. Newham, Mr D. F. Gleeson, Miss Ann Neary, Captain F. Forde, Ms R. O'Connor-Moulder, Sr Teresa Anthony, Sisters of Charity, Mr P. Collins, Fr E. J. Quinn, Miss Sheila Costello. The Keeper and staff of the State Paper Office, Director and staff, National Library, Keeper of Public Records of Northern Ireland, Librarian Central Catholic Library, staff of Trinity College Library, the Ulster Historical Foundation and the staff of the Kildare County Library. Permission to quote from original sources in all of these Institutions is acknowledged. I am especially thankful to Michael Hewson, director of the National Library, for assistance with the proofs, and to Brian McKenna for help with the illustrations.

Botany Bay.

(From *The Voyage of Gov. Phillip to Botany Bay*, 1798. National Library)

Introduction

The contribution of the Irish to the making of Australia over the last two hundred years has been the subject of much research and comment. That the character and influence of the men and women from Ireland was different from those from England and Scotland has been observed. As in the United States of America, a major institution which has retained substantial Irish qualities is the Roman Catholic church.

But it is not the intention of this book to investigate the lives and legacy of the 290,000 free emigrants who sailed from Ireland to Australia in the nineteenth century; it is to be a consideration of the 45,000 involuntary exiles who went to 'Botany Bay'* in the convict ships during the 77 years that the transportation system of punishment lasted. The questions that will be asked, and it is hoped answered, will be: Who were the convicts? Why were they transported? How did they fare in the colonies?

Before exploring the questions posed, a general look at the social conditions in Ireland at the end of the eighteenth century and in the first half of the nineteenth century should give some background to the scene. Perhaps the most remarkable occurrence was the increase in population from 3.6 million in 1772 to over 8 million on the eve of the famine of 1845, after which, within a few years death, emigration and transportation reduced the population by 20%.

Unlike Great Britain, Ireland did not benefit from the Industrial Revolution to any great extent, and the vast majority of the people lived on small holdings, their existence dependent on the land, or from labouring for hire at low wages. Despite frugal living conditions with no prospects for improvement, marriage was contracted at an early age. In a small mud cabin erected on the sub-divided family plot the young couple set about producing a family which would guarantee their sustenance in old age.

* Botany Bay was the destination of the first convict fleet. On arrival there, it was found unsuitable and the settlement was made instead at Sydney Cove. Nevertheless, in Ireland and Britain, the name 'Botany Bay' became synonymous with a convict colony in New South Wales. In Trinity College, Dublin, an early nineteenth-century residential square was named 'Botany Bay'. According to undergraduate tradition this was after the convict colony, because of its unruliness.

The poverty and squalor in which the landless masses lived was commented on by every visitor who recorded his travels. The possession and tenancy of land was the single most important factor in life, being literally a matter of life or death. Frequent famines had proven that reliance on a single crop, the potato, was disastrous. But, in a country with few industries, there was no alternative to dependence on the land. The ancient oral tradition of recalling the glories and tragedies of the past kept alive the not very distant Cromwellian and other confiscations of estates, and the replacement of the Catholic owners by Protestant settlers. By 1778 only 5% of the land remained in Catholic ownership, though at the beginning of the previous century they had held 90%.

Husbanding their plots, the greater part of the population lived in constant dread of rent-day or eviction. When landlords attempted to increase rents, to evict unsatisfactory tenants or to enclose more land for cattle grazing, they met with fierce opposition from the threatened and desperate tenantry who formed secret societies to protect themselves. The most violent crimes were committed on anyone who sought to implement the landlord's intentions, such as that reported in the *Freeman's Journal* on 2 December 1813. After the agrarian secret society known as The Ribbonmen had administered their oath to a man named Connell, who lived a few miles from Athlone in County Westmeath, he informed on them. He was attacked in his home and pounded to death with stones, after which his body was thrown on the manure heap with a pitchfork through his heart. His wife was shot through the head at such close range that her eyes were blown from her face.

The brutal murders, burnings and cattle maimings perpetrated by the various agrarian societies indicate a complete disregard for property and the law. This might be explained by the centuries of wars and social upheaval which had left the people with little respect for the institutions of the state, and by the lack of sympathy shown by the Protestant Ascendancy towards the Catholics. Penal laws made the practice of the Roman Catholic religion difficult, a fact which united the priests and the people. The influence of the priest on his flock is believed to have prevented even worse excesses on the part of the agrarian activists, but the people constantly disregarded clerical exhortations to cease these disturbances. As with the refusal from the majority to pay tithes to the Established Protestant Church, the priests could also suffer if they angered the populace by making excessive demands for dues. After the coadjutor bishop of Meath had admonished his congregation from the altar, a group of Whiteboys raided his house and the bishop shot dead one of the intruders. That was in 1776; some twenty years later three men broke into the parochial house at Abbeyfeale in County Limerick, and burned the parish priest with a hot iron in an effort to procure his money and to force him to lower his fee for officiating at marriages. It was a violent society in which 'justice' was administered swiftly, if not always justly.

During the period under consideration the majority of the crimes committed in rural Ireland were due to proverty or to disputes over land; in Dublin, the only major urban area, the crimes were similar to those in cities elsewhere. Combined with the unending agrarian agitation, the political movements which led to the formation of the United Irishmen and the Young Irelanders and the consequent Risings of 1798, 1803 and 1848, produced another type of offender, often well-educated and landed. However, the number of political prisoners transported was but a small fraction of the total which would have come from the class associated with the more common offences.

Some historians have thought the Irish convicts similar to those from England – criminals deserving punishment. But once they had arrived in the colonies the Irish were seen to be very different. Despatch after despatch to the home government sought to curtail the transportation from Ireland on the grounds that the prisoners were notorious, seditious and rebellious, unskilled and 'horrid characters'. These, however, were the views of the colonial officials, sometimes Anglo-Irish, but mainly Englishmen who had brought with them their traditional prejudices towards, and ignorance of, Ireland. They might have even come from the army which had served in Ireland, endeavouring to support a political system based on an ascendancy class which was, in general, out of sympathy with the majority of the people. Captain David Collins came from such a background, and his severe judgement of the Irish convicts was one of the earliest published. Further prejudice against the Irish came from the fact that the majority of them were Roman Catholic, or from their speaking of their native Gaelic language. Modern research, based on original source material such as the convict records in Ireland and in Australia, has done much to alter this old view of the Irish and of conditions in the convict colonies. In his recently published

Letters from Irish Australia 1825-1929, Professor Patrick O'Farrell supports Dr J. B. Hirst's view, expounded in *Convict Society and its Enemies*, that 'convict society in New South Wales was a much freer, happier and humane one than traditional judgements have allowed'.

The contemporary prejudice against the convicts is understandable. Coming from deprived, impoverished, strife-riven rural areas, accustomed to violence, and with little regard for the law or its instruments, they naturally associated the colonial officials with those who had endeavoured to enforce the law at home. Without the humanising influence of their womenfolk (and one in every five deportees was married) or the constraints of their Church, it could be expected that the men would be even more lawless, drunken and demoralised than they had been in Ireland. They sought to escape from the chain-gangs and the barracks in the vain hope of returning home. Like the early Christian missionaries from Ireland, the convicts yearned for their island homeland, and the many ballads expressing this longing are now part of Irish and Australian folk literature.

But all the Irish did not wish to return home. There is considerable evidence of those who succeeded in the colony and who sought to bring wives or families out. Indeed, it was not long before it was rumoured in Ireland that men and women deliberately committed crimes in the hope of being transported, and thus being able to enjoy a better life in Australia.

Duncannon Fort, Co. Wexford
(drawing: M. Hooper 1793 from *The Antiquities of Ireland* by Francis Grose 1795).

An eighteenth century drawing of the Pigeon House Fort in Dublin Bay (National Library).

1 First Sailings, 1791-1797

On the morning of 26 February 1791 the Dublin newspaper, the *Freeman's Journal*, carried the news that 'the jailer of Limerick set off for Cork with a number of prisoners, where a large transport is preparing to carry all the convicts in the Kingdom to Botany Bay'. Another newspaper commenting on the transportation reported that, when the prisoners were being removed from Dublin's new prison: 'none of the women seemed to have less feeling for their situation than the men, and Rositer, the woman who had been condemned to die for robbing one of the rooms at the Linen Hall, called out to the soldiers "clear the way" 'til she mounted her landau.' Rositer, with the other prisoners, was bound for Cork where the convict ship *Queen* was waiting at Cove[1] to transport them to Australia.

While Rositer was clearly much happier to be exiled rather than to mount the scaffold, she was but one of the 22 women and 130 men for whose transportation the vessel had been engaged. The cost per head was £17, plus the provision of rations for the passage and the maintenance of the convicts for one year in the colony. While the destination of the prisoners was a new one, transportation as a system of punishment was long established and, despite the assertion of the *Freeman's Journal* that the transport was 'to carry all the convicts in the Kingdom', this was not the government's intention then, nor at any period while the system lasted.

When the prisoners assembled at Cork were put on board the *Queen*, a receipt, dated 11 April 1791, signed by the Naval Agent, was given to the Mayor and to the Sheriff of the City of Cork (Sir Henry Brown Hayes, Knt). The Indent lists, giving details of the transportees, did not reach Sydney until eight years after the arrival of the convicts. This delay in the forwarding of lists, and the general poor documentation of convicts from Ireland caused much adverse comment from the Australian officials during the early years of transportation. Over the next five years four more vessels brought convicts from Ireland to New South Wales. Two sailed in 1793 and one each in the years 1795 and 1796. They carried 520 male and 185 female convicts, of whom 240 of the men are thought to have been guilty of agrarian offences.

The sentence of transportation, as a punishment for crime, had been awarded in England and Ireland since the sixteenth century. In Cromwellian times thousands of Irish people were sent to the West Indies. Following the 'Transportation Act' of 1717, which it was intended 'would deter criminals and supply the colonies with labour', some prisoners were shipped to America. This arrangement was ended by the war of 1776, and a new outlet for the prisoners had to be found. Consideration was given to locations in Canada and in Africa, but finally it was decided that New South Wales should be the beneficiary. Establishing such a settlement in Australia, it was hoped, would get rid of convicts to as distant a place as possible and it could be commercially profitable; it would facilitate the exploitation of business links with Asia, and possibly prevent other European powers from engaging in such activity. Access to important whaling grounds would be opened, while the virgin lands of New South Wales could support traders and merchants. But a labour force would be required, and what more suitable work might be found for the hordes of convicts crowding the jails of England and Ireland?

In London a government order was issued in 1786 authorising 'that convicts, with the usual officers, should go to the eastern coast of New South Wales and establish a colony there', and in the month of May 1787 the first convict fleet was ready to sail from Spithead. It reached Botany Bay on 20 January 1788 after a passage of 252 days. That same year two convict ships sailed from Dublin, but they never reached their destination, which was probably Nova Scotia. One vessel was taken by the convicts, many of whom eventually returned to Ireland, the other off-loaded its human cargo at New Jersey and Connecticut. Nevertheless, in the following year, two more transports set sail from Ireland; their convicts were taken by one vessel to the West Indies and by the other to Newfoundland as the captain discovered that they had developed fever. From Newfoundland many of the prisoners found their way back home, some to be imprisoned again.

The Irish government now decided to follow the example of London and laws were introduced enabling convicts to be transported to New South Wales, and the 'Act for the Better Execution of the Law' was published in the daily newspapers. It was generally agreed that the cost of £70 per head to send a convict to 'Botany Bay' would be well spent; it would lessen the strain on the jails and dispose of part of the troublesome section of the population.

Some of the crimes for which the prisoners on the *Queen* were transported included: 'taking a drab cloth coat, value 10s; for stealing a copper kettle, value 3s; for stealing a pair of blankets, value 3s; for stealing one silver tea spoon, value 2s; for stealing a black hat of silk, value 1s,' all of which offences rated seven year sentences, which showed how seriously these now minor crimes were then considered. James Blake, a Dublin youth aged twelve, was exiled for stealing a pair of silver buckles. He died within four months of arrival at Sydney. Also transported at this time was Robert Flanagan, from Newry, who had been prosecuted for robbery. His case was unusual in that there had been a public subscription to pay the prosecutor and five gentlemen wrote to the authorities requesting that Flanagan should be transported. Their letter, dated April 1791, stated that he was 'a desperate, riotous and lawless villain, and a robber of most infamous character'.

The receipt issued for the convicts on the *Queen* at Cove, in Cork harbour, was for 133 men and 22 women with 4 children, but the Indents when they reached Sydney in 1799, listed 159 adults, adding that 3 men had died and 1 woman had escaped before the vessel had sailed. Over half of the prisoners had received their sentences in Dublin, and 38 of the total had life sentences. During the passage of just over five months the convicts were given short rations, and when the ship arrived at Sydney an Inquiry was held into certain allegations made by convicts. It was established that 'it appeared beyond a doubt that great abuses had been practised in the issuing of the provisions'. The cook said that there had been a shortage of salted provisions, and it was found that much of the storage space had been taken up with stores belonging to the officers. These stores they intended to sell in the colony. That such abuses could occur illustrates the lack of organisation in the management of transportation. The unscrupulous and mercenary character of some of the ships' masters caused the convicts additional suffering by reducing the prison area and restricting the already inadequate ventilation system aboard.

On arrival in Sydney the exiles found that the settlement was already beginning to look well-established. Barracks for both officers and men had been constructed from bricks manufactured at a works on the Parramatta road. Farmers settled on small-holdings were developing the land, and by the end of the following year over 170

settlers held some 8,000 acres. But the new country did not appeal
to the Irishmen as an official dispatch of November 1791 indicates:

> Of those who have been received from Ireland in the *Queen* transport,
> from 15 to 20 have taken to the woods and, though several of them have
> been brought in when so reduced that they could not have lived a second
> day if they had not been found, some of these very men have absconded
> a second time, and must perish.

Some of the escapees believed that it was but 'a tolerable walk' to
China, where they would be free; one convict who persevered in the
search believed that he had reached China when he came to a habitation. To his surprise he saw there the commanding officer of the New
South Wales corps whom he greeted, according to traditional lore,
with the words: 'Long life to you, colonel, what has brought your
honour to China all the way!'

Such naïveté amused the officials. It is not so surprising that men
who had never left their native parish until they were apprehended,
and who were probably illiterate, should be ignorant of geography.
It has been estimated that possibly only one-third of the Irish convicts
were literate, with even a lower average for the women.

The four other ships which sailed from Cove after the *Queen* were
the *Boddingtons* and the *Sugar Cane*, within a couple of months of
each other in 1793, the *Marquis Cornwallis* in 1795, and the *Britannia*
in the December of the following year. In his book *Transportation
from Ireland to Sydney, 1791-1816*, Dr T. J. Kiernan analysed the
Indent lists for the various vessels, showing age of the transportee,
the place of trial and if it was an area of agrarian disturbance, and the
term of sentence. If there was any special mention of the vessel or its
convicts in official records, this was also quoted. The *Boddingtons*,
for example, carried a large proportion of men from Ulster, a province
much disturbed by the agrarian rivalries of the Defenders and the
Peep-of-Day Boys, and many of the men had been given life sentences.
Three-quarters of the prisoners on the *Sugar Cane* had been tried in
Dublin or Cork, and one-fifth had life sentences. Of the women, who
were one-third of the total and aged between 15 and 43, it was said
that, like the men, they could be classified as common malefactors.
As the conviction lists did not accompany the vessels, Governor
Hunter (1795-1800) complained that:

The manner in which the convicts are sent out from Ireland is so extremely careless and irregular that it must be felt by these people as a particular hardship, and by government as a great inconvenience. Every ship from that country have [*sic*] omitted to bring any account of the conviction or terms of transportation of those people they bring out. . . there are many in the settlement now who have repeatedly petitioned to be allowed to leave the country, or to labour and provide for themselves in it, their time, as they say, being completed.

Sometimes the convicts succeeded in convincing the officials that their sentences had expired when they had not. This caused the governor to issue an order that as some of those who came out on the *Boddingtons* and the *Sugar Cane* were now found to have life sentences, and that certificates given to them on false evidence should be disregarded; settlers were directed not to employ them. 'Imposters' was the term used to describe prisoners who had failed to have their certificates renewed, and 'all persons who are friends to good order' were exhorted to bring to headquarters such imposters.

No doubt it must be assumed that some of the convicts would have endeavoured to capitalise on the deficiencies of their records, just as others endured longer sentences for the same reason, a fact acknowledged by the authorities over twenty-five years later.

Even without the additional hardships aboard the convict vessels, such as confinement, lack of ventilation and poor diet, sea journeys under sail were hazardous. If the master of a convict ship was a strict disciplinarian, sadistic or avaricious, the lot of his cargo was even more disastrous.

Before sailing from Cove the *Sugar Cane* was stricken with fever, and both attendants and convicts suffered. When she was about six weeks at sea there was a rumour that the convicts had sawn off their irons and were about to mutiny, with the assistance of some of the sailors and of members of the guard. To suppress any such attempt one man who was found to be out of irons was executed and others were punished; 'These measures,' it was recorded, ' as might well be expected, threw such a damp on the spirits of the rest that no more was heard of intentions to take the ship.'

After the *Boddingtons* had docked a similar story was told by the convicts themselves, 'that all the officers were to have been murdered, the first mate and the agent excepted, who were to be preserved alive for the purpose of conducting the ship to port, when they likewise

were to be put to death'. An official comment on this information was
'that the guard (especially when embarked for the security of a ship
full of wild lawless Irish) ought never to have been composed of young
soldiers, or of deserters from other corps'.

With such stories being told in the colony it is not surprising that
soon the Irish were being described as the 'Hibernian Gentry' or, less
flatteringly, as 'worthless and turbulent characters called Irish Defenders'. One man possibly so described was Laurence Davoran, a 31-
year-old attorney from Ann Grove in Queen's County, who had come
on the *Boddingtons*. He was given a life sentence in Dublin in 1791,
but his offence is not known; during the controversial governorship
of Captain William Bligh (1806-1808) Davoran wrote, in support
of Bligh, 'A New Song, made in NSW on the Rebellion', to the air
of 'Health of the Duchess'. After he was pardoned in 1814 Davoran
returned home.

'Several of the male convicts were known by the name Defenders,
and the whole were of the very worst description,' was an official
opinion on the 152 male and 70 female convicts who disembarked
from the *Marquis of Cornwallis* at Sydney on 11 February 1796.
Eleven men had died during the passage, and, of those who landed,
90 were classified as agrarian offenders, 63 of them had life sentences,
and they represented all four Irish provinces. Within a month of the
vessel sailing from Ireland there were rumours on board of a conspiracy by the convicts and some of the military to seize her. Sergeant
Ellis, of the New South Wales detachment, who was believed to have
been involved in the plot was 'arrested, flogged and ironed to Private
L. Gaffney'. The men were handcuffed, thumb-screwed and leg-
bolted together until the sergeant died nine days later; then Gaffney
was removed from the corpse and ironed to another convict until the
ship docked, a period of over four months. After some 50 men who
were suspected of being implicated in the conspiracy had been flogged, they tried to strangle the informers amongst them. This fracas
caused the guard to fire into the prison. At the subsequent inquiry
evidence was given that the female convicts intended to assist in the
conspiracy 'by preparing pulverised glass to mix with the flour of
which the seamen were to make their puddings'. The ship's captain
was found correct in the punitive action which he took to prevent
the mutiny. On disembarkation the prisoners were described as 'in
general healthy, but some of those who had been punished were not

quite recovered, and were sent to hospital'. They were 'for the most part, of the description of people termed Defenders, desperate and ripe for any scheme from which danger and destruction were likely to ensue, the women were of the same complexion – what an importation!' As Roman Catholics they were even more suspect and, having been organised to some degree at home, and possibly involved in agitation, the Defenders would have been less amenable to convict discipline.

In Ireland preparations were being made for the sailing of another convict ship. Sir Jeremiah Fitzpatrick, a County Westmeath born doctor and Inspector General of Prisons, inspected the transport *Britannia* at Portsmouth before she sailed for Cove. A couple of years earlier the inspector, who was dedicated to reform of the whole convict system, had remarked that all the convict officials, the doctors, contractors and other officers, were leagued together in a system of favours and defalcation. On the *Britannia* he had improvements made in the manner in which the convicts might be segregated, by sex, health and behaviour. Ensuring that they were issued with clothing bags, tea kettles and tin mugs, he hoped that 'the voyage of these unhappy wretches should be rendered as comfortable as possible'.

Thomas Dennott, the master of the *Britannia*, had different views from those of Fitzpatrick. Fearing difficulties, such as those on the *Marquis Cornwallis* and on other Irish ships, he wrote to the chief mate at Cove:

> As the convicts will be on board today or tomorrow, I shall just mention a few points on which I must beg you will pay particular attention; that there be a constant guard kept over them during the day, and that one officer with ten armed men strengthen that guard during the night; that their irons be searched twice every day with the greatest minuteness, and in case any convict should have attempted to get his irons off, for the first offence he be punished with no less than six dozen lashes, with a right and left cat, if able to bear so much. During the punishment that a guard be drawn up on the quarter-deck with bayonets fixed and loaded muskets. If any instrument should be found on any convict, that he be immediately punished with four dozen lashes, and if found in any of their berths that the whole belonging to the berth be punished in like manner, without they declare the culprit. If the convicts should refuse to clean their different berths, the person so offending be punished with two dozen lashes. . .

A less unpleasant letter concerning the *Britannia* was that referring to '13 large cases, containing 6 large looms' for shipment to the colony.

These would soon prove useful for the employment of the many skilled weavers transported after 1798.

The five and a half month passage of the *Britannia* proved, despite the efforts of Inspector Fitzpatrick, to be one of the most brutal in the history of transportation; 10 men and 1 woman died during that time, reducing the number that were disembarked to 134 men and 43 women. Believing that there was about to be a mutiny on board, Master Dennott ordered that the most savage punishments should be awarded. Sadistic by nature, the master did not hesitate to order that James Brannon should be given 300 lashes, followed by 500 the next day. Several men endured 300 lashes, but Patrick Garnley died on the morning after he had received 400. The details of the brutality of the punishment on successive days are shocking, and the floggings were made more severe with the master's insistence that the cat should be made more cutting with the addition of horse skin, and that men pleading for water were not given it. 'I will not hang you,' Dennott roared at some of the prisoners, 'it is too gentle a death, but I will cut you to pieces.' Of the 10 men who died, 6 were as a result of floggings, and 2 others who had also been flogged died from drinking their own urine when refused their water ration.

The females were also harshly treated; several were publicly beaten with a cane, or had their heads shaved. Others were ironed, chained or placed in the neck-yoke. Mary Cogan, who had already attempted suicide while in jail in Dublin, succeeded in doing so on the ship while she was awaiting punishment from the master. Neglect on the part of the ship's surgeon aggravated the plight of the unfortunate prisoners. He did not attend the punishments and he rarely visited the prison. If the women came to him for medicines he refused them and, it was rumoured, sometimes beat them.

So outrageous were the complaints about the *Britannia* that, on its arrival, the governor of the colony John Hunter ordered an inquiry. It was found that the master had been too severe with punishment, and that the surgeon, Augustus Beyer, had been negligent to such a degree that he was an accessory to the master. But neither of the officers was punished, except in that they were no longer to be employed in the convict service.

Like their countrymen of six years before, the newly arrived men could not adapt to the rigorous life of the colony and they made repeated attempts to escape. When spoken to by the governor the

Defenders showed 'a considerable degree of obstinacy and ignorance'.
He decided that 'no better argument could be used to convince them
of their misconduct than a severe corporal punishment, which was
inflicted, and they have since been strictly looked after at their work'.
Six of them, having made their fifth attempt to escape, were again
captured, tried and hanged.

In general the Irish convicts who had arrived so far in New South
Wales were seen as

> turbulent and refractory, and so dissatisfied with their situation that, with-
> out the most rigid and severe treatment, it was impossible to derive from
> them any labour whatever. In addition to their natural vicious propensities,
> they conceived an opinion that there was a colony of white people which
> had been discovered in this country, situated to the SW of the settlement,
> from which it was distant between three and four hundred miles.

Some of the men hoped to escape and their naïveté drew the observation: 'could it be imagined that, at this day, there was existing in a
polished civilised kingdom a race of beings (for they do not deserve
the appellation of men) so extremely ignorant, and so little humanised
as these were, compared with whom the naked savages of the mountains were an enlightened people?' These remarks, expressed by Captain David Collins, in his book *Account of the English Colony in New
South Wales*, published in 1802, may have influenced other less
experienced observers of the convict colony. Having arrived on the
first fleet, Collins was knowledgeable on the situation there, but his
opinion of the Irish may have been biased on account of his family
background. The son of an English major-general who had settled
in Ireland, possibly on a government granted estate, Collins was born
in the King's County in 1756 and sent to England for schooling at
an early age. It is doubtful if he ever acquired any affection for his
birthplace, and the 'polished civilised kingdom' to which he referred,
if he meant Ireland, was not the kingdom of the greater majority of
the population.

Sometimes Governor Hunter (1795-1800) did show sympathy for
the Irish, remarking that 'the ignorance of these poor deluded people
would scarcely be believed if such positive proof of it was not before
us'. One group of men who had seized a boat in an escape attempt
had been drowned, and another large party tried to reach the 'white
colony' with the aid of a compass on a piece of paper. When they

were captured the governor ordered that, 'for the sake of humanity, four of the hardiest, to be selected by themselves, should be sent on a journey of discovery'. He gave them guides, but these were withdrawn when it was found that the convicts planned to murder them. Instead soldiers were sent to the mountains with the Irishmen, 'but they all turned back, sick of the journey'. On another occasion the governor singled out an individual for praise: 'I could not get a mill erected until I found an ingenious Irish convict who has finished a very good one, and as an encouragement I gave him £25'.

In general, however, complaints were more usual to the authorities at home about the documentation of the convicts and about the quality of the men: 'If so many Irish are sent here it will be impossible to keep order'.

However, an exception to the latter generalisation must have been Henry Waldron, born in 1755 at Maynooth, County Kildare, the son of a respectable, silversmith and his wife, a midwife and dressmaker. The cost of his education was undertaken by a local clergyman on account of the poverty of the parents. At the Blue Coat School in Dublin Waldron stabbed another pupil during a brawl. Before he ran away from the school he took with him whatever valuables he could find, and so started his career. Joining a group of touring players he changed his name to George Barrington, and he supplemented his meagre income by picking pockets. Moving to London he became a professional gentleman pickpocket and was successful for a time.

When he was caught he was confined in a hulk on the Thames, but after he was released he was soon back at his old occupation. When he was next apprehended, despite an eloquent plea from the dock, he was sentenced to seven years transportation. During the voyage out he helped to quell a mutiny, and so gained the confidence of the captain. Soon he was reading the Sunday service for his fellow convicts.

On arrival in New South Wales he ingratiated himself with the authorities and in two years he merited the first Warrant of Emancipation that was issued. He was appointed Chief Constable at Parramatta and Superintendent of Convicts. His free time he devoted to writing plays for the Sydney Theatre Royal, at the opening of which in 1796 he is said to have spoken the prologue; part of it went as follows:

Through distant climes, o'er wide spread seas we come,
(Though not with much eclat, or beat of drum)
True patriots all; for it be understood,
We left our country for our country's good.

He is credited with the authorship of *A Voyage to New South Wales
(with a description of the country; the manners, customs, religion etc. of
the natives, in the vicinity of Botany Bay)* in 1796, and two histories
of the new land. He died a respected citizen, but a lunatic, in 1804.
He is remembered in Australian folklore as 'The Crown Prince of
Pickpockets'.

In the autumn of 1796 as more prisoners were being assembled
on the brig *Elizabeth* at Cove, to await the arrival of a transport ship,
many of them sought friends or scribes to write petitions to Dublin
Castle in an effort to secure a reprieve or a remission of sentence.
Others sent information to the Castle in a desperate attempt to gain
clemency. One called Murphy gave a list of Defenders in County
Louth, complaining that it was their ill-will that caused him to be
transported. Some others gave information on their fellow prisoners
on the brig, while a number of Kildare men communicated with their
county gentry offering to make disclosures of various descriptions,
and in particular of the Defenders' depot of arms; for their co-operation
Laurence Drennan, Edward Byrne, Pat Connor and Michael Galavan
petitioned that they should be allowed to join the fleet. Commenting
on this information Mr J. Wolfe of Forenaghts, Naas, recommended
that the men should be interviewed at Cove to see what they had to
say; Galavan, he added, had been given £20, raised by friends, to
bribe the ship's captain to allow him to escape.

Fearing the possibility of an invasion by the French, and concerned
by the increasing organisation of the United Irishmen, the government formed a corps of loyal yeomen; already much concerned with
the French wars, London could commit no further troops to Ireland.
The passing of the 1796 Insurrection Act was intended as a further
deterrent to unrest; it gave magistrates considerable discretion in the
sentencing of offenders, and it was possible for them to transport men
on very little evidence. When the Lord Lieutenant proclaimed disturbed counties, where agrarian disturbance was common, a night
curfew was imposed with the intention of preventing illegal gather-
ings, restricting the administration of oaths to such tenant-rights
societies as Whiteboys or Defenders, and curtailing attacks against

persons or property. Anyone abroad by night, or guilty of offences, could be sentenced to exile by two magistrates, without a jury. Military courts also had wide powers, and in 1797 one Dublin Castle official voiced the opinion that the awarding of lesser punishments would but excite offenders to seek revenge, and that all prisoners in jails should be transported.

Another important factor in Irish political life at this time had been the founding of the Society of United Irishmen in 1791. They sought to gain parliamentary reform, a more just administration, a lowering of taxes and an improvement in trade, through the pressure of public opinion. Roman Catholics, too, were seeking emancipation from oppressive laws, and agrarian discontent continued. With the outbreak of war between England and France the more radical leaders of the United Irishmen believed that, with help from France, this was the time to gain reform, emancipation and independence. Plans were made for a rising in the month of May 1798 but, despite some serious engagements between the government troops and the rebels in both the north and south of the country, the day was lost. Soon the United Irishmen were being rounded up and disposed of by execution, exile or imprisonment.

Though no other transport ship sailed from Ireland until the month of August 1799, when many of those on board were sentenced as a result of the Rising of the year before, the contemporary County Wexford Catholic historian Edward Hay wrote: 'For months previous to the Insurrection groups of from 12 to 15 cartloads of persons, condemned to transportation in other counties, passed daily through the county Wexford on their way to Duncannon fort.'[12] In the month of July 1798 a witness said he saw 'many floggings in Carrick-on-Suir, after which salt was rubbed into the wounds', and he observed transportees en route to Duncannon from Clonmel passing through Carrick. One such prisoner was described by Mrs Barbara Newton Lett: 'this horrid creature dined every day with our servants, and was a person whom we never should have suspected as the author or maker of deadly weapons. He was tried for his offence, and transported for life.'

Historian Hay himself narrowly escaped transportation. He had surrendered with the hope of being sent to America, but he was delayed and false charges were laid against him.

Without trial or investigation I was marched to the Custom House Quay and put on this hulk. Two sloops had already been prepared as prison ships [by the rebels], and one of them had been condemned as unfit for a pig, named *The Lovely Kitty*, it was hauled to one side of the [Wexford] harbour, where for leaks it sank, and so escaped when the other sloop was set on fire.

On the hulk he continued:

a little dry straw was shaken over what remained in her hold, and when walked on it became dung. We could not sit for the damp, or rest on the sides as the planks were soaked; some of the men were bitten by rats. The stench of rotten malt, and the heat of crowded bodies made it impossible to see from one end of the room to the other.

When it rained the men were further soaked, and the stinking water had to be constantly pumped to prevent the vessel sinking. There were 21 men on board *The Lovely Kitty* in conditions which, Hay believed, 'could not be paralleled by any dungeon in the world'. He complained about the situation and was told: 'That as the vessel had been fitted-out by the rebels, she was good enough for them'. His companions Hay regarded as 'desperate villains, the scum of the earth'. One of the guards on the sloop Hay recognised as a carpenter who had worked for his father. This man from the Shelmalier Infantry, a County Wexford yeomanry corps, offered to bring Hay his bed, but the captain of the guard, a former friend and neighbour of Hay's, refused him this privilege.

Another prisoner on *The Lovely Kitty* was 13-year-old James Letts, a near relative of the United Irish leader Bagenal Harvey. This boy had shown great courage at the battles of Ross and Foulkesmill and when he was captured he was told that he would be hanged if he did not petition to be transported. He was released later. Hay spent thirteen months in confinement, of which five weeks were spent on the sloop and the remainder in jail. Hay secured his release by submitting evidence that he had not been involved in any of the battles, and that his only weapon was his pistol, as the rebels had taken the others from him. He pleaded that, in fact, he was prepared to fight against the rebels, and that he had taken dispatches for the army, and that the whole business of his confinement was a mistake.

The *Princess*, the vessel arranged to transport prisoners from Wexford to Cove, was crowded with 282 men, of whom 142 had been committed without trial. Fifty of the men were said to require medical

attention, and they were all confined in the prison which measured 90′ x 30′ x 7′, and in which there was a shortage of hammocks and bedding. There was a fear that, due to overcrowding, fever would break out. There was no medical officer. There was also concern that the 39 army recruits on the vessel might be influenced by the prisoners, 'some of whom had committed no crimes, while others had offences of the most heinous nature'. The prisoners plotted to seize the vessel and run her ashore, but when the 'Rev. Henry Fulton, a Protestant clergyman and Mr O'Meara, a Roman Catholic priest', discovered the plot they informed the commander. As a result the plot was aborted, and the two clergymen prisoners were recommended for indulgence by the commander: 'I consider myself under the greatest obligation to those two clergymen. . . if the plot had come off few of us would be alive.'

This action of the parson and the priest illustrates the complexity of the relationship between the clergy themselves and the people.

Fr William O Meara, Parish Priest of Nenagh, with Fr Talbot of Castletown Arrah and the Rev. Mr Fulton, had been accused of taking the 'Defenders Oath' and were imprisoned at Limerick. Neither of the two priests was transported, and local tradition at Castletown Arrah, Portroe, near Nenagh, keeps alive the memory of Fr Talbot. He is said to have condemned publicly the immoral life of the local Protestant landlord, who secured Catholics to give false evidence against the priest. Tied to a tree in the landlord's demesne and then flogged, Fr Talbot was taken to Duncannon, and from there to Cove where he died on the hulk, due to ill-treatment. Nor, the story concludes, did the landlord prosper. Soon after this incident he fell from his horse and was killed.

When the *Princess* arrived at Cove, in the month of May 1799, the prison was fumigated and white-washed. The bedding had to be destroyed, and it was recommended that, before new bedding was issued, the men should be 'combed, and well washed with soap and water'.

Soon after the Rising started, on 20 May 1798, General Dundas from his camp at Castlemartin, near Kilcullen, County Kildare, complained that 'the jail and guard room at Naas are full. . . many of those (imprisoned) were sentenced to transportation, and some who have had the death sentence mitigated to transportation. What am I to do with them?' By August General Nugent, in Belfast, was suggesting that those prisoners who had surrendered themselves should be allowed 'to transport themselves to America'. Any of the military themselves who had shown disloyalty were severely punished; John Malone, a private in the 5th Royal Irish Dragoons, found guilty of 'trying to entice others to desert to the rebels', was given 500 lashes and ordered 'to serve His Majesty abroad, for life'. Yeomen also were found to have attended illegal meetings, to have violated their oath, to have conspired on the life of fellow yeomen, or to have had arms at illegal meetings. Daniel Greer, accused of all of these crimes, was sentenced to 500 lashes and transportation; later, on account of his youth, he was permitted to go to America. Other less fortunate yeomen were executed.

Two United Irish leaders in Ballymoney, County Antrim, John Gunning and Richard Caldwell, were sentenced to death, but the former was allowed to go to America, while the latter went to New South Wales. So did Caldwell's neighbour, William Johnson, but first he endured a sentence of 500 lashes. In the parish of Glin, County Limerick, the United Irish leader Tom Langan, also known as Captain Steel, was given the death sentence. On the intervention of the Knight of Glin the sentence was mitigated to seven years in 'Botany Bay'. Langan returned to Glin in 1817, again due to the influence of the Knight.

While the arrival of vessels to transport prisoners to New South Wales was awaited, the jails and hulks continued to be packed with more transportees. As an example to others punishments were sometimes inflicted on individuals in the jails or hulks: on 25 September 1798 Daniel O Meara, a farmer from Lorrha, County Tipperary, was given 150 lashes. He had been sentenced to 400 lashes and transportation for 'endeavouring to procure arms'.

The terror of the Rising and its aftermath did not quiet the country. In a country town in the month of February 1799, for maiming and houghing cattle, a man was given 'a thousand lashes on his bare back by the drummer of the garrison with a cat-o-nine tails', and then hanged. A Limerick city merchant, Francis Arthur, imprisoned and awaiting transportation to Australia, who had also been fined £5,000 for alleged involvement in the Rising, petitioned Dublin Castle on the grounds that he had been convicted on the false evidence of a perjurer.

All of those under sentence of banishment were not in the political or agrarian category. Thirteen-year-old James Connor was one of four boys from Dublin sentenced to transportation for life. His parents pleaded that 'he was playing marbles on the steps of the parliament house when, during a friendly scuffle, one boy said that three pound notes were taken from him'. Connor and his friends were transported. Such juvenile 'criminals' did not necessarily get compassion on account of their youth, and many of them begged to be allowed to go to America, or to enlist in the Services rather than to be sent to 'Botany Bay'. They might have been surprised at the better quality of life to be found in Australia, where there was no poverty, but many opportunities for advancement. The availability of free convict labour made it unnecessary to employ the young at the laborious tasks as at home, and they were not exploited.

A shoemaker from Monaghan was sentenced to seven years transportation when prosecuted by his sister for stealing sheep from their father. Three brothers from County Wicklow were convicted of concealing stolen goods; one of them was transported but, despite a petition from the inhabitants of Clonbullogue that only one of the others should be hanged as a warning, both were executed.

Another solution to the problem of the troublesome section of the population was proposed in March 1799. It was that all fit Irish rebels would be taken as privates by the King of Prussia, 'a good way of getting rid of them,' commented a government official. The Prussian officer seeking the soldiers said 'I only want young, well-looking and tall men, at least 5' 4", under 30 years of age. Rebels only, no rogues or thieves; I will take 200.' They were to be collected at New Geneva,[3] and engaged for ten years, after which they might return home with an honourable passport. They could bring their families with them as 'otherwise no good will be got of them'.

Perhaps he was speaking from knowledge of the Irishmen who had served in Prussia earlier in the century. King George I, in 1721, had sought volunteers, of whom he wished to make a present to the King of Prussia, to complete his royal regiment of grenadiers. Then the physical requirements had been higher and the volunteers had to be not under 6' 2", though they could be either Protestants or Catholics, providing they were gentlemen.

But all of the men destined for Prussia were not volunteers, as this story from Cox's *Irish Magazine* for the month of February 1815 illustrates. In 1798 one of the prisoners at New Geneva was a young man named O'Neill from County Antrim who had been a student for the priesthood. His mother undertook the long journey from the north to visit him, as 'he had been sold to the King of Prussia as a slave for the salt mines'. Having bribed a sentry Mrs O'Neill gained entry to the barracks, but just as she greeted her son she was taken and brought before the governor. Following a long questioning by Colonel Scott and his wife, Mrs O'Neill was handed over to Highlanders from the Garrison to be 'blanketed'. They stripped her naked and, in the presence of the colonel and his lady, eight of them tossed her in the blanket for twenty minutes. Observers outside the barracks saw the unfortunate victim appearing above the wall for that time. Afterwards she was taken to a nearby village, where she died the next day.

The blanketing of Mrs O'Neill, 1798, in Cox's *Irish Magazine*, February 1815 (National Library).

Kingstown Harbour, from the *Dublin Penny Journal*, 15 January 1834.
The hulk *Essex* is the mastless vessel in the foreground (National Library).

2 United Irishmen, 1798-1799

Following the Rising of the United Irishmen in 1798 it has been estimated by Dr Kiernan that about 775 political prisoners were among the 1,067 men transported in nine ships between 1799 and 1805. Seven ships carried over 172 female convicts, but as at least one of these, the *William Pitt*, which sailed from Cove on 31 August 1805, may also have carried women from England, an exact figure is not available.

Both the *Minerva* and the *Friendship* left Cork in August 1799 with a total of 321 men and 26 women, all victims of the unsuccessful Rising. A glimpse of the preparations for the passage is given in a letter from Matthew Sutton, on the *Friendship*, to his father. 'We have been stripped, scrubbed and dressed in canvas shirts; then ironed together.' Fever, he said, had already infected the long room where 120 men were confined, and several died. Six men also died on the *Minerva* while she was waiting at Cove, and 8 were discharged; 3 more died during the passage, and 7 women gave birth. A list of the 162 male and 26 female convicts who disembarked from the vessel at Sydney in January 1800 shows that 7 men had surrendered themselves for transportation, 76 were thought to be political offenders. Among the professions represented among the prisoners were army officers, a doctor, a teacher, two attorneys, a Protestant and a Catholic clergyman. Trades represented amongst the 71 skilled men included blacksmith, apothecary, silversmith and engraver, cotton and linen printer, jeweller, cutler, tallow-chandler and soap boiler, coppersmith, iron-founder, carpenters, mill and wheel-wrights, stonemasons, plasterers, distillers, tilers, nailers, publicans and tobacconists, painters, woolcomber, cotton-spinner, baker, carpet maker, hosier, shoemaker, gardener, cooper, butcher, gentlemen's servant, and 20 weavers. All these craftsmen must have proved of considerable use in the infant colony. Even the governor, in the midst of the 'Irish conspiracy' of September, 1800, admitted that 'some good workmen are among the Irish convicts lately brought here, in the flax and weaving'.

Aboard the ships which left Ireland in August 1799 were some of

the men who were to become best known in the history of transportation from Ireland. All sentenced for political crimes, they were Fr
James Harold, and Fr James Dixon, Rev. Mr Henry Fulton, Dr
Bryan O'Connor, James Meehan, Joseph Holt, Captain St Leger
and Captain William Alcock. The two latter gentlemen had been,
respectively, in the 24th Light Dragoons and in the Wexford Militia.

Fr Harold was parish priest of Rathcoole, County Dublin and his
house at Rathcoole was burned by the militia in 1798. Accused of
complicity in the Rising, he was tried at Kildare and, at the age of
55, given a sentence of transportation for life. Holt, from County
Wicklow, was a 'strong Protestant' farmer who had seen his house
burned by the yeomen. Joining the rebels, he soon proved to be a
good leader with a notable victory over government forces at Bally-
ellis. With the failure of the Rising, Holt surrendered unconditionally
to Lord Powerscourt and, at the age of 39, was sentenced to transportation for life. Dr O'Connor at Cork and Rev. Fulton at Tipperary
received the same sentence. A contemporary account of the departure
of Holt is that 'he swore, blasphemed and inveighed most bitterly
against this breach of his treaty', as he had expected to be sent to
America. Handcuffed, double-bolted and encompassed in an 'iron
circumference', according to one report, Holt left the Pigeon House[4]
in Dublin for transport to Cork. His own version of his departure
claims that he refused the fetters. As the vessel bringing the convicts
south passed down the Wicklow coast Holt mused: 'If I had known
the misery of this vessel, no lord or lady would have influence enough
to induce me to surrender.' Sleet, rain, short rations, including lack
of water, made life miserable. The stinking bilge water, and 'a tub,
meant as a toilet for 80 persons and only emptied every twenty-four
hours, kept in a constant state of evaporation by the movement of the
ship' added to the squalor. When they put in at Ballyhack, and later
at Cove, the local people came on board to see Holt, 'the general'.

Waiting to greet Holt also were his wife and children, their arrival
arranged by Mrs Latouche, a wealthy acquaintance of theirs. She had
given 120 guineas to purchase passage on the *Minerva* so that his
family could accompany him. With Mr Fulton's family they shared
a cabin off the steerage, and there Mrs Holt gave birth to a son. Six
other women, of the 34 on board, of whom 26 were convicts, also
gave birth before the vessel sailed. Captain Alcock's wife came to visit
him, and he signed over his property to her; later Holt remarked that

Alcock 'carried a locket with her picture and hair in it, but in the fourteen years he spent in exile she never once wrote to him'.

While the cause of the captain's wife's failure to communicate is not known, the distress of Alcock must have been extreme. Such lack of contact between the exiles and their families was an additional anxiety to them, and pathetic protests from convicts whose letters home had not been answered are to be found in the state archives in Dublin.

The destitute and desperate state of the convicts on the *Minerva* is shown by the fact that when they discovered that they were to be issued with new clothes they sold the old ones; each man got two each of trousers, jackets, shirts, pairs of socks and shoes, with a rug, a blanket and a flock bed. When the heads of the prisoners were being shaved Holt refused to have his done. He was brought ashore to meet General Meyers when, he boasted, 'a crowd of 400 gathered to see him'. The general, according to Holt, offered him his freedom 'if he turned over', but he said that 'he would prefer to try his fortune in a new land'.

During the passage the *Minerva* anchored at Rio de Janeiro for three weeks to take on fresh supplies. There, too, the ship's captain, whom Holt described as 'a kind master', made some money 'by selling watches which he had brought from Dublin, and which he had engraved during the voyage by two Dublin convicts'. Having gained the captain's confidence Holt was put in charge of the convicts while they were on deck, when the United Irishmen were allowed an extended recreational period. 'Unpleasant characters on board included two informers from northern Ireland', remembered Holt; one of them told the captain that there was a plan to scuttle the vessel, but Holt exposed him. There was also some comedy aboard. When the *Minerva* drew close to purchase supplies from a passing sloop, Holt bought fruit and pepper. The latter was a great novelty, and after he had burned his mouth, Holt offered the pepper to Alcock and Fulton, causing the parson to cry out, 'Holt, you have poisoned me'; to which Holt replied, 'Call up the priest to anoint him'.

There was no such frivolity when the ship docked at Sydney. They were greeted by the sight of the skeleton of a murderer hanging from a gallows on top of a hill. When a convict tried to come on board the vessel he was shot by a soldier from County Cavan, who was later tried for his 'vigilance' and sentenced to the penal colony on Norfolk

Island. Holt was employed to manage a farm, and the family adapted to the new life. Then, in the September of 1800, there were rumours of an insurrection by the Irish and, with other alleged conspirators, Holt was arrested and confined for a while.

Within a few months of the sailing of the *Minerva* and the *Friendship*, official correspondence indicates that at home the state of the country remained unsettled. The sheriff of Limerick requested a military guard to accompany convicts to Cork as 'it was not possible to travel otherwise'. Another guard from the Sligo Militia was detailed to travel with the prisoners from Wexford jail to New Geneva barracks where they were to await shipment to Cork, en route to New South Wales in December 1799. One of these prisoners, Thomas Cloney, who was in poor health, travelled on a horse given to him by a friend; through Taghmon and Foulkesmill they came to New Ross, where they were kept overnight in the guard room. Early the following morning, Cloney wrote, 'a Gun Boat took us down the river to New Geneva, a dark and loathsome prison, it really exceeded any description I could give of it for filthiness and want of every sort of comfort'. There were three priests with Cloney; he found that the intolerable smell in their sleeping place 'baffles description, so it was impossible to eat'. But he was fortunate, and after twelve months imprisonment at Wexford his petition for clemency was successful and he was released.

Another man in the barracks of New Geneva in the winter of 1800 was Christopher Fallon whose transportation had been delayed for nine months as he was found fit and suitable for work there. In the hope of obtaining a pardon he gave the information that the 250 convicts on board a ship in the harbour were 'in general, robbers of the most desperate character; they would have many times annihilated the officers and crew but I told the colonel, and they were caught and punished; glad I was to save many lives. I abhor rebels. . .'. Just a year earlier the evidence of another informer, Bridget Dolan from Carnew, was doubted by the Lord Lieutenant. He recommended that the sentence of death imposed on a number of men at court-martial should be mitigated 'to general service abroad, or transportation for seven years', as Dolan's 'testimony has been so often impeached'.

The convicts from the *Minerva* and the *Friendship* were not long at Port Jackson in New South Wales before Governor Hunter expressed his views on them; 'With respect to labourers, notwithstand-

ing the number brought from Ireland by the last two ships, we have
received no great accumulation of strength. Many of those prisoners
have been either bred up in genteel life, or to professions, unaccus-
tomed to hard labour. Those are a dead weight on the public store;
and really, nothwithstanding, we cannot fail to have the most determined abhorrence of the crimes which sent many of them here, yet
we can scarcely divest ourselves of the common feelings of humanity
so far as to send a physician, a formerly respectable sheriff of a county,
a Roman Catholic priest, or a Protestant clergyman and family to the
grubbing hoe or timber carriage.'

Suitable employment was found for James Meehan, who had
arrived on the *Friendship*, in the surveyor's office. Gradually he
became a trusted official with responsibility for almost all the land
surveys and road and town plans in New South Wales and in Van
Diemen's Land. When he retired in 1820 he held the position of
Deputy Surveyor of New South Wales; described as 'a most excellent
land surveyor, a man of strict honour and dignity', he was given an
annual pension of £100. Later Meehan Valley, in Tasmania, bore his
name, and a school was established in his former home.

Also transported in the *Friendship* was Michael Hayes, from Enniscorthy, with a life sentence for his part in the Rising. Some of his
correspondence home has been preserved, including a letter from the
ship in which he mentions that he had become friendly with Fr Dixon
whom he found to be in bad health and short of money.

Regarded with suspicion and suspected of plotting insurrection,
the Irish were investigated by a court of inquiry convened to consider
information received concerning assemblies in the colony. It met in
September 1800. After about a week's sitting it found that 'various
unwarrantable consultations and seditious meetings have been assembled by several of the disaffected Irish convicts, tending to excite a
spirit of discontent which was fast ripening to a serious revolt and
consequences the most dreadful. . .' Though no evidence of this plot
was produced, and no arms were found, the examining magistrate,
the Rev. Samuel Marsden, reported, 'We have not been able to come
at any of the pikes yet; whether we shall or not is uncertain. I think
there will be sufficient evidence. . . to justify some severe examples
of punishment.' Eighteen of the Irish were sentenced to removal to
Norfolk Island; of these, 9 were to be flogged, 5 receiving 500 lashes,
the remainder 100 each.

'James Harold, called priest', was the first to be examined; found
to be sympathetic with the conspirators, he was given a seven year
sentence to Norfolk Island, but first he was to be 'publicly brought
in person as a culprit to attend and bear witness on the said several
sentences being severely carried into execution, as a peculiar mark of
infamy and disgrace. . .' Fr Harold was made to stand with his hand
on the tree to which the men being flogged were tied, and thus to
observe at close quarters the terrible punishments.

An eye-witness account of the flogging of 40-year-old County Cork
farmer Maurice Fitzgerald describes the scene:

> The two floggers, a right handed and a left handed man, were given the
> task of administering the punishment. I never saw two threshers in a barn
> move their flails with more regularity than those two mankillers did,
> unmoved by pity. The very first blow made the blood spout out from
> Fitzgerald's shoulders, and I felt so disgusted and horrified that I turned
> away from the cruel sight. One of the constables employed to carry out
> this tremendous punishment came to me and forced me 'to look at my
> peril'. I have witnessed many horrible scenes, but this was the most appal-
> ling sight I had ever seen. The day was windy, and although I was 15
> yards to leeward from the sufferer, the blood, skin, and flesh blew in my
> face as the executioners shook it off their cats. During the time Fitzgerald
> was receiving his punishment he never uttered a groan, the only words
> he said were 'Flog me fair, do not strike me on the neck'. When it was
> over two constables took him by the arms to help him into the cart. He
> said to them 'Let my arms go', and struck each of them in the pit of the
> stomach with his elbows and knocked them down. He then stepped into
> the cart unassisted. The doctor remarked that the man had strength
> enough to bear two hundred more. . .

Fitzgerald, who was not a political prisoner, survived this ordeal and
was given a pardon in 1812.

Despite the suppression of the rumoured insurrection the fears of
the officials continued, and on the last day of September another
inquiry was appointed. This resulted in 34 men being sentenced to
be 'transported to some secluded isle belonging to the territory, there
to remain for the term of their original sentences, employed in hard
labour, and ordered to the strictest discipline to reduce them to due
obedience, subordination and order'. Before the end of the year they
were on Norfolk Island, a thousand miles east of Sydney, where very
soon they were again suspected of being involved in another insurrection. During the week before Christmas, 2 men were executed;

24-year-old John Woologhan, who had been convicted at Cork, and 40-year-old Peter McClean, from Cavan. Twenty-one others were 'severely punished'. An official report on this incident concluded that 'the lives of every person who would not assist them in forwarding their intentions, was to have been taken. Their intention was forcibly to have made themselves masters of the island, and for that purpose they had prepared a number of pikes. The officers were to have been put to death, they even proposed to murder the women and children. . .' While Joseph Holt did not then go to Norfolk Island, to which he had been sentenced, Fr Harold did. He spent seven years there. His reputation amongst his countrymen would not seem to have been high; fellow convict Michael Hayes found him 'a learned man, and a great orator, but he did not practice all he preached; he was avaricious and petulant to a degree for which others rebuked him. . .' No doubt, there must also have been criticism of the priest when, on 12 September 1800, two Irish prisoners were apprehended on information which he gave. They were discharged as the accusation was deemed to be 'malevolent and groundless'. After he was pardoned in 1810 Fr Harold went to America, and five years later he returned home. He worked in Fairview parish, in Dublin, where he died in 1830.

Two others who suffered for the unrest of 1800 were William Maum, from Cork, and Benjamin Carroll, from Roscommon. Both were Catholics, and they had life sentences. Carroll, 38, and a distiller by trade, was found in possession of 'a pike, completely finished': he was sentenced to 500 lashes and gaol ganged for life. Maum, a 21-year-old teacher of Greek and Latin, had been employed as an usher by Fr William Dunn of Charleville, County Cork. He was also sentenced to 500 lashes. An official view of him was that 'his atrocious conduct while in Ireland cannot be unknown to you. I shall, therefore, make no remark on him than by observing that his principles and conduct have changed as little as the others. Nor can time or place have an effect on such depraved characters.' This report suggests that the priest at Charleville must either have been ignorant of his employee's activities, or sympathetic to them. Nevertheless, Maum revived his luck and from a farm of fifty acres which he had been granted at Parramatta, he moved to a farm at Clarence Plains in Van Diemen's Land where he raced horses with some success.

Rev. Marsden, the magistrate responsible for much of the inhuman treatment of the convicts at this period, was termed 'the Christian Mahomet of Botany Bay'. Of him a fellow magistrate remarked, 'I have known him to order 500 lashes, and the punishments afflicted by his authority were more severe than those of any other magistrate in the colony.' In an effort to discover where pikes were hidden Marsden ordered a young Irishman to be severely punished. Of this flogging Marsden wrote: 'Though a young man he would have died upon the spot before he would tell a single sentence. He was taken down three times, punished upon his back, and also on his bottom when he could receive no more on his back. He is not in a situation to be send down to Sydney yet.' This unfortunate victim was probably 20-year-old Paddy Galvin whose punishment was also witnessed by Joseph Holt:

> He was tied up next to receive 300 lashes. The first hundred were on the shoulders, and he was cut to the bone between the shoulder blades, which were both bare. The doctor then ordered that the next hundred be inflicted lower down, which reduced his flesh to such jelly that the doctor ordered him to have the remaining hundred on the calves of the legs. During the whole time Galvin never whimpered or flinched, if indeed it was possible for him to have done so. He was asked where the pikes were hid. He answered he did not know, and that if he did he would not tell. 'You may hang me,' he said, 'if you like, but you shall have no music out of my mouth to make others dance.' He was put into a cart and sent to hospital.

Galvin recovered, and in 1810 merited a free pardon.

The subsequent fate of other prisoners who had travelled on the *Minerva* with Patrick Galvin is also known. Captain Alcock had his sentence reduced, and was given the post of assistant engineer. John Lacey, a 20-year-old iron-founder in Dublin when convicted, had been allowed to bring his wife with him. Given a grant of land, by 1810 he was described as having 'numerous infant family', and eventually he became the owner of 1,080 acres, with two houses. Wicklowman Alfred Byrne, who was 20 at the time of the United Irish rising, who was described as 'intelligent, sober, honest and industrious', was freed within six years of arrival in the colony, and with his wife and three children he lived on a grant of land near Botany Bay. By 1822 he had six children, and he had acquired more land and a 100 head of cattle. A most successful man was Richard Dry, a Protestant woollen draper from Dublin, who had been given a life sentence for political offences in 1797. From an original grant of 500 acres he eventually held 12,000. From being a store-keeper of 'much propriety'. and married to a 'Currency Lass',[5] he became an official with the British and Foreign Bible Society, and was a founder of the Tamar Steam Navigation Co., and of the Cornwall Bank. His son, who was an active anti-transportationist, was knighted.

Two men from the King's County, Edward McRedmond and Farrell Cuffe, also enjoyed moderate prosperity. The latter, a school-master from Edenderry, was aged 24 when he surrendered himself for transportation for life. Following the alleged Irish Conspiracy in the autumn of 1800 he was sentenced to '500 lashes of the cat', but he survived that experience and in 1828 was again teaching, and he lived on a thirty acre farm with his wife and son. McRedmond, a Protestant and a 32-year-old labourer when he was awarded a life sentence, had, thirty years later, been granted 135 acres on which he lived with his family. Those men who had trades generally found their skills in demand. Such a one was John Flahavan, a Waterford carpenter, transported for life at the age of 56, and still working as a carpenter in Sydney when aged 78.

Similarly it is known that among those who disembarked from the *Friendship* some prospered in the new land. William Davis, a blacksmith from the King's County, having acquired a pardon in 1814, had, by 1828, 1,700 acres, 700 cattle, 200 sheep and 2 houses. He was active in the affairs of the Catholic church. James Lyons, a former private in the Longford Militia who had been charged and convicted for joining the French in 1798, ended up as a constable[6] in Sydney, and he also worked for Fr J. J. Therry. On the other hand, Anthony Curran, a Protestant from County Mayo, and who worked as a self-employed mason, was murdered in 1823. After his widow received compensation she remarried.

A shoemaker who did well was Patrick Mason, from Saintfield, County Down. Given a conditional pardon by Governor Macquarie on 31 January 1816, he practised his trade, and by 1828 he was farming 100 acres and owned a dozen cattle.

Even more successful, and certainly more celebrated, was Denis McCarthy from Wexford. Within a decade of his arrival in the colony he was a constable at New Norfolk where he received Governor Mac-quarie when he visited there. The governor praised McCarthy's com-fortable farmhouse at Birch Grove, where he stayed a night, though within a few years he may have doubted the integrity of his host when he was awarded a sentence of twelve months for smuggling. While he was absent bushrangers raided Birch Grove and stole property, as a result of which McCarthy successfully pleaded for a reduction of his punishment. In addition to farming, McCarthy owned a schooner in which he explored the south-west coast and discovered coal. Despite the loss of the schooner he managed to acquire further vessels, and he also undertook contracts for the making of a road from Hobart to New Norfolk. But he seems to have been of a turbulent nature and, in addition to being accused of assault on one occasion, the quality of his road work was disputed. Though he acquired considerable land and property, his farm at Birch Grove was up for sale in 1820 when he was drowned, and there were rumours of foul play.

County Antrim man William Orr, a watch-maker from Creevery, was transported on the charge of lifting arms in 1799. His mother continued to plead for him on the grounds that he had been punished on a false charge, but that the ship had sailed when this was discovered. As a ballad said, he was gone

> From the emerald island
> Ne'er to see dry land
> Until they spy land
> In sweet Botany Bay.

3   Priests and Rebels, 1800

In the month of April 1800 the convict transport ship *Anne* lay at Waterford preparing for the passage to New South Wales. Part of the inspection report on the vessel was that 'it was found necessary to remove all provisions and stores to have the ship smoked to destroy the rats'. The damaged stores, it was ordered, should be replaced at Cork before the convicts embarked. One of those unhappily waiting for embarkation at Cork was Eleanor Moore who had already spent two years in jail. While she admitted that she stole house linen to make up into articles which she had pawned, she now pleaded for clemency.

Miles Byrne, a United Irishman from County Wexford who later served with distinction in the Irish Legion in France, saw many of his companions transported. Some of them he remembered in his *Memoirs* including 16-year-old Miles Breen who witnessed his father and brother being shot before he was 'sent on board a transport ship in the harbour of Dublin'. Three blacksmiths, 'James Haydon, William Butter and D'Alton', were transported on account of their trade, as it was feared that they would manufacture pikes. A man named Mallowney, who had been wounded at Castlebar, Byrne regarded as 'more fortunate'. His sentence of transportation was lifted to enable him to be sent to the Prussian army, where he reached the rank of sergeant-major. Byrne remembered Mrs Keogh whom he met after she had taken leave of her husband 'just put aboard a vessel in the river waiting to sail'. She cried that she 'was doomed never to see her dear husband more'. He also met men who had returned from New South Wales. In Paris he encountered Paul Murray, of Kilmurray, near Wicklow and, on another occasion, an informer named Morgan, who had been given a sentence for robberies and other crimes. Edward Gibbons, the son of a gentleman from Newport, County Mayo, also joined the Irish Legion in Paris. He had been condemned to be hung, and the rope was about his neck, when some humane person interceded on his behalf and had his sentence commuted, and he was transported to 'Botany Bay' for life. His crime, and that of his father, had been to allow their horses to transport General Humbert's baggage when he landed in Mayo in 1798. Gibbons senior fled to France where he got a commission in the Irish Legion also. Nevertheless, the great majority of those banished remained in Australia. Anticipating emancipation, many of them encouraged their wives and families to join them in a new life in a land of opportunity.

The *Anne* sailed from Cove on 20 June 1800, and there was much disturbance during the passage of 240 days. She was part of a convoy as far as the Canary Islands, then she was alone and about three weeks out of Rio de Janeiro, when the prison was being fumigated, a convict shouted 'Death or Liberty', and grabbed the ship's master, James Stewart, by the throat. Though order was restored within a few minutes, one convict had been shot dead. After the master had discussed the incident with his officers it was decided that the ringleader should be shot. Marcus Sheehy, identified as the man who had led the attack on the officers, was executed by firing squad, before the assembled convicts. Sheehy earned the dubious distinction of being 'the only prisoner thus executed on a convict ship', as they were usually hanged at the yard's arm. Christopher Grogan, the leader of the attack on the deck, was given 250 lashes.

Another version of this incident was given by a priest, Fr O'Neil, who was being transported for alleged complicity in a murder in County Cork. While Fr O'Neil found the master of the *Anne* to be kind, he described the mate as a brute, and it was he that the priest blamed for the trouble. After a convict spilled something on the deck the mate struck him with a cannon ball and killed him. This caused the other prisoners to revolt, but Fr O'Neil succeeded in having them submit to the officers. A few days later the convicts saw what they believed to be justice done when the mate fell from the mast and was killed. For the remainder of the passage the master ordered that the irons should be removed from the convicts, and they were only put on if a British warship was sighted, and before the *Anne* reached Sydney. While the ship had called at Rio Fr O'Neil had been allowed to go ashore; there he had said Mass, and purchased requisites which enabled him to celebrate Mass regularly for the remainder of the voyage. When the ship was endangered by a severe storm, and again by an iceberg, he called on his flock to pray. Master Stewart admitted that, in general, the conduct of the prisoners was good. Most of them he thought, 'were guilty of no crimes, but were charged with political crimes into which they had been led unwittingly by secret societies. . .'

The official account of the attempt by the convicts to seize the ship blamed the two deaths on the necessity to quell the affray. A vice-admiralty court which sat on the incident honourably acquitted the ship's officers.

On disembarkation at Sydney Fr O'Neil was surprised to be greeted by a well-dressed lady who, tearfully, told him that she had been a servant in his own house at Ballymacoda. Later, while working in Youghal, she had been falsely accused of theft and transported. When the real culprit was apprehended an order had been issued for her release but by then she had married well, and elected to remain where she was. Fr O'Neil penned a 'Remonstrance to the Nobility and Gentry of County Cork', giving details of his arrest and treatment, and this is believed to have influenced the decision to permit him to return to Ireland within a couple of years of arrival in the colony.

The lists, giving the sentences of the 133 male and 24 female convicts disembarked from the *Anne* after she arrived at Sydney on 21 February 1801, did not arrive in the colony until 1819, when an official order was received to the effect that any of those who had arrived on the *Anne* and whose sentences had expired, should be released. The prisoners, 15 of whom had died on the passage, were victims of the 1798 Rising, with sentences from courts-martial, or without any trial.

This influx of fresh convicts from Ireland was not welcomed in the colony, and Governor King (1800-1806) wrote back to London that, since the suppression of the Irish Conspiracy five months before:

> We have been very quiet until the arrival of the *Anne* transport from Cork, with 137 of the most desperate and diabolical characters that could be selected throughout that kingdom, together with a Catholic priest of the most notorious, seditious, and rebellious principles – which makes the numbers of those who, avowing a determination never to lose sight of the oath by which they are bound as United Irishmen, amount to 600, are ready, and only waiting an opportunity to put their diabolical plans in execution.

Then, having praised the discipline and good behaviour of the New South Wales corps, and of the greater part of the English inhabitants, he pleaded that 'no more men of a violent Republican character, and particularly the priests (of whom we have now three), should be sent'. Accepting that the colony had been established for 'the reception of such characters as could not with safety be kept in Ireland or England', he emphasised that the infant state could not absorb any more such persons. 'If more Irish Republicans are sent I do not know what will be the consequences. They have hitherto kept us in a constant state of suspicion.'

The 'notorious Catholic priest' complained of by the governor was Fr Peter O'Neil, the parish priest of Ballymacoda, County Cork, who was aged 33 when transported. He had been accused of involvement in the death of an informer and brought to the 'stinking black-hole in Youghal'. General Loftus, who was presiding there, said that he 'would make the popish rebel groan', and he ordered that Fr O'Neil would be flogged with a cat which had scraps of tin knotted into it. In the handball alley at Youghal the priest was stripped and put on the triangle; six soldiers, two at a time, left- and right-handed men, flogged him until he had been given 275 lashes.

> My back and the points of my shoulders were quite bare of flesh. . . After a pause a wire cat was got; the first lash, as it renewed all my pains, made me shake the triangle, indeed, a second infliction penetrated my loins and tore them excruciatingly. The third maintained the tremulous exhibition long enough, the spectators were satisfied.

Repeatedly asked if he was guilty, he replied, 'I would rather die.' Showing him the bloody bodies hanging on the gallows, the officials threatened that they would hang him and cut off his head and throw his body in the river, if he did not reveal the names of the United Irishmen which he knew from the confessional. As they failed to extract any information from the priest, he was sent to Duncannon, and from there to Waterford where he was put on board the *Princess Charlotte*. There he met another priest, Fr T. Barry, who died before the transportation vessel was prepared. Another prisoner on the ship was Thomas Cloney, who was later to be released. Transferred to the transport vessel *Anne*, where he was confined for ten months, Fr O'Neil knew that a Court of Inquiry was being held into his case at Youghal, but when a letter instructing that he should be taken off the convict ship reached Cove the *Anne* had sailed for Australia.

Fr O'Neil, with the two other Irish priests Fathers Harold and Dixon, was among those recommended for conditional pardon by the governor in the month of August 1801. But the Lord Lieutenant wrote from Ireland that he was not in favour of the priests being allowed to return home: 'It does not appear to me that I am enabled to form a competent judgement of the circumstances under which any one of the persons mentioned have *(sic)* been transported,' he wrote. However, a year later it was agreed that the three priests could be employed either as schooolmasters or in the exercise of their priestly duties. When, in November 1802, permission came from Ireland for Fr O'Neil to return home, the governor expressed sorrow at his departure, even to the extent of offering him a salary of £200 to remain. Fr Harold saw his colleague as 'a kind and faithful friend, who had brought with him property sufficient to afford us the necessities of life, and had only just left as much as would pay his passage home. Every shilling he could spare he left us, but any consideration of this nature is but a miserable compensation for his absence. . .' Despite the fact that the local Orange Men protested when he returned to Ballymacoda, Fr O'Neil remained there until he died at the age of 89 in 1846. Local tradition holds that all of those who informed against him met bad ends, through hanging or suicide. Of the man who held his horse when he was arrested, it was said that 'the grave received his hand seven years before his body', as due to an accident, his limb had to be amputated.

The character of the convicts in the colony during the time that Fr O'Neil spent there was remarked on by a long-time resident: 'Their worst trait is the ill-feeling they display to all except their own class. A spirit of freemasonry exists among them to a great extent, and the greater the ruffian, the greater the pet he is. A man who endeavours to reform, or to give satisfaction to his master is barely tolerated, while he who has been subjected to excessive punishment at the penal settlement is considered a hero.' The police were very much despised by the convicts, and those convicts who became constables were seen to have betrayed their mates.

The fear that the Irish rebels would again revolt is evident from a Proclamation issued by the governor in the month of April 1802. Aware of the fact that two recent attempts had been made to revive seditious meetings, it was ordered that no meeting of more than twelve people could be held, and then only with permission, and having given public notice. If two or more persons met contrary to this order, and did not disperse within half an hour of being told to do so, they should suffer death. Those found administering or taking oaths, for a mutinous or seditious purpose, should be given 1,000 lashes, and transported to a penal station and employed in the gaol gang.

A glimpse of life in Sydney in 1802 is given in a letter by Michael Hayes to his sister in County Wexford. Enclosing a lock of his hair, he said how much he wished that she could join him in Australia, but he could not yet afford to send her the passage money. He gave his opinion of the eleven hundred women in the colony: 'there are not twenty virtuous ones among them. Previously they used to be flogged and led through the town by the executioners, with a label on their backs telling the crime. Now they are mostly shaved and ducked, and sent up to hard labour with the men.' Mentioning some fellow prisoners, who were neighbours from Enniscorthy, he told of one man from that town who had been drowned while crossing a river in a native canoe. Hayes finished his letter by requesting his sister that 'three small firkins of butter be sent from Passage,[7] as presents for the governor'. Thirteen years later he was still an exile, and he wrote saying how much he would like to send his 6-year-old daughter home to Wexford. A couple of years after that, in a letter to Edward Hay complaining about the cruelties inflicted on those transported, he added a note asking that porter might be sent out to him for re-sale in the colony.

Three farmers from County Wexford who had also disembarked from the *Anne* in 1801 found a modicum of success in New South Wales. Two brothers from Barrymile, Moses and Michael Brennan, and James Doyle had been confined with other croppies[8] at New Geneva while awaiting transportation. On 31 January 1813 the Brennans were given conditional pardons, but Doyle had to wait a further five years for the same privilege. By 1828 both of the Brennans were married and living on farms, while Doyle had found employment with a miller in Sydney. Another transportee from the same vessel was Wicklow man James Byrne; when free he lived on his 200 acre farm at Appin with his wife and four children. Other old rebels found work as servants, such as Patrick Farrell, from Carlow, who was a farm labourer, and the Ulster Presbyterian weaver Robert Chambers, still employed as a servant at the age of 87.

In County Wexford today possibly the best remembered exile of the 1798 period is Fr James Dixon, who was a curate in Crossabeg parish after he returned from his education on the continent. Various traditions survive concerning his arrest; one is that he was hearing confessions when taken, another, that on the evidence of an informer, he was accused of having administered the United Irishman's oath, of singing a rebel song, and of wearing a medal inscribed *Erin Go Bragh*[9]. Lodged in Duncannon fort, he was sentenced to death, but this was commuted to transportation for life.

Captain Thomas Dixon, a leader of the United Irishmen, and the master of a vessel, decided to avenge the injustice to his cousin the priest. He went to the town jail and took out the informer and two other prisoners and brought them to the Bullring. There he forced the two men to shoot the informer and to dump his body from the quay. Though Fr Dixon continued to enjoy the confidence of a local landlord and of the Protestant clergyman of Crossabeg, they could not save him from transportation. In the company of 133 other croppies, many of whom were also from Wexford, he left Cove on the *Friendship* on 24 August 1799. While there are no records of complaints against the master, Hugh Reed, there were nineteen deaths amongst the convicts on the voyage, that is one death to every seven men embarked. But that all may not have been well on the *Friendship* is suggested in a letter home to Wexford from another prisoner named Thomas Flood of Clonmore. He wrote that 'Fr Dixon during his journey out on a boat that took six months to do the trip was chained to a dead black corpse until the rats ate the flesh off the bones (of the corpse)...'

After a few years in the colony Fr Dixon was permitted to say Mass publicly. A government proclamation of 19 April 1803 announced this fact, and ordained that during the service, which was to be at 9 o'clock on Sunday morning, there was to be 'no seditious conversation which might cause disturbance', nor were Protestants to behave in an anti-Catholic fashion. The priest was to be held responsible for the conduct of his flock both during Mass, and while the congregation was coming to and going from the location. At the first public Mass, on 15 May, Fr Dixon wore as a vestment an old damask curtain. There was no altar stone, and the chalice had been made from tin by a convict. His server was his friend Thomas Flood. A year later Governor King remarked that the regular Masses 'have had a most salutary effect on the Irish Catholics, and since its toleration there has not been the most distant cause for complaint among that description who regularly attend divine service'. In appreciation, Fr Dixon was given £60 per annum.

However, the Irish did not long remain in the good repute generated by the governor's remarks. In March 1804 there were again rumours of an Irish insurrection, and it would seem that Joseph Holt was determined not to be involved. He warned his countrymen that 'you saw in Ireland that even there you could not depend on each other, and I am sure it would be worse here. An insurrection will only add to your misery, or bring you to the gallows.' Lecky, the historian, might have been echoing Holt's words when he wrote: 'it is curious to note how, beneath the Southern Cross, as in every disturbance at home, the familiar figure of the Irish informer at once appeared'. An old Irish rebel, who declared he had suffered so much in rebellion that he would never again be implicated in it, gave the first information of the designs of the conspirators. Holt went so far as to tell the agitators that he would have nothing to do with them, and 'would be on the side of the governor'.

But the insurrection at Castle Hill went ahead with the rebels shouting that 'they would be free or die'. (They called it Vinegar Hill, after the battlefield of 1798.) Martial law was proclaimed and several of the rebels were shot. Prisoners were taken, eight of whom were 'strung up like dogs'. Holt's later account of the affair was that about 300 men, led by a Kerryman named Cunningham, took part. Cunningham was killed and his body was put on public display as a warning to others. A 'one-armed Monaghan man named Neil Smith' gave false information about Holt; his house was searched twice, and then Holt was lodged in jail where the jailor was 'one Daniel Macaleese, the former hangman of Trim, in County Meath'.

An Englishman who had been transported for forgery, mindful of 'the flame of sedition' lit by the Irish a few years earlier, found that

> discontent had taken root, and its eradication was a matter of more difficulty than could have been foreseen. The most unprincipled of the convicts had cherished the vile principles of their new companions, and only waited for the maturity of their designs to commence the execution of schemes which involved the happiness and security of the whole colony. Men of such desperate characters as are to be found in this colony, are not to be intimidated by punishment, nor discouraged by failure from the pursuit of that career of depravity, which is become dear to them from habit; nothing short of death can destroy in those minds, the affection for vice, and the determination to gratify their ruling passion. . .

Major Johnston, it was reported, suppressed 'a rising of 400 unhappy patriots by the use of musketry fire and bayonet, killing 20 and taking twice as many prisoners'. In the operation the following arms were seized: 26 muskets, 8 reaping hooks, 4 bayonets, 2 swords, a fowling piece, a pitch fork and a pistol.

Within a week of the insurrection Governor King admitted that 'excepting a brutal violence to one individual, no act of atrocity marked the conduct of these deluded people, who, there is not the least doubt in my mind and in that of the principal officers civil and military, were actuated and guided by some clever villains. Not a blade or grain of wheat was injured, nor was any property except arms, ammunition, and a few trifling things invaded. . .' Governor King suspected that Joseph Holt 'was principally concerned in these proceedings, yet there not being sufficient evidence to convict him before a criminal court, altho' sufficient to establish his guilt, and from the circumstances of his not being found with arms in his hands', he was exiled to Norfolk Island. Holt himself believed that false information was given about him by a Kerryman named Walsh. Eight men were executed, two of them being hung in chains; nine men were sentenced to a total of 3,084 lashes, of which they received 880, one man being given 284 and another 200.

Despite the fact that Fr Dixon accompanied the officer who sought to persuade the Castle Hill rebels to surrender he was suspected of plotting with them and, for a time, his salary was withheld. He had the unhappy duty of attending those who were hanged and during the floggings, the horror of that punishment caused him to faint when he was forced to hold the hands of the victims at the triangle. Back at home in Wexford, it was rumoured that he himself was tied to a drag-cart and flogged.   .

In 1809 Fr Dixon was granted permission to return to Ireland, to see his parents, where he was joyously received by his parishioners. They built a presbytery for him beside the church at Crossabeg. But the exile was not welcomed by a local parson who complained that a man who had been convicted of treason and transported should again be in charge of souls. When Fr Dixon died as parish priest of Crossabeg in 1840 he was aged 82. During all of his years there he refused to talk about life in the convict colony, always replying to those who sought information: 'What good will it do you to know. The less you know about these punishments the better my child.' His grave, close to his church, became a place of pilgrimage, and pious people came to pray and take away earth from the grave. His remains were reinterred in 1913, and a fine memorial was erected over the grave which was visited by Archbishop Mannix of Sydney in 1927 during a visit home.

Following the departure of Fr James Dixon from Sydney there was a lapse of eight years before another priest came there.

'About 40 of the worst' of the Irish rebels from Castle Hill were sent to the coal works at Newcastle where, it was rumoured, they made a plan to kill the military guard and to make their escape. However, the plot was discovered and 'Francis Neason, and Neil Smith, the chief instigators and leaders of the conspiracy', were sent double-ironed and handcuffed back to Sydney, and the leaders were given severe corporal punishment, an average of 200 lashes, with 500 inflicted on a man named Tierney, 'for the murder plan'. Some time later it was decided to send twenty English convicts to the coal works as the governor had advised that 'by mixing them with the Irish you have, I promise myself less evil will arise, than if they were all Irish'.

Joseph Holt recalled later that during his time in the penal colony on Norfolk Island he believed

> that the usage I have seen men receive exceeds in cruelty any thing that can be credited. There was, in particular, one poor man named Michael Cox from the County of Cork; he was compelled to walk about and work with a chain, weighing twelve pounds, on his leg, and while labouring under a dysentery was driven up to his middle in the sea, and obliged to bring heavy packages ashore. He soon became too weak for work, and too late had his irons knocked off. Cox died a few days later. I hope he obtained mercy for his crimes in heaven, as none was extended to him on Norfolk Island.

Some of the officials on the island were also Irish. Both of the doctors were from Ulster, D'Arcy Wentworth and William Redfern, but 'they seemed to be afraid to exempt a man from work'. Peter Walsh, an overseer, was from Wicklow, and Holt knew his family at home. For company, Holt had Rev. Fulton, and the story was told that one Sunday while the latter was reading the bible to his flock an order was given 'to launch the boat', at which all the men ran to assist. This caused Holt to remark to the parson that 'I perceive Tony Chandler's word has more power than the word of God. . .' Holt also claimed that, when a French fleet appeared off-shore, 'all of the Irish were locked up, and arrangements were made to have them burnt to death, if the French attempted to land'.

Having endured '19 months and 2 days on the accursed island',

Holt came back to Van Diemen's Land; there he was entertained by a man from Wexford named Carty, and he found that the governor, Lieutenant Colonel David Collins, from King's County, was a cultivated and mannerly man, very much liked by the inhabitants. Though but holding a brevet rank, Collins had the distinction of being the founder of the new penal settlement at Port Phillip in south Australia, and of laying the foundation stone of Hobart. Judging by Holt's good impression of Governor Collins it would seem that he no longer judged the Irish so harshly as he had done a few years before in his book on New South Wales. Back in Sydney Holt was again troubled by informers; Hugh Byrne, a first cousin of Michael Dwyer, and also from Wicklow, and a Lieutenant Cummins, reported him to the authorities for distilling brandy illegally, for which he was bound over. But Holt could also be on the side of the law, and he helped to trap two Kildare men, Dick Troy and James Staines, who were dealing in stolen cattle.

Following the appointment of Captain William Bligh as governor of New South Wales (1806-1808) Holt was pardoned. His eldest son was then 21, married and settled on a 100-acre farm. Joseph himself held over 200 acres, with 400 sheep, 50 cattle and 7 horses; when he was granted a further 110 acres, it was measured out by his friend, the surveyor James Meehan, and he called it *Holt's Fancy*. In 1811, when given his free pardon, Holt sold his farm for £2,000 and set out for Ireland with his wife and son, and three servants, including John Byrne, who had worked for the Holts for ten years, and for whom Holt had secured a pardon so that he might return to his wife and seven children.

The cost of the passage home was £30 per head, the passengers having to provide their own food. For the latter purpose Holt killed a bullock and three hogs. Specially-made wheaten biscuits, tea, sugar and rum completed the store. In the steerage he had a cabin built for his family, and he procured a room for the men, on the *Isabella*. In February 1813, the ship ran on rocks near the North Cape. The life boats were lowered and the *Isabella* abandoned. The Holt family sheltered on an island with the crew and passengers. Back in Dublin in April 1814, Holt opened a tavern and set about writing his *Memoirs*. While the police questioned the exile's return, by the people he was regarded as a celebrity. Holt himself, it was believed, regretted leaving Australia where he had been respected and prosperous.

4 A Sheriff and a General, 1801-1802

The only other Irish prisoners to reach Australia in 1801 came on the *Minorca* (part of a fleet which included three convict ships) which sailed from Spithead on 21 June and arrived on 14 December, after a voyage of 176 days. The 15 Irishmen, aged between 23 and 40, had been court-martialled on the *HMS Gladiator* at Portsmouth for having held mutinous assemblies while serving aboard the *HMS Defiance*. It was alleged that they had taken this oath:

> I swear to be true to the Free and United Irishmen, who are fighting our cause against tyrants and oppressors; and to defend their rights to the last drop of my blood, and to keep all secret; and I do agree to carry the ship into Brest the next time the ship looks out ahead at sea, and to kill every officer and man that shall hinder us, except the master; and to hoist the green ensign with a harp in it; and afterwards to kill and destroy the Protestants.

Of the 25 men accused of the mutiny, 19 were sentenced to death, but 8 had their sentences commuted to transportation, and thus they joined 7 others who had been given a similar punishment; five of the sentences were for life, the remainder for seven years.

As the fleet which included the *Minorca* sailed for the antipodes, preparations were being made in Dublin and Cork for the departure of two convict vessels. One of those people awaiting transportation was the United Irishman, Napper Tandy, whose death sentence had been commuted. While the 64-year-old Tandy was trying to prepare himself for the passage his son was pleading that his aged parent would not survive the journey 'on a transport with the low and vile of all descriptions to Botany Bay'. The plea was successful and Napper Tandy was allowed to go to France.

The vessels being prepared at Cork were the *Atlas* and the *Hercules*, and Sir Jeremiah Fitzpatrick, the Irish born army physician and penal reformer, requested that he should be sent from his base at Portsmouth to Cork to supervise the work as he was very concerned at the neglect attending the shipments of convicts from Ireland. His anxiety was justified when the passage of those two vessels proved to be particularly disastrous. Evidence of the maladministration is reflected in the official correspondence between the supervising officers and Dublin Castle. In January 1801 Dr Harding complained to the Chief Secretary that he had already lost £1,000 in his treatment of the prisoners; he urgently requested £500 to enable him to continue working. Dr Trevor, the Superintendent of Convicts at Kilmainham, claimed that he was due £200 for thirteen-months attendance. That the problem was not new was illustrated by the statement that in 1798 the sheriff of Cork had lost £1,000 in expenses.

On 29 November 1801 the *Atlas* and the *Hercules* sailed together from Cove, both newly built and possibly on their maiden voyages. The transports were not long at sea when they separated. Then, early in the following month, as the *Hercules* was passing Cape Verde, it was rumoured that the 141 male and 25 female convicts on board had plotted to seize her. At lunchtime on 29 December, while the ship's officers were still dining, some of the prisoners overpowered the sentinels and took the quarter-deck. Within an hour the mutiny had been suppressed, with 13 convicts dead. Two men who had freed themselves of their irons were brought on deck; an informer identified one of them, Jeremiah Prendergast, as the leader, and he was shot by the ship's master.

When the *Hercules* arrived in Sydney on 26 June 1802, after a passage of 209 days, the convicts who had been kept in close confinements after the mutiny, were seen to be emaciated and filthy. In all, there had been 44 deaths on the ship, and more than half of those disembarked required medical attention. A Vice-Admiralty Court investigated the killings during the mutiny, and the master Luckyn Betts was acquitted. On a second charge of shooting Prendergast, he was found guilty of manslaughter and fined £500. As he returned to England, it is possible that he avoided this punishment. An analysis of the backgrounds of those on the *Hercules* found that 66 of them were from Ulster, 18 from Kildare, 12 from Westmeath, and the remainder from 23 other counties. Life sentences had been awarded to 84 prisoners, including 3 women, while 59 men and 22 women were to serve 7 years, and one man got 14 years. It was assumed that a high proportion of the sentences were for involvement in the rising of 1798. During the passage, apart from the mutiny, the prisoners suffered from overcrowding and filth as the officers had packed the vessel with stores intended for sale in the colony. The quarters were never cleaned or fumigated, and the convicts had their water ration reduced, while their food was always short, due to false weights being used by the quartermaster.

The 220 day passage of the *Atlas* was also a bad one with only 85 men and 26 women disembarking from the total of 153 men and 28 women who had embarked at Dublin and Cork; again, most of the prisoners were from trials held after 1798. Typhus and dysentery had already killed two of the convicts before the vessel sailed, and the health of the remainder deteriorated during the journey as the *Atlas* had also been packed with private stores and the prison, in which the convicts were confined, so lacking in ventilation that candles would not burn for lack of oxygen. For the entire voyage the unfortunate transportees were confined with heavy irons on their legs and around their necks, secured with a padlock weighing one and half pounds.

When the deaths on the *Atlas* were investigated at Sydney it was found that they had resulted from 'the want of proper attention to cleanliness, the want of free circulation of air, and the lumbered state of the prison and hospital'. The master, Captain Richard Brooks, explained the long passage, with calls at Rio and the Cape of Good Hope, as being necessary to suppress a mutiny, and to have necessary repairs made to the ship. The convicts, he said, had a plan to poison the soldiers. Officials at Sydney claimed they were horrified by the condition of the prisoners, some of whom were lying dead with heavy irons on them – 4 more died soon after arrival, and 20 were so ill they could not immediately be brought ashore. As a punishment for the neglect of his prisoners, the master was forbidden to unload and sell the stores which he had brought. Otherwise he escaped punishment, and he returned to New South Wales as master of the *Alexander* which transported convicts from England in 1806.

Three young brothers from Limerick survived the troubles on the *Atlas*. The four Aherns had been tried as 'croppies' in Limerick at the summer assizes of 1800. John, Mathias and Michael had their death sentences commuted to banishment for life. (The fourth brother, Murtagh, may have been gaoled, or allowed to join one of the services.) By 1828 Michael Ahern was a constable at Holsworthy; he had the lease of 30 acres, and owned 18 head of cattle.

John Lyons from Tipperary was another croppy. When he had

merited a conditional pardon, he farmed 79 acres at Wilberforce with his wife and family. Michael Ryan, who had come from Queen's County, had a more modest holding of six acres at Hunter River, where he lived with his family. For him, too, the small-holding was progress, as previously he had been a hired man.

Among the transportees from County Cork were the two Doulan sisters, sentenced 'on account of rebellion', and Sir Henry Brown Hayes who had been found guilty of abduction and condemned to death, but reprieved.

In his capacity as Sheriff of Cork, Brown Hayes has received receipts for convicts handed over for transportation to the Naval Agent. Now that he himself was among the transportees he managed to come to a financial arrangement with the master of the *Atlas* by which he was allowed to travel apart from the convicts, and to dine in the cabin. A captain in the South Cork Militia, and a prominent figure in Cork society, Sir Henry was a 35-year-old widower when, in 1797, he abducted a 21-year-old Quaker heiress named Mary Pike. Having procured a compliant priest he forced the girl to go through a form of marriage. However, when she resisted his advances he left her. She went to England. A reward of £1,000 was put on the head of Brown Hayes, but he evaded arrest. After a couple of years, believing that his popularity would save him, he surrendered, it was said through the agency of his barber who was to collect the reward. When the opinions of no less than twelve judges had been sought he was found guilty of abduction, and four months later, in the summer of 1801, he was condemned to death, but this was commuted to transportation for life. Epigrams and verses were written about him, including the following sample:

> The fate of Sir Henry is sure a hard case,
> Unable in Cork to exhibit his face,
> Pursued by the Brethren, proclaimed in the papers,
> Though his boyish mis-deeds were mere boyish capers;
> Since mercy, high goddess, revisits these climes,
> And rebels and traitors are pardoned their crimes,
> Tho' different his guilt, let them all share alike,
> He was not United, and gave up his Pike. . .

Another humorous ballad on the same abduction also showed sympathy with the culprit:

Sir Henry kissed behind the bush,
Sir Henry kissed the Quaker,
And if he did, and if he did,
I'm sure he didn't ate her.

But there was also concern from more responsible citizens that the popular sheriff might escape punishment. Mr Philip Heatcote circulated a printed letter addressed to the government. It complained that while Brown Hayes was confined in Cork city jail he behaved like a mountebank, making his guard drunk, and appearing at a window to harangue a sympathetic mob. It was pointed out that a man named Murphy, convicted of the same crime as the sheriff, had been executed. 'There is in Ireland,' wrote Heatcote, 'scarce any instance of a man of repute being executed by sentence of law, with the exception of state prisoners. . .' Now, it was demanded, justice should be done and Brown Hayes transported.

Sir Henry was transported on the *Atlas* where he encountered Mr Jamison, Surgeon General of New South Wales, who was returning to the colony. Sir Henry so insulted the surgeon that, when the ship reached Rio, Jamison transferred to the *Hercules* for the remainder of the passage. On arrival at Sydney the Surgeon General laid charges against Brown Hayes of 'threatening and improper conduct', for which he was given a six-month sentence. It is not surprising to find that, in a dispatch, the colony's governor wrote: 'to confirm the accounts I gave in my last letters of the general, quiet and orderly behaviour of the Irish convicts and indeed of every other person of that description, except one or two individuals, among whom is Henry Brown Hayes, a restless, troublesome character who has twice been imprisoned for six months by the Bench of Magistrates.'

Given a ticket-of-leave, i.e. a certificate which excused him from compulsory labour, which permitted him to work on his own behalf, Sir Henry settled at Parramatta. There he farmed on an estate he called 'Vacluse', and built himself a comfortable house which he protected from snakes with soil which he had especially imported from holy Ireland. He kept a small sailing boat, and was attended to by his man-servant Breakwell, 'a young person who gave Sir Henry much comfort', according to the sensitive young English convict John Grant who had been indicted for shooting a man. Grant, who remarked on Sir Henry's 'remarkable whiskers', enjoyed visiting 'Vacluse' where he found the living was 'as civilised as that of a country

squire'. The squire himself he thought was a 'much injured and
amiable gentleman' who had been much harmed by the governor,
being jailed three times, and sent to work with the hoe, and who was
by every means endeavouring to break his noble spirit and increase
his sufferings'. In 1805 Grant wrote a melancholy poem for Sir Henry,
of which these are two lines:

> Soon must the curtain drop between us two;
> I can but wish a long good-night to you.

Grant was generally in sympathy with the Irish, remarking in the
letters which he wrote in French that, soon after his arrival at Sydney
in 1804, he was greeted by the sight of the corpses of Irish rebels
hanging from the gallows – 'me thought I smelled the bones, and
heard the groans of dying patriots'. They were, he believed, no more
than political prisoners, who kept the government in constant alarm.

Brown Hayes created further friction when, in defiance of the law,
he formed a Masonic Lodge. His financial independence enabled him
to import whiskey from Ireland and to boast that his estate, 'Vacluse',
was worth £5,000. But when he was accused of complicity in the
Castle Hill Insurrection his wealth did not save him from a period
on Norfolk Island. John Grant also spent a time there and he was
particularly sorry for two Irish convicts he met. Michael O'Hogan,
who had struck a particularly objectionable prison officer, 'was led
through the streets at the cart's tail to be beaten into insensibility'.
The other man, Charles Boyle, whom Grant described as 'a handsome
vast man', he had first met on the *Coromandel* during the passage
from England. Then he had seen Boyle publicly flogged and confined
in solitary confinement for the remainder of the journey, after he had
struck a guard who was hitting the convicts with a knotted rope –
when he came to Boyle's common-law wife, who had just given birth,
the Irishman lost his temper. Meeting again on Norfolk Island, Boyle
told Grant of his time in the bush, into which he had escaped with
a woman whom he had 'taken out of compassion', as she was being
ill-treated. When, at Port Jackson, Boyle, who had only one arm,
provoked the guards by not completing his allotted amount of hoeing,
a row started. 'I turned round,' boasted Boyle. 'I seized and wrested
the musket from one and tripped up the other's heels, and would
have got away with their arms but for the fact that the man on the
ground got my little finger in his teeth, and with his hands squeezed

my private parts so hard, and others coming up to assist them, they took me.' Given 100 lashes and a sentence of two years hard labour in double-irons with the chain gang, he was dispatched to the penal island.

In the neighbourhood of 'Vacluse' John Grant met one of the Doulan sisters, who had been transported from Cork; surprisingly, Sir Henry was not friendly with them. Both girls had married and settled on farms, but Bridget's husband, a Frenchman, had been deported to England from Sydney after the Irish Insurrection of 1804. When Grant encountered Bridget he found her 'about 24-years-of-age, she has a lovely face, black eyes, and is a little inclined to be plump'. She lived in a neat cottage 'with an open hearth instead of a fireplace, as favoured by the Irish peasantry', and she had a high moral reputation. Despite his courtship, Bridget declined Grant's offer to come and share his house; eventually she was given a free pardon and returned home. The girls were probably the daughters of a Mrs Doolan [sic], convicted of murder, kept in Naas jail in 1801 and later executed. In his report of a visit to the jail the Inspector General of Prisons in Ireland noted that this prisoner's two girls were transported to New South Wales.

Through the Masonic brotherhood Sir Henry Brown Hayes would have been acquainted with Richard Fitzgerald who was associated with the introduction of the craft to Sydney. Though transported from England in 1791, Fitzgerald is believed to have been connected to the noble Leinster family of the same name. His expertise in farming caused him to be made a supervisor on government farms in the colony. He progressed to being director of the crown agricultural settlements, a high constable, a banker and a prominent citizen. When he died in 1840 his estate was valued at £34,000.

When pardoned Sir Henry returned home too, travelling on the *Isabella* with Joseph Holt and his party. Holt later reported that when the vessel was shipwrecked 'Sir Henry Brown Hayes and his man grabbed the small boat and rowed ashore. . . as a result the women had to get off by accommodation chair.' More critical of the knight's behaviour, one of the *Isabella*'s officers in his journal wrote that Hayes had endangered the lives of the other passengers. While the ship-wrecked party was sheltering on the shore it was decided to form a council to govern themselves. Holt remarked that 'Sir Henry had ingratiated himself to the marines on the ship. . .' By playing *Hide the Botton* and other games with them he had been elected a member of the council, and when he ordered that no one should leave the island until all could go together, Holt replied, 'You have as much command over me as you had over Miss Pike when you attempted to take her out of her carriage.'

Despite the rancour, both men arrived back in Ireland where they were greeted with this comment in Cox's *Irish Magazine:* 'These two eminent gentlemen have arrived from Botany Bay. It is singular enough that the two were transported for the Pike business, Sir Henry for stealing a pike, and the general for bestowing pikes.'

A story rather similar to that of Brown Hayes is told by Sir Jonah Barrington in his *Personal Sketches.* It concerned James Fitzpatrick Knaresborough, 'a young man of tolerable private fortune in the County Kilkenny'. He was accused of a capital crime by a Miss Barton and sentenced to death, which was remitted to one of 'perpetual transportation'. Taking what fortune he had with him Knaresborough went to 'Botany Bay'. After a time there he managed to get away to Africa and America. Then he returned home, but was apprehended and lodged in Newgate from where he petitioned the government that he might be hanged! During his time in jail he won two lotteries for large sums of money and he was eventually released.

No doubt Knaresborough's wealth had made his confinement more tolerable than that of the ordinary prisoner, such as William Burke. 'Confined without the air of a yard, or any other place that is comfortable, but a dismal room. . . my poverty here is unsupportable. It is with a flood of tears I write you these few lines,' cried William Burke from Limerick city jail to his mother on 13 July 1802. Awaiting transportation, and already confined for six months, he begged that she would try to have the judge influenced, so that his sentence might be commuted. Asking for the price of a shirt – 'I have not the tack of a shirt to my back,' he added. 'It would grieve my heart full sore to leave you and my poor father in your old days, as if it is the will of God to spare me to ye, it is my intent to stick by yer and my sisters and brothers while I have life, and until they are able to do for themselves.'

When Burke sent this pathetic letter to his mother one of the two convict ships which sailed in that year had already left, and the other was not to leave until November. Both the *Atlas II,* which sailed on 30 May, and the *Rolla,* which sailed on 4 November, were new vessels, and they completed their passages in 153 and 189 days respectively. They carried a total of 339 convicts, of whom 38 were female, and of the men 206 had life sentences. The Indent for the *Atlas II*, which had sailed from Waterford, was sent with that of the *Rolla*, on the *Rolla*.

One of the prisoners was Tristram Moore, a 30-year-old County Derry Presbyterian who, as a United Irishman, had been sentenced to death by court-martial in 1798. Now on a life sentence instead, he seems to have thrived in the new land as by 1828, farming 100 acres, he owned a horse and 18 cattle and he was living with a housekeeper named Catherine Johnson.

Andrew Doyle, from the *Rolla,* also prospered in the colony. Exiled for his part in the 'troubles', this Wicklow man was fortunate in that his wife and three children followed him on another vessel. In 1804 his wife was given a grant of land at Toongabbie, and within another five years he was in a position to purchase land near Lower Portland on the Hawkesbury river where he built a house and set about raising a family of seven. By 1828 he had been given a grant of a further 300 acres, and owned in all 1,220 acres on which were 14 horses and 130 horned cattle. His children were good settlers and one of them, Cyrus Doyle, was active in public affairs in Maitland, where he also bred race-horses. Surprisingly, Andrew himself is remembered as a water-colourist and some of his paintings of botanical subjects survive. He had been asked by Governor King to paint pictures of the natural shrubs of the colony and he painted a series of wild flowers on lengths of ribbon for the governor's wife.

With the arrival of *Atlas II* the number of Irish convicts in New South Wales was estimated to be a quarter of the inhabitants and they were again causing trouble. On 15 November, while employed in agricultural labour at Castle Hill, near Sydney, 15 men escaped. It was later recorded in the *Historical Records of Australia* that 'they were misled by rumours of a settlement to the west of the Blue Mountains, and of an overland route to China. After obtaining arms and food from the houses of two settlers, they crossed the Hawkesbury river but were captured near the foot of the mountains.' Some of the contemporary newspaper accounts of the escape were more graphic. The *Sydney Gazette* reported that the men 'committed many acts of violence and atrocity'. In one dwelling-house they took arms, clothes, provisions and 'spiritous and vinous liquors, a quantity of which they drank or wasted in the house'. Coming to another house they 'wantonly and inhumanly discharged a pistol at a manservant, which so shattered his face as to render him a ghastly spectacle, in all probability during the remainder of his life'. In Mrs Bean's house they 'gave aloose to sensuality, equally brutal and unmanly. Resistance was of no avail, for their rapacity was unbridled.' The *Gazette* concluded: 'Justice to the prisoners at large in the colony requires that we should observe that this banditti is entirely composed of Irish prisoners, brought by the *Hercules* and the *Atlas*.'

Fourteen of the escapees were captured and came up for trial on 15 March of the following year. Witnesses who identified the men or some of the stolen property were called. Francis Simpson was identified by a servant named Mary Tirley who said that 'he had compelled her to fill two glasses of wine for him during which interval she had taken much notice of his countenance'. All fourteen men were condemned to death and three of them, including Simpson, were taken for execution at Castle Hill where stood 'the fatal tree, which had been purposely erected near to the spot on which they had committed the offence for which they were about to atone'. The parson was in attendance as the three men mounted the vehicle which was to be driven from under them. One of them was reprieved but Simpson and his friend died. The reprieved and the other eleven men were given life sentences. Simpson, according to a newspaper report, 'died truly impenitent and hardened', while his companion 'behaved himself with a penitence becoming to his situation'.

Another man from Ireland who was destined to become notorious in convict folklore arrived in Australia about six months after the execution of Simpson. He was an ex-soldier of the 4th King's Own Regiment, a giant of a man, six feet six inches tall, named William Buckley. He was among the 307 male convicts who had left Spithead on *HMS Calcutta* for the new settlement of Port Phillip on 24 April 1803. Managing to escape into the bush with a few companions Buckley succeeded in remaining free for thirty years. His companions were never seen again, and it was rumoured that Buckley had eaten them! Joining a tribe of aborigines, Buckley took to himself a wife and remained with the natives until one day in 1835 'a startling figure clad in possum skins, displaying long hair, bearing spears, shields and clubs' met a hunting party. Brought back into convict society, at first Buckley was not able to speak English; after a time he was given a job as gate-keeper to the women's factory, and afterwards a pension. Sometimes employed as a tracker, he spoke of a white woman who had joined the aborigines. The search party which went to seek her displayed notices in English and Irish advising the woman that she was being sought but she was never found and, like Buckley himself, became a legend.

Among those who arrived at Sydney on the *Atlas II* in October 1802 were Murtagh Fortune and Thomas Connell. The former was one of 23 men from Wexford on the vessel, while the latter was with 24 companions from Tipperary. Thomas Connell, aged 24, a labourer from Bakerstown in Holycross parish, he had been accused of attempting to rescue a prisoner from the yeomanry and he served four years in New Geneva before transportation. After he was pardoned in Australia he farmed on the Goulburn Plains with his wife and two children, owning three score cattle. Fortune had also been a labourer and by 1810 he was employed by the police in Sydney. Another Wexford man, William Lett, having been granted a conditional pardon in 1815, opened a shop at Kent Street in Sydney and he also owned a small farm.

5   Dr Trevor and Michael Dwyer, 1803-1812

One important consequence of the failed rising of 1798 was the confirmation in the minds of the English establishment that, now more than ever, Ireland was a serious political problem. Not alone did it offer a back door through which Britain might be attacked by an enemy, but the continuing unrest and agitation in Ireland absorbed too much effort and money. A union of the parliaments of Britain and Ireland was proposed and by persuasion, propaganda and bribery the Act of Union was passed. Ireland became part of the United Kingdom on 1 January 1801.

Within a few years there was yet another attempt to change the political scene. Robert Emmet led an abortive rising on 23 July 1803 in Dublin, but he was captured and, with 21 of his followers, executed. It was the end of the United Irish movement.

In his stronghold in the Wicklow mountains the local leader, Michael Dwyer, came to terms with the situation. His father was already confined in New Geneva for two years, and some male relatives were 'exposed to the fury of the easterly wind' aboard a tender off the Pigeon House in Dublin Bay for 15 weeks. Baltinglass jail was the home of Dwyer's sister and other members of the family, and there was a reward of £500 on his head. With the hope of being sent to America, Dwyer surrendered to Captain Hume of Humewood just before the Christmas of 1803. On 12 December the *Freeman's Journal* reported that 'Dwyer, the noted Insurgent, was brought into town on Saturday evening last to the Castle,[10] between four and five o'clock, escorted by a party of Captain Hume's Cavalry Corps of Wicklow. He was dressed in country style, in a white frieze Jockey, and appeared to be somewhat inebriated. The noble captain was much displeased at the mob gazing at him and used some ruffianly and angry expressions. He has been lodged in Kilmainham jail'.[11]

At Kilmainham, Dwyer was under the custodianship of Dr Edward Trevor, Master of Kilmainham, Prison Inspector and, later, Inspector of Hulks. St John Mason, a barrister and a cousin of Robert Emmet, was also lodged in Kilmainham and later he published two pamphlets exposing conditions in the prison. He was particulary critical of Dr Trevor, whose treatment of the prisoners he considered inhuman; they were starved, kept under disagreeable circumstances, almost destroyed by vermin. Trevor denied them medical treatment, and frequently confined them in double irons; 'one man was thus confined for 8 months in an effort to force him to ask to be sent to Botany Bay'. According to one story it was Trevor who told Dwyer of his fate; asked by Dwyer when they would sail for America, he replied, '. . . you will never put your feet on American soil, to come back when you like to raise another rebellion. You are to go to Botany Bay.'

In July 1804 a judicial inquiry, prompted by St John Mason's submissions, was held into the management of Kilmainham prison. It led to the admonishment in private of Dr Trevor, and the findings that, apart from a few minor complaints, 'everything was satisfactory'. The judge who had presided at the inquiry continued to receive complaints of ill-treatment in the prison, including one from the 'State Prisoner Dwyer. . . who states that, since he gave evidence at the investigation, Dr Trevor has sought him out for bad treatment and particular annoyance, notwithstanding the confidential charge which we gave him to perform his duties in a more humane and better manner'. In fact, Dwyer and Mason, with others who had given evidence, had been incarcerated in the felon's side of the prison, on a starvation diet and in chains, for eleven days after the inquiry. From the tone and content of later correspondence from Dwyer to Trevor, it would seem that the Wicklowman had learned that it was better to fawn on the all-powerful doctor than to try to expose him.

Mason, however, continued his campaign against this medical gaoler whom he saw as a travesty of justice and compassion. It was rumoured that not alone did Trevor supply Dublin Castle with information gathered from his spies within Kilmainham, but that with one of the Castle officials, he profitably owned the bakery which supplied the prison with poor quality bread. After he was released from prison Mason succeeded in having the Irish playwright and member of parliament, Richard Brinsley Sheridan, raise the maladministration of Kilmainham in the London House of Commons. The outcome of this airing was the appointment of a Royal Commission to inquire into prison abuses in Ireland. When the Commission met in Dublin, the conditions imposed on the submission of evidence were so strict that St John Mason and his witnesses despaired of a fair hearing and left the court in protest. The case against Dr Trevor was dismissed causing hostile demonstrations to be held at Kilmainham and before his house. The verbal battle between Mason and Trevor continued with the publication of a *Vindication* by the latter, which was answered by the barrister's *Prison abuses in Ireland. The Oppressions and Atrocities of Dr Edward Trevor and his associates upon State Prisoners of Kilmainham during the Earl of Hardwicke's administration in Ireland.* No further inquiries were held, and Dr Trevor retired to the city suburbs, where he died in 1837, leaving a fine sum of £36,000. The prison at Kilmainham is now a museum where the memory of many patriots is cherished, but where Trevor is remembered as a tyrant.

By the early summer of 1805 preparations were well under way for the sailing of another transport to New South Wales. A report in *Faulkner's Dublin Journal* of 23 May said that 'on Monday several convicts from the New Gaol were escorted by the military to the water side, where the prisoners were put on board a vessel which is to proceed to Botany Bay'. The vessel concerned was waiting at Poolbeg,[12] in Dublin Bay, to convey prisoners to the *Tellicherry* at Cove. A few weeks later another report in the same newspaper said that some of the convicts on the vessel at Poolbeg 'made a desperate effort to escape, they were fired on by the guard, and three or four were wounded'.

At Cove there were problems. Inspection of the *Tellicherry* revealed that though the men's prison was sufficiently large, it was not properly ventilated. 'If this vessel was to take the usual number of men, five for instance to a berth, on board, half of them would be suffocated. For four to a berth she is not sufficiently ventilated, and should have more scuttles cut in her sides.' It was recommended that more forms should be put in the prison as, otherwise, in bad weather, the men would be 'continually laying in their berths and by consequence contaminating the air'. While the women's apartment was considered small, this was not found to be of much moment, 'as they generally sleep in different parts of the ship'.

Those awaiting transportation in the Cork city jail were also inspected. 'Of the 13 just arrived from Clonmel, 5 had the itch, and others were suffering from sore legs from the bolts.' One of the 12 women was found to be 'excessively weak, and Ann Farrell was a dreadful object'. Those unfortunates confined on the *Renown* at Cove were 'very badly off. They have no straw, save a little scraped together for the sick. The other convicts are lying on the ballast. The day is fine and yet the hatches are down on the middle hatchway, and a boat over them. The air is very bad in the prison, and they allow but 12 on deck at the time. The consequence is that the fever has broke out and is spreading. . . half of them are full of the itch. I ordered the hatches off and the wind sails to be set on both hatches.' Soap, which cost 17s6d, was issued to the convicts.

Michael Dwyer was still confined in Kilmainham and from there, on 29 June, he wrote to Dr Trevor: 'Honoured Sir, I beg you will accept my warmest thanks in return for your kindness towards my children as nothing lies in my power more than to thank you for your kind and humane assistance, and be assured I would sooner ask you for that favour, than any of my fellow prisoners, though perhaps you would not think so, even if it lay in their power.' By 13 July further preparations for the exiling of Dwyer and the others who had surrendered themselves had been made as the *Dublin Evening Post* announced that 'on Thursday the 11th Capt Michael Dwyer, Martin Burke, Hugh Byrne and Arthur Devlin, who were said to have surrendered on condition of emigrating to America U.S., received orders to go on board a transport prepared for their reception in order to proceed to Botany Bay'. A few days later *Faulkner's Dublin Journal* was less complimentary to the men when it described them as 'the rebel robbers'.

Knowing that the ship to Australia was due to sail within a couple of months Dwyer submitted a plea that his family should be allowed to accompany him into exile. On 20 July he sent this further ingratiating letter to Dr Trevor (original spelling retained):

Respected Sir,
With a heart felt gratitude and fully sensible of how far I am from deserving any kindness from your Honour, I make bold to return you my sincere thanks for your kindness to me, and the consolation you gave me by promising your interest to send my children after me to Botany Bay, and your own humane mind will tell you there is nothing so distressing to the parents as parting of their children, especially me, who had the misfortune to forfeit them and their country, and I declare to you that I never was sorry untill now, for offending the govrnment untill I see their kindness in forgiveing the injuries done them and considering the wants of those that were guilty, of such offences, now I am sorry to the bottom of my

heart for having offended so good a govrnment and shall for ever exclaim
against any man or men if I hear any of them speak or act against the
govrnment, this I declare to be my real sentiments at this moment and
will till the our of my death for I never saw my erer untill now, as for my
children I shall leave it to yourself for it would be to much boldness of
me to ask you for so great a favour and I so ill deserving of any, but I
sincerely lament for it and still hope from your humanity that I may expect
my children and shall find myself happy in earning them bread and they
and I shall be for ever bound to pray for your wellfare.

> and I remain
> yours etc. etc
> Michael Dwyer
> July 20 1805

When Captain Hume realised that the men who had surrendered
to him were not going, as they had expected, to America he hastened
to Dublin Castle where 'it required all his zeal and energy to obtain
from the government a paltry sum in lieu of their flagrant breach of
faith'. The sum of £350 was sent to Captain Richard Sainthill, the
Victualling Agent at Cork, who acknowledged it, saying that he
would 'pay it to the men as you directed, as yet I believe they are not
arrived at Cove'. Two days later, on 2 August, Sainthill was able to
report that:

> the convicts, and Dwyer's gang, will be put on board the *Tellicherry*
> tomorrow, the latter say government have agreed with them they shall
> not be put in irons, or put with the convicts, and that their wives and
> children are to go with them, I hope it is not true, as I am sure the captain
> of the *Tellicherry* would not comply with it, as the ship is so completely
> filled he has not room to make such accommodation, and in the next place
> it would put the safety of the ship's crew in great danger, to have such
> men at large!

Sainthill added that he would request the captain not to put them in
irons at present but 'when he is at sea he of course will do what he
considers most proper'.

Within ten days 130 men and 35 women were on board the transport, with one of the latter, Mary Grady from County Kerry, on a
life sentence, and the others on sentences of seven years. Fifty-nine
of the men had life sentences. Others of the prisoners who had been
confined awaiting transportation had been allowed to enlist in the
marines or the navy, and 17 had been found to be either too old or
too ill for the journey. Three men from the *Renown* had managed to

escape by stealing that ship's boat. Of those that embarked on the *Tellicherry* 1 woman and 5 men died during the passage of 168 days.

Dwyer was seen to be 'well satisfied' when he received the government money, but he, and Hugh Byrne, were even more pleased when they discovered that they might bring their families with them. The families were to be accommodated in one of the *Tellicherry*'s hospitals, an arrangement which displeased the inspecting surgeon, Dr Robert Harding. He complained that 'altogether this fellow's gang takes up the room of 12 men. When the hospital becomes crowded he will have to move'. In other accounts there were protests from the ship's surgeon that 'the medicine chest is incomplete, particularly so, as to the quantity of medicine'. Further, he thought that the prisons were overcrowded and with insufficient air. His solution was to keep the prisoners on deck whenever the weather allowed.

On 17 August the Secretary at Dublin Castle wrote to Governor King of New South Wales informing him that the Lord Lieutenant had, that day, signed the Warrant transmitting the convicts to the colony, and that 'among the number are five men, Michael Dwyer, John Mernagh, Hugh Byrne, Martin Burke and Arthur Devlin who were engaged in treasonable practices here and who have requested to be allowed to banish themselves for life to New South Wales to avoid being brought to trial'. As it was 'deemed expedient to make such a compromise with them, they are sent there'. In the colony they were to be 'subjected to all the laws and discipline, and any further indulgence was to be earned by their behaviour'.

Having sailed from Cove on 25 August 1805 the *Tellicherry* travelled with a squadron as far as Madeira and reached Sydney on 15 February 1806. On the homeward voyage, while en route to China to load tea, the *Tellicherry* was lost, though the crew escaped. She had the distinction of being the first transport lost on the return journey. Though the outward passage of the *Tellicherry* was uneventful it was, nevertheless, the subject of rumour. In a private letter dated 7 April 1806 (when the ship had completed her voyage two months before) it was said that after the *Tellicherry* had parted from the squadron she had been 'run ashore on the southward of the All Saint's Bay, the captain and officers murdered by the mutineers. . .', who had been led by Michael Dwyer!

Having departed from Cove on the same day as the *Tellicherry* the *William Pitt* did not reach Sydney for a further two months, with her complement of 116 female convicts. She was with an expedition sent to reduce the Dutch settlements at the Cape of Good Hope, which was reached on 4 January 1806. *William Pitt*, after a passage of 222 days anchored at Port Jackson on 11 April having lost one convict due to smallpox, an epidemic of which had affected the vessel.

Immediately after the arrival of the *Tellicherry* Governor King wrote sternly to the authorities: 'I cannot conceal that the arrival of the five United Irishmen, who appear to have been considerable leaders in the late rebellion in Ireland, without any conviction, added to the number of disaffected of that class here already, will call forth the utmost attention of the officers of this colony.' In a further epistle he added: 'Well knowing the capricious disposition of the Irish character, I have very clearly explained to them the footing they are on, and on their promises of being circumspect in their conduct and not giving cause for any complaint, I have allowed them to become settlers, with the encouragement generally given to free settlers sent from England. How far these indulgences will operate on their apparent turbulent dispositions time will show.'

Some time later the Rev. Samuel Marsden also expressed his views on the Irish: '. . . the number of Catholic convicts is very great in the settlement; and those in general composed of the lowest class of the Irish nation. . . they are very dangerous members of society. . . They are extremely superstitious, artful and treacherous. . . They have no true concern whatever for religion. . . but are fond of riot, drunkenness and cabals; and was the Catholic religion tolerated they would assemble together from every quarter not so much from a desire of celebrating Mass, as to recite the miseries and injustices of their punishment, the hardship they suffer and to enflame one another' mind with some wild scheme of revenge.'

The United Irishmen were but a little over a year in the colony before their 'turbulent' dispositions were being investigated. They were accused of treasonable practices in having endeavoured to instigate rebellion several times during the past year. They were all sentenced to removal to penal stations, though it was admitted that 'no arms had been found, our information leading only to declared plans'. Michael Dwyer was believed to have been the leader of the rebels and he was sent to Norfolk Island. After six months there he was transferred to Van Diemen's Land for a further two years. On his return to Sydney, Dwyer was given a grant of a 100 acres at

Cabramatta, and he was appointed constable in charge of that district in 1813.

After Dwyer's death in 1825, his widow, with her three daughters, kept house for Fr Joseph Therry and in her old age she lived with one of the girls who had married a bank manager. When Mrs Dwyer died in 1861 the Sydney *Freeman's Journal* described her as an 'estimable woman, the relict of one who struggled with all his manhood vigour for a noble cause some sixty-two years ago'. Her funeral was attended by 'a large number of city and country clergymen. The bishop's carriage was in the cortège, a mark of respect for departed worth.'

The men of 1798 are remembered with a memorial in Sydney. In Ireland their memory remained alive, and such ballads as 'The Banished Defender' recalled that the hero suffered '. . . in cold irons, in Van Diemen's Land'. A century later songs were still being written about them: Padric Gregory, in 1917, penned a 'Ballad of the '98 Heroes' which included the line 'the treacherous foe. . . sent Dwyer to Botany Bay'.

Though no further convict ships were to sail from Ireland until January 1809, sentences of transportation continued to be handed down and petitions for mercy continued to be written. 'God Save the King,' concluded James Armstrong, 20-years-of-age, five feet eleven inches tall, 'free from all eyesores and blemishes' in his plea to be allowed to join one of the services. He was in Naas jail, 'quite naked for want of clothes', awaiting transportation on a sentence of 7 years. Confined at the same time at Newpass, Edgeworthstown, was John Monks, who had been convicted of forgery at Mullingar and whose death sentence had been mitigated to one of permanent exile. There was a complaint that allowing him to remain at Newpass was 'an injury to the country, his friends think he will be liberated, and those who wish to disturb the peace of the neighbourhood look to him as a leader, if he should escape punishment he will be more harm to the country than in any way he already was'. It was recommended that he should 'be removed immediately and transported at the first opportunity'. The first ship on which he might have been transported was the *Boyd* which sailed from Cork on 10 March 1809. The *Experiment* which had departed six weeks earlier carried only female convicts. Mick Duggan, one of the 139 men on board the *Boyd* (about half were believed to be agrarian offenders), made a last desperate bid for freedom, but he was drowned.

What the new arrivals might expect to find in Sydney was a town with a population of 3,000, the streets of which were 'made a danger and an inconvenience to horse and foot passengers by pigs, goats and dogs being permitted to wander at large' throughout the place. Preparations were being made to have the streets widened, and pathways laid, and an order was issued that 'pigs which might be found in the street or about the water tanks, where they render it unfit for use, would be sold for the benefit of the orphan fund'. The colony was spread over 1,460 miles, with a population of 7,500, five-sixths of whom were of convict origin, and one-third prisoners. Only 360 of the 1,412 women were married, and of the 1,801 children under nineteen years of age, 908 were illegitimate. A short time after the arrival of Governor Macquarie (1809-1821) one observer of the scene described it as 'a population of idle prisoners, paupers and paid officials. . .' By the time Macquarie left office the colony had become 'a large free community, thriving on the produce of flocks and the labour of convicts'. He had done much to humanise society there, introducing such sports as horse-racing, athletics, and cock-fighting. The Irish reel, it was observed, was a popular dance.

Such frivolity was far from the mind of Dr Trevor in Dublin when in June 1810 he was insisting that the regulations as specified by the Navy Office in London governing the preparation of convict transports should be adhered to. When the vessels arrived at Cove they should be carrying the clothing, provisions and necessaries for the passage. He pointed out that the *Elizabeth*, then waiting at Cork to embark female convicts, was not thus equipped. To add to his annoyance, Trevor found that the sloop with the women had already left Dublin for Cove. The *Elizabeth* did not sail, and another convict ship did not depart Ireland until early in 1811 when the *Providence* embarked 140 men and 40 women, of whom about a quarter could have been sentenced for agrarian crimes. At least one forger was among them.

He was Edward Eagar, the son of a land agent from near Killarney. County Kerry. Eagar was sentenced to death at Cork Summer Assizes in 1809 for uttering a forged bill. Introduced to Methodism while in jail, he adopted that faith and he is credited with its introduction to Australia. In 1962 when the one hundred and fiftieth anniversary of this event was celebrated the church in Australia had a membership of 1,000,000. Having disembarked from the *Providence* Eagar was assigned to a clergyman as tutor for his children. When not encouraged to pursue his legal profession he adopted the Emancipist cause. After he had been granted an absolute pardon in 1818 he was sent to London to plead that cause. In a pamphlet which he published on the subject he argued that 'transportation had proved a successful punishment and was quite compatible with free settlement'.

Forgery was a common crime in Ireland at that time; for example, at the Summer Assizes in Limerick in 1810, five men had been convicted of the crime. Perjury was also a frequent crime in a society where the taking of oaths was casual. Membership of any of the many secret societies required such oaths, and the people's disregard for the administrators of the law lessened their respect for the oath. Transportation records suggest that only from Ireland were persons transported for this crime. Other convictions there were for rape, assault, wife-killing, house-burning, pig- and goat-stealing, and for 'burglary and terrorising a family and carrying off an informer's daughter'. The making of counterfeit bank paper and illegal watermarks was a common activity until the introduction of printing with steel plates in the early nineteenth century.

A bonus for the colony came with the skills of the transported tradesmen such as paper-makers. They contributed to the development of that trade when a paper mill was established, and men banished for forgery were also found useful there.

Following the departure of the *Providence*, there was the usual tidying-up to be done with those left behind due to illness or infirmities. They could not be lodged in the House of Industry, as the inmates there were already four to a bed, and it was not a secure place to house convicts anyhow. Already the numbers awaiting transportation were increasing almost daily and in June there were 145 men and 50 women assembled. One of the latter was Joan Ready who 'for having in her possession a forged bank post bill of the Bank of Ireland, she well knowing the same to be forged', was sentenced to 14 years in New South Wales at the Clonmel Spring Assizes. Having spent almost a year in jail she was transported, with 53 other women and 147 men, on the *Archduke Charles* on 15 May 1812. Seven years later she was granted a free pardon. During the time that the ship was being prepared for the passage several of those under sentence made last efforts to get reprieved. Tadhg Kelly's plea was refused, but two women were released. They were Ellen Markey from Cavan, convicted of stealing a bullock, and Bridget McDaniel from Longford, who stole goods from a shop in the town. Before the *Archduke Charles* weighed anchor many of the prisoners were stricken with pains, fever, dysentery and worms. Some of the costs of this transportation are recorded; for transporting Anthony Gallagher from Sligo to Cork, a distance of 190 miles, £30, according to an account submitted by the jailor of Cork. The Victualling Agent, Mr Sainthill, was still worrying about the non-payment of the accounts for sailings some two years before, and he claimed that he had not been reimbursed for sundries supplied to the *Boyd* and the *Experiment*

When the *Archduke Charles* had departed the officials at Cove turned their attention to the detainees left behind. John Halligan, who was nearly 80 years old, and suffering from tuberculosis, had not been transported as he would be 'a burden to the colony', reported the doctor. Other men, he added, were suffering from venereal disease, had fits or were spitting blood. More desperate characters had burned their legs to make them sore, and they had continued to keep them sore in the hope of a remission of sentence. One John Fitzgerald was allowed to have 'a bed to himself as he caught his leg in the wheel of a car on the way here, and is in a very bad condition'.

As after previous sailings, there were complaints about the slowness or non-payment of accounts. It would seem that quantities of rum, wine and sugar supplied to the *Archduke Charles* had not been paid for nor, indeed, had payment been received for the same rations supplied to the *Providence* eighteen months before.

The procedures for the transportation of convicts from Ireland were outlined by the Inspector General of Prisons to the *Select Committee on Transportation* on 8 July 1812. After all petitions concerning a prisoner had been considered, those convicts to be transported were medically examined, to prevent 'persons infected with epidemic disease or such debility as would endanger life' from being sent to depots at Dublin or Cork, as it was intended that none 'unfit by age or infirmity should proceed on the voyage'. The proportion of male to female transportees was about three to one, and those who had their death sentences respited were transported for life. Some men, 'if their cases are of a favourable nature', were permitted to join the army or navy. It was estimated that the proportion of those transported to those sent to the penitentiary houses was 'nearly as $2\frac{1}{4}$ to 1'. Con-

victs were detained in the county jails, unless they were too overcrowded or insecure, until a direction was received to send them to
the ship. Those from the west and north, and from around Dublin,
were brought by open cart to the city to be put on a vessel to bring
them to Cork. Those in the south were sent to Cork, and then down
the river by boat to the port at Cove for embarkation. Each convict
was to be supplied with two full suits of clothing, and the same provisions for a soldier or sailor. Women were allowed tea and sugar,
and all the necessaries were to be provided by the agent at Cork. The
report concluded that 'the good effects of this compassionate consideration for those unfortunate exiles are exemplified at the termination
of the voyage, not more in the general good health in which the Irish
convicts are landed, than in the superior condition of their clothing,
stores, etc.'.

Organised and efficient as the transportation system appeared to
be, according to the Inspector General's report, in reality the collection and dispatch of the convicts continued to cause serious problems
for the administrators. The 'good health' of the transportees depended
very much on the treatment which they received during the passage
and, as history testifies, they did not always arrive in a satisfactory
state.

Not all the petitions submitted concerning prisoners were intended
to be in their favour. The Earl of Longford, writing from Pakenham
Hall in January 1813, complained that fellow countyman William
Kearns, though loyal, Protestant and a yeoman, should not have been
released as he was troublesome. Awarded a 7-year sentence of transportation for robbery, Kearns was given his freedom, but with the
proviso that if he got into more trouble, he would be apprehended.

⑥ Preparations and Passage, 1813-1817

On 22 August 1813 the *Catherine* arrived from England at Cove to collect female convicts. Only two years old, the vessel was inspected on the day she arrived and was found to have 'a good roomy prison and berths made up for a hundred females, and there may be more. Her hospital is a good one, except being placed in the bows; it is tolerably well ventilated. She had a table in the centre of the prison which must be removed and forms placed there'. Thirty women were put on the *Catherine* on the twenty-fifth, and 20 more went on a couple of days later, followed by another 10 on the twenty-eighth. Twenty-five came to the vessel from the Cork city jail, and after 10 more arrived on 1 October there was a total of 90 women and 4 children. Most of the women were to serve 7 or 14 years, but Ann Rorke from Dublin and Catherine Geran from County Limerick, had life sentences. The occupations of the women included servant, house-keeper, needle-woman, shoe-binder, cutter, confectioner, shop-keeper, dealer, mantuar, upholsterer and country work.

The *Three Bees* was also inspected at Cove, on 23 August, when she had just come to anchor. The 'large and spacious prison' had berths for 220 convicts, but was not well ventilated. The hospital was also badly located, too far forward, had but 8 berths and it was also badly ventilated. Again, there were no forms in the prison. Just a month after the arrival of the *Catherine* and the *Three Bees* the hired brig *Atlas* came from the canal docks in Dublin to Cove in thirty-nine hours with convicts for transfer to the two transports. In general the prisoners were found to be in good condition, though many had the itch, and 'Wogan had a fever'. The itch was also present among the females, but otherwise they were in good shape except for two 'who suffered from old complaints'. As the transfer of the men to the *Three Bees* began, they were issued with new clothing and shaved. By 10 October there were 219 men on board.

Some of the accounts submitted for the inspection and administration of the convicts during this time give a glimpse of the day-to-day work of the officials:

To examining 317 convicts, at 1 crown each:	£85.17.1.
To visits to jails,	
16 January to 26 October: at £1.1: each visit:	£150.3.0.
To visits to *Catherine*, *Three Bees*, etc.	£91.0.0.
Soap for males and females:	£4.7.8.
Burying convict's child:	11.0.
Barber's account:	£9.15.0.
Washing for male convicts:	£6.17.6.
Burying child A. Smith, convict:	12.0.
Apothecaries bill (enclosed):	£56.17.2.

Both the *Catherine* and the *Three Bees* sailed on 8 December 1813, and they arrived within a couple of days of each other at Sydney in the first week of May 1814. Scurvy was rampant on the *Three Bees* during the passage and 9 men died. At Sydney 55 more were admitted to hospital 'in a dreadful state'. It was estimated that of the 219 men, 57 of whom had life-sentences, about 70 were agrarian offenders. They came from all four provinces, with 59 from trials in Dublin; their occupations included: weaver, carpenter, quarryman, currier, bricklayer, fisherman, shoemaker, stonemason, glass cutter, slater, plasterer, coachwheeler, paper maker, leather dyer, watchmaker, tailor, locksmith, book binder, cooper, cabinet maker, butcher and millwright.

It was just a year later that the next convict vessels sailed from Cove. They were the *Francis and Eliza* and the *Canada*. The first named carried 69 women and 54 men, 11 with life-sentences. An unusual characteristic of this group was age, half of the men were over 50, and most of the others over 40. All of the women were over 25, and 14 were aged between 40 and 60. Some of the men were agrarian offenders, such as 35-year-old Thomas and 70-year-old John Beirne, from Roscommon. There was a high number of prisoners, male and female, with such currency offences as 'forging, having forging implements'. Evidence of political unrest in County Roscommon is found in an official report of July 1814. Michael Murray and Peter Banaghan had been apprehended for breaking into the house of Patrick Ruane at Elphin, and for administering 'Trasher's Oaths'. They were sentenced to be transported for life, having been pilloried at Elphin. Up to 5,000 people gathered to see the men being pilloried, during which, according to an official report, 'a priest of the name of

Salmon went to them as a duty. I said there was no need as their life was not in danger; he said they were innocent, and that it was his duty to make it known. When he started to make a speech I removed him by force.'

It took the *Francis and Eliza* 246 days to reach Sydney, causing Governor Macquarie to write expressing his anxiety for her safety. One reason for the delay was that, on 4 January 1815 at sea, she was captured by an American privateer, the *Warrier* and detained for twenty-four hours. The vessel's guns, ammunition and some of the cargo were taken by the captors, and a number of the crew deserted to the Americans. The convicts were not interfered with and they assisted with the navigation of the *Francis and Eliza* when she was released. Putting into Teneriffe, Captain William Harrison sent those crewmen who had been troublesome back home and he took on new men. Joining up with the *Canada*, the *Francis and Eliza* was escorted to Sierra Leone by a British frigate and there a military guard was found for the latter transport. The *Canada*, with its complement of 156 male convicts, reached Sydney three days before the *Francis and Eliza* and when the governor learned of the good behaviour of the Irish prisoners on the troubled ship, they 'having conducted themselves with great discretion, moderation and decency at the time of the capture, and while the vessel remained in the possession of the enemy, and while the crew had been mutinous', he recommended conditional pardons for all the convicts; but this was not acceptable to the authorities in Dublin Castle.

Another convict, whose arrival on the *Baring* from England in September 1815 must have pleased the governor, was Thomas Whyte. Born in Dublin and sentenced at Edinburgh, he was a Master Mariner and he was quickly assigned to the Colonial Marine. In 1820 he was granted 300 acres at Longford, on the Norfolk plains of Van Diemen's Land, but he was forced to sell his farm and solid house within a few years when he lost valuable goods in the wreck of a ship coming from Sydney. Whyte then decided to go back to his seafaring and he joined the Van Diemen's Land Colonial Marine. In the service he was given the task of pursuing bushrangers and escaped convicts and on one such expedition he was ambushed and robbed by fellow countryman Matthew Brady. Brady, who had arrived in the *Juliana* just after Christmas in 1820, suffered 350 lashes for his escape attempts. He succeeded in escaping in 1823 and for a few years himself and his gang evaded capture, but in 1826 he was taken and hanged. He soon become part of colonial folklore and he is remembered also south-west of Cressy in the placename Brady's Outlook.

Of the two ships that sailed from Ireland in 1815, the *Guildford* was making the first of three such voyages from Cork, and during her eight passages from these islands between 1812 and 1829 she ferried a total of 1,500 men into exile, with the loss of a dozen people. On this voyage she carried 225 convicts, of whom 90 may have been classified as agrarian offenders. The *Alexander* carried 84 women, of whom 3 died en route. Following a voyage from England which decimated her officers and convicts when typhus raged on the vessel, great care was taken to make the *Surrey* healthy for the transportation of 150, including 61 agrarian, prisoners when she arrived at Cove. The vessel was ventilated and thoroughly cleaned, and the prison was regularly fumigated. Wine was issued as an anti-scorbutic and, during the passage, half of the men were allowed on deck at one time. Given classes in reading and writing, and employed at oakum-picking, they were given rewards instead of punishments. At night they were permitted on deck 'to recreate with music for their general good conduct. . . with dancing, and as an anti-scorbutic'. If it was found necessary to punish an offender, for such petty crimes as theft or disorderly behaviour, no more than 18 lashes were ever given. Not surprisingly, the *Surrey* landed all her men in good health, but with 8 in single irons. The ship's log recorded that, on being disembarked, the convicts 'cheered repeatedly and expressed the liveliest gratitude for their treatment'. Amongst the 40 men from Tipperary aboard the *Surrey* were Edward Ryan from Clonoulty, near Cashel, and his cousin Roger Corcoran, both in their mid-20s. With 8 companions they had been accused of destroying a house which had been used as a barracks – an offence which had been classified as agrarian. Both Ryan and Corcoran prospered when they settled at Boorowa, and in subsequent years several members of their families came from Tipperary to join them.

After the *Surrey* had left Cove on 14 July 1816 the routine work of assembling those to go on the next sailings continued. By September there were 51 women in Newgate prison in Dublin, aged between 18 and 50, with an average age of 30; their crimes had been robbery, forgery, burglary, or the theft of such items as stockings, ribbon, hankies, plate, money, watches, muslin, and a prayer book.

Male prisoners at the same count numbered 93, aged from 16 to 50, with an average age of 45. Sixteen of them had been convicted of forgery, and other crimes were listed as the stealing of plate, beef, paper, money and horses.

In the spring of the following year three ships were being prepared for departure at Cove. They were the *Pilot*, the *Canada* and the *Chapman*, between them destined to bring a total of 392 convicts, of whom 89 were women, to the colony. The vessels were subject to a demurrage fee; for the 558-ton *Chapman*, the largest of the three, it was £446.8.0. per month. Accordingly there were complaints about the delay in having the convicts embarked. In the case of the female transport *Canada* the delay was caused by official indecision as to the fate of the children of some of the women. While waiting some 63 of the women were confined on the sloop *Dumfries* for eight days sleeping on filthy straw, which had been on the sloop since she had left Dublin. As the *Dumfries* was also rat infested it was not surprising that many of the women were ill, the condition of most of them being described as dreadful. Ellen Dixon, from Galway, was placed in men's heavy irons by the doctor 'to make her appear more culpable' when she told him that she had venereal disease. The disposal of the children of the female convicts had caused much heartsearching on the part of the authorities: what was to be done with them, particularly those from distant counties? Some of them aged 7-8, were lodged in foundling hospitals, the remainder, it was recommended, should be allowed to go on the *Canada* as there was room for them. It was argued that 'they cannot be taken from their mothers and thrown in the streets, as there is room on the ship a small allowance of provisions would be the only expense to the government, if allowed to travel, and it would be a great comfort to the poor women'.

When the women were taken on board the *Canada* they were found to be 'weak and irritable, scrofulous looking', with some of them suffering from asthma and haemorrhage. There was confusion about the identity of a few of the women as they were known by their maiden-names although married. Ann Hoar was thought to labour 'under a peculiar female obstruction which renders women particularly irritable and their circulation easily excited, and this had been her case for near two years'. When the ship's surgeon discovered Ellen Dixon's complaint he treated her more kindly than had her last physician. He gave her medicine when she told him that, while confined in the jail at Galway, the gaoler had cohabited with her and she had a miscarriage. As he had venereal disease she thought that she must have contracted it but he kept her in solitary confinement for two months so that she would not complain. The *Canada* left Cove on 21 March, just nine days after the *Pilot* and four days before the *Chapman*.

There was illness, too, among those awaiting embarkation on the *Chapman*, causing the inspecting doctor to report that 'James Neal, I fear, will get around me as he has taken tobacco water and is now in high fever. . .' This vessel was low below deck causing one officer to suggest that only small men and boys should be placed on her. This proposal led to disagreement as another official held that the *Pilot* was even lower! While awaiting transportation the convicts were allowed 6*d* a day to feed themselves and another 6*d* per head was given to the jailer and the sheriff; it was rumoured that the delay in the sailing of the ships was caused by the victuallers wishing to extend their profits. The report of a party of Commissioners who were sent to Cove to inspect the *Canada*, *Pilot* and *Chapman* found that the berths and the soldiers' quarters were very dirty on the *Pilot*, which also carried unauthorised women, children and pigs. Though the convicts were forbidden to have spirits, the inspectors found evidence that they consumed them and they were not pleased with the supervising doctor, as he would not reveal his income. The two Cork sheriffs, they noted, got a gift of £50 between them after the ships had sailed. Before the men had been put on the ships, a turnkey informed the inspectors that he had bought supplies cheap for them which they cooked themselves. But no spirits were allowed he said, 'except sometimes, after the men had had their heads shaved, they got a glass of whiskey, to prevent colds, if they could afford it'.

While the women on the *Canada* may have had moments of hope when the vessel was forced to put back into Cove, due to contrary winds, these were dashed when she sailed on 21 March. On the other hand, the 200 men on the *Chapman* were entirely without hope from the time that they boarded the vessel. For Captain Drake, master of the ship, this was his first command and he was highly nervous of his cargo. Even while the *Chapman* lay at Cove, he permitted only 12 men on deck at a time, for an hour. After she went to sea he continued the same practice and when the men were being brought on deck for inspection or for their wine ration, they were hurried up the main and down the fore hatchways. In the prison they were con-

stantly in irons. Consequently it was not surprising that the ship was
at sea for but a week when there were rumours of a mutiny. Then,
in the third week of April, an informer named Michael Collins told
the captain that it was the intention of the prisoners to capture the
vessel and sail for America. When, at eight o'clock on the evening of
17 April, a cry was raised that the prisoners were breaking out, the
guard fired into the prison for about three-quarters of an hour. Despite
the moans of the wounded, they withdrew leaving the prisoners un-
attended until the next morning. Then it was found that three of
them had been killed and 22 wounded. About ten days later there
were further rumours of trouble and again the prisoners were fired
on. This time one was killed and four wounded.

Another account of these tragic occurrences came from a convict
named Tom Ryan who, on the recommendations of the captain and
surgeon of the *Chapman*, had been given employment in the office
of the colonial secretary at £30 per year. In a letter home to Dr Trevor,
in which he pleaded for a pardon, and a return to Ireland, having
'truly repented for a trivial offence', Ryan wrote:

> I am sorry to inform you of the disturbances wherein 12 unfortunate
> prisoners fell victims to the cold blooded assassins to whose care they were
> committed, about 30 severely wounded, two of whom died since, as also
> two sailors who were placed in a boat astern of the ship and fired on by
> 12 soldiers on the suspicion of their intending to aid the prisoners in
> taking the ship. The cause of all this was the consequence of two villainous
> prisoners giving private false information to the captain and doctor, of the
> prisoners intending to mutinise and massacre the ship's crew. Instead of
> the captain taking precautions to guard against such evil, he kept it secret,
> on the night it was supposed to happen they fired on them from all quarters
> and destroyed the poor unfortunate wretches as they lay in their births
> *(sic)* and on the deck where they lay for coolness. Then floggings on
> suspicion ensued, and upwards of 1,000 lashes were inflicted on them
> frequently. They were taken up on deck by Baxer, the third officer, and
> flogged severely. The boatswain would not be permitted to flog for fear
> he would not be severe enough. In addition 14 were put in irons, double
> handcuffed and chained to the poop since the night in question 'till they
> arrived here, and the remainder chained in the prison with a chain cable
> between their legs. If they made the least noise with their chain they
> would be flogged. If they made water between decks they would be flog-
> ged, which was often done as they were afraid to move about the deck.
> For upwards of a week three men were kept in the hold, chained to the
> pump, on bread and water, brought up once a day and told to pray as
> they had only a few minutes to live, armed soldiers were put before them

to shoot them. Asked if they were ready, they replied, 'Yes, and better for us if we were put out of this punishment long before now.' Now the officers thought it better to inflict corporal punishment, they were severely flogged, and one of them named Leo, after flogging, was tied up to the main yardarm and towed overboard until almost dead, and the ship running at the rate of 10 knots an hour. After some time he was brought on deck and salt rubbed on his back, after which he was chained to the poop without any surgical aid. I must remark also that the doctor would not dress the wounded, but let their wounds mortify. The men were also starved, and arrived here in an exhausted state. Soon after arrival a committee was appointed by Governor Macquarie to investigate the matter, the result of this was that Lieutenant Busteed of the 69th Regiment on the *Chapman*, and the surgeon superintendent, Alexander Dewar, were ordered to be sent home to England under close arrest, as well as three soldiers of the guard who have been charged with murder and the ship's captain to give bail for their appearance in London at the end of two years. For the prosecution, 12 convicts and 9 soldiers were also sent home as evidence.

Having added that, for speaking Irish and for making noises, another man was flogged twice, Ryan offered Dr Trevor his services in the colony, 'I will feel the greatest pleasure in informing you by every opportunity, if you favour me with a letter stating the particulars you would wish'.

The men who were sent to England for trial came before an Admiralty Sessions in January 1819, and were acquitted when it was found that 'upon the evidence the conduct of the convicts was of a nature to excite in the minds of the officers and crew such an apprehension of danger as could excuse at least, if not justify, the several acts of homicide laid to their charge'.

Following the three sailings of March 1817 the doctor who had supervised the departures wrote to Dublin Castle, 'The ships have sailed, and an ease it is to us, for every day almost produced new enquiry'. There had been complaints that the convicts had been issued with old clothes, of their conditions in the jails, and that they were not getting full rations. 'We have been held up in a newspaper here, the editor of which pays occasional visits here; it is however, now silent, how long it will be I cannot say.'

Very soon reports were being sent to the authorities about the crowded state of the prisons; Monaghan held 160, many of whom were ill. Some of these, it was decided, could go to Kilmainham, but first, they should be cleaned, free from itch and given clean clothing.

Then they would be ready for New South Wales. Others, such as one John Murphy, were sent to Cork city jail. He was amongst those who walked from Clonmel to Cork, a distance of 60 miles, over three days on a daily diet of a pint of porter and half a loaf of bread. In Cork jail an official report found crowding 'to excess. . . rendering the apartments loathsome', with dishonest turnkeys and short rations.

From Trim, in July, came the report that overcrowding was so great, many of the prisoners had to sleep in the common hall, but at least there was no fever. Of the total of 209 confined there only 13 were awaiting transportation. Carrickfergus jail was so full it was suggested that the town guard and the garrison must be increased to contain the prisoners, some of whom had escaped by the use of a skeleton key. In August Sir John Stewart requested that the transportees should be removed from the County Tyrone jail as it was packed with 340 prisoners. Similar requests were being made from Londonderry, Lifford, Downpatrick, Tralee, Monaghan, Sligo and Kilkenny. In the latter city the prisoners had attempted a break out and in Limerick, after breaking the furniture and utensils and setting fire to the place, they had also tried to escape. Fever was rampant in many of the jails, a factor which intensified the demand for the transfer of transportees to the vessels in Dublin. It has been thought that the ending of the Napoleonic and American wars brought a wave of 'post-war crime in both England and Ireland' and from 1817 transportation became a common punishment for larceny, the stealing of animals, coining, burglary and forgery. Thus the numbers for shipment increased.

The *Guildford*, making her third passage to Australia and her second from Ireland, was the only other convict ship to sail from Cork in 1817. Departing on 11 November she arrived at Port Jackson on 1 April of the following year. The captain of the *Guildford*, Magnus Johnson, was 'a prudent and conscientious master, and he treated the convicts humanely'; 198 of the 200 convicts were disembarked.

An unexpected arrival from Ireland in New South Wales in 1817 was a Cistercian priest, Fr Jeremiah O'Flynn, who had come as a settler, on funds provided by Dublin Catholics. He had a chalice and vestments supplied by the Congregation of Propaganda in Rome. He was welcomed in Van Diemen's Land, where he celebrated Mass in public and officiated at baptisms and marriages. But in New South Wales he was not so well received. Governor Macquarie feared that he might 'disturb the minds of the touchy Roman Catholic community which had become so docile that some of its members had formed the habit of attending the Anglican church': it was even thought possible that 'a designing artful priest. . . would bring back among the local Irish the old spirit of rebellion of 1804'. So Fr O'Flynn was lodged in jail and within a year of his coming was on his way home.

His departure caused genuine regret amongst the Catholics. Michael Hayes, writing to his mother, said that there were 'about eleven hundred children not baptised, including his ten-year-old son, and also many wanted marriage'. Another old inhabitant of the colony recalled that 'the priest had the sweetest and swiftest tongue of Irish I ever heard', adding that he never spoke a word of English himself until it was made punishable with 50 lashes to speak a word of Irish. Fr O'Flynn left his books behind and, more importantly, the Blessed Sacrament in the house of a friend. People came to pray before the sacrament, and it was 'remarkably beautiful to contemplate these men of sorrow around the Bread of Life. . . not a priest within ten thousand miles'. Another commentator saw the Irish differently, and when about 20 men escaped to Port Stephen they were described as 'piratical. . . largely Hibernians and partisans of the exiled Fr O'Flynn.'

The Cistercian had also expressed his views of his fellow Irish in the colony:

> Half the population are Roman Catholics, whose conduct will show you how successful the government has been in making them Protestant. Those that are free in the country and such as have been emancipated, never go to [the Protestant] church, nor do they get their children baptised. As to prisoners, you will be surprised to hear of the compulsory manner in which they are forced to church, in which their conduct, as I am informed, is not very regular; one will take out a pack of cards, another a novel, or any convenient book, another will be prepared with a variety of tricks to raise the mirth of his neighbours, another will provide himself with needle and thread to mend his clothes, another will endeavour to sleep all the time; but of all the latter is least indulged, as there are three or four constables, with scurges in their hands, who are constantly rousing them from sleep. Notwithstanding the great dis-edification shown by the Catholics they are mustered rank and file every Sunday by the governor, and in case of absence from church are confined from church time until work-time on Monday morning.

The pardoned convict Michael Hayes also wrote about the compulsory attendance at Protestant services, and after the departure of Fr

O'Flynn he said that those living on the land were 'disconsolate for their own ministers and rituals', they refused to be married in the Established churches and so lived together unwed; their children were not instructed in their religion and 'when the Sectaries visited the families to moralise them, they did not attend to their admonitions, not having faith in them. Such is a faint portrait of the situation of the Catholics in New South Wales, which would not be so calamitous if the Catholic priests were admitted to come here at earlier times.'

Dr Portia Robinson, who in recent years has studied the status of the female convicts, supports the views of family-life expressed by Hayes early in the nineteenth century. Despite the fact that the Irish Catholics declined to be married in the Protestant churches, they maintained long-lasting unions and their children generally retained the faith. These unions were encouraged by the availability of land grants, which could be increased, depending on family size. Traditionally the character of the convict woman had been accepted as that expressed by colonial officials, such as Mr Marsden, as immoral, abandoned and unskilled. In reality the majority of them had been convicted of minor crimes, and as single, unprotected women they were naturally treated with suspicion by conservative, and often hostile, officials. Most of the women were wives and mothers endeavouring to care for their families as they would have done at home. Several of them became self-supporting, as boarding-house keepers, public-house owners, servants or laundresses. The image of the average inmate of the Parramatta factory may have been accurate for some, but it included only those convicted of crimes or in transit to assignments. While it may be true that such incidents happened as that in which women raised their skirts to expose their posteriors as the ultimate insult to harsh officers, it must be realised that such a gesture of disapproval was known to be employed in Ireland also. Like Peggy Brophy from Nenagh, who is mentioned in the ballad 'Van Diemen's Land' and who married a planter, the majority of women (in a land where, the same ballad tells us, there were twenty men for one woman) settled down to the oblivion of domestic life, as did their sisters elsewhere. The fact that, compared with the British convicts, the Irish included a greater proportion of women was significant. It meant that the Irish women played an important part in the development of family life in the colony, and they succeeded in transmitting to their offspring the values and traditions of 'the ould sod'.

7 Gaelic-speaking Rockchoppers, 1818-1820

On New Year's Day 1818 the *Minerva* sailed from Cove, the first of five convict-ships to leave Ireland in that year. Between them they brought 101 female and 663 male convicts; 157 of the latter were disembarked at Hobart in Van Diemen's Land. But even as the first vessel left Cork harbour preparations were already underway to assemble bodies for the next. Petitions were dictated to the scribes or written by those so capable for dispatch to Dublin Castle. One came from Nancy Haigney, who had been sentenced in County Galway for stealing clothes, pleading not to be exiled as she suffered from convulsions.

By the month of February there were 466 men and 82 women in the jails throughout the country. Those with sentences of 14 years had been convicted of crimes such as forgery, or in place of the death sentence – for robbery. Seven-year-sentences were awarded for stealing a hat, wine, candles, butter and a looking-glass, and to 10 men at Cashel for insurrection. At Newgate in Dublin 98 men under sentence of death, aged from 14 to 55, 37 of whom were 20 or under, were remitted and sentenced to permanent transportation. Their crimes were vagrancy, or stealing food or clothing. When medically examined a few of them were found to be suffering from venereal disease.

The Keeper of Cork jail advertised for clothes for the inmates; 'grey cloth jacket, lined with linen and trousers of the same, 17s10d; leather cap lined with linen, 1s5d; stockings, 1s8d; shoes of strong description, 5s'. This outfitting of the prisoners locally was not satisfactory to some of the supervising officials who recommended that 'in future, when the convict ships arrived from England that they should be provided with clothes and provisions for the voyage and for after arrival in the colony'. In the Cork jail 172 prisoners were crowded into the space for 62, and fever raged; among the crowd were 14 boys who were being transported for vagrancy. Conditions were worse in Kilmainham prison in Dublin. Due to the fact that the hospital roof had been burned the keeper considered the place to be unsafe and he requested iron fetters in which to secure the prisoners. The Inspector of Prisons did not agree that the prisoners should be fettered before embarking as it was an unnecessary hardship; instead, he thought, more watchmen should be employed.

In February the accounts were submitted for providing for the *Guildford* and the *Minerva*; these show that advertising for contracts in *The Advertiser* and the *Southern Reporter* cost £5.17.0. Other expenses were: straw, £3.19.0; locks £3; cutlery £3.10.0; tinware £11.2.8; 18 lbs chocolate £4.10.0; portable soup and charcoal £131.19.0; barley £9.7.5; handcuffs £13.10.0; mustard £13.4.0; vinegar £14.2.2; tobacco, £18.8.0, and 'wine from Gerard Galway, 18 dozen, £38.14.0. Victualling convicts: £251.8.5.'

Early in the summer of 1818 it was planned to begin the movement of the Dublin prisoners by road to Cork. Travelling by stages, they were to be accommodated in the jails en route overnight. The procession, growing in numbers at each town, as more prisoners were collected and accompanied by the gaolers and a guard was expected to be an example, 'the men in chains would be a great deterrent'. Another official view of this was 'that tumult might ensue, and too many military would be required to line the road'. Finally it was decided to take the prisoners by sea, and two vessels were procured; the *Kitty* and the *Isabella* between them transported 230 men to Cove. But now there was trouble in Tipperary; the jail, crowded with 341 convicts, was insecure as the walls were decayed. To make matters worse, the well in the jail had run dry and it was found necessary to draw water from the river. At night a guard was mounted at the jail and this required the service of 40 soldiers. Generally, the structural condition of the jails was deplorable, and the squalor of the cells extreme.

When the ship *Elizabeth* anchored at Cove in June it was expected that she would carry the stores as requested but she did not and there was a delay of a month before the supply-ship came, consequently the embarkation of the 101 female prisoners could not begin. When the stores were received each woman was issued with a cloth jacket, waistcoat, a woollen hat, a linen bag, a coarse rubber, hankerchief, shoes, and two each of shirts, stockings, linen trousers and combs. Nor were there stores on the *Tyne* when she arrived to load 180 men. The wives of an officer and four soldiers travelled on the *Tyne* with their menfolk. The *Earl St Vincent* was then also standing by to take

160 men, but before she sailed with the *Tyne* at 6 am on 7 August 1818, one prisoner was drowned in an escape bid. After the guard discovered him in hiding under the ship's head he called out, 'My life is in your hands' before he fell into the water and was carried away by a strong tide.

On 3 September following the departure of the vessels, Dr Trevor (whose salary for managing the convict depot was £1,000 per annum) submitted to his superiors a *Memorandum* for his supervision of the ships *Tyne, Earl St Vincent, Elizabeth* and *Martha*, saying unctuously that 'as I feel that you are aware of the importance of my exertions on these occasions I shall not trespass on your time detailing them, but merely add that they have been attended with much advantage to the public and that the four embarkations were despatched in less time than two months'. He emphasised that, including his visit to London to make arrangements with the commissioners of the navy, the entire business took him 102 days. Within a short time of forwarding this report Dr Trevor was requesting Mr Secretary Peel that, as his son was 'now of age' he wished him to be considered for an office appointment.

Despite the fact that five ships left Ireland in 1818 the crowded state of the country's jails continued to cause apprehension to the government. At Cork in October, the county sheriff protested that there were 61 prisoners, including 21 boys aged from 10 to 18, in the jail; by Christmas the situation was worse with food and clothing for the inmates in short supply, the bills had not been paid and the building itself was falling down!

In early spring of the new year of 1819 it was intended that female convicts would be moved by road from Kilmainham to Cork, and an order was issued to outline the procedure. Hackney jaunting cars with sail covers were to be provided and a military escort was to accompany the convoy which would move by stages, with overnight accommodation in the jails at Naas, Carlow, Kilkenny, Clonmel and at the military barracks in Fermoy. A free woman who was prepared to join the female convicts was Fanny Fannagan. She begged to be allowed to go to her husband at 'Botany Bay' as she had three small children and, having no support, was in great distress. Her story might have been that told in the ballad 'The Convict Child' which was published by 'Alx. Mayne, High Street, Belfast'. In four verses it expressed the agony of separation of a convict father from his child and the mother's grief also:

> Her tears might flow in vain,
> For on that day her husband sailed
> She ne'er would see again.
> She pressed her infant to her breast
> And again at her it smiled
> 'I live for that dear boy,' she cried;
> Alas! her convict child.

Conditions in Cork jail had not improved and in April Dr Trevor said it 'was filthy, the men filthy, unshaved and without haircuts, their conduct on the streets of the city, en route to the transports, was disgraceful', with many of them drunk. The women embarked on the *Lord Wellington* were 'well-clothed and behaved. . . due to the visits of a lady while in Kilmainham jail. Fourteen of them could knit'. Worsted was put on board that vessel, with needles to make 12 dozen pairs of socks, which were to be given to those who made them. Extra soap, writing-paper and pens, ink and Testaments were also supplied. A lady in Cork sought to visit the women, causing Dr Trevor to observe 'The priest who attends the depot prid *(sic)* at the idea of any interference. I do not think it prudent to make any arrangements with regard to the females, other than keeping them at work.'

Between April and December 1819 seven ships left Ireland for Australia with 1,028 convicts of whom 226 were female. One of these vessels, the *Castle Forbes*, took its prisoners on to Hobart where, after disembarkation, 28 of them planned to seize the ship while she lay at anchor. An informer revealed the plot and the conspirators were apprehended.

With the arrival of the English convict-ship *Prince Regent* early in 1820 new hope was given to the Catholic community in the colony. The vessel brought two young Irish priests who had volunteered for the Australian mission in response to the debate in the House of Commons in London concerning the circumstances in which Fr O'Flynn had left New South Wales. It was decided that chaplains, with a salary of £100 per year, should be sent out, and so Fr John Joseph Therry from Cork and Fr Phillip Conolly from Monaghan decided to go. Fr Conolly served for two years in Port Jackson before moving to Van Diemen's Land to minister to the convicts.

Fr Therry's interest in the colony was said to have been aroused by the sight of a wagon-full of handcuffed prisoners going through the streets of his native city on their way to the convict ship. He purchased prayer books for the prisoners and resolved that one day he would accompany them into exile. Working in Sydney Fr Therry at first had difficulty with some of the officials, such as in procuring access to Catholic children in state institutions. It was held that all the children of convicts were legally orphans and should be reared in the government orphan school, which taught the Protestant religion.

One of the priest's greatest ambitions was to have a church built for his congregation and this he finally achieved with the aid of the two former convicts, James Meehan, who chose the site, and Francis Greenway, who designed St Mary's. But Fr Therry was especially concerned for the convicts; visiting them in the prisons, hospitals and chain gangs, he became known as 'the felon's friend'. Always at their call, he went long distances to comfort men who were condemned to death. His popularity with, and endeavours on behalf of, the convicts did not improve his standing with the authorities or with the Established Church and he was dismissed from his post as an official chaplain.

From his experience in the new land Fr Conolly wrote to a priest friend at home in Ireland describing the type of priest who might be selected for the Australian mission. They should be 'from country parishes [where] their habits of exertion prepare them in a great measure for the labours they should undergo here, and a missioner should speak the Irish language without which he would be at a loss to hear confessions'. Of course, the convicts also had their views on religion, and one of their ballads on the subject advised:

Let Romanists all at confessional kneel.
Let the Jew in disgust turn from it,
Let the mighty Crown Prelate in church pander zeal
Let the Mussulman worship Mahomet. . .
Let psalm-singing churchmen and Lutherans sing,
They can't deceive me with their Blarney;
They might just as well dance the Highland fling,
Or sing the fair fame of Kate Kearney.

While the writer of this ballad seems to have taken a cynical view of all religions, it was to be expected that the Protestant English colonial officers would bring their suspicions of the Irish Catholics with them to New South Wales and Van Diemen's Land. The term

'Rockchoppers', applied to the Roman Catholics, possibly came from the initials RC or maybe from the employment of some of the convicts at stone breaking.

In the year before the arrival of Fathers Conolly and Therry another Irish clergyman had disembarked at Sydney, but as a convict. Laurence Halloran, D.D., who was born in County Meath in 1765, had worked as a Protestant minister in England and at the Cape of Good Hope and in both places he made himself unpopular by the publication of slanderous doggerel. The father of a large family, he was constantly in financial difficulties and in 1818 he was convicted of counterfeiting and sentenced to transportation for 7 years. On his arrival at Sydney in 1819 he was immediately given a ticket-of-leave and proceeded to establish a private school. When his family came to join him, Halloran appeared to be about to establish a successful lifestyle but soon his litigious habits caused him problems and over the next decade he was forced to close and reopen his school several times. In 1825 he founded a Public Free Grammar School in Sydney but within a year it had to close. A ballad which he had written in 1801 might well have served for his epitaph when he died in 1831; it was entitled *Lachrymae Hibernicae*, or *The Genius of Erin's Complaint*.

⑧ Defenders and Whiteboys, 1821-1824

By 1821 the population of Ireland had reached 6.8 million, almost twice what it had been in 1772, and with the ending of the French wars in 1815 the demand for agricultural produce decreased causing great hardship to the hundreds of thousands of people depending on the land for income. A decline in the demand for homespun textiles threw another section of the community into poverty, thus adding to the misery of a people already subject to periodic famine. In 1814 there was another Insurrection Act with Limerick and the regularly troublesome County of Tipperary being proclaimed. Demands from the Established Church for their due tithes inflamed the already desperate situation, and the secret societies of 'Whiteboys', 'Defenders' and others multiplied, and became ever more violent in the hope of improving the lot of the impoverished. Not surprisingly, the courts were full of agrarian offenders or other social delinquents some of whom eventually found their way on to the convict ships and thus to Australia.

During 1820 five convict ships sailed from Ireland and, though the system of transportation to Australia had then been employed for 30 years, the arrangements for collecting the prisoners was still bad and the conditions in which they were confined reflected the general disarray of the prison system which was incapable of housing the culprits from the ever increasing population. At Passage, in July, the detainees were 'in a state not to be wondered at. . . they made well-groomed complaints which would cause clamour if they reached the ears of certain individuals. . .' It was urged that a vessel should come to Passage to remove them. This was arranged and in the following month the *Almorah* arrived. While the soldiers' wives washed the convicts linen on shore, the hold of the *Almorah* was whitewashed and the bedding straw was changed. Then 160 men were put on board for passage to Cork. There two transports, the *Prince Regent* and the *Lord Sidmouth* were being prepared for departure. It was recommended by Dr Trevor that the agent who was providing the food and necessaries for the ships should be paid £80, and while he knew that the agent was being allowed 1s3d per day to feed a prisoner, he believed that they could be messed for little more than half of that sum. The scale of messing for 6 men each day was 4 lb of beef, vegetables, oatmeal and salt, to make broth, and 1 lb of bread. As usual, many of those about to be exiled tried for mercy. Such a one was Catherine Stafford, from Cork, with a 7-year sentence for coining. The mother 'of eight fatherless children' she protested that she was but a lodger in the house where evidence of coining had been found.

But efforts were being made to improve the prison system and, as the complaints about the condition of the prisoners at Passage were reaching the appropriate officers, the final preparations had been made for the opening of the newly-built Richmond Penitentiary in Dublin.

After the penitentiary was functioning for some years *Observations* on the cost of this innovation in the penal system were published. These included the belief that 'the predominant qualities of the depraved population of this country are a disposition to mischievous combinations, a restless desire of change and innovation, daring, or rather a defiant contempt of death, all of these are forwarded rather than repressed by existing criminal law, and it is recommended that convicts for transportation to Port Jackson commit special crimes in order that they may be transported. Arrived there, with tickets-of-leave, they have full range of the colony.' This belief that conditions in Australia might be better than at home was given credence by some of the letters from the exiles.

In the spring of 1821 prisoners were again on the move, and the conveyance of Newgate convicts to the Pigeon House in Dublin Bay led to a recommendation that the jailer should be repremanded as many of the prisoners 'were in a shameful state of intoxication, and produced great clamour and irregularity'. Some delicate men had been held over in the prison, though the doctor suspected that they were consuming tobacco water and he warned that he would soon find out. Dr Trevor was also complaining a couple of months later when a female convict was moved by canal to the jail in Dublin, in order to await transfer to the Pigeon House for shipment to Cork. This passage of women under a military guard could, the doctor believed, cause irregularities. He recommended that three men should be employed for the work at a wage of a guinea a week and their expenses by road back to Dublin. Presumably Dr Trevor's opinion of the soldiery was a common one but his efforts to protect the morals of the women failed once they were on board the convict ship.

The eighty women for whom he was concerned were for embarkation on the *John Bull*. Before they embarked the surgeon vaccinated the women and their children and a supply of the vaccine was taken on the vessel. In the course of the 146 days-passage to Sydney of the *John Bull* there was trouble with the crew when the master tried to prevent prostitution among the convicts. The second mate was put in irons when it was discovered that he had accommodated a female in the cabin throughout a Sunday. Despite more such trouble with the sailors, the *John Bull* reached port safely.

The transferring of convicts by sea from Dublin to Cove would appear to have been an improvement on the former method of sending them by road and Dr Trevor claimed credit for this innovation. Thanks to this arrangement, he submitted, and by reducing the stay of the convict ships at Cove, in addition to his improvements in the victualling system, a considerable saving had been effected to the public purse. Frauds committed by the sheriff of Cork and by the city jailer had been detected but further irregularities needed to be halted. The Chief Secretary's Office remarked on unexplained erasures on the convict lists and other documents given to the ships' masters for delivery to the governor in New South Wales. Again Trevor had a solution: the documents should be of vellum, and sealed in a tin box.

Conditions on the convict ships themselves were also being improved and when the *Isabella* sailed on 4 November 1821 with 200 male convicts it was equipped with materials for the education of the men: 1 gallon of ink, 300 quills, 3 dozen cutters, 2 dozen each of slates and primers and 1 dozen spelling-books. However, the port officials at Cork had managed to prevent the sending onto the *Isabella* of religious books requested by Fr Conolly. He had written home saying that, due to the shortage of texts, his mission was rendered useless and recommending that 5,000 books of instruction, prayer books, testaments and catechisms should be sent out. Apart from the *Isabella* three other Irish ships brought 361 male convicts to Sydney in 1822. The fastest of these was the *Countess of Harcourt* which made the passage in 109 days, just two days over the record of the *Lord Sidmouth* in the February of the previous year.

The endeavours of Dr Trevor and other officers to improve the

arrangements for transportation would seem to have been successful
to the extent that when a Special Royal Commissioner visited the
colony about this time he commented on the fact that on arrival in
New South Wales the Irish were generally in a very healthy state and
that during the passage they were found to be more obedient and
sensible of kind treatment than any other convicts. However, he also
noticed that the separation from their native country, both on departure and during the voyage, made a greater impression on them than
on any others. If the standards of the convict officers in Ireland had
risen, those in the colony had not. According to the Commissioner's
report the officials seized every opportunity to cheat the convicts,
particularly in the matter of issuing of and accounting for rations.

With the re-introduction of an old law, that persons abroad at night
could be transported, in 1822 the jails continued to be crowded and
the guarding of the prisoners difficult. In Londonderry jail, where
the inmates were considered to be bad characters and ill-conducted,
an escape attempt was made requiring the under-mining of the jail
walls. Some impression of the type of criminal confined may be formed
from the petitions which they were submitting. Anne Donnelly,
described as a woman of weak and credulous mind, who had been
incited by an accomplice who had gone free to rob a bleach green,
pleaded that she had a deaf husband and three small children. William
Henry, from Omagh, a blacksmith who had been at sea for 14 years
and had been sentenced for stealing his master's shoes, gave the excuse
that on a dark morning he had put on the wrong pair! John Kelly,
an itinerant tailor who was transported for vagrancy, made the case
that he was not a vagrant, but that he could earn his subsistence by
moving from farm to farm and exercising his trade. There was a
'youth of tender years who was induced by wicked company at a
wake in Golden Lane, Dublin, to try and sell a petticoat which had
been stolen', and, of course, there was a man offering information in
return for clemency. To escape his sentence for sheep-stealing John
Currans, from Kilkenny, was prepared to give details of outrages
committed in the previous two years.

One of the five convict ships to sail from Cork in 1823 was the
Earl St. Vincent, making her third passage to New South Wales and
one of the 156 men disembarked from the *Earl St. Vincent* at Sydney
was Dennis Mahony a native of Dunmanway, County Cork, where
he had left a wife and four children. The separation of husbands from

wives and children was a cause of great anguish as the family was broken up and left without a bread-winner; such was the case with the Mahonys, and within a couple of years a magistrate certified that they were mendicant and destitute. From Botany Bay, where he was employed as a servant near the wharf, Dennis Mahony petitioned the Lord Lieutenant in Dublin and various gentlemen, a priest and a parson, that his family might be sent out. His request was recommended by the governor and the priest, and he exhorted his wife to travel and said that if their oldest son was not able to get passage she was to have the second boy stay with him in Ireland. During the passage on the *Earl St. Vincent*, he wrote he had never been ill and he explained that if his wife came he could get £50 a year and half that for son Johnny if he worked for a settler; they could live better than those at home who paid £100 in rent! Before leaving home, Mrs Mahony was to seek to have his sentence reduced and she was to write to him giving news of her plans, with copies of the letter to the Superintendent of Barracks, to his employers, and to Fr Therry. The importance of the priest to the people, as a leader and intermediary, continued as at home, and Mahony instructed his wife to ask for the priest as soon as she came ashore at the wharf close to where he himself worked. And he did not forget his mother, sending her the message that he hoped that 'I would never die until I see her again'.

To alleviate the crowded condition of the prisons it was decided in 1824 to follow the English example by accommodating convicts on dismantled vessels anchored in harbours. The hulk *Essex* was put at Kingstown,[13] and the *Surprise* at Cove, to 'which all prisoners convicted and sentenced to transportation shall be transmitted with all practical expedition'. However, this arrangement did not solve the problem, and within a short time the hulks were also overcrowded, and thus they remained for their time in service.

Several prisoners who were to become well known in convict tradition arrived in Australia in 1824; in that year and in the previous year, 8 ships brought 951 male and 202 female prisoners from Ireland. Convict John Graham, who was sentenced to 7 years transportation at Dundalk in March 1823 for stealing six-and-a-quarter pounds of hemp, had a foretaste of the possible violence of life in a penal colony while aboard the hulk *Surprise* at Cork. In November when 157 convicts from Dublin were being taken on board the *Surprise* one of the guards shouted out to the convicts already on the hulk, 'Take care of yourselves, the Dublin convicts have arrived.' The men from Munster had been anticipating the arrival of the Dublin convicts for some time and had prepared themselves with hammock-batons, shackles and loaded canvas bags for use as weapons. Due to cold weather the men from the south were not in full irons and they attacked the newcomers. During the riot the prisoners from Ulster on the vessel were also assaulted and at the end of the affray 100 men were found to have injuries, from which one man died. Graham was the subject of a book by Robert Gibbings in which his account of rescuing of a Mrs Fraser, who had been shipwrecked and lived with an aborigine tribe, is a true episode. When the riot on the *Surprise* was being investigated Dr Trevor offered the opinion that it could have been avoided if proper discipline had been observed. He believed that if the convicts were usefully employed on such tasks as cooking, washing clothes and cleaning the vessel, there should be a considerable saving to the government.

A ballad called 'The Town of Passage' mentions the hulk *Surprise*, which lay there:

'Tis there's the hulk that's well stored with convicts
Who were never upon decks till they went to sea;
They'll ne'er touch dry land, nor rocky island
Until they spy land at sweet Botany Bay.

Just a year after the *Surprise* came into use it was described as being able to accommodate 350 men, and to be in 'an extremely healthy condition'. In the twelve years that the vessel served as a hulk it accommodated some 5,500 men awaiting transportation.

The original 'Wild colonial boy', Jack Donahoe from Dublin, was also transported in 1824. Within two years of his arrival in the colony he had escaped into the bush where he became the most notorious bushranger of the time. The 'Stripper', as he was known, was caught while attempting to rob two carts, for which he was rewarded with two death sentences! He managed to escape and roamed free for a couple of more years until he was shot dead during a gunbattle with the police. Several ballads were composed to his memory, and his death mask was used as a model for pipe bowls. Donahoe himself was said to have written one ballad, part of which read:

Then hurl me to crime and brand me with shame
But think not to baulk me, my spirit it tame,
For I'll fight to the last in old Ireland's name.
    Though I be a Bushranger,
    You still are the stranger,
    And I'm Donahoe.

Frank Macnamara, from Cashel, County Tipperary unwillingly reached Australia, possibly sentenced as a forger, about the same time as Donahoe. Macnamara composed and recited poetry, some of which has been published. This is a sample:

I was convicted by the laws of England's hostile crown,
Conveyed across swelling seas in slavery's fetters bound,
For ever banished from that shore
    where love and friendship grow.

Bernard Reilly, another transportee of 1824, also expressed himself in verse but not until he returned to his native Ballinamore, County Leitrim where his admonitory *True history. . . with an account of his sufferings, etc., etc.*, was printed and published. An excerpt from the seven-page story reads:

When I came home my friends all leaped for joy,
To see once more returned their convict boy,
I am happy blown by their Southern Gales,
From the land of the Heathen called South Wales,
Let this to all young men a caution be,
To avoid night rambling and bad company,
Lest they should meet the same unhappy fate,
And rue like me when it might be too late.

He also wrote:

My master was a wealthy Gentleman,
Mr Luke Dillon a transport from Dublin.
One hundred crown slaves are on his estate,
And those of good behaviour he did treat
With kindness and attention, Wages good he gave,
And told us carefully our store to save,
So that they might return home free,
And of our master independent be. . .

A full report of the trial of Luke Dillon was published in the *Freeman's Journal* when he was accused of having raped a Miss Frizell, the daughter of a man of substance, at a Capel Street hotel in Dublin.

Then aged about 23, Dillon was condemned to death but following petitions from, among others, the girl's father, the sentence was commuted. From a minor landed family, of Mount Dillon in County Roscommon, Dillon was a former student of Trinity College, Dublin and a 'man about town' when the incident occurred. Having qualified for a conditional pardon in the colony Dillon managed to escape, and he is believed to have died at an asylum in Dieppe.

Alexander Pearce died in a more public way at Hobart at the end of July 1824. Attended on the gallows by Fr Conolly, Pearce asked that his confession should be read out publicly. As the 33-year-old County Monaghan Pearce, who had been exiled for theft, awaited the noose the assembled crowd of freemen and convicts heard a horrific story. Having escaped into the bush with another convict named Cox, Pearce, when they were starving, killed his companion and ate his flesh. This unnatural appetite, he revealed, he had developed during an earlier escape when starvation forced him, Mathew Travers and others, to kill and consume some of their fellows. Even the most hardened characters who listened to Pearce's story were revolted by his extraordinary confession. Perhaps it was not so surprising to find Hobart described in that year, when Sir George Arthur assumed governorship of Van Diemen's Land, as a very neglected town in a colony seen as 'a wretched sequestered spot peopled by the refuse of Newgate'. Around the same time Governor Brisbane of New South Wales (1821-1825), in an endeavour to have more priests sent out, expressed his opinion that since his arrival there every murder or diabolical crime had been committed by a Roman Catholic. It was hoped that more active ministry might improve moral standards among the Irish convicts.

Now the town of Sydney was developing into a substantial one with hewn stone houses and warehouses by the waterside and with accommodation, it was boasted, equal to that of any English country town. But there were also many 'grog shanties' where the less respectable of the residents found solace.

Another station for convict labour was established in 1824 when Moreton Bay, far to the north of Sydney, was opened. Many of the first convicts to go there volunteered, in an endeavour to break the normal cycle of drudgery and boredom in New South Wales. After a couple of years, with Port Macquarie and Norfolk Island, Moreton Bay was designated a Penal Settlement and so remained until 1842.

When a convict merited a further punishment and was exiled to one of the penal stations it did not mean that his original sentence was made longer and he was still entitled to his release on the termination of that sentence. The additional exile was simply intended to make his life even more unpleasant.

Records preserved at Brisbane include those of Irishmen who spent time at Moreton Bay. Thirty-five-year-old William Walsh from County Wicklow, who had been transported on the *Guildford* in 1817, was a 5′ 4½″ Roman Catholic tailor. Sent to Moreton Bay for larceny, he was dead within a year of going there as the result of an attack by Tomas Allen and Thomas Mathews. Two men who escaped for a while from the settlement were a former white smith from Limerick named Bulbridge and a carter from Dublin called Fegan. While they were free they robbed a hut near Port Macquarie but were caught and sent back to Moreton Bay where they were hanged in January 1831. Life in Moreton Bay inspired one balladeer, who had also served time in chains in the other settlements, to moan:

> Moreton Bay I found no equal,
> For excessive tyranny each day prevails:

That the writer was Irish is evident in the lines:

> I am a native of the land of Erin,
> And lately banished from that lovely shore:
> I left behind my aged parents,
> And the girl I did adore.

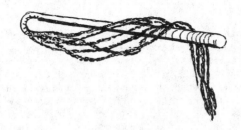

⑨ Bushrangers and Balladeers, 1825-1832

Back on 'Erin's lovely shore' more involuntary emigrants were being collected. Among the women were a 15-year-old girl, convicted of stealing runlets, another for taking a gown worth 8s, and a woman who had stolen an ostrich feather. She sought clemency on the grounds that she was the daughter and the widow of a soldier, and that five of her uncles had fought at Waterloo. Saying that she was but a trivial offender, the mother of 5 orphans and with an old mother to care for, she begged remission as she had already been confined for 5 years. A Dublin poulterer whose crime had been the theft of a wild duck, value 1s and 10 turkeys, value 3s and with a 7-year sentence, pleaded that without his support his wife and four children would be 'reduced to the utmost distress and misery, and be a burthen on the public'. In the winter of 1826/7 there was a record number of prisoners on the hulk *Essex* at Kingstown. The 249 unfortunates were afflicted with fever and dysentery and confined to the vessel's prison for 16 out of each period of twenty-four hours. This vessel, formerly a fast-sailing frigate in the United States navy, had been captured by the British in 1814. A decade later she was towed into Kingstown harbour to be used as a prison for convicts awaiting transportation. This is how a visitor to Ireland described the *Essex* in January 1834:

> Here the hulk, a convict ship – the well trained sentinel slowly pacing its deck, surrounded by other military men, while many a heavy heart beats mournfully below, as memory brings to view scenes never again to be beheld – the mourning parent, the bereaved wife or sorrowing child; and where hope can scarcely picture anything beyond a life of servitude and disgrace, on some far distant and unknown region of the globe. Dwell not on such scenes, however, but observe at a little distance the beautiful yacht, belonging to the Lord Lieutenant.

During 1825 and 1826 twelve ships brought some 2,011 convicts to Australia from Ireland, of whom only 212 were women. In 1827 eight vessels disembarked 1,257 male and 192 female Irish prisoners.

John Troy, a Dublin city man, was on the *Asia* which docked on 22
February 1825. On a 7-year sentence for burglary and felony, he was
later the subject of an annoymous ballad. Escaping with a few others
into the bush, Troy became a benevolent bushranger, robbing only
the rich and helping the poor. But his kindness did not save him and
when apprehended he was hanged.

> Upon the tenth of April upon the scaffold high.
> His friends and all that knew him wept for this fearless boy;
> There goes our young hero by name of Johnny Troy.

Laurence Frayne, another Dubliner, suffered much for his repeated
escape attempts having arrived in the colony on the *Regalia* in 1826.
He recorded in his diary the agony of enduring 150 lashes after which
his shoulders were 'actually in a state of decomposition, the stench of
which I could not bear myself, how offensive then must I appear and
smell to my companions in misery. . .' On Norfolk Island he was
forced to carry salt beef on his mutilated back, making him long for
death. But worse was to follow. When he incurred the wrath of the
colony's commandant he was sentenced to 200 lashes, to be administered over 12 days. Not surprisingly he considered the island
to be 'worse than the blackest dens and caverns of hell. . . I began to
question in my own then perverted mind the infinite mercy, nay the
justice, of Deity itself.'

A happier exile at that time was Patrick Hanraghan, farming 50
acres in 1828. He appears to have been a widower as his 23-year-old
housekeeper was caring for his five children, aged from 17 years to
a baby of a few months. With his two brothers Hanraghan had been
tried for murder at Loughrea, County Galway in 1801. All three got
the death-sentence, two were executed and 17-year-old Patrick was
transported.

The reformative character of the innovative Richmond Penitentiary
was questioned by the Archbishop of Dublin, Dr Daniel Murray.
The purpose of that institution, he pointed out, was 'to correct and
purify prisoners, and restore them to society' while awaiting the convict ship or having been pardoned from the sentence of exile. His
information was that those confined there were being ill-treated, with
some prisoners gagged with spiked iron keys, chained up, put on a
diet of bread and water, or confined in stocks in the 'piggery', as the
solitary cells were called. An even more serious allegation was made

by Mary Frazer that, for 14 weeks, she had been chained down to a rack and forced to renounce her church. Afterwards, when in the prison chapel, she rose up and proclaimed that she was being sent to Botany Bay because she was a Roman Catholic. For this revelation she was put in solitary. Even in the chapel there were spies, listening to hear if the priest preached heresy, and it was further alleged that prisoners were forced 'to profess a religion which they despise in their hearts or become hypocrits'.

An official inquiry was ordered and it found no evidence of proselytising by cruelty and concluded that there was no religious discrimination. Five years late, on the order of the Lord Lieutenant, the penitentiary was closed.

If conditions in Richmond penitentiary were bad, they continued to be unsatisfactory on the transports also. While waiting at Cove in December 1827 the men on the *Florentia* went sick with typhus. Those in good health begged to be allowed to join the army or navy, and the pathetic widows told their stories. One from Downpatrick who had lost 5 sons in the Peninsular Wars, begged that her only remaining son should be spared from the 7-year sentence given to him for stealing money. A 15-year-old orphan in Carrickfergus jail had been given the same sentence for embezzling a small sum of money, as had Stephen Brennan for being in possession of a pair of trousers. His father, from an address at 17 Fade Street, Dublin, pleaded for leniency for this, the last remaining of his 9 children. A reference from a priest accompanied Richard Burke's petition from the jail at Clonmel. He had been sentenced for manslaughter during a riot between country people and Orange Men at Cloughjordan. Fourteen-year-old Francis Carney was facing 7 years abroad for stealing handkerchiefs.

Samuel Hammon from Navan, County Meath, convicted at Trim court on a charge of highway-robbery and given a life sentence, in 1827, left a wife and 3 children behind when he was transported. After he had settled in the colony he decided that his family should come out, but repeated letters to his wife received no reply. Finally, in 1835, he wrote to a gentleman at home asking for news of his wife; he was concerned that she might already have left to join him and could have been among those lost on the *Neva*. Expressing regret for his crime, Hammon wrote that if she joined him they could make a good living and be happy. In 1836 Mrs Hammon, with her children, sailed from Cork for the Promised Land, as did the family of Thomas Helion, who had waited 4 years for their coming. Employed as a shepherd, he was able to send his employer's assurance that, as he was such a good worker, employment would also be available for his sons when they arrived. On a 7-year sentence, Helion had arrived on the *Cambridge*, the fastest of the eight ships from Ireland that sailed in 1827, completing the passage from Dublin to Sydney in 107 days.

Other convicts like those from Nenagh, County Tipperary, commemorated in the ballad 'Van Diemen's Land', were convicted of poaching and given 14 year sentences, as was Peggy Brophy, from the same town, who married a planter. Some of the men were named in the nine verse ballad:

> Poor Thomas Brown from Nenagh town,
> Jack Murphy and poor Joe
> Were three determined poachers as
> the county well does know. . .

Martin Cash, who entered Australian folklore as the 'Gentleman Bushranger', arrived in New South Wales in 1828, one of the 1,084 convicts from Ireland (including 80 women) to disembark from the six ships that arrived that year. On one of those sailings the *Mangles* created a new record for the passage when it reached Sydney in 100 days. Eighteen-year-old Cash, a native of Enniscorthy, County Wexford, who had been transported for housebreaking, did not adjust to life in Van Dieman's Land, and made a bid to escape. He was not successful, and was awarded further banishment to Port Arthur for four years. There he met Lawrence Kavanagh, from Rathdrum in County Wicklow (whose mother had voluntarily followed him to Australia) and they planned another escape. This time they succeeded and Cash became the leader of the little gang, and his gentlemanly manner to those they robbed gained him his nickname. In one escapade, while attempting to escape, Cash shot a policeman and was captured. Luck was with him again when his death sentence was commuted to one of imprisonment on Norfolk Island. For eight years, until that station was closed, he remained there, then he returned to Van Diemen's Land, where he was employed as a constable and worked a small farm. His life story, said to be autobiographical, was published in 1870, and he was the hero of a ballad which concluded with the sentiments.:

He's the bravest man that you could choose
from Sydney men or cockatoos.
And a gallant son of Erin, where the sprig of
shamrock grows.

In the year that Cash arrived to enliven the colony an experienced convict ship's surgeon published a book in which he recorded his impressions of the Irish. Peter Cunningham's *Two Years in New South Wales* has been much quoted as a balanced account of the transportation system and, in the present context, his views are of interest.

During the passage he observed that the Irish convicts were more happy and contented than the English, and although they were unhappy at leaving their country, many of them admitted that they were better off than ever before in their lives. He thought it amusing that in their letters home they detailed their diet, as well as the garments they had been issued with; the fact that a man had a bed 'to my own self entirely' seemed to the convicts a novelty. Surgeon Cunningham found the Irish more agreeable and willing to oblige than the English, and the only sign of religion he saw on the ships was among the Catholics. They repeated the prayers from their book and said the rosary when they were confined for the night. He noticed that while the English divided themselves into *townies* and *yokels*, the Irish sub-divided into *Dublin boys*, *North boys* and *Cork boys*; but his general impression of the Irish was that 'a great portion of them were poor simple peasantry, transported for very trumpery offences'.

A flattering account of the 1798 men still alive in the colony at this same period was that of the Irish-born Roman Catholic judge of the Australian Supreme Court, Sir Roger Therry. Among them he knew 'truly good men' who had brought relatives out from home, or who regularly sent back money. One particular man, a blacksmith transported for making pikes, when pardoned became a rich property owner who willed considerable sums for religious and educational purposes. Therry sympathised with the exiles, believing that they were the victims 'of the unjust laws that ground them down'. But Governor Darling (1825-1831) of New South Wales did not look so favourably on the sons of convicts, who, he believed, had 'feelings just the reverse of those of the Lower Orders in England and Ireland', proud of their convict parentage and reluctant to enter the army or to join the police.

Perhaps Governor Darling had in mind William Charles

Wentworth, a son of Surgeon D'Arcy Wentworth and convict Catherine Crowley. She had been sentenced to 7 years transportation at Staffordshire in 1788 for 'feloniously stealing wearing apparel', and she travelled on the same vessels as Wentworth to Sydney and to Norfolk Island. While a pamphlet published in 1819 alleged that Wentworth had also been transported as a convict it has since been established that he had voluntarily opted for 'Botany Bay' when he had been acquitted of four charges of highway robbery. His father was an inn keeper from near Portadown, County Armagh, where D'Arcy served in the Irish Volunteers while apprenticed to a doctor. Moving to London to find employment, he became acquainted with his noble kinsmen of Wentworth Woodhouse and, not being wealthy, perhaps sought another way to raise funds. In New South Wales he prospered, eventually filling many important posts, including that of principal surgeon, and was awarded a total of 17,000 acres. In 1817 he was on the court of inquiry which investigated the mutinous passage of the *Chapman* from Ireland.

William Charles Wentworth (1790-1872) was sent to England to be educated and there he also met his Fitzwilliam cousins. Qualified as a barrister, he returned home where he was soon involved in supporting the emancipists[14] in their call for more rights in the colony. He campaigned for a reform of the constitution and of the legal system, and he furthered the establishment of schools and a university. His liberal views brought him into conflict with Governor Darling, but he worked well with Governor Bourke. He married the daughter of an emancipist blacksmith, Francis Cox, possibly the unhappy man who suffered 300 lashes during the troublesome passage of the *Britannia* in 1797. William and Sarah Cox purchased 'Vacluse', the property once owned by the celebrated sheriff of Cork, Sir Henry Brown Hayes. There they raised a large family, and established one of the dynasties of the new land. In 1910 *Vacluse* was declared a National Monument, in memory of W. C. Wentworth.

Judge Therry, recalling the type of prisoner who had come from Ireland before his own arrival in the colony in 1829, said that many had been transported for agrarian disturbances during the suspension of the *Habeas Corpus Act* and under the *Insurrection Acts* or other coercive measures. That a large number of men had deservedly been banished for outrages that merited such punishment he did not doubt, but he found that it was no less true that very many were sentenced for the infringement of severe laws, some of which would have merited but a few months imprisonment thirty years later, when he was recording his memories.

Confirmation of Surgeon Cunningham's belief that convicts improved their lot by being transported might be found in the rumours current in the New Year of 1829 to the effect that several of the women transported on the *Edward*, which sailed from Cove on 1 January, had committed offences in the hope of being sent to 'Botany Bay' where their husbands were already exiled.

Three men whose families did not accompany them were James Brogan from Scarriff, County Clare, Thomas Montgomery from Enniskillen, County Fermanagh – who had taken part in the battle of Macken, and Alexander Boyce from Belfast, who arrived on a 7-year sentence on the *Sophia* on 17 January 1829. All three later petitioned to have their families brought out and Brogan's employer wrote on his behalf, explaining that there was plenty of employment for those who were honest and hard-working. Brogan himself advised his 35-year-old wife Ellen that if the eldest boy of their 6 children could not travel with her that he should seek work as a crew-member on the vessel. In 1835 Mrs Brogan sailed from Cork on the female convict ship *Roslin Castle* and her grown up sons came on a later ship. Montgomery, who had earned his ticket-of-leave by 1838, was disappointed that his family had not arrived, but within a couple of years his wife had made up her mind to undertake the great journey. This indecision on the part of a woman is understandable. Apart from the fact that in all probability she had never ventured outside her own parish before, the fear of the long passage, doubts about life in Australia and the realisation that it was unlikely that she would ever see her relatives in Ireland again must have made the decision to undertake the journey traumatic.

It was not indecision, but death, that prevented Boyce's 'beloved Eliza' from replying to his petulant letter of 25 January 1835. It was three years since he had done himself 'the pleasure of both writing to you, as also to my beloved children', and of requesting the Home Government that they might join him. He said that he was surprised at her neglect and silence, and that day and night he thought of her and of his children – 'my panting bosom and extended arms are every moment open to receive ye.' Explaining that he had his ticket-of-leave and extolling the salubrity of the climate and the fertility of the soil, he expressed a most positive view of life in the colony. The fact that Boyce did not know that his Eliza had died a couple of years before he wrote this letter and after she had been granted a free passage, illustrates the difficulties and unreliability of communications. Now, when officialdom decided that his 17-year-old and 9-year-old daughters might join him, they declined to travel. This decision, no doubt based on fear of the unknown and reluctance to join a parent whom they could hardly remember, must have caused further heartbreak to their father. His kindness is evident in a note to his father, which he added to his letter of 1835, requesting him to try to locate the illegitimate son of Sarah Cramshee, a convict. A neighbour of theirs in Belfast, she had left the child in the poorhouse and now she sought to find him.

The *Edward* was the first of the six vessels that went in 1829 with a total of 370 women and 758 men, and on some of the vessels wives and children were allowed to accompany the men. Despite the efforts of Dr Trevor and his fellow officers to improve the efficiency of the system, there were still errors and omissions. The Indents were not always sent on the ships, and there was a case of men with 7-year sentences being sent for life. Only 120 women were sent out in 1830, with the 958 men in the half-dozen vessels that departed that year. But they did not all sail without incident. In June the men confined to the hulk in the harbour at Kingstown attempted to escape by setting fire to the vessel. Prompt action on the part of Lieutenant Pyke, of the *Despatch*, a sloop-of-war anchored nearby, extinguished the fire and prevented the escape.

If the new arrivals in New South Wales were in any doubt about the quality of life there the *Sydney Gazette* of 30 November 1830 left them in no doubt. All prisoners were fed with the coarsest food and subject to rigid discipline and to the will of 'stern and frequently capricious' overseers. At summary trials they were given severe punishments, including floggings and re-transportation. When assigned to work under a master they might be lucky, if he were kind, or they could be treated little better than slaves. The same newspaper had earlier published a ballad in five verses which expressed an Irishman's longing for home. Telling the story of the writer's labour in an agricultural settlement at Emu Plains, near Sydney, it began:

O! farewell, my country, my kindred, my lover;
Each morning and evening is sacred to you,
While I toil the long day, without shelter or cover,
Full often I think of and talk of thee, Erin,
While chained to the soil on the Plains of Emu.

Despite the facts, there was a common myth which suggested that the convicts in Australia had a merry life, which was in itself an encouragement to others to commit crimes in the hope of reaching the same Hy-Brasil. The origin of such a belief might be found in the reluctance of many of the convicts to give a true account of their circumstances in their letters home, as they did not wish to cause further anguish to their distressed families.

Or it could have come from the letters of the more fortunate men whose masters were humane and who encouraged them to bring their wives and families out from Ireland and from the correspondence of freed convicts who had acquired land or found secure employment and who likewise sought passage for their loved ones. For them life could indeed be bountiful and, if they succeeded in bringing their families out, happy. By contrast the convicts in the penal stations suffered deprivation and brutal treatment; being of a more sensational nature, life in Norfolk Island and the other punishment locations attracted more public attention and came to typify 'Botany Bay' to the outside world.

One prominent member of the Establishment who had no illusions about the penal system was the Protestant archbishop of Dublin, Dr Richard Whately, who published pamphlets which were highly critical of the system in the early 1830s. It was his belief that the prisoners would be better kept at home in penitentiaries and given useful employment, such as draining bogs. The prelate suffered much ridicule for his views, even from Australia, where Governor Arthur at Hobart remarked that 'the Archbishop, from his chair in Dublin, was doing the colonies all the mischief he can by checking emigration to them'. It was even argued that the transportation system, far from being worse than death, was 'actually a benefit to the culprit, who was much better off than soldiers, or labourers'.

Public criticism, including that of the Archbishop, was having its effect and in June 1831 the Lord Lieutenant ordered that the Richmond Penitentiary should be closed after but a decade of use. When the inmates had been transferred to the penitentiary at Cork, except those who had been in some degree reformed, or whose sentences of transportation had expired, the staff of the institution, which numbered 27, were to be put out of work. The closure had resulted from 'causes not within the control of the government. The objects in view with the formation of this establishment had in a very great degree failed.'

Apart from the accommodation available in the Cork penitentiary, it was necessary to retain the hulks. Dr Trevor examined 100 women on the hulk *Rowena* in Cork harbour, prior to embarkation on the *Palambam*; it was the first of eight vessels to sail for New South Wales in 1831, with 925 men and 445 women. In early summer the doctor had found that many of the prisoners were suffering from the itch, which spread on the vessels, making it necessary to destroy much of the bedding. Others had incurable diseases, such as consumption, and died as soon as they reached Cork. Conditions on the hulk *Essex* at Kingstown were as bad. It was infected with dry rot, and in great need of repair. The movement of convicts from the north and east of the country to the *Essex* was effected as the result of instructions issued from Dublin Castle on a standard letter format, leaving blank spaces for the insertion of such details as dates, names of the ships and hulks etc. It was specified that during the movement of prisoners by road commanding officers on the routes were to have the way lined with troops. Before being taken from the various jails the convicts were to be medically examined to ensure that they were not ill, were free from itch and fit for the passage; they were to be clean, and have their hair cut. Certificates were to be sent with them stating that all these conditions were fulfilled. Only children at the breast were to be permitted to travel, and there was to be no movement on Sundays, nor was liquor or tobacco allowed, as these were forbidden on the hulks. Knives and money were to be taken from the convicts, a receipt being issued by the keeper of the hulk, who was to hold the money. The scale of issue of clothing was specified, and it was to be of a cheap quality and care was to be taken that none of it was to be sold on the road.

Conditions on the hulks remained terrible, causing some of the concerned officials to express serious doubts about the system in the autumn of 1833. Up to 150 men and boys of all ages, all unemployed, were locked down at sunset in one dark deck without any supervision even to quell the fights which inevitably took place. When the keeper

of the hulk *Surprise* was questioned about the routine he admitted
that even if there was a serious disturbance he feared that it would
be impossible to control it as he dared not venture among the convicts
after they were locked up.

The misery of the men about to be exiled was accentuated by the
knowledge of the presence of some of their womenfolk and children
on the nearby shore. This graphic description came from a British
official:

> The first sound I heard as I approached the Irish coast was the accent of
> distress. As the vessel rounded the harbour of Kingstown, she passed
> under the stern of a convict ship moored near the shore. On the opposite
> rocks were some women, miserably attired, with infants in their arms and
> in a state of grief and wretchedness. One of them shouted in Irish to the
> ship, from which we heard the voice of a man in reply. The prisoners on
> board were rioters, who having been sentenced to transportation, were
> thus taking their last farewell of their desolate families.

The state of the country during this unhappy period was sum-
marised by Thomas MacNevin in a 'Letter to the Earl of Roden',
published in 1838. Looking back to the beginning of the century,
he outlined the repressive legislation enforced at different times; from
1800 to 1802 the Insurrection Act; Martial Law from 1803 to 1805,
the Insurrection Act again between 1807 and 1810, though this time
no areas were proclaimed. When disorder revived in 1814 Counties
Tipperary and Limerick were proclaimed under another Insurrection
Act, and similar Acts were again invoked from 1822 to 1825, when
Special Commissions could give sentences. Special courts were set
up in the disturbed districts under the 1833 Coercion Act. Agrarian
outrages continued to decline from 6,374 in 1832, 4,020 in 1833,
3,091 in 1834 to 2,185 in 1836, which was 760 less than the previous
year. Between the years 1832 and 1836 an average of 1,060 convicts
were transported annually of whom about one-sixth were women.
1836 was the year in which the maximum number of women were
banished, when three ships transported 394.

Despite the high crime rate the law reforms continued and in 1832
the punishment of transportation for life was substituted for the death
penalty for certain offences. This extract from the reforming statute
lists the crimes meriting banishment:

An Act for consolidating and amending the Laws in Ireland relative to Larceny, and other Offences connected therewith, it is among other things enacted, that if any Person shall steal in any Dwelling House any Chattel, Money, or valuable Security, to the Value in the whole of Five Pounds, or more, every such Offender, being convicted thereof, shall suffer Death as a Felon; and it is also by the said last mentioned Act enacted, that if any Person shall steal any Horse, Mare, Gelding, Colt, or Filly, or any Bull, Cow, Ox, Steer, Bullock, Heifer, or Calf, or any Ram, Ewe, Sheep, or Lamb, or shall wilfully kill any of such Cattle with Intent to steal the Carcass or Skin or any Part of the Cattle so killed, every such Offender shall be guilty of Felony, and being convicted thereof shall suffer Death as a Felon: and whereas it is expedient that a lesser Punishment than that of Death should be provided for the several offences herein-before specified: Be it therefore enacted by the King's most Excellent Majesty, by and with the Advice and Consent of the Lords Spiritual and Temporal, and Commons, in this present Parliament assembled, and by the Authority of the same, That so much of each of the said Acts as inflicts the Punishment of Death upon Persons convicted of any of the Felonies herein-before specified shall be and the same is hereby repealed; and that from and after the passing of this Act every Person convicted of any of the Felonies herein-before specified, or of counselling, aiding, or abetting the Commission thereof, shall be transported beyond the Seas for Life.

Nevertheless the suffering and misery of the individual was not much alleviated and first offenders, such as 17-year-old Cornelius Driscell from Cork, and 76-year-old Patrick Donohue, from County Galway, were transported on the *Portland*, which arrived in Sydney in June 1833. The youth, a cabin-boy, had a 7-year sentence for stealing from the person; the old man went for life. Described as a Roman Catholic, with no education, married with 7 children, and by occupation a shepherd, his crime was houghing sheep.

Two other men transported in 1833 were John Tighe from Sligo on a charge of manslaughter and Dennis Dogherty from Derry for mutiny. Tighe had to wait 20 years before his family joined him on his farm at Wollongong. When his wife Mary, and daughters Mary and Honora arrived they had sad stories to tell of the famine years in Heapstown, when they had been evicted from their cabin and taken in by Mrs Tighe's brother.

Dogherty's fate was better known as he was mentioned by Anthony Trollope in the book which he published following his visit to Australasia in 1871-2. In the prison at Port Arthur the writer talked with the Derryman who claimed that he had been confined for over forty years, during which time he had endured almost 3,000 lashes.

In 1876 he was given his freedom, and he is immortalised by Trollope who wrote 'I did feel for him and when he spoke of himself as a caged bird, I should have liked to take him out into the world and have given him a month of freedom. He would probably however have knocked my brains out at the first opportunity. . .'

10 Nuns and Other Females, 1833-1838

Governor Bourke (1831-1837) of New South Wales estimated that in 1833, of the convicts who had arrived in the previous seven years, about one-third were Irish Roman Catholics. With their families they then formed about one-fifth of the population. Their spiritual welfare was in the care of a vicar general and two priests and it was hoped that four more priests would be available in the following year. In Sydney a 'large and handsome RC church', towards which the government had given £1,600, was not yet completed and private subscriptions were enabling the building of chapels at Campbell Town, Maitland and Parramatta. Government grants were given towards Catholic schools, which were regulated after the manner of the schools in Ireland.

This improvement in the status of the Catholics was mainly due to the arrival of the new governor in 1831. He was Richard Bourke, from Dublin, a humane and reforming officer who soon found himself unpopular with both the officials and settlers of more conservative views. Bourke believed that transportation would soon be ended and he was especially critical of the assignment system as he thought it created 'a slave mentality' in the settlers. Cruel and unnecessary punishments he considered evil, while admitting that a certain severity of rule was necessary. Having restricted the power of the magistrates, he set about improving the general standard of education, endeavouring to have adopted the system instituted in Ireland by the *National School Act* of 1831. His *Church Act* in 1836 confirmed the principle of religious equality and government funds were made available for church buildings.

While the progress was welcomed by such personages as his fellow Irish, though Roman Catholic, Solicitor-General J. H. Plunkett and Commissioner of the Crown Roger Therry (who was to become a judge of the Supreme Court of New South Wales), it was condemned by others like H. C. Butler from Belturbet, County Cavan. A government surveyor in Sydney since 1829, Butler believed that standards in the colony had fallen with the arrival of Bourke. Not alone did the governor encourage communication with the convicts but he also invited persons of an inferior social status to Government House! Bourke himself ably answered such critics in 1835 when he wrote:

> those inconsistent persons, who have attained wealth by the service of convicts, who, up to the present moment, are emulating each other in frequent and urgent application for more convict servants; who are continually travelling to their farms and remote stations over roads of great length and difficult construction, wholly formed by the labour of convicts; yet spend their lives in cavilling at the evils by which these advantages are inevitably accompanied, and charge them on the government.

The esteem in which Bourke was held by the people of New South Wales was proven by their erection of a statue in his honour, on which was recorded 'his able, honest and benevolent administration'.

An unofficial observer of the scene believed that the number of convicts was in proportion to the populations of their respective countries, England, Ireland and Scotland. Further, he expressed the view that while the Irish were better workers than the English, they were abandoned, careless, unsteady, reckless of crime and its consequences and always ready to enter any plot no matter how absurd, 'but bound together by no tie, so that they would sacrifice a friend or brother without the smallest remorse'. The English were idle but attached to each other, and when combined, dangerous; their females were 'the most thoroughly depraved to be found in any country'. Of the Scotch, it was held, they were the best workers but the most vicious and desperate characters of the whole. A settler who had 15 Irishmen among his workers thought they had the strangest names he ever heard and that they were all admirers of O'Connell, after whom a public house had been named in Sydney. St Patrick was given the same honour with his name over a public house in Clarence Street.

While the *Lady Kennaway* was waiting at Cove in the month of October 1834 the 280 English convicts on board continued to be subjected to illness as they had come from Portsmouth with cholera on board. During the vessel's stay in Cork 31 more convicts were embarked, 18 were landed sick at Haulbowline, and 17 died.

On the passage there were two more deaths. When the English convicts were disembarked at Hobart the 31 from Ireland were sent on to New South Wales. If any of the men serving out their time in that colony committed offences which merited further punishment they could expect to receive harsh treatment, as specified in administrative regulations just issued. Men working in the ironed-gang stockades were regularly searched and their irons inspected twice daily. When they were confined in their huts, on Sundays, wet days or at night and where no drinking or gambling was permitted, they were also subject to regular checks. For their comfort a tub of drinking water and a cup, and a urine tub, were provided. The ration scale specified that, in a 24 hour period, men in irons were allowed $1\frac{1}{4}$ lbs of white bread, 1 lb of flour, 1 lb of beef, 8 oz of maize meal, 1 oz of sugar, $\frac{1}{2}$ oz salt and the same of soap. The annual issue of clothing for a man was 2 each of Parramatta frocks and trousers, 3 striped shirts, and the same number of pairs of shoes, a straw hat, a cap and a blanket, with an extra one allowed in winter.

But the newly arrived convicts might, if they had education, find encouragement in the career of the pardoned Edward O'Shaughnessy, a graduate of Trinity College, Dublin who in 1835 was appointed editor of the *Sydney Gazette*. Of course, there was some objection to this elevation of an ex-convict, but O'Shaughnessy merited and was successful at, such employment. At the age of 26 he had been convicted in Dublin on a charge of 'obtaining money under false pretences', and sentenced to 7 years transportation.

Encouraging words on future prospects in the colony could have come from Peter Fitzgibbon who had been given a life sentence for agrarian offences at Ennis in his native County Clare in 1832. In a letter to his wife at home in Kilmore he urged her to try and have his sentence commuted, or, failing that, to come with their children to him. Explaining how some of his companions were thriving in the colony, he asked his wife to bring their certificate of marriage with her, as then he could be assigned to her and would be almost as well off as a free man. With a free pardon 'a man could earn £25 a year. . . and as much as he can eat of everything. If you and the children could come out I could support you here without one shilling better than I could if I had 20 acres of good ground at home.' Some indication of the poverty which he knew in Ireland is expressed in his promise of plenty.

Despite his knowledge of the system, Fitzgibbon neglected to procure a certificate of good behaviour from the governor and, as some women who had come out had been left to the charity of the colony, her free passage was delayed. Explaining the duration of sentences, he wrote that a lifer such as himself could be free after 8 years, and those with 14 or 7 year sentences were pardoned in 6 and 4 years; then they could earn £25 a year, with as much food as they could eat! No doubt, this latter bonus, in addition to the good pay, was like manna to those coming from destitution at home.

Similar expressions of hope are to be found in the letters of Thomas Fallon and Timothy Regan to their wives in 1835. Regan, then a free man, had procured a free passage for his wife some years before but, possibly due to postage difficulties, had not had her reply. 'God,' he wrote, 'has prospered my industry and exertions, and I have now the means with a continuation of industry to obtain a comfortable living much more so than I could in Ireland. . .' Fallon, on the other hand, was still awaiting his liberty when, he believed, he could earn 10s a day. 'This is as fine a country as there is in the world for eating and drinking. If you were in this country you could be worth a pound a week by your own labour,' he wrote encouragingly. He even suggested that his wife might bring her sister with her as 'there are some fine girls coming out as emigrants'.

The Dublin newspaper, the *Freeman's Journal*, on 8 December 1835, announced that from a recent arrival from Sydney it was learnt that the Irish convict ship *Neva* had been lost, with a total of 214 souls drowned. This figure included 150 female-convicts, 55 children and 9 free women. The *Neva* was one of the two convict vessels out of the total half-dozen which sailed in 1835 that were wrecked. The *Hive,* which ran aground on the coast of New South Wales on 10 December, lost but one member of her crew, all the others being saved. These included the two sons of the widow Mary Browne from Henn Street, Killarney, 'doomed to exile for life on a charge of Assault and Robbery for a piece of corduroy worth a few shillings'. Mrs Browne made a plea on behalf of Edmond and William but before it was considered the *Hive* had sailed and her hope to have her sole supporters imprisoned at home was frustrated.

The *Neva*, with children, free women and convicts on board, left Cove on 8 January 1835 and she was 125 days out of Cove and in the Bass Strait when she struck a rock. Though every effort was made to stabilise the vessel, high seas hindered this and the panic-stricken women caused the boats to capsize. Within four hours the *Neva* had broken up and only 15 of the convicts and crew managed to reach the shore. Five of the women died soon afterwards. The subsequent Court of Inquiry decided that the ship was lost 'due to unavoidable circumstances', which included the strength of the tide. The slowness of communications in the early nineteenth century is evident from the lapse of time between the tragedy and its notice in the Irish press. Further information on the wreck appeared in the *Freeman's Journal* on 17 December when the death of the ship's surgeon in the wreck was the subject of a sad report. With 20 years' service on the convict ships, Dr Stephenson, though unwell, was on his last journey. Carried from his cot when the ship struck, he was placed in one of the boats only to be drowned when the boat was rushed by the women convicts. It had been the doctor's intention to wed on his return home and, indeed, his betrothed would have been on the *Neva* with him but the rules of the service forbade such arrangements. 'Thus providentially his intended escaped a watery grave,' commented the *Freeman's Journal*. When the Select Committee on Shipwrecks considered the loss of the *Neva* the question was asked, 'Had the vessel been surveyed as seaworthy? When it was reported that she was, discussion took place on the design of the ship and it was enquired whether if she had had a solid bottom would she have held together long enough for the crew to be saved?' This, it was decided, was doubtful as it would have depended on where the concussion had occurred.

Hundreds of petitions continued to reach the office of the Lord Lieutenant in Dublin each year on behalf of individuals hoping to avoid going to 'Botany Bay'. Women frequently pleaded for their menfolk, such as the mother, in 1836, whose son had stolen a shirt valued at 1s, or another for a 13-year-old child who had stolen linen worth 2s. Mary Leary, from Killarney, submitted a plea that the man who was being transported for raping her should be allowed to remain at home.

Other crimes for which Kerrymen were imprisoned during that year, according to the official records, included stealing cows, pigs, sheep, larceny, stabbing a person, robbing a person; and, for embezzlement, two men were hanged. The ages of the male prisoners were from 19 to 50, with an average of 21. There were 6 women in jail in the county, aged between 21 and 24, and their offences were robbery or larceny. At the other end of the country, County Antrim, men were gaoled for life for horse stealing or house robbery but the

majority of crimes were larceny, assault or receiving stolen goods.
The average age was 23, the youngest offender being 14, the oldest
48. Of the 26 female criminals, 2 had been sentenced for sheep stealing, the remainder for larceny, and they aged from 14 to 52. About
this time there was a decrease in agrarian offences and not until 1840
were any appreciable numbers again transported for such crimes.

When they arrived in Australia some individuals continued to write
supplicatory letters in an endeavour to be returned home. One such
epistle from an exile employed as a constable at Port Macquarie
expressed his fear that he would become, like his terrible companions,
depraved and abandoned. Those he described as lame, blind, insane
and epileptic, the language of whom was worse than their bodily
infirmities. Fearing that some one who did not like him might try to
have him punished without reason, he believed that, for him, all would
be over as the flogging would damage his mind more than his back.
As he did not wish his family at home to know of his situation he
had not written home and he thought that it was fortunate for Ireland
that so few ex-convicts returned there as, having served a sentence
in the colony, they would be unfit to be admitted into civilised society
again.

Other residents saw life differently, like Thomas Made from Charleville in County Cork, whose letter to his wife is quoted in Patrick
O'Farrell's *Letters from Irish Australia*. Made was fortunate to have
an honourable master in John Macarthur, and his satisfaction with
his lot is evident in this extract from his letter:

This is a very fine country not a finer in the world and a very wholesome
climate. . . you need not be any way uneasy of the voyage as it will be the
outside of it if you are three months on sea, I am with the best gentleman
in this colony and the wealthiest. I want for nothing. . . The two Egans
are here with me on this farm where I am stationed. The two Egans are
doing well. They are both in good health and desire to be remembered
to their friends. The climate is purty *(sic)* hot. The Blacks are very numerous in this country and are quite savage. This is a very fruitful country.
There is three crops in the year growed here so me wife there is nothing
troubling me but for want of your presence which I hope I shortly will
have. I hope that you wont delay as soon as you receive this that you will
answer it. . . the gentlemen I am with they are I assure you very fond of
me that whatever I require from them they give it to me. We have got
only one clergyman in this country which I am sure there would be ten
wanted there the country is so large.

A major investigation of the transportation system was made public in 1838 when the report of a committee appointed from Members of the House of Commons was published. It found that the punishment of transportation did not deter crime and that rather than reforming, it further corrupted those who underwent the experience. The committee recommended that transportation should be abolished and that some modification of the penitentiary system should be substituted in the home countries. As an immediate measure in the colonies it was believed that a method of reward and punishment, linked with the possibility of future advantage, should be initiated. Van Diemen's Land was to receive no more convicts than could be employed there, and other locations for such labour were to be considered, including Cape Town and the Falkland Islands. From the end of 1839 no more prisoners were sent to Norfolk Island and what was expected to be the last convict ship to Sydney arrived there in November of the following year.

Some views on the character of the Irish were expressed by witnesses called to give evidence before the 1837 Committee. An extensive landowner believed that many of them profited by the exchange, being much better off than they were at home; and a naval surgeon was of the opinion that the moral condition of the Irish was 'very low indeed'. In general it was found that many of the convicts were so miserable that they committed crimes in the hope of getting a change of location, even if it were to a road gang or penal settlement. Those men who had merited pardons and who had gone into business were often subject to harassment or blackmail by the police, for whom such activity was a considerable source of revenue. If men did succeed in having themselves transferred to one of the penal stations, they would regret it. So severe were conditions on Norfolk Island, a witness testified, that 'some men injured their mates with the intention of being executed, in the belief that it was better to hang than to live in such hell'.

Doctor Ullathorne, the English Benedictine who had been appointed Vicar General of New South Wales in 1833, was not a witness called before the House of Commons Committee, even though he had expressed his views strongly on the subject in his book *The Horrors of Transportation* in 1837. It was his opinion that many distressed, ignorant people committed crimes in the hope that they might benefit themselves in the new land. From the colonies they wrote to their wife or husband, encouraging them to join them but without revealing the true nature of the place. If a spouse did venture out they found their partners slaves. The bishop wrote of a blind man who thanked God for depriving him of the monstrous horrors of the place. Ullathorne was particularly critical of the punishments, citing the floggings inflicted on two Irishmen; both had been punished previously. Andrew McMahon, who was found drunk and disorderly, was given 50 lashes with a regular cat; he bellowed at every lash, writhed in agony and bled more than any victim seen before by the bishop. The second man, who was younger than McMahon, got the same punishment. He was Francis Hayes, whose offence had been disorderly conduct and arguing at work. Ullathorne wrote that he 'cried out and struggled all of the time. Blood came at the fifth stroke. He prayed to be taken down, and was given water'. As the majority of his flock were Irish it was to be expected that the Vicar General would endeavour to understand their character. With the exception of those from the larger cities, he believed the others were banished for the infringement of the penal laws, for agrarian offences or for minor delinquencies. In contrast, the English convicts, with rare exceptions, were being punished for direct aggression on person or property.

Another English Benedictine, Dr Polding, who was appointed Australia's first Catholic bishop in 1834, had a different view of the Irish, remarking that there was 'sufficient reason for supposing that the great majority were persons of wicked life'. But he also said that the transportation system was the most horrible punishment ever devised. Some years before Polding reached Australia an Irish man living there had given his impressions of his countrymen in a letter to the Roman Catholic archbishop of Dublin. It was with regret that he told of some unfortunate and wretched individuals who were foremost in perpetrating the shocking crimes in the colony; 'the blood-thirsty and treacherous acts of the ruffians are enough to make the genuine Irishman hide his face in shame'.

The punishment described by Dr Ullathorne was a well organised one, during which the flogger was supervised by a constable who counted each stroke and who could have the flogger himself flogged if he was found to be negligent. It was intended that 50 lashes could be inflicted in 4 minutes with a whip made of flax, though in some places whip-cord was used. One sadistic justice of the peace recommended that the lash should be knotted and waxed to inflict more pain. The average number of lashes given was either 25 or 50, the smaller number being awarded for such offences as absence, drunkenness or disturbance. Naturally, the victims of this barbarity re-acted in different ways; some wept or cried 'no blood', others fainted or remained silent, and there were those who could just not stand up, or who cursed and blasphemed.

The maximum punishment of death was considered preferable to flogging or to further exile in the coalmines or chain-gangs of Norfolk Island or Port Arthur, and many of the 102 people executed in Sydney between 1833 and 1836 thanked God for the relief of oblivion. The Chief Inspector of New South Wales had voiced the view that it would be better to burn men alive than to send them to Norfolk Island, while a convict who endured time there cried: 'My heart has been taken from me, and I have been given the heart of a beast'.

What were the views of the Irish themselves on their circumstances in the colony? These ranged to the cry of County Cork-born Mickey Donohoe that the system made him a wild beast, never hearing a Christian word, and of that exile who would not write home as he did nor want to tell his family of the conditions he endured. However, there was another side to life in the new land, and from the small number of letters from emancipists or from men soon to be pardoned, a different vision emerges. From letters written in the 1830s by or on behalf of convicts encouraging their wives to come out and to bring the children and other relatives, the colony seems a more attractive place. The good climate, fruitful soil and the opportunities for advancement are extolled; if joined by the family, they 'would never see a poor day' as employment would be readily available for the wife and children of working age. In several letters it was emphasised that they would be better off than those at home holding 20 acres, or who assumed £100 rent.

A County Mayo labourer, transported for 7 years on the *Middlesex* in 1840, urged his wife to join him, bringing the twins who had been born after his departure; his brother also should come as Australia was 'the best country under the sun. . . I am very thankful for my prosecutors for sending me here, to the land of liberty and freedom'.

That the local gentlemen in County Clare could be helpful in securing mitigation for those in New South Wales is evident in the success of a Mrs Moore in procuring such a benefit for her husband

William. Unfortunately, three years later, when Moore was again
encouraging his wife to come out, he was unaware of the pardon and
word of it had not reached the colony. Recommending that his brother
should also come out, he advised that if their son John was too old
to travel on the women's ship that he could be put on 'the prison man
ship'. Moore informed his wife that, even if pardoned that he would
not wish to go home for another few years as in the colony he could
make enough money to support him at home without work for the
rest of his life! He was happy in the factory making soap and candles,
and he assured his wife that when she came she too would be 'as
happy as you were in all your life'. It can only be hoped that she was
as, before she left Corofin with her 4 daughters for the transport to
Cork in 1836, to be followed by her son John a short while after, the
local clergyman described the family as wretchedly poor. Offering to
provide the Moores with clothing, he sought payment from the convict office in Dublin for the expense.

The extreme unhappiness of those who did not receive answers to
their letters home was expressed by such letter-writers as Thomas
Made to his wife in Charleville, County Cork, and Robert Boyd to
his family in Carrickfergus, County Antrim. In his sixth unanswered
letter Made told his wife that they would 'never see a poor day either
yourself or myself', if she came out, having first made an effort to have
his sentence reduced. Despite many letters home Boyd also had no
replies and now he neglected to send the governor's recommendation
which meant that his request would not be received in Dublin. Telling
his wife how miserable and anxious he was on account of not having
heard from her, he implored her to come with their children, adding
that he had 16 cattle and 'had you been with me, I could have thrice
as many'.

Boyd, if he was musically inclined, could have enjoyed concerts in
the late 1830s by the Waterford-born musician Vincent Wallace, who
had settled in the colony as a sheep farmer. Sir Richard Bourke, the
Governor of New South Wales, was said to have paid for his seats at
one concert with a gift of 100 sheep to the musician. Even with such
benevolence, Wallace did not prosper and one morning the newspapers announced that 'Mr Wallace, the Australian Paganini, had
left the colony in a clandestine manner, having contracted debts'.
Despite being ship-wrecked Wallace eventually arrived back home
and he was to achieve lasting fame as the composer of the opera

Maritana.

Another auspicious day for the Roman Catholics of Sydney was New Year's Eve 1838 when the *Francis Spaight* docked. It brought Dr Ullathorne back from Europe where he had assembled a group of priests and students to accompany him to his mission. The ship also disembarked four Irish Sisters of Charity whose superior and founder, Mother Mary Aikenhead, described their vocation as to 'a church like those of the first ages'. Sr Mary John Cahill, one of the pioneers, had long had this work in mind and had often wished to accompany the wretched convicts on the ships.

When the nuns had established themselves in a house given to them as a gift by a benevolent citizen they commenced work at the factory for female convicts at Parramatta. There they found that 400 of the 600 prisoners were Catholics living in an atmosphere of noise, ribaldry and obscene conversation and employed at sawing wood and breaking stones. Soon things began to change. A school was opened for the children and the employment of the women was made that of laundering and needlework. It was arranged that a priest would visit to administer the sacraments and within a year 200 of the inmates were confirmed.

The women were divided into three categories. Firstly, those whose conduct was reasonably satisfactory and who could be assigned to families as domestics; secondly, the mothers of ill children; and thirdly, the 'poor degraded creatures who were under severe punishment and were sometimes subdued by the soldiers, whom they attacked with stones'. An additional bonus for the women of the first class was that, if a ticket-of-leave man came to the factory to find a wife, they could be offered an opportunity to meet him. They would have been instructed by the nuns and they would have received the sacraments. The women were summoned to the factory parlour where the prospective groom examined them. He called the one he fancied and they were allowed a private conversation. If they agreed to marry the appropriate clergyman was sent for and the knot tied. Many of these unions, it transpired, were very happy and the arrangement was probably not too objectionable to the women as at home too their marriage would have been arranged, and at Parramatta there was the added bonus of escaping from the confinement of the factory.

Before the arrival of the Sisters of Charity the marriage arrangements for the women was more haphazard. An anonymous ballad entitled *Botany Bay Courtship* told the story of Molly McGuigan, who had been given the death sentence at Newry for stealing her mistress' watch and gown. It would seem that she was addicted to Cooper's best gin and she was then in the stocks for having beaten her mistress, Mrs Cox. Nevertheless, Molly was the lass that the ballad-maker adored and 'he sighed and cried at the factory gate that she might be soon released'.

An orphanage caring for 80 children was opened by the sisters. At the end of the first year, when the progress of the institution was being assessed, it was noted that, as the orphans had been familiar with crime since they were tots, those of 7 years old got up at night to pick the pockets of the newcomers; gradually the sisters were discouraging this practice. Another task undertaken by the nuns was the visitation of those confined in the condemned cell. They consoled Mickey Donohoe from Clonakilty, who was regarded as dangerous and 'little better than a beast'. He cried when the sisters came, protesting, 'I am not a wild beast, but they would make me one. Nothing for me but irons and the lash, never a Christian word.' After the nuns had left him he wrote to his mother and he died with courage. Another unfortunate being instructed in his faith told a nun that if he had known as much about his religion twenty years before he would now 'not have to suffer a disgraceful death'.

During the first year that the Sisters of Charity were in the colony 2,400 convicts arrived in Sydney of whom about a third were Catholics. It was arranged that before the latter were distributed to the various locations they spent a time being instructed by the nuns and being prepared to receive the sacraments. Encouragement for the hard-working nuns came in the month of May 1840 when the foundation stone for the new church of St Patrick was laid in Sydney. Banners made by the nuns were displayed and a crowd estimated at 14,000 attended the ceremony. The celebratory banners may have been made by the convict women in Parramatta as when a couple of years later Bishop Polding visited there they made an embroidered picture of the scene.

Such rallyings of the Irish were not usually appreciated by the colonial officials. The celebration of St Patrick's Day, for example, was seen as a possible source of disorder and perhaps as an occasion for intrigue.

11 The Famine Victims, 1839-1848

During the last three years of the 1830s over 3,000 Irish convicts went to Sydney, of whom 873 were women. This regular imbalance of the sexes created a situation in the colonies which was only commenced to be corrected with the importation of several hundred free young women from Ireland. By the month of May 1850 eight vessels had brought 1,295 orphan Irish girls, of whom less than 50 were Protestant, to Australia. Aged from 14 to 19, they had been chosen from the various work-houses and the girls' discipline, education and general appearance was found to reflect great credit 'on the conductors of those humane institutions'. But there was not a general welcome for them in the new country. The editor of a Melbourne paper described them as 'a set of ignorant creatures whose sole knowledge of household duties barely reaches to distinguishing the inside from the outside of a potato, and whose chief employment hitherto has consisted of some such intellectual occupation as occasionally trotting across a bog to fetch back a runaway pig'. Another critic saw them as of 'the most abandoned character, the sweepings of the Irish work-houses'. But the chief objection to the girls was their religion; the society into which they were introduced was dominated by English Protestant officials, many of whom had little education themselves and whose natural prejudices found little opposition from the majority of the Irish other than through violence when sufficiently provoked. It was believed that the influx of Roman Catholic girls would not benefit the colonies, as theirs was 'a religion unfavourable to the development of liberty, of safety, of public happiness or progress, everyone of these girls will one day be the centre of a Roman Catholic circle. . .'

One change made in the Irish penal system in the 1830s was the abandonment of the hulks, which the Lord Lieutenant believed was 'a most pernicious system . . . a worse form of prison could scarcely be devised. . .' During the decade 1825-1835 it has been estimated that some 5,251 persons were confined on the *Essex*, of whom 67%

had been convicted of theft. Only a small percentage of the balance were classified as political offenders; there were about 50 murderers and even fewer sexual offenders.

A report on these vessels, from Capt W. J. Williams, an English Inspector of Prisons, from about this time noted that both the *Essex* and the *Surprise* were

> similarly fitted, and are nearly of the same size; they are arranged upon the very worst form of prison discipline although not the worst for security: the upper deck is part fitted as a hospital, and before the mainmast as a mess or dining room: the lower deck as a sleeping room: the plan strikes one as precisely that which would be adopted for securing and lodging wild beasts: upon the upper deck they pass the day, lounging in idleness or basking in the sunshine, or when it rains in taking shelter under the awnings which project over the sides and walls of their airing yard: and at close of day they are mustered and passed into their sleeping room through a confined aperture, admitting the entrance of one at a time with difficulty, and thus rendering a rush outwards next to impossible – in this place they are locked up for the night. A glimmer of light is furnished to their apartment by a lamp placed behind an illuminator in both the fore and after bulkheads, and should disturbance take place during the night, these lights are instantly extinguished: but no one dares to venture into the prison. There are no means of finding employment on board, none of inciting the prisoners to habits of industry by uniform or routine occupation: none even of fatiguing the body, so as to diminish the activity of vicious minds by inducing sleep: no means of classification in separation, the youngest boy associating with the most hardened felon or murderer – there is an attempt at a school on board each ship, but it would appear that by far the greater part of a convict's time is passed in recounting his adventures in vice and infamy to his less wicked companions, and if this may be supposed to be particularly checked during the day by the presence of a Civil Guard overlooking the airing deck, it must be admitted that during the whole of the night their conversation is uncontrolled.

While Capt Williams found little disease among the prisoners in either hulk, and that consequently the hospital expenses were very low, he believed that 'the personal condition of the inmates of both hulks appears to present such a contrast to that of the lower classes of Irish generally that transportation upon the system now prevailing would seem to be the greatest boon that could be bestowed upon an Irish labourer'.

Commenting on William's report, W. Branch Johnson, the author of a book on English prison hulks, remarked:

Williams seems to assume that all of the occupants of the *Essex* and the *Surprise* were felons brought to their present situation by law-breaking. That was certainly true of some. Felons they were in the sense that, in time of famine, they had stolen sheep or cattle in order to keep body and soul together. It is noteworthy that, next to sheep-stealing and cattle-stealing, a very large number of prisoners were hulked for what was termed 'insurrectionary offences' – in other words, they had been driven to dabble in extremist politics. But by far the greatest number had been put on board for reasons that were officially 'not particularised'. They were in short, not criminals at all but political suspects, who, after a period at Kingstown or Cork were transported. . .

Branch Johnson estimated that during the years of service of the two hulks 10,763 prisoners passed through the vessels, of whom 9,650 were actually transported. These included 1,847 men aged beween 16 and 20, 292 youths aged between 14 and 16, 118 aged between 10 and 14, and two boys under 10 years of age. The *Essex* was closed as a prison in 1836, and the *Surprise* two years later.

Prisoners remaining on the hulks were taken ashore to prisons which were scarcely less crowded than the vessels and which were also health hazards. At Wexford, in July 1838 the prison's 18 cells held 33 women and 12 children. Emphasising the danger of disease in the hot summer it was urged that some of those confined should be moved to the depot at Grange Gorman Lane, in Dublin, and this was arranged.

During the passage disease continued to take its toll, and when necessary, discipline was dispensed. Reporting from the Cape of Good Hope on 21 July 1838, Surgeon Smith of the *Clyde*, which had sailed from Dublin on 11 May with 216 male convicts, wrote that they were about to take on supplies of beef and vegetables. Apart from some minor complaints there were no signs of disease, except for infection of the gums in the case of some of the men. It was hoped that the refreshment that all on board would receive while at the Cape would hinder any further illness. There had been little need for punishment as the men were well behaved, but one man had been flogged for stealing, and several who had been quarrelling and fighting were 'rope's ended', and those who had committed minor offences were confined in the box. The principal complaint from the surgeon was that the clothing which had been issued to the convicts was of a very poor quality, and they were then in a most ragged state.

An explanation for the low standard of clothing which had been issued might be found in the report of an Inquiry into the alleged abuses of the transportation system in 1841. After the death of Dr Trevor in 1837, Major James Palmer, with 17 years of experience in the convict service, took over the office of Inspector General of Prisons and he was suspected of being corrupt. The turnkeys alleged that they were not getting their full pay and it was believed that in the movement of prisoners within the country false expenses were being claimed. Palmer was absolved of all charges other than that he had employed his brother-in-law in the jail at Kilmainham, and in being rather lax generally. Another official was found to have managed to have his three sons and his son-in-law recruited into the system, and this nepotism resulted in the Inquiry recommending that 'members of one family should not be employed, as it is difficult for them to check each other'. Major Palmer's great defence was that he could operate the system much cheaper than Trevor had done; for example, in the expenses of the convict depot for one year Palmer claimed to have saved £2,283.2.7, the total of his account being £4,895.8.10, against Trevor's £7,178.11.5.

While Major Palmer may have been pleased with his efficiency in coping with the costs of the convict accounts, other public officials were concerned at the constant high rate of crime. A Crown Solicitor on the Munster Circuit, Matthew Barrington, voiced his views in 1839. Land, he believed, was at the centre of all the trouble. The peasants desired to own land as their existence depended on it. The outrages, he said, were perpetrated mainly by 'the lowest description of labourers and farm servants, persons without land or employment'. Other commentators on the state of the nation agreed that the misery of the poor, their destitution when turned off the land and without any other means of existence, would naturally involve them in criminal endeavours to procure a means of maintaining their families. All of the west of Ireland was then subject to periods of great hardship as the population was constantly increasing and the poor people could not procure land on which to grow their potatoes as the landed gentry had too many cattle. 'The land is the cause of all the murders' was a common conclusion. Rural crime continued, though about half of those transported were first offenders. County Tipperary remained a troublesome area and in 1844 it was estimated that a quarter of all the outrages in the country were committed there. Urban crime in Belfast had increased over that in Dublin, and of those transported in the six pre-famine years only about one-sixth of the 3,000 are thought to have been offenders in the agrarian category.

If the ever increasing population, dependant on the potato for basic sustenance, became more agitated as land for growing the crop became more scarce and was a source of rural disturbance earlier in the nineteenth century, it became the cause of a major tragedy in the 1840s when the failure of the potato crop in successive years caused widespread and severe famine. It was estimated that the population of the country in 1845, when the famine started, was 8 million; six years later it had been reduced by 2 million, half of whom had perished, the others emigrated overseas, including about 4,000 transported to Australia.

During the actual years of the famine, from 1845-1849, the numbers of people transported annually fell, reaching their lowest in 1848 when but 139 were disembarked; the average figure for the three previous years was 600. Undoubtedly the general state of disaster in the country disrupted the efficiency of the law and the constant movement of starving hordes in search of food, bringing with them disease and death, discouraged unnecessary physical contact on the part of the officials. Those crimes that were committed were mainly due to the desperate efforts of famished people to procure food for themselves and their families. From the end of 1848 and during the following year transportations increased and 9 vessels brought 2,153, of whom 700 were women, to colonies at Hobart, Moreton Bay and Sydney.

Perhaps the most celebrated of those banished during the famine times were the Connery brothers from Bothaduin in County Waterford. In a local agrarian dispute they dressed as women and attempted to shoot a land steward but failed. They were informed on, arrested and lodged in Waterford jail, from where they managed to escape. Eventually they were caught again, charged with possession of arms and transported. After a time in Australia they earned pardons and prospered. At home in Waterford they became folk heroes, and the subject of poems and stories in both Irish and English.

In one poem the man who informed on them is condemned:

Curse and misfortune on you, O thieving, lying rascal,
May the day of your death soon come without the grace of the Son of God.
You willingly took the bribe and falsely swore the oath,
That sent the Connerys over the sea from Bothaduin of the trees.

The first of the four verses of the Gaelic poem *Muinntir Conaire* actually names the informer:

> Cursed Comyn! on thee, may misfortune be, and bitter hate,
> And on all beside, to thee near allied, both soon and late;
> For 'twas you that swore, though my heart you tore, the lying tales
> That sent the Connerys far across the seas, to New South Wales.

From the neighbouring county of Tipperary came another transportee of this time whose son was destined to become the greatest hero in Australian folk-history. John Kelly's crime has never been identified but it has been said to have been an attempt to shoot a landlord or participating in a faction fight or 'for stealing two pigs, the property of Mr Quainy'. Whatever it was, Kelly found himself in Van Diemen's Land and when he merited his ticket-of-leave he moved to New South Wales where he married the daughter of an Irish emigrant. Ned Kelly (1854-1880) was one of their children and his exploits as a bushranger led to the coining of the expression 'as game as Ned Kelly'. One of those who introduced Ned to the violent life was Waterford-born Henry Johnston who, like Kelly senior, had been released from Van Diemen's Land. Under the name 'Harry Power' Johnston was involved in a gunfight with the police in Victoria when he was caught and put on the hulk *Success* at Melbourne. Escaping from there he took to the bush and his adventures are remembered in a six-verse ballad called *Bushranger Jack Power*. It ends with the lines:

> The pluck that is in him
> Is beyond all belief,
> A daring highwayman
> A professional thief.

The other end of Ireland was the setting for the story of Peter Magill who was accused of the murder of a rent collector whose body was found in a bog hole in County Antrim in 1845. The principal witness for the prosecution was Magill's own son and the judge was so surprised that a son could so coolly testify against his father that the jury disagreed and Magill was transported for life. It is to be hoped that in Australia he met his neighbours from Mallaghbawn who had been exiled for illegal assembly. A ballad still sung in Ulster recalls the exploits of 'The Boys from Mallaghbawn'. Another broadside published in the 1840s concerns a man from County Limerick:

to some foreign country I was sent as a slave,
Since in my own country I would not behave.

But he had left his girl back in Limerick and he promised that as soon as he gained his liberty he would bid adieu to Van Diemen's Land and return to her.

The Limerick man's ambition to leave Van Diemen's Land can be appreciated if the regulations for convicts, published in 1847, are studied. They might not wear long hair or whiskers, their clothes must carry their convict number and they might not have fancy belts, buckles or knives. While marching to and from work they had to keep silent and in their free time dancing, gaming, swearing and immoral talk were forbidden. They might consume only what rations the government issued them with. In the year before these rules were issued an official paper on the colony put the convict population at 8,603, in 9 probation and 8 punishment stations. The latter places included the railroad and the coalmines. Men on hard labour worked on the thread wheel, at house, road or fence building, or as blacksmiths or boat crews. Those employed at barrack duties carried wood or water, or were bakers, cobblers, tailors or servants. Of the 1,119 females, 465 worked with wool or the needle and others were servants or nursed children.

While the regulations for the conduct of the convicts should have created some order in the stations, the Bishop of Tasmania found that the system instead of improving the men made them worse. Advocating that it should be abandoned he wrote: 'It let loose on a young society a body of depraved characters with evil influence, despite the efforts to counteract it.' One of the chaplains at Hobart saw '1,200 men congregated together like beasts, the most disgusting crimes that ever stained characters of men are perpetrated there. There is no way of preventing it, there are no divisions in the sleeping wards as they are overcrowded.' Norfolk Island, the bishop believed, was particularly depraved. He had heard of 150 couples 'who habitually associate for this most detested intercourse, they are said to be married. In the hospital at Tasman's peninsula there were diseased victims of unnatural crime and that vice had even been detected among the women.' Indeed, the bishop and the chaplain were but repeating a common assertion about the colonies and it had even been thought at one time that the climate of New South Wales had a tendency to dispose convicts to unnatural practices. So shocked was one convict by what he found in the stations he admitted, 'I began to be staggered in my belief of the existence of God; if he existed he would not suffer such infamy to exist.' However, it was the one vice of which the Irish were believed to be innocent. Governor George Gipps of New South Wales (1837-1846) remarked that the crime prevailed 'almost exclusively among the prisoners of English birth. . . and the Irish are (to their honour) generally acknowledged to be untainted by it. . .'

Again, the contrast between conditions in the penal stations and elsewhere in the colony is shown in a letter written on behalf of Roscommon man Patrick Mally in 1847. Addressed to a gentleman at Kilbride, who had promised support for the family, the letter indicated that Mally had managed to save a small amount of money, and that Mrs Mally could find employment as a washerwoman. It was arranged that, with her small boys, she could find passage on a female convict vessel.

At Fremantle, in Western Australia, where the first group of the Irish Sisters of Mercy arrived in January 1846, in the company of the first bishop of Perth, life was more simple. All the inhabitants of the whaling station had gathered to greet the bishop but the nuns were disappointed with the station, 'a place of miserable cottages'. They were more impressed by the aborigine chief who wore an enormous crown of cockatoo feathers, and they also saw a 'band of savages chained together on their way to prison'. In time as they worked amongst the natives the sisters came to love them, finding the aborigines intelligent and gentle but not wishing to hear about religion 'on account of the cruelties practiced on them by the Protestants'.

Michael M'Donald, a farm worker aged 34 from the midlands, who was transported for a burglary at Maryborough in the Queen's County, was one of a number of prisoners from whom statements were taken at the barracks in Hobart in September 1849. These accounts of life in a famine stricken countryside present a bleak picture. M'Donald had at first been employed at an annual wage of £5, rising to £7, and was married with two children when, due to the famine, he could no longer find employment. Before being apprehended he had been a wandering beggar for two months; after sentence he was confined in Maryborough jail where he was one of the 300 prisoners who attended school for 2 hours daily, to learn catechism, and he was able to continue his regular practice of attending Mass each Sunday. With a diet of oatmeal and buttermilk for breakfast and bread and new milk for dinner, M'Donald was employed at stone-breaking and had a cell to himself. Life in Maryborough, he admitted, was not too severe during the 7 weeks that he spent there. Transferred to the Smithfield Depot in Dublin, where he worked at oakum-picking for 5 months, he was sent to Spike Island for a further 18 months in the company of 1,300 other prisoners. The work there was quarrying, building and mat-making, but M'Donald was given the task of wardmaster. For embarkation he was brought to Dublin from where the *Hyderbad* sailed with 300 male convicts on 23 May 1849.

Another man who was confined for two years before embarkation was 22-year-old bachelor John Mooney, a stable hand from Waterford. Also illiterate, as was M'Donald, and a regular Mass-goer, he had never been to school until he went to jail in Waterford. There he worked as a weaver and he was rewarded with extra bread if he completed more than 5 yards a day. Confined four to a cell and two to an iron bed, Mooney blamed bad company for involving him in the theft of a cow, for which he got a 7-year sentence. While the attendance at school was a new experience for him, he said he learnt nothing there, as the teacher was another convict.

Other men at Hobart told similar tales, of crime-free lives, no schooling, regular Mass-going and hunger. Patrick M'Hugh, a 24-year-old from Belmar in County Mayo, claimed that he 'committed the crime from being in a state of starvation', as did Lawrence Kehoe who was tried, like M'Hugh, for sheep stealing. The official Irish records of *Crimes and Sentences*, for 1847 carry a note that

> the criminal tables show an increase of 12,717 committals, a result which was to have been anticipated from famine which prevailed for the entire period, and the social disorganisation consequent on a state of distress. The prisons have been crowded by a class of person hitherto of good character, who have committed offences by families, with a view to obtaining the support which they failed to procure from legitimate sources of parochial relief or charitable contribution. Cattle stealing was so frequent as to require the check of transportation at the closing session of the year.

While the foregoing sentiments suggest a certain sympathy with the afflicted population, it is apparent from the address of the Lord Chief Justice to the Grand Jury, at the opening of trials held under a Special Commission for the County Limerick on 4 January 1848, that persons involved in outrages would be severly disciplined. Endeavouring to suppress the wave of crime afflicting the country, Her Majesty's Government,

> on full and mature consideration of the actual state of things, have issued this Special Commission in order that justice may be speedily administered, the urgency of the case being such as not to admit delay until the ordinary period for administering the criminal law... Gentlemen, it further appears, that the principal object of this combination, and this illegal confederacy, is the destruction of the rights of landlords; fraud, violence and intimidation are recurred to and even murder itself is perpetrated, in order to prevent or frustrate landlords in the execution of their legal rights and remedies...

Juries were summoned and the Chief Justice himself presided at Limerick when the trials commenced. One case heard there was that against William Frewen. It was held that he, 'knowing one William Ryan had feloniously committed a murder, did feloniously receive, harbour and maintain him'. Though the defence claimed that Frewen was ignorant of the fact that Ryan was a murderer, the jury, without leaving the box, found him guilty. Before imposing the sentence the Chief Justice admonished Frewen, telling him that

> the crime of which you have been convicted may be considered in a degree the main source of all the frightful calamities with which this unfortunate country is visited. It is the duty of every loyal subject, to the utmost extent in his power, to aid in the execution of the law... You have screened and protected a murderer! a man who slew the father of a family in the presence of his wife and children – a murder so barbarous and brutal that it is impossible not to shudder at the mention of it! The sentence of the Court is that you be transported for the term of your natural life.

Presiding at similar trials at Ennis, in County Clare, the Lord Chief Justice sentenced John Slattery to be transported for 14 years, commenting that 'if a severer punishment had been inflicted (by the Court), it would have been well merited'. Slattery had been convicted of being one of a party of armed men who 'had unlawfully and maliciously assaulted the dwelling house of Thomas Hennessey at Ballyboy, on 25 September, 1847'. Hennessey had been 'dragged from his bed in a state of perfect nudity in order to procure fire-arms'. Slattery's sentence reflected the fact that he had 'acted with a greater degree of violence and barbarity' than the other prisoners. Of the latter, Michael Murphy was to be transported for 7 years, Daniel

M'Namara got 12 months' hard labour and three others were acquitted.

Also at Ennis, four men were given sentences of transportation for 'maliciously assaulting the dwelling house of William Walsh, carrying away a gun, the property of William Walsh, at Truagh, in the County Clare, on Sunday 1 August 1847'. Knowing that Walsh was at church the men broke into and ransacked the house, threatening the women-folk, as given in evidence by Mrs Walsh and one of her maids. Mrs Walsh said that 'I was at first greatly shocked, but I soon recovered. I was more alarmed for my little child than for myself!' The maid, who had taken shelter in the parlour with her mistress, when asked by the court if she could recognise any of the accused, said that a man had come behind her and caught her by her hair, and that she was much too frightened to remember any of them! Addressing the four accused the Chief Justice announced, 'I will at once relieve you from all doubt as to your fate, by telling you that you are to be transported for fourteen years. As to admonition or advice, you are beyond its reach: your sentence will put you beyond mere advice, for you will be deprived of the power of doing injury. . .' It was not for their benefit, he added, that he addressed them, but for the sake of others.

Such men and other casualties of the famine years formed the bulk of the 300 men transported on the *Pestonjee Bomanjee* from Kings-town on 20 September 1848. The governor of Van Diemen's Land was notified of the necessity to transport these prisoners as there was no suitable accommodation for them in Ireland, where the prisons and the depots were full to overflowing. The suspension of transport-ation for a time was first given as the reason for the increase in numbers now. Dublin Castle emphasised, in a letter to Whitehall, that those transportees were not ordinary criminals, that they had not been guilty of serious offences, or that their offences all exhibited mitigating circumstances. Of previous good character, their conduct in the depot was satisfactory. It was recommended that on arrival in the colony that they should be given tickets-of-leave and that their employers should be men of good character. It was hoped that the exiles could contribute to the fares of their families when they had repaid the cost of their own passage. The Lord Lieutenant believed that there was no greater boon to such men than being united with their families, in fact he could not anticipate any successful results with them until they were united!

So concerned was the Lord Lieutenant for the welfare of those

transported that he arranged for the appointment of religious instructors to accompany the convicts on the ships. On the *Pestonjee Bomanjee* this office was held by Fr Robert Downing and the journal which
he kept each day during the passage is preserved in the State Paper
Office at Dublin Castle. His flock consisted of 270 Roman Catholics
among the 300 men on the vessel. For the first couple of days after
sailing the men were occupied in fixing up their billets, then, by order
of the Surgeon Superintendent, morning prayers were commenced
on 22 September, after which the priest gave a lecture. It was intended
to have evening prayers that day also but as many of the men were
sea sick they were cancelled. This routine of regular prayers and
lectures was established in the prison, except on wet days when all
the convicts had to be confined in the prison. Fr Downing frequently
recorded in his journal how attentive the men were during services,
meditation or Mass on Sundays. Usually about 10 men came for
confession and an average of 17 communicated.

Early in October a school was started in the prison during the
mornings. Each of the 3 classes of 12 men had a monitor, prayer-books
and catechisms were issued and on the day following the first assembly
of the school a further 4 classes were formed. 'It gave me much satisfaction,' wrote the priest, 'to perceive the anxiety which they showed
to learn.' He was also impressed by the fact that usually all the men
also attended morning and evening prayers. He was also called on to
give the last rites to John McConnon and Thomas Molloy who died
on the passage and were buried at sea.

When the ship arrived in Hobart Harbour it was inspected by the
governor and then, having been given bibles and spiritual books, the
men disembarked. Summing up the results of his endeavours during
the journey, Fr Downing wrote that the conduct of the men had been
good and that while all those who attended school had improved, 90
had learnt to read and 60 to write. But the governor Sir William
Denison (1846-54) did not appreciate the quality of the new arrivals
and he wrote to the authorities at home in July complaining that the
men had been landed as ticket-of-leave or comparatively free men,
although they had been but a short time in prison in Ireland. Now,
it seemed they admitted that they were much better off than they had
been at home. The governor finished by saying that 'their natural
indolence is enhanced by easiness of procuring livelihood'. His real
grievance was that prisoners were arriving without having to undergo

a probationary period which would improve and prepare them for employment. Of those from the *Blenheim*, which arrived on 2 February 1849, he said that they had no previous training or discipline; ignorant and insubordinate, they were not likely to prove desirable additions to the labour market.

Irish convicts were also found amongst those sent from England and in 1848 nine with tickets-of-leave were included with 300 dispatched to the Cape of Good Hope. A recommendation from a priest accompanied the nine explaining that, 'while their crimes were serious, they were driven to theft by dire distress and famine and the political offences were committed in fear and excitement, they were mere creatures of others, ignorant of what they were about'. Two shiploads of Irish prisoners arrived at Bermuda in June of the same year causing the governor there to write to Whitehall that the *Medway* and the *Bangalore* brought 704, many of whom were convicted of food and grain stealing, no doubt attributable to the dreadful calamity which befell the poorer classes of people during the last two years, while others had been guilty of agrarian offences, due to bad example, in time of desperate need. It was proposed that when 'comparative tranquillity returned to Ireland' a commission should be appointed to select Irish convicts from Bermuda to go to Australia on conditional pardons or tickets-of-leave and to be replaced at Bermuda by convicts from England. This suggestion was later put into effect.

The humane character of the Bermudian governor was evident for his understanding of the 'friendless men, of good conduct'. He was particularly sympathetic to the young boys, 68 of whom were under 19, 12 of whom were under 16, and one of 13 with a 15-year sentence for sheep stealing. Their childish appearance, be believed, was not alone due to their age but also to 'the hard things of their infancy'. He sought to have them 'removed quickly from a mode of punishment which had serious risks'. A more appropriate punishment for them, he ventured, would have been 'a sharp private whipping, as boys are usually corrected, and a short solitary confinement on short diet and hard work under good guidance'. Putting them on hulks was a particular disaster and their condition on release from such association was appalling. In the meantime, while awaiting a reply from London, the governor intended to separate the boys from the older men, and have them instructed in a trade. Convicts from Ireland, he recommended, should be over 20, and fit for hard labour.

12 Young Irelanders, 1849-1850

Arrangements for the passage of the *Hyderbad* in 1849 were similar to those for the *Pestonjee Bomanjee* in that a religious and moral leader, in the person of Fr C. McCarthy, was appointed to accompany the 300 male convicts. Dublin Castle officials again arranged that the transportees should have tickets-of-leave as, 'with few exceptions, they have not been convicted of any breach of law; their deportment is quiet and submissive'. Further, in the absence of a reformatory penitentiary in Ireland, such as there was in England, and as the prisons were crowed, 'arising from distress and destitution', the status of the men on arrival was considered appropriate. Coupled with the Lord Lieutenant's request to the governor at Hobart that the prisoners might 'not be placed in circumstances of much difficulty or exposed to trials, which, from their imperfect training in this country, they will be unable successfully to resist', the opinion could be formed that, in fact, these men and their fellow transportees on the other vessels of this period were part of a government plan to resolve the problem of displaced and poverty-stricken people in the aftermath of the terrible years of famine.

Ninety-five days after leaving Dublin the *Hyderbad* reached Hobart, 3 men having died en route, only to be greeted with less than enthusiasm. 'They are landed upon the shores of this country ignorant of all the peculiarities of climate, or of the cultivation which characterises it.' The settlers would not hire them as they were unskilled and their only use was that of stone breakers. The governor, Sir William Denison, expressed himself strongly, explaining that all convicts should be of benefit to the colony by their labour, particularly the Irish. Nor did he want immigrants from Ireland as 'their want of industry, insubordination and subservience to their religious instructors render them apart. They are unfitted as settlers here, where luxuries are cheap and easily procured.'

Support for the governor's disapproval came from the superintendant of the convict barracks at Hobart within a few weeks of the *Hyderbad*'s arrival when only 15 of the men had been hired. He saw them as 'Inefficient workmen. Striking indications of ineptitude and want of intelligence were observable in the majority of them, to which the settlers, object. I have seen no other body of convicts in the colony so deficient in their capacity for labour, only the best of them can do second-class work.'

However, the opposition to the importation of convicts to Van Diemen's Land embraced those from England as well as Ireland. In 1849 a public meeting was called to support the abolition of transportation. The colony was prospering and the need for convict labour diminishing; it was becoming a respectable community which could boast no less than 111 places of worship, the majority of which were Protestant, but there were 4 Roman Catholic churches, and 2 synagogues. Schools had been established and in the convict quarters the sleeping arrangements had been improved and the quality of the rations raised. Convicts who wished to bring out their families from home were encouraged to do so, and that year 10 Irishmen made such a request, which was recommended by the governor.

The protestations of the Australian authorities were being heard in Downing Street and in June 1849 a reprimand from there was directed to Dublin Castle: 'If the Irish convicts are not effectively punished before sending to the colonies the system will fail, and transportation from Ireland instead of being a punishment may be looked on as a reward, and as free emigration.' It was even suggested that crowds of people would start committing crimes with the intention of being banished. Shortage of prison accommodation made a probation system impossible, the Lord Lieutenant countered, and he again reminded the government that the huge rise in crime was 'due to destitution and the suffering of the lower classes in four consecutive years'.

Official figures of the prison population on 1 June 1849 show that there were 3,489 male convicts in the various jails, which were intended to accommodate only 1,863. In the years 1848-49 2,153 prisoners had been transported, while the average in the three years before 1846 was but 673. The bulk of those confined in 1849 were on the recently opened Spike Island[15] and a new Model Prison was under construction in Dublin and almost ready for occupation. The Under Secretary of State, Thomas Redington from County Galway, who would have understood the circumstances and characteristics of his countrymen, concluded his report on the Penal System by giving his views of the convicts. They differed widely from the English, he wrote, as the crimes of the Irish were 'mostly not as a result of habitual profligacy and vicious contamination; they were not hardened offenders, whose reform is always difficult and sometimes hopeless, nor are they usually in gangs under leaders for well planned crimes. Most of the thefts were as the result of distress, and the more violent crimes, including murder, were almost always connected with the possession of land, which was regarded as the first necessity of life', or with local feuds or faction. 'These crimes,' Redington believed, 'are not considered by people to involve the same degree of turpitude as they would in England, and perpetrators, when not excited by these causes, are not men of irreclaimable character. Until last year transportation was viewed with horror in Ireland, the severance from home and family, except where there was starvation, was regarded with more horror than any term of imprisonment.'

A modern study of the convicts of Van Diemen's Land between the years 1840 and 1853 by J. H. Moore accepts this contemporary view that the Irish could not be considered as hardened criminals, that they were mainly first-time and petty offenders living in far greater poverty than their comparative class in England. Making comparison between the 28,000 male and female convicts from both countries in the years surveyed it was found that the Irish were mainly from rural areas, unskilled farm labourers who had never before left their home parishes. Generally they were older and more likely to be married than the English and they adapted better to the colonial system than did urban transportees.

Dealing with the famine years, Moore noted that the crime most common was that of theft and that the minimum sentences of exile were given; 'It was not unknown,' he commented, 'for men to commit crimes in the hope of being transported out of the country.' The latter comment might have been based on evidence submitted to the Select Committee on Poor Laws, Ireland, in 1849. An Assistant Barrister, who was a judicial officer in County Mayo, said that he was regularly asked by defendants, some as young as 12 years of age, to sentence them to transportation. He gave as examples two 'honest people's children from Clare Island, John and Charles Ruddy'; aged 12 and 15 they were convicted of sheep-stealing and sent away for 7 years. They said that one-third of the island's population had died of famine. When Owen Eady was asked if he knew what transportation was, the youth replied that, even if he had chains on his legs, he would have something to eat. 'Anything was better than starving and sleep-ing out at night.' It was the barrister's view that the boys had no alternative but starvation or the commission of crime. Elsewhere in the country it was the same story. Jeremiah Quinn, at Cork in the January of 1848, was transported for 7 years for stealing a handful of barley. Later he brought his wife and children out to the colony.

After a lapse of nine years another shipload of 225 Irishmen, all with tickets-of-leave, arrived in New South Wales on 3 October 1849. Officially transportation there had ceased almost a decade before, and when the *Mount Stewart Elphinstone* arrived at Sydney she was directed to disembark the convicts at Moreton Bay. A month later the *Havering* brought 334 men to Sydney after a passage of 96 days from Cork. She had the distinction of being the last convict-ship from Ireland to New South Wales and henceforth it was no longer accurate to refer to 'Botany Bay' as a penal destination. But the threat inherent in the ballad of that name was still real:

All you young men a warning, a warning take by me,
I'll advise you to stop night walking, or else you'll rue the day;
I'll advise you to stop night walking, and shun bad company,
You'll be sent on transport, my lad, you'll be sent to Botany Bay.

While the *Mount Stewart Elphinstone* lay at Sydney she disem-barked two prisoners, Kevin Izod O'Doherty and John Martin, the first of the 7 members of the Young Ireland movement transported after the Insurrection of 1848, to reach there. Before the end of October they were in Van Diemen's Land, to join their political col-leagues William Smith O'Brien, Thomas Francis Meagher, Patrick O'Donahue and Terence Bellew McManus who arrived on the *Swift* a few days earlier. John Mitchel did not reach Hobart until 5 April 1850, though he had been the first of the Young Irelanders to be exiled, as he spent almost a year aboard a hulk at Bermuda and then a while at the Cape of Good Hope.

O'Doherty and Martin had 10-year sentences for High Treason. Martin, a landed gentleman and a Presbyterian from County Down, had studied at Trinity College in Dublin and was a brother-in-law of Mitchel. His offence had been the founding of a journal, *The Irish Felon*, which was considered to be subversive. When he was given his ticket-of-leave he went to live with Mitchel and he later returned to Ireland. O'Doherty was a Catholic, and a medical student, who

Cottage of William Smith O'Brien at Port Arthur. c. 1950.

NORFOLK ISLAND.—THE CONVICT SYSTEM.

Convicts at work on Norfolk Island, from the *Illustrated London News*, 12 June 1847 (National Library).

contributed articles to *The Tribune* which were said to be seditious, and he was able to continue his studies at Hobart until his release in 1854. Back in Dublin he took a Fellowship at the College of Surgeons and commenced to practice. But he decided to go back to Australia where he settled in Brisbane. After some years he again came home and was elected as an MP for North Meath; but his restlessness brought him back to Australia once again, where he died in 1905.

William Smith O'Brien, from the ancient Thomond family, had also been an MP. His 14-year sentence had resulted from his arrest following an abortive raid on a police barracks at Ballingarry. He was sent to Maria Island, north of Tasman's peninsula, when he refused to take a ticket-of-leave. Maria Island was notorious as a place of punishment, but O'Brien was accommodated in two rooms and a garden, 'better than many officer's quarters', according to an English visitor. However it was not to O'Brien's liking; as the garden was planted with potatoes there was only a rough, narrow path for exercise, and he was not allowed to communicate with anyone. His letters were censored and he was under the constant gaze of a sentry. Not surprisingly, when John Mitchel later visited him he found that O'Brien's health was failing due to the close confinement. An escape attempt by O'Brien almost succeeded, but instead he was moved to Port Arthur where he was again in close custody. There he was a little more content as he had a small library and could do some gardening. After he took a ticket-of-leave at the end of 1850 he was employed as tutor to the family of a doctor and four years later he was pardoned, on the condition that he would not return to Ireland; but the intercession of sympathetic Members of Parliament gained him this permission. His observation of his countrymen in Australia caused him intense satisfaction; he found they had 'distinguished themselves by industry, intelligence, enterprise and good conduct'.

'When we tread Van Diemen's Land, transported to that shore, in prayer we'll bless our native land, as Paddies evermore,' murmured Thomas Francis Meagher after he had been given a similar sentence to O'Brien. The well-educated son of a Waterford business man, he was given a ticket-of-leave on arrival, but confined to the Campbell district. There the local hotel was kept by a widow from County Kildare; in her sitting-room Meagher felt at home, beneath pictures of Brian Boru and Daniel O'Connell. He met an Irish girl and married. They settled on a farm, but he was not happy. Leaving his wife with relatives he succeeded in getting a passage to America. When his wife set out to join him she came to meet his family in Waterford and died there when just 22. In America Meagher became a general in the Federal Army during the Civil War, and he was later acting governor of the Territory of Montana. He was drowned in 1867.

Two of the other arrivals in Van Diemen's Land in the autumn of 1849 were Terence McManus from County Monaghan, and Patrick O'Donohue, both Young Irelanders. McManus escaped to America in 1851 and, after several attempts, O'Donohue did likewise a few years later. A law-clerk from Dublin, O'Donohue kept a diary during his passage down under; he described their schooling, when they read aloud from the classics, or from Moore and Byron, or the men gave talks on their occupations. Charles Quinn, a brassfounder, spoke on that trade and O'Donohue sometimes expounded on the evils of drink. Described as 'a true disciple of Fr Matthew', he believed that 'many of the political, social and moral evils of Ireland were due to the baneful vice of drunkenness'. Indeed, he may have even repeated the story that, during one voyage to Australia, on St Patrick's Day, a child was baptised and named after the national saint. In a more sober mood the next day the father of the infant came to the priest and revealed that it was a girl, and she was renamed Mary Patrick! During the long journey into exile O'Donohue longed for Ireland and when he first glimpsed Madeira he immediately was reminded of the Hill of Howth and Lambay Island. With a ticket-of-leave in the Hobart district, O'Donohue founded a newspaper called the *Irish Exile*, which was not popular with some of his companions. One report on him suggested that he abandoned the ideals of Fr Matthew and was frequently in trouble for being drunk. An English visitor saw him while he was serving a sentence of confinement. O'Donohue was 'reading in bed, dressed in blue flannel hospital dress, having been injured in a fight with another Irishman'.

The leaders of the abortive insurrection of 1848 had sought, once again, to right Ireland's troubles; all Irishmen, regardless of religion or origin, were to be united in an independent nation. The well educated and eloquent men left behind them a legacy of words and of thoughts which was to influence subsequent generations. The most remembered of the leaders is the Ulster Presbyterian solicitor, John Mitchel; his newspaper, *The United Irishman*, advocated passive resistance by the small farmers with resort to violence as a final measure.

Convicted of treason-felony and given a 14-year sentence he was lodged in Newgate. From there he was moved to Spike Island before transportation to Bermuda where he was confined on the hulk *Dromedary* for almost a year. There he saw the most barbaric punishment of apprehended escapees; so severe was the flogging of the men that their screams reached Mitchel in his cell where, as he wrote, 'I have been walking up and down all day gnawing my tongue.' While he did not disapprove of the mangling of felons to preserve discipline, as a matter of personal taste, he remarked, he would rather be out of hearing. As he wrote in his *Jail Journal*

> but what enrages me more than all, is to think of the crowd of starved Irish, old and young, who have taken sheep or poultry to keep their perishing families alive in the famine, sent out to Bermuda to live in a style of comfort they never knew before even in their dreams, and to be initiated into mysteries and profound depths of corruption that their mother tongue has no name for.

Following another period at the Cape of Good Hope, Mitchel was brought to Van Diemen's Land on the convict ship *Neptune* which reached there on 5 April 1850.

It had been intended that the 300 convicts on the *Neptune* should be landed at the Cape but the governor there refused to have them and the ship continued to Hobart, where they were also unwelcome as it was seen as a breach of the understanding that no further convicts were to be placed there. Six Irishmen died during the passage and after Mitchel had joined them at Bermuda he found that about 200 of the men were compatriots, many of whom did not know a word of English. At night he found their *caoining* very mournful and he cursed the system which sent 'boys with fine open countenances, handsome, with ringing laughter, not yet 12 years of age, into exile'. Mitchel's only consolation was the company of a cheerful County Clare woman, who was accompanying her husband, Sergeant Nolan, to Australia. Mitchel admitted that 'Only that she is old, say half a century, I should fall in love with her'. He was then 34, and his health had suffered during his confinement, so much so that when Meagher met him he was shocked. 'I would not give ten shillings for his life,' he noted.

Before the *Neptune* arrived the governor of Van Diemen's Land, Sir William Denison, had been informed that all the convicts, with the exception of Mitchel, were to have conditional pardons. He was to be given a ticket-of-leave, which would be withdrawn if he attempted to leave the colony. The climate suited Mitchel and his health improved, but he hated the place; he resented having to report to the police once a month and thought that if he was on the footing of a genuine convict he would be happier, as then he would escape, and he felt that every colonist on the island would help him. After a time when his wife and family joined him and they settled at Nant cottage, near Bothwell village, he felt happier and another daughter was born there. When just over three years in exile Mitchel escaped. Having purchased a horse from a police officer he surrendered his ticket-of-leave, as he did not wish to break the trust which this implied. 'Pleased with the idea of having my enemy's horse to ride off on', Mitchel found shelter in various farms until he was able to board a ship at Hobart under an assumed name. His family was already on board and they all safely reached America. In his new country he again published newspapers, and he returned home in 1874. Elected as MP for Tipperary, he died at his old home at Newry in March 1875. During his time in America Mitchel published his *Jail Journal*, regarded as a classic in prison literature. Of the transportation system he wrote

> It is the very worst scheme of criminal punishment that ever was contrived; and I seriously think it was contrived by the devil, with the assistance of some friends. If it turns out to be no punishment for the criminal population generally, it is on the contrary, a far too severe punishment, far worse than the cruelest death, to the unhardened and casual delinquents.

While absent from Ireland he was remembered in ballads, such as 'Blackbird':

> John Mitchel brave was my blackbird's name.
> In 'forty-eight he is bore away,
> In a felon's chains for his country

Continuing to seek some further abatement of the disorder of the famine years the Irish authorities proposed in April 1850 that a further consignment of 300 male prisoners should be sent, with tickets-of-leave, to Van Diemen's Land. Permission was also sought to dispatch a further 300, 'of greater offence, whose deportation was essential to the country', to Bermuda and Gibraltar. Both of the latter destinations were refused, as 'they were not suited to hardened criminals, and those Irish already sent to Bermuda were not suitable for hard labour in a hot climate'. Procedures were initiated to transport the men to Australia, with the intention that they would arrive there in November. Those transported were to be only those convicted of crimes resulting from distress, and whose previous character and conduct, while in the Convict Depot, was good. As it was realised that they would not be in any way skilled in mechanical labour a quantity of leather was to be put on the ship with the intention of having them trained in its use during the passage. The cost of the leather was to be repaid to the convict office, with any profits to be at the disposal of the ship's surgeon to give awards to any prisoners who merited them.

The *Hyderbad*, which had brought convicts from Dublin to Hobart the previous year, was again chartered and she was ready to sail from Cove on 13 September with her complement of 287 men. Following arrival in Van Diemen's Land 91 days later 200 of the men went to probation stations to be employed at public works, 69 were given tickets-of-leave and 18 were imprisoned for bad conduct. Those men lodged at the probation station were subjected to a strict regime, the routine being:

04.45: Rise, fold beds, to be aired if weather fine.
05.00: Cells unlocked; wash under supervision. Prayers.
05.45: Work parties formed. March off.
07.55: Breakfast, grace. Smoke in yard.
08.40: Work resumed.
11.55: Dinner.
12.50: Work.
17.00: Return to station.
18.00: Prayers; school; intellectual recreation.
20.00: School over. To bed.

In the billets a light was kept on all night and there were frequent rounds by an overseer. Over the years a more ordered system of controlling the convicts had evolved and many of the disciplines imposed were similar to those employed in the army and the navy. Dr Archibald Allison, having observed the convict system, wrote about this time that 'it has often been observed by those practically acquainted with the working of the transport system, that the Irish convicts were generally the best, the Scotch, beyond all question, the worst who arrived'. The type of person in jail in Ireland in 1850 can be judged from the *Convict Books* of the various institutions. Kilkenny city jail held only 4 men, 2 of whom had 15 year sentences as a result of having escaped from jail when under sentence of transportation; the other 2 prisoners had been found guilty of robbery and of obtaining money by false pretences. Two women in the jail had been convicted of larceny, and of theft from the person. The county jail of Kilkenny held 39 men, and their crimes were stealing animals, arson, manslaughter and lesser offences. Female confinees had stolen sheep, burgled, robbed or injured others. Some of these women, no doubt, were among the 259 females transported on the *Blackfriar* on 24 January 1851.

The women on the *Blackfriar* came from every county in the country and the majority of them had 7-year sentences, though a few went for life, 34 for 14 or 15 years, and twice that number for 10 years; 49 children of the convicts accompanied them on the passage. Miss Charlotte McCullagh was matron in charge of the women and she was assisted by Miss Elizabeth McCullagh and Miss Catherine White. Again the citizens of Hobart objected to the arrival of yet another convict ship as being a violation of the Queen's 1847 pledge to discontinue the system. However, within a month of disembarkation, 167 of the women had been hired. The fact that the new arrivals were Irish was a further cause of annoyance, as the majority of the convicts in the colony already were of that nationality. A Roman Catholic teacher named O'Halloran had been appointed to teach the 200 children, but the adults also needed improvement. It was recommended that they would benefit from a period of educational and industrial training before being allowed to private employers.

Governor Denison went even further in his disapproval; the women, he said, 'were unfit for any type of useful household labour, and it had been recommended early in 1851 that neither male nor female Irish should be sent there'. By the middle of that year some 285 male, 259 female and 93 Irish children had come there and none had left. Of the men, who had arrived on the *London* just after St Patrick's Day, only 178 had been hired, due to their general lack of training. But there was the occasional encouraging story, such as that of the wife of George Hull, an ex-convict and a farmer; she was reputed to have been 'a deeply depraved woman while in Ireland, but her conduct had been exemplary since arrival in the colony and she was now the mother of six beautiful children who go two miles or more to school each day'. The ultimate fate of Kerryman Daniel Connor, transported in 1853 for petty larceny, was also a happy one. Having been pardoned he became a pedlar, but he managed his affairs so well that he soon was the owner of considerable property in Western Australia, and at his death in 1898 his estate was worth a quarter of a million pounds. The Sisters of Mercy benefited from his success, and his family prospered, one of them coming back to Trinity College in Dublin to become a doctor, after which he returned to Australia and, like his father, entered local government.

Interesting observations on life in New South Wales are found in the writings of contemporary authors; Mrs Louisa Meredith lived, in 1851, forty miles from the nearest village with but a ticket-of-leave gardener and a pardoned convict for company on occasions. She wrote:

> I think it must be very evident that the country cannot be the den of horrors it has of late been painted, where a female only so protected can sit in her quiet country house with doors and windows left open the whole day through, and sleep safely and peacefully at night, without a bar or bolt or shutter to a single window, every room being on the ground floor.

About the same time, G. C. Mundy remarked that

> A person newly arrived here feels no little curiosity, perhaps some little uneasiness, on the subject of the degree of influence exerted on the social system by the numerous body of affluent emancipists, which the lapse of time and their own reformed characters have formed in the community. It seems almost incredible that, living in the very midst of this community – in many cases in equal and even superior style to what may be called the aristocracy – possessing some of the handsomest residences in the city and suburbs – warehouses, counting houses, banking establishments, shipping, immense tracts of land, flocks and herds, enjoying all the political and material immunities, in common with those possessing equal fortunes, of the more reputable classes – they are, nevertheless a class apart from the untainted.

13   Fenians, 1851-1876

Between the sailing of *Blackfriar* in the first month of 1851, and the *Midlothian*'s arrival at Hobart just over two years later, the last 8 convict ships to bring Irish men and women to Van Diemen's Land deposited 1,518 male and 548 female prisoners in the colony. While the administration of the system was now better organised there were still rumbles from various concerned parties. Sometimes the cause of complaint was that men sentenced to be transported had been allowed to go free, as happened in County Westmeath in 1851. There a public fund had been organised to bring cattle stealers to justice and they had been apprehended and given sentences of 7 years in exile. Now the magistrates expostulated that the public fund-raising had been a waste as the men had been released after a short time, and one of them, by name Walsh, since his release, had been part of an armed gang which held up and robbed a respectable merchant. The official response to this complaint was that the conduct of the men while in jail had been good, to which a magistrate laconically replied: 'What else could they do there?'

While the door for the disposal of convicts had been closed in New South Wales and Van Diemen's Land, that to Western Australia had been opened with the first vessel from England arriving at Swan River in June 1850. It was over two years later that an Irish convict ship reached there, and in the 18 years that Western Australia benefited from the concept only two vessels with Irish prisoners went there. The second of these was the *Hougoumont* which included in its cargo 62 of the exiled Fenians. Departing Queenstown[16] on 2 June 1853 the *Phoebe Dunbar*, the last convict ship to leave Ireland, after a passage of 89 days, disembarked 285 Irishmen in the new colony. In the jails those with sentences of banishment continued to submit pleas, and just before the Christmas of 1855 a 22-year-old Tipperary man Jeremiah Tracey, facing a 7-year sentence for manslaughter, begged for 'the brightest gem in the British Crown, that of mercy'. Having already been confined for 3 years and 9 months, he begged to be allowed to return to his aged parents, and 4 fatherless children. But he remained on Spike Island, as his plea was refused. Having committed an unusual crime three and a half years before, 27-year-old Martin Torpy from Dungarvan was also awaiting transportation for 7 years. He had stolen an ass and a cart, having lifted the cart over a wall as the gate was closed. 'The law must take its course' was the answer he got. Sometimes a plea was successful, such as that of John White, from County Clare. His 10-year sentence for sheep stealing was shortened by 4 years.

Well-organised as the procedures now were, there were still difficulties. During 1855, on a few occasions, when female prisoners arrived at the railway station in Cork city the covered carts in which they should be carried to the jail were not there to meet them and they had to be paraded through the streets. In January those from Waterford and Limerick were 'marched through the whole city. . . in a manner calculated to raise disgraceful and scandalous scenes'. During the summer four females from Galway, though escorted by constables from the railway station, were followed by such an excited crowd that a riot was feared. A disorderly mob also accompanied the women from Dublin in October, again leading to a protest from the city's prison officers who blamed those in Dublin for not sending letters of notification of arrival to reach them in time to finalise arrangements. Not surprisingly, the best method of punishment for offenders continued to be a discussion topic for politicians and reformers. A solution offered in 1857 included transportation, but only to the Mullet peninsula in County Mayo; there the salubrious climate was considered to be suitable for agriculture and ship building and repairs. It would also be much cheaper than sending convicts to distant overseas colonies. Practical as the proposal may have been, it was not adopted.

Sometimes the return of convicts from abroad was noticed by the newspapers. When the convict depot at Bermuda was closed in 1863 eight men were returned to confinement on Spike Island. On 13 May of that year *The Irish Times* reported that 'Our readers will remember William Burke Kirwan who was, some years back found guilty of having cruelly murdered his wife at Ireland's Eye'. His death sentence had been commuted to one of penal servitude for life and by the beginning of summer in 1863 he was back in Ireland. Just over four years later the same newspaper carried a letter from 'A lover of fair play' concerning a meeting with a man just returned from transportation. Asked how he found the punishment, the ex-convict replied, 'I never knew what transportation was until obliged to return to my own home again.' The letter writer found that his informant seemed 'quite a changed man in his appearance for the better and, what is more, he has received a plain education since he left. Hearing so much said as to the bad treatment of our convicts, I feel much pleasure in bringing this circumstances before the public, for the sake of our laws, and the Christian manner in which they are executed.'

The last group of Irishmen to be transported were the leaders of the secret organisation known as the Fenians, which had been established in 1858. Nationalist and democratic, the members believed in the separation of church and state and they recruited mainly from amongst small farmers and the working class. They also found members in the communities of Irish emigrants in Britain and the United States. Their planned rising in 1867 was as unsuccessful as that of the Young Irelanders almost 20 years before, and many of the Fenian leaders had been apprehended by the authorities before the fateful day. Very soon more than 60 of them were bound for exile.

'Another chance for the old dreams,' was the comment of John Boyle O'Reilly, the Fenian, when he learnt that his 20 year prison sentence was being altered to that of transportation to Western Australia. An ex-soldier of the 10th Hussars, he was one of 17 military prisoners amongst the 62 Irish political offenders on the *Hougoumont* which reached Freemantle on 9 January 1868 after a passage of 89 days from London. Many years later, after he had escaped from the colony and settled in America, O'Reilly published a novel entitled *Moondyne* which reflected some of his experiences as a convict.

While awaiting embarkation at Portland Dock the Fenians were inspected by the medical authorities and by the prison governor. When being exercised 20 of them were chained together, which experience enabled them to sample the conditions of the common convict. On the day that the Irishmen were being marched to the gangway to begin their exile a harrowing incident occurred, and it was recorded by O'Reilly:

A woman's piercing shriek rose up from the crowd on the wharf; a young girl rushed wildly out and threw herself weeping and sobbing on the breast of a man in our chain, poor Thomas Dunne. She was his sister, and she had come from Dublin to see him before he sailed away. They would not let her see him in prison, so she had come here to see him in his chains. Oh! May God keep me from ever seeing another scene like that which all stood to gaze at; even the merciless officials for a moment hesitated to interfere. Poor Dunne could only lower his head and kiss his sister, his arms were chained; and that loving, heartbroken girl, worn out by grief, clung to his arms and his chains as they dragged her away; and when she saw him pushed rudely to the gangway she raised her voice in a wild cry: 'O God, O God,' as if reproaching Him who willed such things to pass. From the steamer's deck we saw her still watching tirelessly and we tried to say words of comfort to that brother, her brother and ours. He knew she was alone, and had no friends in England. Thank God, he is a free man now in a free country.

Other Fenians on the *Hougoumont* were John Valentine Flood, Denis Cashman and John Walsh. Four from Drogheda, Patrick Wall, Robert May, and brothers Luke and Laurence Fulham had a moderate pleasure in knowing that their convict dress was made from linen manufactured in their hometown. During Christmas 1867 as the ship reached the antipodes Eugene Lombard, a baker from Cork, was thinking of his parents at home, and of how sad his mother must have been to see his place vacant for the first time on Christmas Day. To occupy their time on the passage some of the Fenians produced a newspaper, *The Wild Goose*. Lombard was copyist and Flood editor. Though they were almost half way to Australia by the time they thought of the publication they produced eight issues before they disembarked. Fr Delaney, the ships's chaplain, was a loyal companion to the men and he encouraged their work on the paper.

Even though the Irish prisoners were kept separated from the rest of the convicts they saw and heard the sufferings of those unfortunates. O'Reilly described how, when they were becalmed in the tropics, the women and the man packed in the prison suffered from heat and thirst. When the weaker ones succumbed to the conditions they 'were laid in a row in the port side. Relays of sailors worked at the shrouding and burial. The bodies were wrapped in sailcloth, with a cannon ball tied at the feet.'

Some of the men, in letters to the families at home, gave their impressions of Western Australia. Lombard, with 19 others, had been sent as cook with the party into the bush to build roads. The town of Perth he estimated was about half the size of Queenstown with a Spanish bishop and an Irish chaplain. Later, from another part of the bush, he observed:

You would imagine that civilised man never set foot here, parrots and cockatoos, mahoganies towering to the sky, gum trees. The mosquitoes almost sting us to death, to keep them away we light fires before the tent at night, crack jokes, and sing songs around the fire.' When the priest came to visit them, bringing the necessaries for the celebration of mass in a leather bag strung across his saddle bow, he also brought them Irish novels. 'Now I am reading the life of Gerald Griffin,' wrote Lombard, and he was comforted by the fact that the other Corkmen were working only about 5 miles away. One letter home he concluded with the promise that he would never abandon the idea of seeing his own land before he died.

Quarrying was the employment of Thomas Duggan and John Kenneally, 'heavy work under the burning skies of this country, but better than Portland'. There, prior to embarkation, the men suffered from sore hands from the rough work with stones and bricks and for any misdemeanour they were locked in the black hole on a diet of bread and water. They also resented the searches when they were made to strip naked while their clothes were examined. Duggan hated Australia, describing it as 'a miserable place to live in'. But then, on the occasion that he wrote making that comment, he was suffering from 'the two sicknesses of the place, diarrhoea and sore eyes'. He had also just spent two days in the dark cell, for venturing outside bounds to pick mushrooms in front of the officers' hut.

John Boyle O'Reilly was also engaged on roadmaking, and the story was told that when it was decided to cut down a particularly fine old tree which was in the line of the road, O'Reilly made a plea to have it saved. The chief surveyor was so amused at a convict expressing such sentiments that he told his wife. She came to see the tree and with her extra persuasion it was saved (it survived until 1951). O'Reilly was only just over a year in the colony when he succeeded in boarding a ship and escaping to America. There, with John Devoy and other Fenians, he set about making plans to rescue some of his companions from the colony. The achievement of this ambition resulted in the much-told story of the *Catalpa* rescue in 1876. This vessel was purchased by the escape committee and sent to Bunbury, about 30 miles from Fremantle. The escape of six Fenians caused such a sensation in Bunbury that even the unveiling of the foundation stone for a new Freemasons' Hall did not attract the crowds away from the quays, where they were waiting for news of the efforts to apprehend the escapers. Not surprisingly the ballad written to celebrate the event was banned in Western Australia in the late 1870s. The chorus of it ran:

So come all you screw warders and jailers,
Remember Perth regatta day;
Take care of the rest of your Fenians,
Or the Yankees will take them away.

However, it had not been the ambition of all of the prisoners to escape from the colony and, in 1869 when 45 of them were amnestied, seven elected to remain behind while the remainder returned to Ireland or went to America. Those who stayed in Australia found livelihoods in various ways – Cornelius O'Mahony and Thomas Duggan taught school in Perth and Hugh Brophy was a builder in the same city. He erected a bridge over the Swan river there before he moved to Melbourne where he died at the age of 90 in 1919. In Sydney John Flood, from Wexford, published a weekly newspaper *The Irish People* for about a year prior to moving to Queensland where he worked as a journalist. Michael Cody from Dublin also worked in Sydney as a businessman.

Kevin Izod O'Doherty, who had been a medical student at the Catholic Unversity in Dublin before he was exiled, was employed in the same field before moving to Victoria when he was pardoned in 1854. There, with some of his companions, he sought a fortune in the gold fields, but when he was not successful he returned to Europe and resumed his medical studies in Paris. By 1856 he was married to Eva Kelly, a contributor of verse to *The Nation*, and having been granted an unconditional pardon, returned to Dublin and to the College of Surgeons, from which he obtained a fellowship in 1857. Dr O'Doherty must have retained some happy memories of Australia as, in 1865, he was back with his family in Brisbane where he opened a practice. Soon he was prominent in church and public affairs, but he did not lose his interest in the Irish cause. He was elected a member of the Legislative Assembly in 1868 and he remained in politics until he was invited to return home to represent North Meath as a Parnell party member in the House of Commons. In Dublin he gave a talk in the Rotunda on his life in Australia and was made a Freeman of the city. After a few years he returned to Queensland to resume his medical practice, but he was not very successful. He died there in 1905. His wife had continued contributing verse to publications in Australia, and she was remembered with her husband in a sonnet by the Queensland poet Tom MacBride. This is part of it:

Bricks both, glazed in the fire of tribulation
Bright keystones in the building of our nation.

Epilogue

Various estimates have been made of the numbers and status of the convicts, of whom some 162,000, including 25,000 women, were transported from Ireland and Britain in the years between 1787 and 1868. Irish transportees formed slightly less than 28% of the whole, numbering about 45,000, including possibly as many as 6,000 apprehended and transported from England. Of the 39,000 sent directly from Ireland, 9,000 were women; they were carried on the 212 ships which sailed out of Dublin or Cove from 1791 to 1853. A considerable amount of research has been done into the origins of the convicts. As this narrative has shown, during the decades that Irish transportees arrived in Australia, the colonial officials generally regarded them as being different from the English and Scottish. On the other hand, in 1863, the *Edinburgh Review* dismissed the notion prevalent in England, that Irish crime was 'something simpler, agrarian, or something odd'. Having studied the tables of crimes committed in both England and Ireland the *Review* concluded that 'the offences are just like those of other countries, and quite as large a proportion of burglaries and all sorts of thefts as elsewhere'. Sometimes sympathy was shown by both the officials and settlers to the political prisoners, and they might even be referred to as 'patriots'. But others saw them as 'rebels of life-long disposition, far more troublesome than all the forgers, burglars and thieves with whom the governors had to deal'. While that latter opinion, of the Australian historian Ernest Scott, may have been true of the rebels of 1798, it could hardly be applied to the exiled Young Irelanders or Fenians.

Up to comparatively recent years in Australia a convict in one's ancestry was an embarrassment; now, when the realities of the offences of those transported have been researched and analysed, a better understanding of the character of these people can be achieved. The work of such historians as T. J. Kiernan, J. F. H. Moore and A. G. L. Shaw has placed the transportees in their historical perspective. In his classic study of the convicts Shaw has written, 'In Ireland there was less ordinary crime than in England, except in Dublin', which was then the only large urban area. In general scholarly research has decided that of the total Irish transported only about 600 could be considered to have been convicted of political offences, but this does not take into account those sent without trial; and a further 4,300 might be classified as social or agrarian offenders. This suggests that about 40,000 transportees were in the ordinary criminal class, but consideration should be given to the nature of the society in which these men and women lived and offended, and it may be admitted that inducement to crime was great. While the crimes committed were similar to those of their comrades from England and Scotland it must be remembered that poverty in Ireland was more extreme. Travellers visiting the Irish countryside during the period under consideration invariably commented on the frightful living conditions of the people. At Bantry in County Cork, in 1842, the English writer William Makepeace Thackeray found the wretchedness of the cabins quite curious. An ordinary pigsty in England, he thought, would be more comfortable than the rude stone shelters measuring about 6 feet by 5 feet in height, topped with ruined thatch. 'I declare I believe a Hottentot kraal has more comfort in it, even to write of the place makes one unhappy,' he added.

In the antipodes the majority of the Irish achieved crime-free records, and their contribution to the new society was significant. The professional and skilled prisoners were useful in their respective spheres and, while the vast majority of the Irish were unskilled, their labour was no less important in the creation of farms, and of such public works as roads, towns and harbours. The Roman Catholic and the Methodist churches were introduced by the Irish, and the special character of the former church was unmistakably Irish. The folk history of Australia was enriched by many characters from Ireland, and it may be that it is in that area that the distinctiveness of the Irish was best expressed. In stories and ballads their non-acceptance of authority and their non-conformist views with their advocacy of social change are evident. Tolerant of human weakness, they presented an independent and democratic voice in a community which had inherited its values from eighteenth-century England, with its traditional and rigid class structure and Established Church.

When Judge Roger Therry, who had been the first Roman Catholic official to be appointed in the colonies, looked back on thirty years of residence in New South Wales, in 1863, he had this to say:

It is satisfactory to be enabled to testify that amongst the thousands transported to New South Wales many became reformed and really good men.
This reformation was mostly observable in that class of convicts who were
sent out for offences that did not partake of the character of base crime,
such as burglaries, etc. Transported political offenders were usually a class
of persons whose moral character stood little more in need of reformation
than ordinary citizens at home. . . many exiled for political offences from
Great Britain and Ireland were of this class. . . London pick-pockets and
convicts from Dublin, Liverpool and the large towns of the United Kingdom, who, from their childhood upwards, had been brought up in ignorance, and had led lives of habitual crime, if not from principle, from obvious
motives of interest in the prospect of becoming independent in a land of
abundance, altered their course of conduct and became industrious members of society.'

Forecasting the eventual fate of the Australian Irish the nineteenth-
century nationalist writer *Speranza* (Lady Wilde, 1826-1896)
believed that, in time, they would become as powerful as their American cousins. She even anticipated the day when they would return
to 'free Ireland, and buy up the estates of the pauperised landlords'.
Perhaps her contemporary Charles Darwin was more accurate in his
opinion that transportation as a reformatory system had failed, but
'as a means of making men outwardly honest, of converting vagabonds
most useless in one country, into active citizens of another, and thus
giving birth to a new and splendid country, it has succeeded to a
degree perhaps unparalleled in history'.

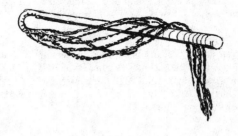

Notes

1. *Cove:* a port in Cork harbour, and an important naval base for the British until 1937. It was named Queenstown from 1849 until 1922. It is now Cobh.
2. *Duncannon Fort:* a seventeenth century fortification in Waterford harbour. Used also as a prison in the late eighteenth and early nineteenth centuries, it is preserved.
3. *New Geneva:* Intended to be a settlement for refugees from Switzerland in 1785, it never succeeded and became a military depot. Used as a jail after 1798 it became infamous for its harsh regime; now a ruin, it is remembered in ballad and story.
4. *Pigeon House:* a packet station, close to Poolbeg anchorage in Dublin Bay. A fort was built there in 1813. It is partly preserved.
5. *Currency Lass:* The daughter of an emancipist.
6. *Constable:* At that time the police force was composed of emancipists, ticket-of-leave-men and convicts.
7. *Passage:* A port in Cork harbour, now Passage West. Passage East is a port in Waterford Harbour.
8. *Croppy:* A term applied to rebels in 1798, many of whom wore their hair cropped.
9. *Erin Go Bragh: Erin go brách,* Ireland for ever.
10. *Dublin Castle:* The centre of British power in Ireland. Important prisoners were sometimes kept there. It is now open to the public.
11. *Kilmainham jail:* Opened in 1796. It held prisoners from the Risings of 1798, 1803, 1848, 1867. It is now a museum.
12. *Poolbeg:* A deep pool for anchorage on the south side of Dublin Bay.
13. *Kingstown:* A harbour was opened in Dunleary about 1760 which, much improved, was named Kingstown following a royal visit in 1821. It is now Dun Laoghaire.
14. *Emancipist:* A convict who has served his term.
15. *Spike Island:* In Cork harbour. A convict depot was established there in 1847, the men being employed in the construction of harbours etc. The prison closed in 1883, but was re-opened in recent years.
16. *Queenstown:* Now Cobh.

Chronology

1788: Arrival at Van Diemen's Land of the first fleet of convict ships from Great Britain.

1791: The first convict ship from Ireland sailed to Sydney.

1798: United Irish Rising.

1801: Union of Ireland with Great Britain.

1803: Rising, led by Robert Emmet, in Dublin.

1818: First convict ship from Ireland to Van Diemen's Land.

1830: Tithe war in Ireland.

1837: Queen Victoria comes to the throne.

1845-1848: Famine in Ireland.

1848: Young Ireland Rising in Ireland.

1849: Last convict ship from Ireland to New South Wales. Vessel from Ireland to Moreton Bay.

1850: John Mitchel arrives in Van Diemen's Land.

1853: Last convict ship from Ireland to Van Diemen's Land. First convict ship from Ireland to Western Australia.

1867: Fenian Rising in Ireland. *Hougoumont* sails to Western Australia.

1876: The *Catalpa* rescue.

Bibliography

Acts of Parliament

1717: 4 George I, c. 2.
1776: 16 George III, c. 43.
1778: 17/18 George III, c. 9.
1779: 19 George III, c. 74.
1784: 23/24 George III, c. 56.
1786: 26 George III, c. 24.
1790: 30 George III, c. 32.
1792: 32 George III, c. 27.
1824: 5 George IV, c. 84.
1833: 3 William IV c. 4.

Parliamentary Papers

House of Commons's Journals
Select Committees and other papers on:
  Transportations: 1776, 1785, 1810/12, 1837/38, 1847, 1856, 1857/58, 1861,
  Hulks: 1778, 1814/15. 1847.
  Penitentiaries: 1784, 1810/11, 1812/14.
  Irish gaols, prisons: 1808, 1809, 1813/14, 1823.
  Prisons, general: 1816, 1819, 1835, 1843, 1850-52, 1863.
  Ireland, State of, Disturbance in : 1816, 1823, 1824, 1825, 1830, 1831/32 1836, 1839, 1845, 1852.
  Ireland, Colonisation from: 1847/48, 1849.
  Van Diemen's Land: Prisons, discipline etc: 1822, 1823, 1828, 1830/31, 1837/38.
  Shipwrecks: 1836.

Irish Parliamentary Debates:
  Reports of the Committees of Secrecy Irish House of Commons and Irish House of Lords: 1798/99.

Correspondence, Accounts, Returns, Papers: 1816-1852

Poor Laws, Ireland. Reports, minutes. 1849.

Manuscripts

State Paper Office, Dublin.
Chief Secretary's Office, Registered Papers: 592, 588aaa, 602, 621, 622, 623.

Official Papers:
508, 510, 513, 515, 518, 527, 529, 531, 538, 544, 550, 554, 560, 568, 569, 576, 588, 588 aab, 595.

Government Letter Books:
Correspondence Books: 1827-1857.

Rebellion Papers:
State of the Country Papers, Outrage and Police Reports: 620
State of the Country: 1796-1831, vi.

Convict Department Records:
Convict Office Letter Books: 1836-51.
Convict Papers: Registers of convicts for transportation.
General Prison Board Papers.
Prisoners Petitions and Cases:
394, 53. 55. 66. 92, 2726, 2730, 2733, 2735, 2736, 2737, 2738, 2741, 2747, 2752, 2753, 3116, 1A 170-4, 1A 17a-4, VI.13. 4-110.
Free Settlers Papers: 1825-1848.

National Library, Dublin

Larcom Mss. 7695/7696.
Ms. 7324.
Ballads: 691, 447. Henry S. *Songs of the People.*
A ballad of '98 Heroes. P. Gregory. 1917.

John Oxley Library, Brisbane

Book of trials, Moreton Bay. Peter Spicer's Diary.
Convict Indentures.
New South Wales Colonial Secretary's Correspondence.

Mitchell Library, Sydney

NSW Colonial Secretary Papers. Vol. 1, 681/1.

Public Records Office, London

HO 10 Convict Papers.
HO 100, 123. Ireland.

Annals of Religious Orders

Annals of the Irish Sisters of Mercy. Vol. II, 1883.
Annals of the Sisters of Charity, 1834-1844.
Notes on the Rev. James Dixon, PP, Crossabeg, in the keeping of the priest of that parish.

Contemporary Newspapers and Magazines

Anthologia Hibernica.
Cox's *Irish Magazine.*
Dublin Chronicle.
Dublin Evening Post.
Edinburgh Review.
Edward's Cork Remembrancer.
Faulkner's Dublin Journal.
Freeman's Journal, Dublin.
Freeman's Journal, Sydney.
Hibernian Chronicle, Cork.
Irish Times.
Irishman.
The Nation.
Post.
Sydney Gazette.

Journals

County Kildare Archaeological Society, XVI, no. 4. 1983/4.
Béaloideas, vol. 6. no. 2. 1936.
Australian Catholic Historical Society, Sydney.
Historical Records of Australia.
Historical Records of New South Wales
Historical Studies, Australia.
Tasmanian Historical Research Association.
The Past, no. 5, 1949; no. 6. 1950.
Waterford Archaeological Journal, No. 14, 1911.

Printed Sources

Allan, J. A., *Men and Manners in Australia* (1825).

Anon., *Ireland in 1831. Letters on the state of Ireland* (1831).

Armstrong, J. S., *A Report of trials under a Special Commission, for Counties Limerick and Clare* (1848).

Arthur, G. *Defence of Transportation* (1835).

Atkinson, S., *Mother M. Aikenhead* (1879).

Australian Encyclopaedia, (1938).

Barrington, G., *A Voyage to Botany Bay* (1801).

——, *A History of New South Wales* (1802).

Barrington, J., *Personal Sketches* (1827).

Bateson, C. *The Convict Ships, 1787-1868* (1959).

Bayley Butler, M., *A Candle was Lit* (1953).

Brady, John, *Catholics and Catholicism in the 18th Century Press* (1965).

Branch Johnson, W. *The English Prison Hulks* (1970).

Brown, M., *Australian Son* (1948).

Brown Hayes, Sir Henry, *Trial of* (1801).

Brosnan, C. (Con Costello), *Botany Bay. Irish Independent* 28.5.1962. – 6.6.1962.

Brunicardi, N. *Haulbowline, Spike and Rocky Islands* (1968).

Byrne, M., *Memoirs* (1863).

Campion, E., *Rockchoppers: growing up Catholic in Australia* (1983).

Campion, J. T., *Michael Dwyer* (N.D.).

Clark, M. *A Short History of Australia* (1963).

——, *Select Documents in Australian History, 1788-1850* (1950).

Clarke, J. *The Story of the Catalpa* (N.D.).

Clery, P. S., *Australia's Debt to the Irish Nationbuilders* (1933).

Cloney, T., *Personal Narrative of 1798* (1832).

Clune, F., *The Kelly Hunters* (1954).

Collins, Capt. D., *An Account of the English Colony in NSW* (1798-1802) 1802.

Connolly, S. J., *Priests and People in pre-famine Ireland* (1982).

Coughlan, R. J., *Napper Tandy* (1976).

Crofton, Sir W., *Convict system and transportation* (1862).

Cullen, J. H., *Young Ireland in Exile* (1928).

Cunningham, P., *Two Years in NSW* (1827).

Daly, M. E., *The Famine in Ireland* (1986).

Dickson, C., *Life of Michael Dwyer* (1944).

Dickson, C., *Revolt in the North* (1960).
Dictionary of National Biography.
Dudley Edwards, Ruth, *An Atlas of Irish History* (1973).
Ellis, M. H. *Lachlan Macquarie* (1947).
——, *John Macarthur* (1955).
Evans, L. and Nicholls, P., *Convicts and Colonial Society, 1788-1853* (1976).
Fitzpatrick, B., *Australian People 1788-1945* (1951).
Flower, R., *The Irish Tradition* (1947).
Gibbings, R., *John Graham, convict* (1937).
Greenwood, G. ed., *Australia, a social and political history* (1955).
Hancock, W., *Australia* (1930).
Hay, E., *History of the Irish Insurrection 1798* (1803).
Henderson, J., *Observations on the Colonies of NSW and VDL* (1832).
Hill-Reid, W. S. *John Grant's Journey* (1957).
Hirst, J. B., *Convict Society and its enemies* (1983).
Hocking, C., *Dictionary of Disasters at Sea: 1824-1862* (1969).
Hogan, J. F., *The Irish in Australia* (1888).
Holt, J., *Memoirs* ed. T. Crofton Croker (1838).
Hughes, R., *The Fatal Shore* (1987).
Kavanagh, P. F., *History of 1798* (N.D.).
Kenny, J., *History of Catholicity in Australia* (1886).
Kiernan, C. ed., *Ireland and Australia* (1984).
Kiernan, C. ed., *Australia and Ireland, Bicentenary Essays, 1788-1988.* (1986).
Kiernan, T. J., *The Irish exiles in Australia* (1954).
——, *Transportation from Ireland to Sydney, 1791-1816* (1954).
King, H. *Richard Bourke* (1971).
Leahy, D., *State of Crime in Ireland* (1839).
Lecky, W. E. H., *History of Ireland in the 18th Century* (1892-6).
Levy, M. C., *Governor George Arthur* (1953).
MacDonagh, O., *The Inspector General* (1981).
MacDonagh O. and Mandle W. F., eds, *Ireland and Irish Australia, Studies in Cultural and Political History* (1986).
Mac Giolla Choille, B., *Transportation 1798-1848* State Papers (1983).
Mackaness, G. *Life of Vice Admiral W. Bligh* (1931).
MacNevin, T., *Letter to the Earl of Roden* (1838).
Mason, St. J. *Pedro Redivivus* (1810).
Meehan, J. B., *The Tyrant of Kilmainham, Evening Herald*

17.4.1961-22.4.1961.

Meredith, Mrs Louisa, *Nine Years in Tasmania* (1851).

Mitchel, J., *Jail Journal* (1918).

Moore, J. F. M., *The Convicts of Van Diemen's Land, 1840-1853* (1976).

Moran, Cardinal, *History of the Catholic Church in Australasia* (1896).

Mulcahy, M. and Fitzgibbon, M., *The Voice of the People* (1982).

Mundy, G. C., *Our Antipodes* (1852).

Murtagh, J. G., *Australia, the Catholic Chapter* (1959).

Newman, J., *Maynooth and Georgian Ireland* (1979)

Observations on Richmond Penitentiary. (1827).

O'Brien, E., *The Foundation of Australia* (1950).

O'Brien, G., *Economic History of Ireland in the 18th Century* (1918).

O'Farrell, P., *Letters from Irish Australia, 1825-1929* (1984).

O'Farrell, P., *The Irish in Australia* (1986).

O'Neil, P., *Remonstrance to the Nobility and Gentry of County Cork* (1804).

O'Reilly, J. B., *Moondyne* (1880).

Perkins, H., *The Convict Priests* (1984).

Phillips, C., *Cry of the Dingo* (1956).

Pyle, F., *Trinity College, Dublin* (1983).

Quennell, P. ed., *Journals of Thomas Moore* (1964).

Reilly, B., *A True History of Bernard Reilly* (c. 1839).

Rice, W., *Memoir of Rev. P. O'Neil, PP* (1900).

Robins, J., *The Lost Children* (1980).

Robson, L. L. *The Convict Settlers of Australia* (1965).

Roche, J. J., *John Boyle O'Reilly* (1890).

Rowe, C. J., *Bonds of Disunion* (1883).

Rude G., *Early Irish Rebels in Australia. Historical Studies* vol. 16, no. 62 (1974).

Scott, E., *A Short History of Australia* (1916).

Shaw, A. G. L., *Convicts and Colonies* (1966).

Smith, C., *Shadow over Tasmania* (1958).

Taggart, N. W., *The Irish in world Methodism, 1760-1900* (1986).

Therry, R., *Reminiscences of 30 years in NSW and Victoria* (1863).

Traill, H. D., *Social History of England* vol. V (1894).

Ullathorne, W., *Horrors of Transportation* (1837).

Wannan, B., *The Wearing of the Green* (1966).

Ward, R., *The Australian Legend* (1958).

Waugh, D., *Three years practical experience of a settler in NSW* (1838).

West, J., *History of Tasmania* (1852).
Whately, R., *Thoughts on Secondary Punishment in a letter to Earl Grey* (1832).
——, *Remarks on Transportation* (1834).

IRISH COUNTRY TOWNS

Edited by
Anngret Simms and J. H. Andrews

Country towns are an important aspect of Irish identity, blending place and time in a unique fashion. Their stories reflect the formative periods of town foundation in Ireland: from Gaelic monastic sites to Anglo-Norman colonial settlements to early modern plantation towns.

The story of each town is here given added interest by a town plan and an evocative black-and-white illustration, usually nineteenth-century. A map gives an overview of all the towns featured in the book and classifies them according to their mode of origin.

The collective history of these Irish towns reflects the complexity of Irish civilisation in a more colourful way than could any chronological history.

The towns included are Kells, Downpatrick, Carrickfergus, Maynooth, Enniscorthy, Bandon, Lurgan, Ennistymon, Castlecomer, Bray, Sligo, Athlone, Dungarvan and Mullingar.

MORE IRISH COUNTRY TOWNS

Edited by
Anngret Simms and J. H. Andrews

A continuation of the first volume – the towns included in this book are Kildare, Carlingford, Bangor, Coleraine, Carrickmacross, Tullamore, Monasterevan, Athenry, Tuam, Westport, Roscrea, Cashel, Tralee, Youghal and Wexford.

THE COURSE OF IRISH HISTORY

Edited by
T.W. Moody and F. X. Martin

Though many specialist books on Irish history have appeared in the past fifty years, there have been few general works broadly narrating and interpreting the course of Irish history as a whole, in the light of new research. That is what this book set out to do; and it is a measure of its success that it is still in demand.

The first of its kind in its field, the book provides a rapid short survey, with geographical introduction, of the whole course of Ireland's history. Based on the series of television programmes first transmitted by Radio Telefís Éireann from January to June 1966, it is designed to be both popular and authoritative, concise but comprehensive, highly selective but balanced and fair-minded, critical but constructive and sympathetic. A distinctive feature is its wealth of illustrations.

The present edition is a revised and enlarged version of the original book. New material has been added, bringing the narrative to the I.R.A. ceasefire of 31 August 1994; the bibliography, chronology and index have been augmented accordingly.

THE GREAT IRISH FAMINE

Edited by
Cathal Póirtéir

This is the most wide-ranging series of essays ever published on the Great Irish Famine and will prove of lasting interest to the general reader. Leading historians, economists, geographers – from Ireland, Britain and the United States – have assembled the most up-to-date research from a wide spectrum of disciplines, including medicine, folklore and literature, to give the fullest account yet of the background and consequences of the famine. Contributors include Dr Kevin Whelan, Professor Mary Daly, Professor James Donnelly and Professor Cormac Ó Gráda.

The Great Irish Famine is the first major series of essays on the Famine to be published in Ireland for almost fifty years.

Beyond the Black Pig's Dyke

A Short History of Ulster

Art ó Broin

Beyond the Black Pig's Dyke is a concise history of Ireland's most fascinating province, from pre-history to the Republican and Loyalist ceasefires and the peace talks at the end of 1994. Drawing on the latest historical sources, it seeks to give an even-handed and accessible account of a region that has become associated with conflict but that has also made an immeasurable contribution to science, to the arts and to the development of liberal nonconformist political thought.

The geological legacy of the Ice Age was a natural barrier of drumlins and wetland between Ulster and the rest of Ireland. Early settlers supplemented nature's work with their own earthworks and the most famous of these barriers was known as the Black Pig's Dyke. In direct contrast, the Ulster planters, mainly Scots, who colonised Ulster in the cataclysmic seventeenth century, regarded the North Channel not as a boundary but as an inland sea. Part of Ireland yet separate, and with adamantine links with Britain, it is small wonder that Ulster's history has been eventful and turbulent.